N
S
TIELORIC OCEAN
NORTH SEA
SANARIKKI
Sindheim
PROUS
SALZHEIM
Salz
Vien River
THE LOW MARSHES
SHIRM VALD
SEA OF MARTYRS
ANNALTIA
Annalt
Istrya
SCHWARZE FOREST
CISNISTRIA MARSHES
NISTRIAN MOUNTAINS
Alba River
Tibor River
GRIFFIN'S CLAW
Ostelar
ARCHDUCHY OF OSBERGIA
BAY OF EMPIRES
Tri-tipped Spear
SOUTH HILLS
KINGDOM OF BADONN
Ren
ISTRYAN'S PASSAGE
Avercarn
AVELLANO MOUNTAINS
Invereid
THE FALL
Palerme
THE BIGHT
ALANIA
SOUTHERN OCEAN
Valenti
TANERIA
Malatesta
THE BRIGHT SEA
Segesia
PROLI
CARTENU MOUNTA
KINGDOM
Vall
Baushar
SABURRIA
SEA OF STRIFE

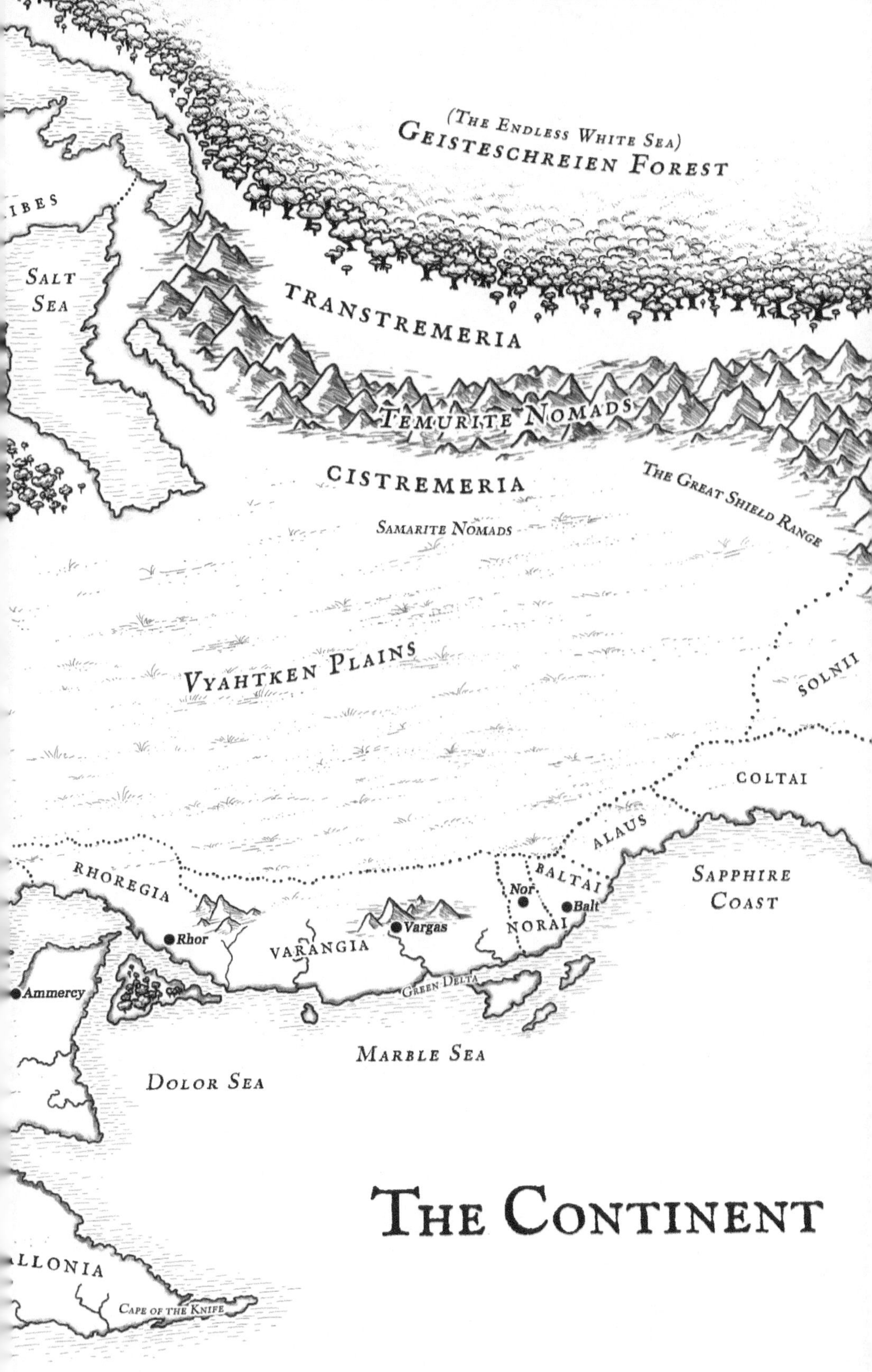

THE CONTINENT

THE PYRES OF VENGEANCE

NC KOUSSIS

By the Author

FOREWORD

This book has graphic depictions of the darker side of disability, abuse, mental illness, and sexual violence. Be warned: this is a much darker novel than my first, *The Sword of Mercy and Wrath*.

I have not done this to beat you over the head with shock like a blunt weapon, but to provide a dialogue into the horrible things that people are capable of and to not shy away from showing the darker side of life. I do this to highlight the brighter side of life: perseverance in the face of inhumanity; dogged persistence of heroism; bravery when all one feels is fear. I say dialogue, after all, and I hope that if you feel something from this story, good or bad, you let me know. I'd love to hear from you, and my email or DMs are always open.

If you feel like you need more information, please see my website at https://nikitaskoussis.com for a full list of content warnings, and please reach out to your sexual violence support line below if you feel you need to:

US: National Sexual Assault Hotline — online.rainn.org or 800 656 4673

UK: Sexual Abuse Support — 0808 500 2222 or 08 08 16 89 111
AUS: 1800 RESPECT — 1800 737 732
Elsewhere: https://ibiblio.org/rcip/internl.html

Nikitas C. Koussis
May 2023

For my father, who never got to see me follow my dreams.

RETURN TO THE CONTINENT...

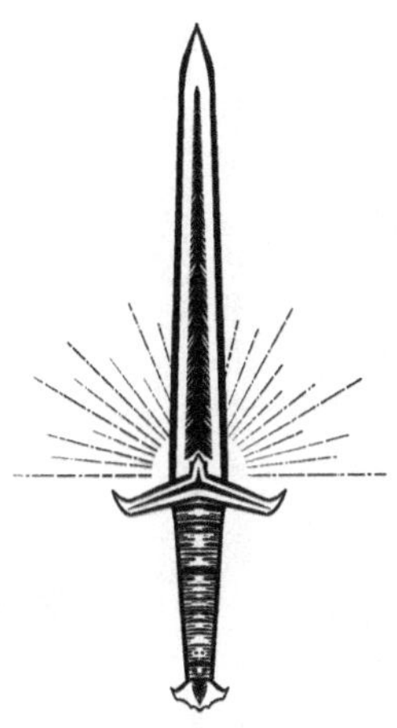

Aestiva
Levitum
Sanguinum
Auctumnitas
Fervum
Effusum
Tribum
Gelum
Vernus
Letum
Aetesta
Ultima
Vernia
Requia
Prima
Bruma

CONTENTS

PROLOGUE
REQUIA, 1045

RICHTER SHOVED A BLADE into his gullet. Right as he did, the sheriff knocked on the door. *These southerners,* he thought as blood poured from his throat like the finest Tanerian red. *No sense for punctuality.*

Life ebbed from his left arm first. Peculiar how that always happened. He slapped it across the table, testing it. Felt like pins poked it, poked the ends, then nothing. Blood continued to splash across the wood and filled the air with a powerful stink.

The knocking came again, more frantic this time, and he slumped his head, unable to support his own weight anymore. He slid out of the chair and made a flopping noise as he hit the floorboards. A nail poked up at him like a rude gesture.

His vision faded to brown, then gray, then he looked at himself and warmth came, peaceful and quiet. He couldn't hear the knocking anymore, only vast emptiness. Familiar but wanting.

It reminded him of his failure.

Fire seared his skin and boiled his belly as he was pulled back inside his body. Fur erupted from every pore and claws as sharp as a lion's pushed their way out of his nail beds, tearing skin to make way. His head shifted, bones cracking and locking into place. His chest doubled in size. Bones had to break, had to restructure, to mend into something made for a predator.

He sighed. *Why do I think the next time will work?*

He considered whether he could kill the god that had cursed him. It seemed unlikely. Relaxing his muscles and his mind, he let the transformation back take hold and threw his clothes on.

When the sheriff knocked on the door for the fifth time, Richter opened it as a man.

"Yes?"

"Your pardon, master," he said. A stray lock of light hair protruded from his stained coif. At his belt, a flanged mace marked his station. "The lord said you were staying here. There's a family what need your curing."

"I don't know about cure, but I'll certainly see if I can help."

"It's said you're a healer." He tried to stick his head over Richter's shoulder, likely noticing the pool of blood drying into the wood.

Richter moved into his path and smiled. "That it is."

The sheriff stepped away and a man in a dirty smock and felted hat approached. He took off his hat and pressed it between his hands.

"Well met, master. I'm Reginald, though the folk 'round here call me Sod. I'm out at the lord's farm a few miles west of here. I'm a freedman, but I work for my liege lord."

Richter raised an eyebrow. "Sod?"

"It's what my mother called me. 'Bloody Sod.' It stuck."

You poor man.

Sod looked down, his cheeks flushing red. "Well... it pains me to ask, you know. But Sigur bless us, my wife's been havin' strange things happen of late."

"Of what nature? Menses?"

"Nay, master."

Richter smiled. "Please, be at ease, friend. I'm Richter, Richter Absault. My father was a Badonnian. Don't hold it against me."

Sod laughed. Richter gestured to the tavern across from his abode, over the main street of passing carts carving tracks through the mud. Feet, human and cloven, had churned the path into muck, frothy at the edges. Richter put his pattens on—wooden overshoes that set you above the muck—and with the farmer he went to the alehouse. The sheriff bid farewell.

They sat at an uneven table and were served warm ale that tasted like old shoes. Richter cleared his throat and the farmer continued.

"My wife, you see... she's pregnant. But she's been having night spells, like she's been 'exed. Like a witch has got her."

"A witch, you say. What sort of night spells?"

"I'll find her in the garden, or down by the riverbed in the morn. She'll be covered head-to-toe in muck, like she'd been crawling in it."

The peasant looked around, satisfied himself that no one was listening, and leaned closer. Richter's eyes flashed with anger. He didn't like the invasion of his personal space, but then he remembered his teachings, passages that would get you through a hard day's work. *The Lightfather places His grace on every child who speaks His name.*

He took a breath and placed his hand on the knife at his belt for comfort.

"One time I found blood on her skirts, too."

Richter pushed down his excitement. He had to remain stoic, impassive. Concerned, even.

"Is that so? This is grave news, then. Menses or no, it requires urgent attention. Where is your wife now?"

"At home, master."

"I see." Richter leaned out of his chair and called for the bill to be settled. "A few miles' ride isn't so bad in this country. If we were near Ostelar, I might be worried to come across Annaltians on the road looking for trouble." *Not that I can't handle a few Annaltians, but this hayseed doesn't need to know that.*

This was Forberg, a little town outside of Triburg. He'd made it his home of late, though his mission required him to move rapidly and very far, often. Traveling healers plied their trade along the roads south of Ostelar after the capture of that city, and it served him as the perfect cover.

"We can take my horse."

"Of course, master. I'd be happy to pay you for your time. I've been saving up in case a man like you crossed my path."

"Oh, what happy luck. Sigur has ordained our meeting, then."

"Indeed, he has, master."

THE FARMER'S HOUSE STOOD on an embankment, elevated from the flood pan on stilts. This part of the countryside often flooded, as he was told by every cowpoke and hayseed the moment he stepped foot here. Richter steered his horse to the front of the house and swung his leg over, helping the farmer down with a gloved hand.

He smelled the blood before he caught the stink of cow shit. Someone had been killed here, not two nights ago. The farmer was lying, or not telling the whole truth, out of some protective notion. Only someone with Richter's nose would know. So, the farmer had thought to cure the curse.

When the Lightfather has delivered these tools unto your hands, you must seize them.

"My wife should be inside," Sod said, and led him up the set of stairs to the front door.

Inside, a woman whistled a tune that some of the Osbergians sang. A tune about a donkey having its way with a woman. He preferred the version where the woman's organs were so bruised, she died from bleeding on the inside.

The farmer's house consisted of a single, sad room, nested with moss-stuffed bedding around a fire, soot staining the ceiling. The farmer's wife tinkered at a small cot and seemed surprised to see them.

Her gaze lingered on the knife at Richter's belt. Around her eyes, he could see flecks of sleep, where she'd clearly had disturbance in the night. Wrinkles settled beyond that, couching the rest of her face in age and worry. But she was pregnant, and that was easily seen. Her belly pouched considerably over her thighs, ripe.

Richter pushed down his excitement. It pressed against his leg, hard against his hose. He remembered the training, what the instructors had beat into him. *What the Lightfather giveth, the Lightfather taketh away.*

"Woman, this is Master Richter Absault," the farmer said. "He's a healer, wot I said I was going out to do today."

"Well met, master."

Richter leaned against the wall. "Well met, goodwoman. I've heard you've been having some night spells? Your concerned husband thinks you've been hexed by a witch."

She shook her head and laughed. "Sorry, I think my husband has pulled a nasty trick on you, master."

A frown. "What do you mean?" He kept his voice level despite the hate starting to build behind his eyes.

She fixed her eyes on his chest. Could she see the pin that he kept tucked in his tunic? Surely not. Even if she was what he thought she was, he hid the thing well enough that a cursory glance wouldn't reveal much. Nothing about him was standard issue for his line of work.

And if she was what he thought she was, that made her very interesting indeed. He'd never seen a pregnant one before.

Blessings come in all forms and sizes and at the most unexpected times, for He is good.

An unexpected blessing indeed. When he woke up this morning, he'd pissed into the remnants of the fire under the stove, relieved himself, then he'd taken the rest of the slop given to him by the good tavernkeeper's daughter into his belly, and shoved a knife in his throat.

He didn't think it would work, but on the off chance... *For He is good.*

The woman placed a crown of daisies that she'd been sewing at the head of the cot.

"My husband has these flights of fancy at times." She smiled. "But it's why I married him."

"Come, woman, enough jesting now. Tell him what you've been doing. The blood on your skirts that time."

"You told him..." She paused and let her hand slip by her side. "You told him about that?" Richter saw movement in her eyes.

In that moment, he moved. The knife at his belt was no common belt knife, used for cutting cooked flesh at the table, or to spread butter on the stale trencher. It went zipping through the air and planted in the woman's throat.

She screamed. The farmer gaped and yelled. It was the last thing he did. Richter shoved a clawed fist through his lungs, punching through the ribs. Sod's throat made a hissing noise.

Richter wrenched his hand free, tearing more flesh open and Sod dropped. He might still be alive, but Richter wasn't taking a chance with the wife, as she sauntered, dazed, around the room, pissing blood on the floor. She screamed as she lashed out at him with a knife. He turned to the side and punched a claw into the woman's eye. The claw sank to the knuckle. He scraped around as she gibbered in excruciating pain. It wasn't just the killing he enjoyed. It was the pain, too.

Something the Lightfather had cursed him with had also blessed him. *For He blesses and curses in equal measure.* Richter had made it his own blessing and seized the tools that He had given him. Using the control he trained himself with, and the Grand Inquisitor's beatings, he could manipulate the transformation at will. One part of him could be human, another part monster.

He chuckled. "Or am I *all* monster?"

She widened her one working eye. He lowered her to the ground and brought huge, club-like fists down on her head, again and again. When he finished, she was unrecognizable as human. Then he took hold of her head, or what was left of it, and twisted. Snapping rang out as tendons and bones twisted. He pulled, planting his foot against her shoulder.

Her head came free. He stared at it longingly and thought to relieve himself of the stiffness pressing uncomfortably against his leg, but then he remembered the other problem.

He looked down. The woman's belly sunk a little laying down, dead as she was, but it was still quite pronounced from the cursed offspring inside. The babe would probably die without its mother to sustain it, but he couldn't take the chance.

He shoved his claws inside her belly again and again. Tearing the small, unborn babe to ribbons.

After it was done, and he'd taken care of the stiffness in his hose, he went outside. The horse waited there, the beast's stupid eyes staring back at him. As though it had not a single fucking clue what went on inside. What evil he'd dealt for a righteous cause.

Lightfather, I have brought war and spared no quarter. Let me be free of this curse.

Sigur did not answer him. He never answered. Still, he hunted the wolf-men, the cursed demons, in the hope that one day he'd be free and he could die.

Have I not done enough?

He shook off his shoulders. He'd need to bathe in the river to get rid of the blood, but it was already getting chilly.

"A little fire would help," he said for Sigur's ears only.

When he rode away, the flames rose high and licked the evening air. He felt good. One more demon dead on the Continent. He would not rest until they were all gone, then finally himself.

VOLUME FOUR

When He hath given you an arm with which to wield a sword, you must wield it. When He hath given you a leg with which to sprint a spear, you must use it. When He hath given you a heart with which to hate the demon, you must hate. And you must make no peace with them, and give no quarter, but war against them; and when the Lightfather has delivered these tools unto your hands, you must seize them. Bring glorious battle against every demon: man, woman, and child. Do not spare any the edge of the sword, or the blade of the axe, for every one that survives takes us further from His Light.

— THE BOOK OF LIGHT, CHAPTER II, VERSE 1-8.

CHAPTER 1
NEW BEGINNINGS
VERNUS, 1045

A world without hope is a world without life.

— VERSE II OF THE BOOK OF THE MOTHER

SELENE KNEW THE WORLD wouldn't wait for them to be ready. She watched the people of Palerme bash at each other with metal bars and fists. Men, boys, and women too. They flailed around; no blocking, no finesse. The sort of fighting that reminded you that most people couldn't fight worth a damn. Standing on the stone walk running the length of the curtain wall, Leon directed their attacks like a general.

"Bash it, Helge! Smash the teeth, Trestinsen! Poke the eyes! Elbows, elbows!"

Tried and true, he'd said. His method for bringing out the wolf in you, but controlled. Less chaotic than the usual, which involved a fire and pitchforks. Or a bolt and a blade.

Frix and his cousins lingered nearby, ready with nets to provide more aggressive means of control.

She was higher still, on the lord's balcony, looking over them all. The air still carried the chill of bruma, though the ice floes had receded, and the rivers ran again. Smiths hammered steel and iron into shape, prentices sharpened weapons on grindstones. At the livestock pens, pigs and goats riffed in the troughs as the boys brought slop to them. Spinsters and little girls carded wool and spun it on the wheel, making more cloth for the next bruma. Quite the vantage she had, out to the horizon beyond the walls, where fir and pine forests enclosed the land like a coverlet.

It stole her breath to think that mere months ago—not even a year—she slew one love and got another killed. Now she was the protector of a little cut of land that was theirs. Belonged to the Althann. Lady, they called her. Selene of some lauded house, now, you'd hear. If you liked to be deceived.

Still, it opened doors that were otherwise forbidden. If it wasn't for her name, Palerme wouldn't exist. Oh, the fort would be here, but it'd be a dusty, barren, moth-ridden rot of a place, like it was when they arrived. Full of ghosts. Now it was full of life, and she smiled for it.

Behind, she heard the door open. Ottille stepped out and closed it again to keep the heat inside. She glanced at Selene's belly. She couldn't help herself; none of them could. The first child born in Palerme would be a boon, and proof of their self-sufficiency. Proof they could survive in the mountains.

Framed by leaded windows, Ottille wore a wimple tight around her hair, and a dress in the Salzheimer cut, while over that an apron tied around her waist.

"Feeling partisan today?" Selene asked, placing her hands on her pronounced belly. "I didn't know you were from Salzheim."

Ottille smiled. "I'm from Triburg, milady. It was a gift from my mother-in-law, who was from Salzheim. The bitch can rot in the hells for all I care, but I kept her dress. It's the only nice one I have."

It was her first day as Selene's dresser; a role she took seriously, it seemed. "You don't have to dress fancy, you know. I'm not some noble lady."

"Begging your pardon, milady, but you are. You're the lady of a fair castle straddling the border of Osbergia and Alania. Duca Alberracin takes your audience when you visit. If that ain't worthy of dressing nice to better your company, milady, what is?"

Selene smiled sadly. She wondered if perhaps if things had been different, if the events and choices of her life took a different path, she might've been in a similar position. *No, I'd be married to a knight or a lord, squeezing out babes. Now I'm simply squeezing out a babe for a dead man whom I once loved, one that I killed because of his inability to change. But at least I have something to show for it all.* Palerme was proof.

"It's well, milady," Ottille said. "I can't think of a better person to dress nice for, anyway."

"You're very kind. How is Sanna? I heard she's been on a few sojourns with those twins."

"Aye, milady." Ottille clicked her teeth. "Silly girl has it in her head that she can find gold in these mountains. We've found iron and naught else, and I've told her as much."

"I'll talk to Gregor. Maybe he can rein in his twins."

"Aye, milady."

The sound of the battle below roared to an apex as a few of the young men transformed. They howled, the thundering blast battered the stones, rattled her teeth. Two calmed themselves, breathing heavy, white breath curling upwards from their long snouts. Folk cheered for them, cleared space, patted them on their furred backs.

The third, Tomas, the ex-guardsman and russet werewolf, looked to be struggling. His feet scraped the ground, pushing up shingle. Strained his muscles, arched his back, looked to be trying to stop himself. Trying and failing. One of Frix's cousins, the tonsured one—a shaved crown, sides left long—came in with a net. Selene covered her belly defensively.

"Control him," Leon yelled. Everyone scattered.

The net tangled around the beast's strong limbs. Four hundred stones of fur and muscle strained against the thick rope, popping strands, but it held. From Selene's time in the Order, they'd learned a better way of constructing the nets from hempen rope. The restraint calmed him, like swaddling a babe, and soon he transformed back.

Those in the yard clapped and celebrated. Selene breathed. Ottille made a noise of relief as well.

"Milady, we shouldn't—" Ottille interrupted herself, looked away.

"Speak."

"We shouldn't do this in the keep, not where children are around. They haven't come into their strength yet."

"I agree, but where else ought we do it? The Order hides their spies everywhere and waits for us to let down our guard."

She'd found one in the woods outside the keep disguised as a poacher. He screamed his innocence, but Selene recognized him from her training days. He remained in the oubliette below the keep, in a tiny cell only fit for rats and the like.

Ottille sighed. "Are things truly that dire?"

Selene nodded and brushed her hand against her belly again. In the deepest part of her mind, she knew that this boy had a dark lineage, one he could never know.

"Arrivals!" One of the lookouts along the curtain wall waved his arms. "Arrivals!"

Selene and Ottille looked at each other with excitement.

"At last," Selene said.

Ottille and her family had been the last for the past few months. Selene was sure it had something to do with the Order, though maybe no one knew about Palerme beyond Triburg, where Ottille hailed from. The Order might've been wiped out in Osbergia, but that was only one branch. They had branches in each province, and their headquarters in Istrya, the capital. Selene wouldn't risk sending anyone out and spreading the word, and so it began to look like Ottille and her family were the last.

Well, not anymore, apparently.

She waddled—as quickly as she could manage—into the lord's chamber, the blast of the hearths making little Trist crawl up inside her. It was an odd feeling, and entirely unwelcome. It came as a bittersweet thought that before long, he wouldn't do that anymore, and he'd be out in the world. Ottille proceeded ahead, opening the doors for her. She adjusted Selene's hair as she walked past.

She tutted. "Don't fuss."

"You don't want to look like a vagabond. These people will look to you for guidance."

When did I get a choice in the matter? But she only thought it and didn't speak. It was selfish, she knew. This was her life, now. The protector and guide for forty Althann, and a handful of humans, and soon to be more of both.

She did long to have some choices in the matter, though.

They met them outside the walls. Leon tucked his thumbs into his belt and looked back as Selene approached. The people of Palerme bowed their heads as she passed. She expressed her displeasure about it often, but many insisted. Anyway, it made things easier in the eyes of the newcomers, and they bowed too.

"Lady of Palerme," the one at the front said. He passed his hand back and pulled a pinch-faced girl in her teen years forward, sixteen perhaps, along with a boy of ten or twelve, who was starting to get fuzz on his chin. Two more strays followed behind, though it didn't look like they belonged to this pack.

"I am Roland Denerim. This is my son Roland, and my daughter Lorela. We've traveled a great distance to be here. Will you accept us with glad tidings?"

He spoke like a northerner, rolling his *R*s like an Annaltian or someone from the capital. Muscular—both him and the boy—they wore tunics and furs dusty from the road, but still in good condition. Made from fine wool. The girl wore a tight-fitted dress with long and baggy sleeves, a fashion better suited to a married woman—it struck Selene as a little strange. But then she realized that the girl probably inherited the dress from her mother, who wasn't here. Dead, maybe. It still fit well, and they were a wealthy family in any case.

But who are these others?

"*Die familie Denerim stammt aus Annaltie,*" she said.

They nodded and glanced at each other with happy surprise.

"I have no love for the archduke or the prince. All are welcome in Palerme."

Still, war raged on the border, it was said, though Osbergia was annexed in all but name. Archduke Albrecht had gone into hiding, seeking refuge in Vallonia and claiming his rule as a government-in-exile, though none cared much. She'd also heard the once noble Annaltian knights roved the countryside along the border, killing, raping, and pillaging. Truly, there was no end to the hypocrisy of the day.

Surely the world has bigger problems than a handful of werewolves making their home in the mountains.

"And you?" She turned to the two extras straggling behind.

One pulled his torn hood tighter across his face, and the other looked like he hadn't slept in a week, swaying on his feet. The one wearing the hood bunched his shoulders up and moved his hand behind his back.

She heard the rasp of swords and saw Frix and his cousins stepping closer out of the corner of her eye. She put her hand out to delay them. The obvious ones were the ones you had to suspect the least, in her experience.

The *girl* pulled her hood down, her hand trembling. A small coinpurse emerged from her back. It rattled as it shook.

"They both joined us on the road," Roland the father said. "The man at Invereid, and the girl about Ineluss. Poor thing was half-starved when she joined us, and she doesn't speak. We don't know what happened to her."

Selene's heart broke for the girl. She looked no older than nineteen and had flaxen, straight hair down to her chest, which unraveled as she pulled down her hood. Older than Selene was when her ward father nearly killed her, and she joined the Order. How life had changed so much the last few years.

"I won't take your money, girl. I do hope that you accept our hospitality, though."

The girl looked uncertainly at Selene before putting her purse back, and Selene thought she saw the briefest of smiles.

"And what of you, master?"

"Dober. Just Dober."

"Well, Dober, if you've arrived with a hearty appetite for work, we have plenty to do. Are you an Althann?"

"Nope. I'm not one of them dogs."

Frix's cousins groused, and above, on the walk, the archers trained their bows on him.

"*Dogs?*" Selene repeated. She admired his gall if nothing else.

"Nope. But I'm lookin' for work, and I'll take anythin' as long as it comes with a roof and a steady meal."

She glanced at Leon, and he shrugged. They hadn't taken in a stray human before, on their lonesome. Not all the people of Palerme were Althann, but those like Ottille's mother, Lucia, came with those who were.

Selene thought for a second. "We have need for workers in the mines. You'd be suited there. Word of advice, though. Don't repeat what you said unless you want your entrails to decorate the trees."

Dober nodded. "Aye, milady. When's sup?"

"The kitchens serve meals at mid-morn and dusk. There's one drink from the buttery after Highest, and one at Lowest. If you want something more to eat or drink, you'll have to barter or trade for it. As long as you're willing to work—"

"Got it, don't you worry, milady." He brushed past them and walked through the gates. No one stopped him.

Roland scoffed. "Charming fellow. But that does run against a slight problem. My family were naught but merchants—and we were damn good at it, too. Until my rival revealed my secret to the folk of Annalt, and we were run out of town. My brother and wife were killed in the flight, I'm sad to report. But yes, what can we do?"

"I'm sorry to hear of your troubles, and for your lost loved ones." She had no reason to suspect he was lying, except for the usual. But why would someone travel half the length of the empire from Annalt, a journey well over sixty days, to lie now? Someone from the Order might, but with children?

"The children can do odd jobs, whatever needs to be done, really. Girl, have you any skill in spinning?" The girl nodded. "We need cloth and blankets for the bruma. Report to Lucia. Boy, we need a stablehand. You look well with a shovel." She thought on what the father said. "Merchant?"

"Roland Denerim of Denerim Brothers Company, at your service. We have stakes in trade ships from frozen Sanarikki in the north to balmy

Saburria. Had." His voice trembled and he looked down in shame. "I lost all my papers when they burned down my office."

His daughter looked up at him, and he smiled again. He seemed more emotional over the loss of his business than his brother or wife.

"Anyway, I have what's left of my family, and I have my life. Which is more than can be said of others in these troubled times."

The girl in the hood who doesn't speak. Something happened to her.

"Alright," Selene said. "We won't turn you away, not after you've traveled so far. There might be something we can get you to do. And you, girl, talk to Gregor. He's the smith with shoulders like big blocks. He'll know what you can do."

The mute girl nodded. As the family thanked Selene and headed inside, she looked to Leon.

"Keep an eye on them," she said. "Especially that Dober." She failed to stop herself from grinning. "New arrivals."

He cheered and shouted, and Frix's cousins joined in. *New arrivals!* They could keep looking forward, to the future! To a future where Palerme was a home, a town, a safe haven for the persecuted, Althann and human alike.

Leon strode up alongside her, giant grin on his face as they watched the merchant family and the girl go inside and be welcomed with handshakes and hugs.

"What is it?" she asked.

"Nothing."

"Out with it, Knight."

"Ain't a knight no more. Well, might still be, but when your liege lord tries to kill you, you start to not feel like such a knight anymore."

"You're avoiding the question."

A pause. "As silly as it sounds, I long to hear the cries of a babe. It'd mean so much after so much death. And these new arrivals, I thought... well, things are looking better than they have for a long time."

She looked at him. "That's not silly."

There was a twinkle in his eye. Maybe it caught the light of the sun as it played across the shingles and the fair stone walls of Palerme.

Frix sang a song.

The Althann walk a thousand

Miles of snow

Gentle land of mountains

Taken in slow

It went on and he and his cousins sang for a spell. For a long while after, Selene was happy.

CHAPTER 2
VIRTUE
VERNUS, 1045

It is built a holy bulwark against the Devil's machinations.
These stones will serve as the foundation for a new, more orderly
world.

— PONTIFF ALCHAEN, FIRST PONTIFF OF THE SIGURITE
CHURCH

RICHTER CONSIDERED HIMSELF A virtuous man, so when he didn't shove a claw into the ear and brain of the shitheel in front of him, he considered that a cunting virtue, thank you very much. He very much imagined doing so. But what was in a man's mind was between him and the Lightfather and not anyone else.

"I told you to come back later," the man said. The bastard was a glorified guard dog. "His Most Holy is busy."

"And I told you, he called me here."

Richter took in the room, as he usually did. He needed to know where the exits were and which jugulars to open, if the occasion called for it. Flicked his dry straw hair out of his face. A hundred little princelings dithered about in white robes, the aborted shits of noble bloodlines, failures in human form.

He stood under a scalloped alcove, at the threshold of the Grand Inquisitor's chamber at the rear of the Holy-Fortress. The fortress was a thumb of white stone that extended out of the Cataline Hill of Istrya like a mummer's prick at one of those bawdy shows. You know the ones—where the lord gets made into a cuckold by a passing minstrel. Richter always enjoyed them. He never enjoyed the Holy-Fortress though.

Not enough cuckold shows.

"That's Inquisitor Beltrand, the Hero of Ostelar, you slobbering prick."

Nials. Richter turned. The man who'd spoken had a face like a dog had eaten it and thrown it back up again. It truly wasn't far off what had happened to him. He spoke Low Istryan like someone born with half a mouth, too.

"Nials, you ugly whoreson," Richter yelled.

He clapped his arms around the inquisitor and slapped him about the back. Nials slapped him, harder, and they made a game of it, seeing which one flinched first. The slapping noises rang out until they turned to hard noises more suited to punches.

But Richter never flinched. Ever.

"Alright, alright, you're gonna break my back!" Nials stepped away. He whistled at the guard.

"Go fuck your sister or something. Just get out of his way."

The guard nodded, wide-eyed, and bowed as he moved.

"Hang on," Richter said. "I'm still talking to my friend here."

"You don't have friends." Nials folded his arms and laughed.

Richter laughed too, but only because he didn't feel like opening Nials's weeping eyes and seeing what goodies laid inside. Too much clean-up, really.

"You're right. But what are you doing here? Last I heard you were in Riga, that ice-blighted arsehole."

"Teaching. Novitiate poisons." He leaned in to speak low. "I hump all the girls that come through. You'd be surprised how flexible the young'uns are, and what they're willing to do to get their confirmation. You want in on the game? I'd even let the Hero of Ostelar have the first bite."

Richter ground his teeth. The ones that came through the academy were human, and young. As young as twelve, in some cases. He never took his pleasure in the families of demons, and scarcely liked killing them if he didn't need to. Killing the skinchangers made sense. They weren't human. He'd only raped a few, and never developed a taste for it.

You had to draw the line, somewhere.

"I'm surprised they feel much," Richter said.

He took Nials's cock in his hands and yanked. He always was faster and stronger than most. Nials grimaced and made a lowing noise, like a cow.

Richter weighed the thing.

"Considering you ain't got much." He let go and Nials whimpered, adjusting himself.

"I just remembered I've got class," he said, and ran off.

Richter grinned and watched the idiot scamper, loping weirdly. He turned.

"Right. Can I see cunting Vetterand, now?"

When Richter entered the room, Grand Inquisitor Ulrich Vetterand swung upside down by his ankles from a torture device. Well, it looked to be a torture device from Richter's reckoning, but Vetterand smiled like he was having fun. *Maybe that's his idea of fun.* It wouldn't surprise him.

The office looked out on a lake bobbing with ships—the pleasure craft of highborns. Istrya was built on a lake, and the Cataline Hill was one of three hills that loomed over the city. The palace was built on another one, and the army citadel on the other. He scarcely cared, only that the Cataline was the furthest from the gate and his legs quite ached. But it was a city made safe by the Order, and the nobles got rich and fat on their sacrifice.

Maybe he'd steal one of those boats one day and crash into a pier, just for fun.

Richter bowed only half-heartedly and slumped into a chair, tucking his flaxen hair behind his ears. Vetterand's office stunk of something vile, like an uncorked poultice. Ulrich's little daughter giggled in the corner, playing with a knife. Richter and the little girl were more similar than he cared to admit.

"Are you going to get down from there?" he said.

Vetterand laughed. "The artificers designed it, do you like it? Blood in the head improves the intelligence. Unlike blood in the other head."

"I see. And what does blood in the other head achieve?"

"Too many pups, I suppose, and not enough intelligence."

Richter snorted. He avoided Vetterand's eye and got up from the chair, restless. Around the office, books bound by chain and leather alike stacked on shelves that stretched up to the ceiling. Some were histories, others esoteric texts on Sigurian worship. Others on hunting. One on preserving werewolves in their demonic state—useful if you meant to study them. Vivisection, of course.

A chinking sound rang out. Richter had to stop himself from jumping. *What happened to never flinching? Come on, Richter.*

Vetterand thumped to the floor, landing on his feet, surprisingly acrobatic for a man nearing fifty.

"I hear someone's been having fun in Osbergia. Leaving burned farmsteads and mutilated corpses in his wake."

He lifted a sheaf of paper and read it with the importance that befitted his important eyes.

"Several magistrates have left angry letters. The families of the slain are demanding recompense. Do you know about that?"

Richter chewed his lip and still browsed the books. Well, pretended to at any rate.

"You'd think they'd have more to worry about with the war."

"That's precisely the problem, the war. With the Order's name tarnished by that fool, Rotersand, and that traitorous beast-humping bitch, we don't have the pontiff's sanction anymore. He's brought a bull forward that all Order actions must be beyond reproach. The war has made everyone panicky, like a flock of hens."

"Why should I care about this?"

"Because we depend on the lords and dukes for patronage."

Vetterand leaned on the table, flexing his thick, ringed fingers.

"I wouldn't expect you to take responsibility for it, though."

Richter swallowed. Sweat beaded on his nose. Why was he sweating? Visions of blood and teeth and knives came as he looked in Vetterand's eyes.

A woman without hands, reaching the stumps of her arms out—

Blazing orange with heat, a set of shears—

Vetterand reached out and closed his grip on Richter's chin.

"Be better. You disappoint me."

Sweat plipped on the floor. The noise brought him back to the office.

"Yesh," Richter said, unable to talk properly.

Vetterand's pup giggled at the funny voice. He released Richter's chin.

"It's time to earn your keep, my boy. The Tanerians aren't happy about a city of demons darkening their doorstep."

Richter laughed. "A city of demons... who heard of such a thing?"

The Grand Inquisitor didn't laugh.

"They've kept to themselves so far, but it's only a matter of time. The Tanerians mislike their relationship with the Alanian duca. Throwing things out of tense republican balance, you see. The Tanerians are paying, and we need a new curtain wall. We're taking anyone that can fight, and there's been a lot of them, since the war. It's your job, my boy, to turn these recruits into fighters."

"Do I have a choice?"

"We all have choices. I could choose to inject you with paralyzing poison and slowly cut out your teeth, one by one. In fact, there's three crossbows loaded and pointed right at you, my darling."

The little girl giggled. How did she even know that that was funny? Richter suppressed a shiver. "Fine, but I want my irritation noted."

"Noted. The first inspection is—"

Vetterand glanced at some mechanism on the wall. A ticker, the artificers called them. An imaginative name, as imaginative as those humorless bastards were.

"Well, now. You'd best get moving, son. Time to earn your keep."

Vetterand patted Richter on the cheek and he flinched. If the Grand Inquisitor enjoyed that, he didn't show it. The girl stared at him as he left the room.

Richter stuck his tongue out and made a face at her.

"About the farmsteads," Vetterand called out.

Richter turned.

"Be more careful next time."

Out in the hall, reliefs of demons hunted by great names stared down at him. Gold paint danced along their crowns and glowing weapons. Named warriors: Martyrs. Brigida, Leonina, Georgius. Ulrich, Sigur's right-hand-man, whom the Book of Light said turned an entire army of werewolves to dust with a stare.

If there ever was a man to rival the Martyr himself, it was the Grand Inquisitor who shared his namesake. Ulrich Vetterand.

Rage came up to his eyeballs. He saw an acolyte cleric holding a stack of chain-bound tomes and roared at him, spittle flying. The acolyte shrieked and the stack went tumbling. Satisfied, Richter kneed him in the face and kept walking.

People left him lying there, bleeding from the nostrils. No one dared interrupt the Hero of Ostelar, not after what he'd done. Though what he'd done and what people heard were two very different things.

CHAPTER 3
MAW

VERNUS, 1045

*It is well known that the Great Devil's reach extends to the
child, reaches into the womb. Thereby you must bring an end
to the mother and the beast that lies within.*

— THE BOOK OF LIGHT, CHAPTER IV, VERSE X

SELENE WOKE IN A cold sweat, reaching for her belly. Little Trist didn't move, his legs not dancing across the inside like usual. She held her breath.

Outside, rain washed against the dark-green windows of the lord's chamber. Darkness swallowed the room in its maw, the hearth burned out. Lightning cracked across the horizon, blinding her momentarily. She closed her eyes and listened to her heartbeat. On some days, she imagined she could feel his, too. Pulling back her linens, she felt her bare middle. Nothing. Another position, still nothing.

Gods, answer me. Is my child dead?

Then he pushed against her palm, and she shuddered with relief. Sweat dripped from her nose.

The door clicked open, and a figure entered, extending a candle on a holder in front of them. Selene reached for the knife she kept under her pillow.

"It's me, milady." Ottille's soft voice. "I heard you wake." Her face came into view as she raised the candle. "I didn't mean to startle you, sorry."

"It's alright. You heard me fussing?" Werewolves held vastly superior hearing to humans, but it was still something she needed to adjust to.

Selene let go of the knife and rolled onto her side to sit up. Though she loved her unborn child, she hated what he'd done to her body. "Of course."

"Milady."

They stood there watching each other for a moment. "I can go—"

"Stay," Selene said. "It'd do well to keep some company for the time being."

"Did you have a bad dream?"

Selene blinked and nodded. Her cheek felt wet.

"I saw Tristain." She touched her belly. "My Tristain, all grown up. He was Althann, like his namesake, and I saw him hunted and shot with so many arrows and stabbed with so many swords he bristled like a porcupine. Then a man tied him to a stake and burned him on the largest pyre I'd ever seen. It consumed the world."

She didn't lie. The forests and the fields and all the cities of the world burned in the wake of the gigantic inferno.

Ottille sat down on the bed and put a hand on Selene's shoulder.

Selene frowned. "I'm sorry. I shouldn't have said anything. I know your husband—" He'd been burned at the stake like her dream, though it wasn't anything near as large. Just a regular pyre, but it had killed him, nonetheless.

"Don't put that on yourself, milady. You had a bad dream, we all have them. I know I do, and they're not too different from yours. You fear for your son, growing up in a world where people hunt creatures like us. You've done what you can, but it's not enough. It might never be enough. But we just have to make it one day at a time and keep living our lives. Every day we survive is another day that we get our revenge against those who would kill us."

That's why they trained. The world would not let them be—if it weren't the Order, it'd be someone else. Hate and vengeance ran deep in the Continent, as deep as the roots of the trees, down to the core of the world.

"How can we end it?" She shook her head and wiped her eyes. "It seems hopeless."

Ottille faced her. "Don't put on so. We've made a home for ourselves now, and that's something we never had before. Not in all the centuries. You've done something special for us, milady, and never asked for much in return."

"I know, but—"

"No buts. Now, how can I help you?"

Her eyes wandered to Selene's belly. No, below her belly, though the mistake was easily made. It was very prominent.

"For my former lady, I often performed such a service, to help calm her nerves."

Selene opened her mouth in a little shock. She paused to consider. "Truly?"

Ottille nodded.

She never before considered such a tonic, but it had been eight long months since anyone touched her. Soren was the last. Between establishing themselves in the mountain, clearing the keep for use, and striking iron, she'd thought little of her own needs or wants. The lord's chamber for a start had a family of enormous rats living in it, and the roof had rotted and had been ridden with mold. Thinking about rats didn't inspire good feelings in her nether regions, and the idea of doing anything right now made her exhausted.

"I don't know how that would go. You don't have a prick, do you?"

Ottille laughed. It was a refreshing sound, something that cleared the tension from the air.

"You don't need a prick to feel good, milady. Men are often useless with the bloody things, anyway. No, I've my own methods. You just lie back and let me take care of you."

Selene nodded, leaning against the headboard of the bed. Ottille folded up her underlinens above her knees and set Selene's legs apart. She laughed a little. She never imagined doing this kind of thing before, and she never saw Ottille or indeed any woman as a prospect, but now it set her belly on fire.

Ottille's hands disappeared under the fold of her linens and Selene felt a sharp jolt. And warm, but then she imagined that werewolf blood ran much hotter than human. In all, it was quite pleasurable.

"Relax, milady." Ottille said, smirking. "I'm not going to hurt you. In fact, I think you'll find it will feel rather good, very soon."

She was right. Ottille started doing circles with her fingers and it sent powerful waves through Selene's body. She arched her back, leaning into the feeling. Strange and different from anything she'd ever felt from a man, but good. Great, even. In her mind, she locked onto that memory of that night with Sorenius, the man she'd killed—though she pushed the killing out of her mind—and focused on everything she felt with him. Pleasure wracked her body, and soon she panted and huffed.

She ground against Ottille's hand with her hips, panting and groaning, imagining it was Sorenius's body. The air smelled sweet, like crushed flowers with a hint of decay beneath. Nothing unpleasant; it was all pleasant, and her thoughts danced and popped and fizzed along the edge of her mind, unable to be caught for more than a moment before fading.

She shuddered and her legs locked as she felt overwhelming pressure in her mind and her loins. Incredible pleasure bubbled over her body. Her skin tingled. It stayed like that for a while, and she never wanted to leave that place. But then her legs felt like they were being stabbed with hot pokers, and she pushed upwards, groaning in pain.

Leg cramps.

Ottille laughed Selene writhed not in pleasure but pain, her thighs wobbling not in ecstasy but despair.

"Sorry, milady," she said, without a hint of remorse.

Selene eyed her. "You bitch. Argh," she yelled as another wave of pain shot through her thighs.

They laughed and finally, when Selene recovered, they sat on the bed. The room smelled of her sex, the covers damp with sweat and other wetness.

But then her thoughts lingered on the Order again. It still bothered her, though not as much. Clarity of what she needed to do pierced through like a spike. Surprised her that she hadn't considered the thing before now.

"How do you feel, milady?"

"Better. Much better, and I rather enjoyed myself until the cramps."

A lingering sense of reciprocation hung in the air, but that notion was dispelled when Ottille stood and fetched her candle.

Selene came to her feet as well. "Wake Frix and tell him to meet me in the oubliette. I want to have a talk."

They'd never stop hunting them. The Althann would never be safe with the Order still on the Continent. But what could she do? It'd be better to know what they were up to. What they planned.

Ottille's eyes widened almost imperceptibly. "Milady."

F RIX MET HER AT the threshold of the narrow stairwell at the base of the keep. He stood with a candle in a cradle, burning yellow at the wick, and wore grease-stained linens. She liked Frix—Frischeid. Like Leon, he never carried any airs of pretense, and he often cracked a joke and could hold a tune. Did the difficult things when she needed him to. He was the one that had hunted out the Sword they held in the oubliette below—that the previous lord of the keep likely had installed for similar reasons as she now used it for. Unlike Leon, though, Frix reserved some talents of his own.

As she approached, cramping pain bit into her back and her sides, from inside and below her belly. She clapped her hand on the mortared stone wall, bending double. *Has Ottille done something? Surely not, she would never. No, it feels similar to what's come before.* Ottille's wise mother Lucia said the pains were because her body was getting ready to give birth. For all their training in healing and treating maladies, as well as causing them, Sword training lacked much regarding childbirth. She knew nothing, and she'd been too young for her adoptive mother to have taught her anything much beyond the basics.

Frix raced over. "Are you all right, milady?"

The pain lasted a few more moments, then passed. "I'm fine."

"Beggin' your pardon, milady, but what are we doing here? It's the middle of the night."

"I ask for your utmost discretion, Frix. You are to speak of this to no one." She didn't know if there weren't more spies in the keep—not that she suspected anyone, but you could never be too careful.

"On my life, milady."

"Good. Now help me down the stairs before I slip and kill myself."

He held her hand ahead of her as the stairs were too narrow to walk side-by-side. A rank smell hit her nose, a mossy smell mixed with sweat and shit. The stones gave way to cut earth, damp from the rain. Water ran down the walls and dripped onto rock.

"Just don't let go, Frix," she said. He laughed.

At the foot of the stairs, Selene breathed and caught a full face of the stench that had been wafting up. She couldn't perceive the source; it was pitch black. Just the sound of dripping water and a low noise, like a dog's growl.

Frix's candle flickered across the room, casting shadows that fingered the earthen, moldy walls. Set into the floor was an iron grate covered with a heavy stone. Frix moved the stone and pushed the light down to illuminate the hole.

A woman who hadn't seen what she'd seen might've run screaming from that room. As it was, a lump lodged in her throat.

The man slumped in the corner covered in grime, bones poking from his white arms. He blinked as he looked upwards, then screamed so hard he retched a violent cough, then kept screaming, as long as his breath lasted. It was a long breath. Selene covered her ears.

Finally, the noise stopped, and she took her hands away.

"Are you finished?"

"No, fuck you!" He took another big breath and screamed more.

Frix slapped the grate with his hands. "Hey! Shut the fuck up! You'll give me an apoplexy!"

"What!"

"Apoplexy—"

He screamed more. Selene covered her ears again.

Something choked him off and he hacked until he threw up. Whatever he threw up didn't look healthy, and it couldn't have been food.

Selene leaned over, balancing on Frix's shoulder. She couldn't quite manage a full bend, not with the vast weight out front. That's what she'd taken to calling her unborn child. He certainly felt like one, sometimes.

"Are you ready to talk? What's the Order planning?"

"How many times do I have to tell you? I'm *not from the ORDER!*"

She shook her head, then a large crest of a cramp pushed up into her spine and she gasped. Worse than the usual, but nothing she couldn't handle.

"I have no time for this," she said when it passed. "Frix, get him out."

"Gladly, milady."

Frix knew better than to question her. He was exactly the sort of man she needed—a man whom, if she ever had occasion to kill someone, would ask "when" and "how." He opened the grate. The man shouted in horror as Frix transformed and climbed down into the pit. The Frix-wolf climbed out again as nimbly, with the writhing man in his grip.

"Get off me," he screamed. "Bastard-cunting-wolf-ugly-fuck-bastard, let me fucking go!"

Frix did, and Selene kicked his knee. She heard a satisfying snap, and he cried out, falling.

"Bitch! Are you fucking slow? I'm not one of them cultists! This is unlawful!"

Those words left a shadow of an impression on her mind though she didn't hesitate. Out came the knife. She wanted to see an end to this, either way. The suffering seemed grotesque by comparison—let in end in death or in truth. Because he was dead anyway. No point in dragging it out.

"Tell me, now." She almost wanted to say a name, but before she could chase it, it left her tongue. "What is the Order planning?"

"Are you going to stick me with that knife, bitch?"

"I might—" Another cramp. This one made her double over and Frix held her arm to keep her upright. "*Fuuuucckkk.*" It was bad. Worst one yet.

The man gave her a confused look. "What's wrong with you?"

"Shut up." She blinked at him through watery eyes. "Tell me or I'll kill you."

"Kill me, then! It would be a mercy!"

She dashed the blade across his cheek, still clutching at her belly. "Fuck you."

He cried out and grasped his face.

She stabbed him in the hand as he did, and he screamed now.

"Tell me, *Ebb—*" *Ebberich!* In her haze, she remembered a kind face, a fat cheek, a blocky head. Now that same face stared back at her with sorrow and hate. Cheeks poked ragged against poxy skin, and sores trailed across his graying head. Thin, long hair flattened across his gaunt skull.

"I know you." *I humped you. Must've been why I didn't remember.* She laughed, put that thought to the side as she thought through the outcomes. "Ebberich. We went through training together."

He laughed. Then scream-laughed, which was quite the trick, and she covered her ears again.

"I was wondering how long it would take you to remember. Was I that unremarkable?"

"You were a terrible fuck."

"I'm surprised I didn't throw up, fucking an ugly one-armed bitch like you."

"One-armed—" She pressed her eyelids together as a spasm crested. She couldn't speak, couldn't think. Barely aware of Frix holding her shoulder, she shoved him off, now violently repulsed by human touch. The pain summited, felt like her insides were turned to mush. Like someone shoved a knife inside her and mixed it around for fun.

"Is this bitch giving birth? You sodding cow!" Ebberich laughed.

Frix smashed him across the mouth with a hand. Ebberich fell, bleeding.

"Get Ottille and her mother," Selene said. "Wake them, just get them here, now!"

"If there's a babe comin', we should—"

She cut Frix off. "*Now!*"

He transformed and raced out of the room, bounding up the stairs two at a time, and curved out of sight. She almost thought to remind him that he needed his candle. But no. *They can see in the dark in that form.*

The pain subsided. She needed to move fast before another one of the bad ones came again.

She pushed Ebberich's shoulder over with her foot. "What is the Order planning?"

He glanced at her. Grabbed her calf, bony fingers digging in deep. She kicked him in the head with her other leg.

He cried out as her boot landed on his forehead.

"You think to take advantage of me like this?"

But he could. If one of those horrid, bone-crushing cramps came again. *Not now!*

She'd have to move quick. Two slashes across his chest and he ground his jaw, making rasping noises with his throat, trying not to scream. Oh, he would scream when she was done, and more.

She could feel the wave building again, below her belly. *Fuck!* Pain exploded in her stomach, in her chest, across her back. She stepped towards him, sweat pouring off her nose, dripping across the floor, her bending double, knife forward. "Bas... tard..."

He grabbed the knife and they wrestled. She squealed as all her strength left her, devoured by that pain in her belly. Then she screamed. The dagger turned on her. She held it back and it came anyway, bit into the skin at her breastbone. He climbed to a knee, pushing it deeper, overpowering her.

She didn't know what was worse. Getting stabbed or the agony cresting in her womb, causing her to shudder. Her arm trembled. He tilted the knife, aimed it down, so it would cut into her belly. *No! No! No!* Helplessness broke over her. Trist stood to die, and she could do nothing.

Ebberich flew backwards and crashed against the wall. He puffed as the wind was knocked out of him. The knife clattered down the hole. She grimaced, panting and gasping, dripping with sweat and blood, and saw two werewolves turning. And an old woman. Frix carried Lucia over his shoulder and she stepped down as he pulled his strength inside his skin again. Ottille tied her linens around her arm before she'd transformed, and though naked now, she pulled them back over her head.

Selene breathed. "Thank you," she said as the pain subsided. "Thank you."

The old woman laughed and looked back at the groaning, dazed man lying at the foot of the stairs.

"No end to the thrills in life, is there? Even in my age, you still see something new."

"Don't speak a word—" It was coming. She knew it. Pain reached into her belly like a cruel hand and squeezed until her eyes watered and kept going. She thought she would shit herself or vomit, or both at the same time. "Of... this." She strained the words out. It was about the only thing she could manage before all she could do was yell.

Lucia came over with a cold cloth and ran it over her forehead, stern look on her face. "We have to get you upstairs. The babe's liable to get sick if we stay here." She jabbed a thumb at Ebberich. "What of him?"

"Bring him upstairs." She panted. "I'm not done with him!"

Ottille and Lucia looked at each other. She transformed again. It seemed to be as easy as slipping out of one dress and into another.

"She's going to carry you upstairs, and Frix can take care of this prick. He'll find out what the Order want with us."

She glared at Ebberich's still dazed face. His eyes spun. "Break an arm or a leg if he doesn't speak."

Frix nodded. "Gladly."

Ottille cradled her in her arms and raced up the stairs, Selene's hair sweeping backward with speed.

CHAPTER 4
CARE
VERNUS, 1045

There are two certainties in this world: death, and accidents.

— CONSTAN VERDELHO, DUCA OF SEGESTA

RICHTER HAD NEVER SEEN a sadder bunch of recruits in his life. Mind you, he'd not seen many recruits or much of anyone from the Order for months, since he avoided them like you avoided the plague, but you could tell with a look. They lined up like pigs at the abattoir, ready for the knife. A few had missing teeth, more had pox. Yet more looked fresh from the alehouse, swaying where they stood. He walked between them, all forty of them, walking up and down their rows.

He could smell their fear, their sweat. In these training halls of stone, bloody marks on the floor like shadows cast without matching light, people died. They probably thought he was scrutinizing them, testing them, but he only wondered which ones would survive if thrown into combat with four hundred stones of angry beast.

None of them.

He shook his head and sighed. *The Lightfather tests the weak and the strong alike.*

He loved to test Richter. Did that make him weak or strong? A question better left to someone smarter than him.

"Which one of you knows what end of a sword to hold?"

A man with a scrunched face and a too-heavy brow stepped forward. He slotted between two women, both of them looking like they'd shared one too many beds with men like Richter and earned black bruises on their faces and arms for their trouble.

"I've heard it you're the Hero of Ostelar." He said it as though he didn't believe the words.

Richter laughed. *Is he baiting me?*

"What's your name?"

"Prannik. Stolten Prannik. I'm from—"

Richter shot him with the hand crossbow hanging from his belt. A hip shot. He was rather proud of its accuracy. The bolt lodged in Prannik's neck, and the idiot grinned, then reached for his knife, patting his thighs, clutching at the glut of blood coming from his throat with his other hand.

Around him, women screamed and bolted, racing out the door, where two wardens waited to coax them back inside with bigger crossbows. The others stood horrified, though Richter noted that a couple of them laughed.

A few more watched silently.

Maybe there's diamonds to be made out of this shitheap, after all.

Prannik stumbled forward, gaping his mouth like a fish that suddenly found itself on dry land and didn't quite know what to make of things. Richter was sure he meant to say something smart, but it just came out a gurgle.

He'd better make a lesson out of things, otherwise he'd have to deal with Vetterand's lectures, or worse.

A pair of hot shears—

Blinding pain across his thighs, unable to die, unable to be killed—

Prannik flopped to the stone floor, and Richter turned and reloaded his crossbow. He could feel their eyes on him.

"You got to be ready at any moment to die. I'd love to tell you that you go to join Sigur in his Golden Hall, but you're just as likely to get sent to the hells, as well. You have to be prepared for that, and make sure to kill the man or the demon that wants to kill you before he can."

He pointed his chin at one of the men who didn't flinch and stepped over Prannik—who was still alive, bleeding out—to get to him.

"You. What's your name?"

"Karl."

"Just Karl?"

"Just Karl."

"Good. Grab a sword. I want to see how hopeless you are at fighting."

Karl raced off to the racks on the wall and selected a short, tapered blade. He tested it by bending the tip and came back to Richter. The novitiates cleared a space for them, except Prannik. They just stepped over him and his growing blood pool. He was dead now, his eyes glassy.

The way Karl held his sword gave Richter pause.

"What were you before you joined the Order?"

"A squire."

"Care to elaborate?"

"No."

Richter smirked. *I like him. It'd be a shame to kill him.* But kill him he would. It just happened. It would be like asking the dead not to shit themselves when they died.

Karl flipped over the blade to half-sword—one hand on the hilt, the other halfway down. Richter nearly drew his knife, then decided not to.

He didn't want to make things too easy and found a matching sword in the racks.

"Have you a mother or a wife, Karl? Anyone I can send your balls to once I'm finished?"

Karl didn't answer—he barely reacted. The man had wisps of blond hair sticking from his black hood and an interesting scar across his cheek that Richter hadn't noticed before. It looked like it had been done with a billhook, a knight's weapon, leaving a curved scar, as if his cheek had once been peeled open like an apple.

Richter found him endearing.

He jabbed with the end of his sword. Karl deflected the blow with the flat.

Richter took a quick step to the right, and feinted left, sweeping under—

The squire caught the blow and shoved the pommel right into Richter's face. If Richter had been a beat slower with his movement, it would've broken it. Instead, the pommel glanced off his ear.

He's good. Richter circled him, probing his defenses some more. Karl waited for the next blow and leveled a counter along Richter's offside, somehow knowing more about his opponent's weaknesses than Richter knew about himself. Richter deflected the blow but put him on the back foot.

He's very good!

Letting his guard relax, he baited an attack from the squire. Karl raised his sword high, going for a killing stroke. *Well, it's now or never.* Richter dropped one hand to his side. As he threw the next blow, Karl took a half-step back and threw one of his own.

The knife came flying out, as quick as a sparrow.

It sliced Karl's ear. Then Karl's blade twisted in the air somehow.

Richter gasped. The edge found its way across his neck.

He stumbled, went to speak but couldn't. The crowd groaned with shock. Richter blinked once, clutched his throat, then fell to the ground, his legs failing. *They sharpen these training blades?*

Richter looked at himself from above as he died. Novitates crowded around him as his spirit left his body. But then, he could never really die.

Fuck.

Searing hot pokers needled his skin as something yanked him back into his body. He stood on that bonfire, that old friend. Pain coursed through his back, his spine, biting into his vertebrae. He arched his back and opened his eyes as he transformed before forty werewolf hunters-in-training.

They shouted and grabbed swords, crossbows. Others still raced for the door as the two wardens on the other side leveled their drum crossbows at him. He really didn't like those things.

"Clear the fucking room," someone yelled.

"You fucking shitheels, it's me!" he roared, but it came out garbled. They didn't care. He was just a monster to be slain—now that they had discovered his secret.

Fuck it. If they want a monster, they've got one.

Quarrels thumped through the air, slamming into the wall behind him. A woman dropped as she was hit inadvertently, and then a man. One of the bolts whacked his shoulder and he roared.

That one first!

He lunged for the warden who had shot him, barreling towards her. She barely screamed as he swiped up through her padded jacket, tearing through layers of fabric and skin, down to the ribs 'neath. He pirouetted and struck her with a backwards fist to the head. She fell a broken heap, her spine poking from her neck, dead-eyed.

A bolt punched into his upper back. They were aiming for his neck, his only weak spot. *I wonder if I could just wear a gorget, everything would be right in the world?*

He turned and snatched at the other warden. Closing both hands around his head, Richter squeezed. The warden screamed bloody and gurgled until it came out a twisted burble. Like a crushed lemon, his head exploded in a shower of viscera and bone. More than blood landed on Richter's face and arms.

He stumbled as his vision spun. Someone stuck a spear in his side, and he stumbled more.

Karl. Richter really didn't want to break his pretty neck, though he really could have.

They had poisoned the bolts, of course. Why wouldn't they? They were Order—even a very dead one could still kill you, like ghosts from the grave. He should know.

"If you kill me," he said. "Pull my head off. I think it's the only way to do it."

But Karl just looked at him confused. As though someone pulled the hood off his eyes and showed him one of the secrets of the world. Because werewolves never spoke, demons never reasoned, and Richter was just another one of those that should just die already and we shall never speak of them again, thank you very much.

Richter went to a furred knee, then another one. Karl shoved him down and three novitiates came over, stabbing and killing with their own spears. Well, killing was a stretch. The poison did its work before he could truly be killed, and his vision went gray, then black.

“W HY?”

The word came from outside him. Outside his conscious-ness. No, inside, but now he was waking up and his inner world expanded to take in his newfound perception. Vetterand stood there as Richter blinked the crusted shit off his eyes. He tried to move his hands and arms, but they were chained up. Along with his legs. Chained with links as thick as his wrist, so there was no chance of getting out.

“Why?”

Vetterand never asked twice. Richter must've truly pissed him off.

“I got killed.”

“You're going to wish you were.” He sighed. “Fuck!” Vetterand snatched at his throat.

Richter swallowed. He was sure he could smell blood where a nail dug in too deep.

“Now I have to explain why I had a *fucking demon* working for me! Why a *fucking demon* is the Hero of Ostelar! You made me look like a fucking joke!”

Richter narrowed his eyes. “The only reason I'm the Hero of fucking Ostelar is because I did what I did. Reynard would have destroyed the Order, otherwise, if he found what Rotersand was hiding. What you told him to hide.”

The worst part of the whole thing was that Rotersand was innocent of it, really. The Grand Inquisitor grimaced.

“Yes. Well.”

He let go of Richter and straightened his robe.

“But I have a plan for how to manage you and solve everything.”

Richter failed not to whimper.

“You know I have to thank Rotersand for one thing: he was a genius with poisons. He made something from atropine that I've never seen, not even our finest poisoners can understand. I can keep you on the edge of life and death for as long as I want."

Richter shrank more. He hated himself for it. He didn't quite understand the hold that Vetterand had over him—then memories came in pieces.

A boy of only ten was found living the gutters of Istrya. Nobles spat on him as they walked past, and people knew him around there as a cutpurse, since he was, using a short knife stolen from his parents to cut purses from belts. No one spared any pity, nor any coin, so he had to make do.

The Gutter, as they called it, was a pit nestled at the lowest point between the Cataline and the Palatine hills, where the palace drifted aloft, suspended on the clouds. At least that's what it looked like from the bottom, where that boy lived. The Gutter always lingered with the stink of shit and the refuse from the tanneries, where it all flowed down hill. Scuds floated on the canal water, and rain picked up the grease and the dirt, filling the air with a moldy smell, so no reprieve could be found there.

In the press that came with the arrival of Fervum and Emesday, when the alehouses and the whorehouses spilled out with patrons, that little boy made a killing. He had friends that helped him, but they were long dead now. When that little boy, only ten, took the purse of a man with a mace on his belt that he didn't see, he didn't expect to die.

But that man with the mace, that sheriff, rounded up the boy's friends with the help of his own, and cornered them behind one of the Gutter's brothels. The sheriff brained each of those kids, and then the boy. But the boy didn't die.

He became a werewolf, tearing through the sheriff and every one of his friends.

The Grand Inquisitor found him, lying in a pool of scattered flesh and blood. Not dead, but powerful. He was given the name Richter, and he was raised by Vetterand. The boy couldn't say his old name, now. He couldn't remember.

That was only the beginning of his problems. Dying became him.

Richter blinked.

"There's a surprise in store for you, my boy. A grand procession; a great honor." He patted Richter's cheek. "And you'll learn just how much I care for you."

CHAPTER 5
THE NEW
VERNUS, 1045

New life is realization that the old can become new again; take on new features.

— THINKER PLANGE TAUSEND

ANOTHER WAVE CAME JUST as they burst into the lord's chamber. Fire burned in the hearth, though Selene barely noticed. She crawled onto the bed as Ottille placed her there and yelled. It felt like her inside might rip apart.

"I have to get my mother," Ottille said. "Just breathe. She'll know what to do—she talked me through Sanna's birth, and I couldn't have done it without her."

Selene waved her hand, flailing, trying to reach for Ottille. "Don't go!"

She dithered, then stayed. "Okay, I won't go. My mother'll just have to climb the stairs by herself." She sat on the bed next to Selene and rubbed her back. "I found this helped."

It did. Ottille pressed into her hips and down her spine. It relieved the spasming—taking it from a scream to a dull roar.

She sat in that half-space of wave after wave, for what seemed like an hour, until finally Lucia arrived.

"How long has it been?" Selene gasped. "It mustn't be long now!"

The water clock on the wall gave ten divisions—thirty made an hour; twenty-four hours made a full day. It had barely been any time at all. "Fuck!"

Lucia said something to Ottille and she had a briefly visible smile.

"What are you laughing at!"

Ottille rushed over again. "Nothing, nothing. Now, can we get you on your back?"

Selene groaned. The bastard inside her—literally and painfully—felt like he was ripping her apart on the way out. She rolled onto her side. That was far enough.

"That's good," Lucia said. She wiped Selene with that cloth again, and Selene pushed up with her mouth like a child hungry at the tit.

"Water. I need water."

Ottille raced out of the room and returned with a bowl of clear, cool liquid. "Thank you."

Before she could get more than a sip, her insides turned out again—felt like it, at least. The water clock still showed the same time.

"Is that fucking thing working—*ahh!*"

She was on her back now. The entire event was a haze. Perhaps she'd fainted. Ottille spread Selene's legs. Her linens were hiked up past her knees.

Like earlier—

Thoughts dashed against the rocks of her pain like a bastard berg that sunk all ships—one that she knew was coming but could do nothing about.

"Fuck you bastard cunting prick cunt bastard ass pig-fucker whore-son—*fuuuccckkk!*"

Lucia brushed her head and laughed. "Sorry."

"Fuck off!"

The old woman leaned over and held the candle low. "I see his head!"

"What?" She craned her neck over, but the size of her belly prevented her from seeing anything. "Where?"

"He's right there!"

Ottille gasped. "Milady! He's there!"

Lucia rubbed Selene's shoulder. "You have to push now. With me, ready?"

The wave crested again. It felt like she wanted to shit herself more than anything in the world. Like she'd do largest shit in the world and it would kill her, but at least she'd die happy.

"Now!"

Selene pushed and thought a little shit did come out. She screamed as she put everything into it.

"Stop, stop, stop! You'll tire yourself."

Lucia put her hand on Selene's belly. "Here, I'll feel. You push when I say."

Another wave. Selene could hardly catch her breath now.

"Now!"

She pushed. Definitely did shit. Something like water sprayed from her nether bits. Ottille made a shocked sound.

Lucia looked over. "It'll get ya!"

Selene bore down. Something primal inside her wanted her to push, something she couldn't ignore. A force as ancient as the stones, the land itself.

It ripped her in half. If she thought it was painful before, now it was as though someone strong put their fingers inside her bits and pulled apart, split the skin and muscle and bones until they bled. Further. She screamed.

She'd been stabbed, cut, poisoned. But nothing compared to this. Getting murdered. That's what this felt like.

"I can see his eyes," Ottille yelled and started sobbing, which was no use to Selene.

"That's it, one more push!"

Maybe I don't want this— "*Put it back in! Put it back in! I don't want this!*" If that was weakness, she didn't care.

Lucia slapped her on the legs. "Come on, are you a fucking woman or not! *Push!*"

She swallowed, pushing down the pity. "*I am fucking pushi—aghhhh-hhh!*"

Something wet and sloppy sounding left her, and Lucia held her hands out to receive the thing. It left a void inside, where the pain eased to a throb. Lucia and Ottille looked at each other.

"What? What is it?"

Lucia turned her hands over. She did something with some purple, gray shape, and smacked it on the back twice.

A squall. A hurricane of a babe, so pale you could see the veins, screamed as it took its first breath. Her son's first breath. Lucia turned the child over, her hands covered in blood and muck, and Ottille came in with a blanket, wrapping the child. Out of his belly, a pulsing, throbbing cord connected them.

Selene saw his little eyes and his little body, his tiny fingers, the swathe of dark, dark hair on his purple, squalling head, and broke. Everything was worth it. She whispered because she couldn't speak, and said, "Give him here."

He squealed as Lucia offered him to Selene. The outside world was a powerful shock to the warm inside of Selene's belly.

"A little boy."

"Tristain," Selene said. Even red and purple and swollen, bawling his head off, she could see the boy she loved and the man she'd gotten killed.

"Get me two lengths of silk," Lucia said to Ottille. "These covers'll do—we're like to be rid of them, anyway. Daughter, cut them."

Selene scarcely noticed. She placed Tristain on her breast and watched, teary, as he squirmed, flapping his arms and legs like a newborn foal. Like a newborn. Her newborn.

She would die for him.

Ottille took the knife under Selene's pillow and tore two lengths of the silk sheets. Lucia tied them tight, leaving a little space between them.

Selene laid back, making sure he still laid in the crook between her breasts. Tiredness washed over her like a strong current, a river washing her downstream. She let it take her.

Lucia shook her awake. "There's one more thing, then you can rest."

Comparatively, the placenta that followed was barely worth a mention pain-wise. Gods, it was strange, though. Pulsing and purple, like an over-stuffed liver, a vestigial organ. Lucia took it.

She offered it to Selene, this time to her mouth. Selene glanced at her like she'd slapped her across the face.

"What are you, a maniac? I'm not eating that."

"It's for the babe, to grow up strong. It's old magic."

"Old magic or not—" She considered it. The Althann were old magic, too. "How old?"

"Older than these trees. From before the westerners came, it's said."

"Althann magic."

Lucia nodded.

Selene leaned forward gingerly. *The Althann deserve their place in this world. It's their legacy, as much as anything else. It's just a small adjust-ment—and if I remain comfortable within my little world as part of the legacy that destroyed them... does that make me just as bad as those who hate them?*

It was slipperier than she expected, and she had to adjust her mouth. It tasted like raw liver. She chewed down using her back teeth, and tore a chunk while Lucia held it. Blood and mess spattered on the bed, further staining it. The whole bed would be burned before the week was out, Selene would make sure.

She chewed and swallowed hard. She gagged holding it down, forcing it down. Then it was in her stomach, and it bothered her nothing.

"If it helps as much as it tastes bad, I'll be doing somersaults in no time."

Lucia laughed an old woman's wise laugh. Ottille came over with boiled cloth from the fire. She rung it out and cooled it off, applying the warm cloth onto Selene's nether bits. She was just numb now, and barely felt it at all.

"It'll heal you up. You've lost some blood, and you'll lose some more before the night is through. And then... for a few weeks on. It'll be like your menses, but all the time."

"Pack my drawers. Got it."

The old woman laughed again, wrinkling around her deep-socketed eyes. White hair poked out from under her white close-worn veil. "You're stronger than most, milady. You'll be fine, but there's no shame in admitting when you need help."

Selene's lip wobbled. She would cry again.

"We have some good news, as well, but it can wait. Rest. This is more important."

Selene nodded and closed her eyes. Little Trist shit himself some black goo, like tar, everyone laughing, and Lucia wiped him clean. Then they let the mother and son rest.

CHAPTER 6
OLD ENDS
VERNUS, 1045

When the Great Devil cast down Sigur, is it said the world
burned for a thousand years. I ask you: where is the sign of this
great conflagration?

— DRAMES, A COLLECTION, 585 AE. D.

ONE WEEK AFTER TRIST'S birth, and the day she'd sent Frix and his
cousins to Alania, Ottille and Lucia came to her in the morning
with the lord's books. Ebberich, after Frix's persuasion, had told them of
the Order's plan to kill the duca and pin the blame on the werewolves
in Palerme. His purpose in the forest was to sneak inside the keep and
retrieve evidence they could use to plant on his body, the poor man. She
sent Ebberich to Alania with them to serve as witness, in exchange for his
life. His freedom was another matter entirely. If he was allowed that, he
might flee back to the Order and tell them everything—how many they
were, the layout of the castle. He'd seen enough to be dangerous.

Trist cried and Selene snapped her eyes around. When she got up, her
underlinens stuck to the bed and her head pounded. She reached out,
waving her hand around for balance. She found Ottille's shoulder, and
Lucia's hand found her.

Selene sighed. "Do you know when the dizziness is supposed to pass?" She looked back at the brown stain, like dried wine, on the bed. "And the bleeding?"

"I rather think one has to do with the other, milady. Four weeks was how long it took me. You've been through a lot."

"Think of it like your body catching up on all those menses you missed," Lucia said.

They laughed. Little Trist shrieked louder. Ottille called the wet nurse. Selene lifted him out of the cot as Galena arrived.

Galena had just weaned her own child, but her milk was still coming in. They'd moved her into the keep.

"Milady," she said.

Selene handed him off gingerly. She scrunched her lip. Like a splinter in her chest, broken and free to go where it liked. Her heart, her lungs, and her breath came quick as baby Tristain's wails silenced when Galena put him to her breast with a deft hand. Selene had failed as a mother, since her milk never came in.

Is it me? Is it because of what I've been through? The question plagued her waking hours. That dream of him being hunted, just like his namesake, plagued her sleep. He looked so pale in the morning light.

"Give him some sun once you're done," Selene said. That pounding settled behind her eyes and she felt like screaming. It wouldn't help much, but it might make her feel better.

Galena nodded. "Milady."

"Milady, Gregor needs a hand to help him in the smithy," Ottille said. She had scrawled notes.

They'd recovered the books from the burnt-out library—having restored it since—while they gave proper account of the landscape, the amenities of the keep, the construction. They'd added their own details, as well as the discovery of the mines. Ottille had proved herself not only skilled with a needle and in women's ways, but also with keeping account. She'd done her husband's books in Triburg, and though they differed in scale, the process was largely the same—or she said as much. The only moment her dear friend became truly shrewish.

"Fine, who's free?"

"The merchant's boy, Roland. Or there's—"

She waved a hand. "Get it done."

Her son fussed at the breast, and Selene reached out and brushed his hair, shushing to try to settle him.

"There're the horses, too. Three of them need to be reshod, but there's not a farrier among us."

Selene lifted her head. Would feeding from a werewolf's tit make him one himself? She almost tore the boy away before the silliness of that impulse told itself. *As my son, he'll be hunted no matter what. If he's a werewolf, at least he can protect himself. If not, I can train him, or Leon.*

She looked at Ottille, pushing those feelings aside. "We'll hire a farrier from one of the towns along the coast."

"None of them want to come here. Too dangerous, they say, though we've tried to bargain."

"Well, bargain harder. Bribe them if you have to."

How long until she could train again? She felt in good form, if not in good spirits. Maybe she'd try today. Every waking second in this chamber grated on her yearning to be free.

Ottille grimaced. "There's also the matter of the coffers..."

Selene grunted and started pacing. Frustration echoed each of her steps across the bare floor.

"I've scarcely broke my fast and problems redouble themselves. What's the matter with the coffers?"

"There's the matter of the upkeep, the rebuilding of the curtain wall, the tools Gregor recently bought."

Selene longed to throw a knife at something.

"The merchant might have some coin."

"He's only been here a week. I didn't want to ask... and he's got two children to care for on his lonesome."

"Everyone must contribute. I—" She was about to say that she was their liege and tithes were needed to keep Palerme from collapsing. Selene's eyes strained with the weight of things. She remembered the twins' game, about chasing gold.

"There mightn't be but iron in these mountains, but if we indeed found some gold, that would solve all our problems."

"It is as Althann says," Lucia said. She had been by the window, sunning herself, but returned now. "The waters and lands will provide."

"Can Althann show us where the gold is in these lands?"

Lucia snorted. Galena finished, and she took him outside, the light cutting across the dim chamber. Then her baby was gone as the door closed. Selene looked at her feet.

Ottille brushed her shoulder. "What's wrong? I've noticed you've been off."

"Where can we get these farriers?"

"Milady."

"We could talk to Alberracin. He could lend us the service of a leal farrier."

"Selene."

"But then we'll owe the bastard another favor, and we already owe him too much—ah, but when Leon and the others arrive, he'll be grateful we told him of the plot on his life."

"Selene." Firmer now. "Don't tell me there's nothing wrong. You don't have to be strong for me. Is it your milk?"

"Of course, it's my fucking milk!"

Ottille looked as though she'd been struck with a whip. Anger and pain seethed within Selene's chest.

Ottille bowed her head. "Yes, milady."

"That's it, isn't it? I have to be strong. I can't show any weakness—when I want to throttle everyone! What in Ginevra's green-fucking-demesne do they know? Everyone has a word to say about his care. Everyone with a mouth in my fucking ear."

She undid the tie around her neck. "Draw a bath, Ottille. I have things to do today."

"Milady." The woman redid her auburn hair and strode from the room. She was hurt.

Selene really wanted to throw a knife at a wall or shoot a crossbow. *When did I become such a wilting flower about things? I've never been particularly motherly—why now?* She thought of her own mother, that woman that sung and did her hair. Trist would never have that. Selene never could be a mother like her.

Lucia tutted. "You're not who you believe yourself to be."

Selene frowned. "What?"

"You." She put a finger to her chest. Somehow, it weighed more than an anvil, and Selene found it hard to breathe. "You think you need to be strong, and guard yourself against everything. That that's how to be strong. Hurt people before they hurt you." She sighed. "That's no way to live."

Selene pushed the old woman's hand away. "What do you know?"

"I've lived on this Continent for sixty-five brumas, girl, and I've got a few good years left in me yet. There's one of you in every place I've ever lived.

But if you only asked for help, you would see that there's a town's worth of people willing to help you."

"I don't need help." Anger raged a war in Selene's chest, as violent and sharp as a werewolf hunt.

Selene could be a mother that taught him to fight, how to defend himself against a brutal world. She needed to teach herself again. She looked down at her still-distended belly, only slightly smaller than when she was fully pregnant, and she vowed it would never be like that again.

"Fine," Lucia said, and she was gone.

An hour later and Ottille returned with a few helpers to carry hot water from the hot springs below the mountain, and by then, Selene had calmed. She held baby Tristain and told him of her fights.

"I tripped up the novitiate," she said. "She was bait so that I could trick the werewolf into attacking her. It worked, and I dashed the werewolf with an acid vial. She was killed too, of course."

Ottille entered the room and Selene quieted. She didn't look at Selene, just instructing the helpers to drag the wool-lined tub into the lord's chamber. The helpers poured the buckets into the tub, steam billowing upwards.

"Milady, the bath's ready."

"Very well. Could you tell Leon to meet me in the bailey in an hour?"

"Milady."

Lucia arrived and took the baby, swaddling him tight and he went to sleep. Selene lowered herself into the bath as Ottille and her helpers departed—two men from the mines who commented on the luxury that the lady lived in. The water flooded around her legs nicely, stung a little going further, turned slightly dark, then she leaned back and let the heat take her.

I should apologize. It's not her fault I can't feed my son. She never thought the feeling would hit so hard, but it had. Sorenius once said she brimmed with determination, and now she only felt grief. Sorrow.

Why am I thinking of that fool? Because you've a broken heart, and he left you with a babe—after you killed him, yourself. Killing the man she loved. Did that make her damned? Broken in spirit and mind as well as in heart?

"Better to focus on what I can," she told herself. Life never waited for you to come to terms with it. It kept coming, and you had to hold on with your fingernails for all you were worth. "A good spot of training, sweat and hard work. That'll make me feel better."

Out in the yard, as golden light poured across the gray ground, Leon tested his arms, giving his axe a few good swings, and the sword in his other hand he whirled around like a water wheel. Selene fiddled with one of her eyelets in frustration. Her old fighting gear sat high around her belly—the awful bloody thing deigning to hurt as she tightened the jacket further.

Leon's beard shot with flecks of gray and he stood shorter than Selene, but as he cast off his cloak, muscled arms fuzzed with hair. Grizzled, but fearsome. They didn't call him the Strong for nothing.

"You sure you're ready to fight, Sel?"

Selene drew her dagger.

He cleared his throat. "All right."

They circled each other. He shifted one leg behind. She wasn't so out of practice that she couldn't see his shoulders square up for a blow.

He swung his axe around, moving a half-step forward. She stepped back and waited for his sword to come around too, but it didn't.

Fine. I'll do it myself. She flipped her dagger around in her hand, point down. The trusty steel blade tapered at the end—she'd had it since the beginning. The blade had slain more people than she could count. A little training with this old knight would be easy, even with her current malady.

She lunged with one leg, a side kick. He blocked it with the axe and she pirouetted, kicking out savagely with her back foot. Something twinged in her hip. She ignored it, pushing past the pain. He stepped back, surprised, and she lunged forward with her dagger. The axe head came around, and she ducked quickly, tucking forward into a roll. As she did, she swiped the blade across his ankle, but only gently. Like a lover's kiss.

They were only practicing after all.

He yelped. She met the rest of her roll and came up behind him.

Then fell to her side, unable to stand on her right leg, feeling it twist underneath her. She dropped her dagger and landed on her wrist. Pain exploded up her palm. She clenched her teeth, trying to push through, because if she didn't, she'd hate herself, more than she already did.

The training had attracted a crowd, and they gasped as she fell.

Ottille raced over to help her up. "Milady, let me help you." Selene shoved her off.

"Get off, I'm fine. I just need to warm up."

She flexed her hand, stretching her fingers. Her wrist ached. The pain and the clumsiness reminded her of her early days, the first time she'd held a blade. Her weakness. She breathed and picked up the dagger.

Leon's ankle bled. He readied himself.

Selene flipped up onto her toes and pushed off again, cartwheeling with her one hand and stamping her feet, somersaulting overhead. Her hip spasmed. Pain sliced into her belly like a knife. But she grinned as she soared through the air, ignoring the agony, regretting nothing. Everyone gasped. Leon put his axe high. She twisted and sliced. He dodged.

An attack like that would've killed a werewolf, she knew, had she been in peak condition. But pregnancy had slowed her, and birth had taken her fitness.

She landed on her toes, and sprung off again, throwing her knife, but careful to throw it hilt-first. Reversed, so it struck him with the flat.

It did. The slapping sound rang out and the people of Palerme laughed and sighed in awe.

She smiled as she lowered her balance to land and caught her breath. Her hips still played up, but she felt warm now.

"Fearsome," some said. "We were worried," others still.

"You should keep up, old knight!"

Leon roared with laughter. "I see you've not tempered your smart mouth a whit!"

"Maybe if you'd scored a hit!"

"But I did, Sel."

She looked down. Her trousers were torn, and jagged, while pale leg showed through. She blinked and laughed.

Training went on until the sun was highest and she could do no more. Leon looked ready as ever, though. When they climbed the stairs to the curtain wall overlooking the bailey, and on the other side the conifer forests of the Avallano Mountains, they talked.

"Do you still think of him?" he asked. "You and him, you're kindred in spirit. Still, you fight like a godsdamned wildcat compared to him. I think you would've beaten him, even as an Althann."

Tristain. "There's no one I think about more." *Except the man I killed.*

After a pause, Leon nodded. "I get it. I blame myself, too. I should've done more to protect him. I'd hate me, too."

"I don't hate you."

This bout of genuine emotion from him startled her. He usually wasn't so candid, preferring solitude and sarcasm. She felt the loss of not knowing what he was like as a knight before his shame and denouncement.

They stood silently on the parapet and watched the wind bend the trees. Smoke drifted on the air, smoke from the cookfires and the kitchens. Luncheon would be served soon, though what the cook Elias called luncheon was little more than a few watery eggs stuck to the bottom of an iron pot, covered in some brown sauce he rendered from the bones of something dead, even though none of the animals had died for months. Still, Selene's stomach pained, and her muscles ached. She'd missed this feeling.

"Tristain chose his path, too, don't misunderstand me." Leon leaned over the edge and peered down. Nothing below but rocks and choked sedge. He sighed, deflating a little and looking ten years older.

"In some ways, I'm still the same man that I used to be. But I've got a few more scars and an aching back just to pull me back down to crushing earth. I'm no Althann, but I want to do everything I can. There's a life here, and you've proven it. Now we just have to hold onto it, and hope none of us kill each other in the meantime." His chin worked as he swallowed. "That's what I'm still afraid of. One of them killing us all. It's what you hear as a kid, and what you grow up with. That stinking fucking *fear*."

She put her hand on his shoulder. "Lycanthropy is such a strange power. But we know the truth of it now."

"We owe everything we have to it. The only reason we're still alive is because of it. But it's cost us everything, too." She sighed. He grabbed her hand and held it tight. "Hard truths are often double-edged."

"Old ends come around, and we're likely to miss the opportunities, unless we grab them. That man we caught in the forest: I knew him from my novitiate days, and he told me the Order plan to kill the duca and pin it on us."

He turned. "Those cunting bastards. Gods take them."

"I sent Frix and his cousins to tell Alberracin. I'm sorry for lying to you."

"Let's hope they get to him before the Order do." He slapped his fist on the stone. "Bastards. They'll never rest until we're all gone."

Selene smiled. *Maybe I should've told him in the first place.*

A girl screamed in the yard. Selene turned and put a hand on her knife out of habit.

The hooded girl, the one that had arrived the week before, screamed as she kicked a boy in the shins. One of Gregor's boys. They looked to be fighting over something. There was always trouble when it came to those boys, but this looked more serious.

Selene paced down the stairs. Her legs ached and she didn't want to call alarm to the situation. By the time she'd met the bottom of the wall, both twins had arrived, and the girl was outnumbered.

One of Gregor's twins, she could never tell them apart, turned. "Milady, we caught her stealing from the kitchens."

"Stealing some bread," the other one said. "She can wait with the rest of us and get what we get. No special treatment!"

The girl shoved the second one and he laughed. She screamed in frustration. Selene would never break them up—if the girl wanted to prove the rightness of her words with a fight, then so be it. But Sanna lingered nearby, at the back of the stable. Ottille's little girl might be able to give the straight and true of it.

"Hold, girl. Is this true, what the boys are saying?"

Sanna lifted her head out from behind roughhewn logs. Rudimentary, but it served its purpose, and cared for it'd last for a century. Safe horses, come winter. Whether that was true for the rest of them was unclear.

"I didn't see it," Sanna said. She was younger than the others and Selene often thought that the twins were hard on the girl. She paused.

Gregor came stomping out of the smithy, crunching dirt under his boots. Lines cut across his hard face, and the muscles of a blacksmith bulged under his homespun tunic.

"What's going on?"

"Da, this girl stole bread from the kitchens."

"Where's the cook? We should ask Dunstad," Selene said. She never imagined she'd be investigating the source of missing bread a year ago. But new beginnings create new problems. *Missing bread problems*, she thought with a chuckle.

"It was them, the twins," the girl said.

Selene frowned over at her. She pointed at the two boys. They turned on her and took up rocks and pelted the girl.

"Hey," their father said, and the girl ran. The twins sped after her. "Get back here!"

"Get your boys under control, master blacksmith," Lucia spat. She'd come from the lord's tower, cross. Her old eyes blazed with a youthfulness so far unseen. "My granddaughter did nothing. You should be ashamed, raising little shits like that."

"Don't tell me how to raise my kids," he roared.

Selene rolled her eyes. Over by the wall, Leon watched with a cringe, worry in his eye. Two furious boys chased a girl, and they were gone from the keep, out the north gate, speeding up the mountain switchbacks.

CHAPTER 7

PRAISE BE

VERNUS, 1045

*The Istryan Empire is built on a hope of a thread of a dream.
It brings together fierce northerners who celebrate their enemy's
deaths by drinking from their skulls, wily southerners who pay
others to kill their enemies, and in between, the most low and
craven of midderlanders in Annalt, Ostelar, and all points
between. It seems to be held together by its own sheer weight.*

— Tomas Verdun, Historical Accounts of the
Pre-Imperial Period

"Praise be."

Richter flicked open his eyes. The woman stared back at him like he was a pig swinging from an abattoir hook, which was but a half-step from the truth. She stood a head shorter than him, gilded crown on her head, silvery blonde hair trailing down her shoulders, woven into plaits with pearls strung together. Rose and bergamot perfume fouled the air. Empress Melusine—the youngest wife yet of Emperor Franz, her breasts cinched high by a bodice arrogant enough to try to contain them.

Next to her with his hands clasped in his lap was Vetterand. Richter flinched. *You'll learn just how much I care for you.*

He sorted through his clouded mind. How long had he been hanging here? At least a week. The empress wasn't known to have many free appointments—the busiest woman in all the provinces and the empire. She'd made time for him. Richter nearly felt privileged.

As for why Richter had cause to know the empress's schedule, well, he was prepared. He made it his business to know his betters. The boy who had died in that dirty alley never truly faded from memory.

Melusine leaned forward, snarling his nose with the strong bergamot-orange smell. In his heightened sense—only a residual compared to his monstrous form—he could hear her heart beat faster. Her breasts were pink and fleshy, wrapped like two cantaloupes at the market. She touched Richter's cheek with the tip of a slender finger. The fingers of a woman who had never known dirt. Though that wasn't entirely true. As the rumors went, she danced in the Gutter at the same time as Richter did, although her dance was of a wholly different nature. It was all he could do to not get lost in her deep blue eyes, and he knew why Franz took another wife.

Oh, fuck.

Her eyes traced downwards. His tunic offered just enough coverage of his soft bits when he had his hands lowered. But his hands were not lowered, and his bits were not soft. She burst into laughter.

"He looks human," she said, incredulous. She was almost sad to tear her eyes away from below as she looked him over. "I wouldn't say handsome, but a gruff sort. Pleasant enough. The scars add something fierce and dangerous to his look."

"Indeed, milady. The demon's trickery fooled even me."

She looked back, gave an amused smile. "Well, if he fooled even the great Vetterand, he is truly formidable."

"That's not what I meant—"

"But it is the implication, yes? He was your man for nearly twenty years, since you found him in the streets of the Gutter."

She knows about me. Richter smiled. *This woman has no idea what she's in for.* You never matched wits with Vetterand. You only hoped that his attention focused on other efforts.

As the rumors also went, after marrying Franz, she'd dedicated herself, body and spirit, to the worship of Sigur. Proved shit for the emperor, but a man like that had many mistresses, and he could ply any woman with enough gold to guarantee their silence. Rumors also went that Melusine had taken her own mistresses too.

"What are you smiling at, demon?" She still wore that pleased look. "You won't be smiling after you see what the Grand Inquisitor has in store."

Richter grinned wider. "Is that so?"

Vetterand snorted as the empress turned to him, uncertain.

"Don't worry, milady. The cure will work, and the curse shall be purified from his body."

What cure? Many secrets laid within the walls of the Holy Fortress, where artificers and clerics messed with the fabric of reality. Well, that was a stretch. But they certainly tugged on the bitch's threads. Did they have a cure? Surely not.

Melusine laughed, though it contained only mild amusement.

"Goodbye, demon. I hope we never meet again."

"Same to you, woman."

Melusine didn't deign to answer that barb. "Make sure you cure him or kill him," she said to Vetterand. "These demons will kill us all if we let them."

She left the room, hips swaying with a practiced motion. Two big inquisitors that Richter didn't recognize filed in after. They carried iron staves, loops of thick rope bound to thick iron tips. They slipped the ropes around his neck, and Vetterand approached, fishing a key out of his robe.

Richter laughed. "Are you afraid I'll escape?"

"I know you won't. This is just for show."

"What makes you think so?"

"Because the Order is the only thing that gives your life purpose. I can give you that back, but you have to do what I tell you."

He unlocked the chain fastening him to the roof and his arms dropped. He could reach out and kill both of these inquisitors, and Vetterand. If he moved quick enough. And he hadn't met a man yet that was quicker.

The Lightfather giveth, and the Lightfather taketh away.

"Fine."

The two inquisitors scrunched their noses.

"Are you sure your cure will work, Grand Inquisitor?" one of them asked.

"I will assume you didn't say that, Jonas."

They pulled him forward at the length of their staves. The ropes tightened around his neck, biting, and he growled. If he transformed now, if he escaped, it wouldn't matter. He'd be left with nothing—he'd have to go back to the Gutter, back to that boy that had nothing. Or worse. Thrown into the deepest pit and forgotten forever, more likely. He'd be hunted to the seas and beyond. The Order gave him everything and it fucking broke him to think that he could've had anything else. Yes, he had his mission.

For He is good.

But it would be so much harder without the authority of the Order. What was this cure, then? It was nothing Richter hadn't faced before, and then he could get on with the business of killing werewolves.

He stepped out of the stairwell to find a crowd hemming the edges of a guarded aisle, lined with inquisitors in gray armor—a path for him and his captors—that led straight down to something at the far end. A scalloped stone door, bleeding light. They were still in the Holy Fortress, then.

The crowd yelled, angry and anguished. A demon in their midst, and they all wanted a piece of him. Nials—that dog's breakfast—spat at the floor. But it wasn't just Swords. Men in cinched doublets, fat-chinned yet waspish around the waist, yellow and grinning. Their guts pulled in as if by magic, or corsetry at the very least. Women in tiny hats and huge dresses, their bodices leaving ample displays. He was flattered they all came for him.

They pelted him with rotten fruit and stale bread, soiling his clothes. He wondered if he'd those clothes, soon. He'd enjoyed his share of executions to know when one was coming.

A breeze whistled through the doors and blew up his tunic, leaving his bare ass and bits wobbling. The crowd laughed, all pointing at him, drawing endless entertainment from his misfortune.

Bring judgment on the creature, ruin to his form.

He turned to Nials as he passed. Richter twisted his head, groaning as his bones broke and shifted and fur grew until it resembled a wolf. The crowd gasped. They weren't laughing now. As he stepped forward, pulling the ropes tight, he smelled their fear. Smelled like stale piss and blood. Swords drew their weapons. He roared at Nials. Spittle flew from his mouth and coated a small woman between them. Nials grinned at the challenge.

Where was life without a bit of fun? He couldn't hate them—they were all scared of him. Creatures like him destroyed whole towns for fun. That's why they hunted him and that's why he hunted others like him.

He didn't attack them. They didn't need to know he couldn't be killed. Vetterand knew that, probably. But no one else needed to know—and he would go along with this cure. Only the gods knew if it would work. Though Vetterand seemed convinced. Richter turned back to human, ready to face what awaited.

Outside, when the bright day resolved in his eye, he saw a pyre. A big pyre. The center held an iron cage big enough for him, filled with kindling, while around logs were piled high. Sigur's sword—made from bundles of wood tied together—pierced the sky.

Power may be found in the darkest reaches, where only His light may penetrate.

His neck rubbed where the ropes had him. Chafed. He was all too glad when they undid the ropes and shoved him inside. The crowd filed out of the hall and onto the white flags. Gulls wheeled above and screamed in the air, waiting for the feast. Maybe there was an eagle there too, soaring higher, seeing its pickings among the crowd.

The emperor in his stupid crown, gilded and handsome. The nobles, fawning and ambitious, stuffed with wine and grinning with murder. This world needed men like him, men like Richter. Hard men who did the unpleasant things to keep them safe, so they could continue to live behind their high walls and in their high palaces, stuffing themselves with duck liver and ambition.

An inquisitor locked the gate, chaining it shut, then they piled wood in front of the door, winking the light and the crowd out of view. Faint slivers of day still blued in cracks between the layers. Stinking of dry timber and sap, and rot underneath, the little room would burn soon. Burn him.

Stab him that praises His name, burn him that praises His name, kill him that praises His name. He shall not die.

Richter waited. He closed his eyes. As his stinking breath and the stench of sweat mixed in his nose, he remembered that day. Vetterand found him—a boy of no more than ten. Days he was hammered with training, learning how to fight. Nights he was hammered with words, months of memorization. He barely slept. Vetterand wanted him for his dream, to be the greatest hunter of all the demons on the Continent.

He fulfilled that dream. Now what? Richter wanted nothing more than to free himself of his own curse, and to understand why the god that cursed him drew breath. Vetterand's mission. Richter's mission. They were one and the same.

Sweat dripped from his forehead and down his chin, nestling in his beard and chest hair. Then poured. He could hear cheering. It was hot. Soon his pits were saturated and everything else. Smoke leaked through a gap in the wall. He held his breath. The fire would need to purify him.

Fire is the cure for the beast.

The cure would work. How couldn't it?

He laid down. The wood felt hot on his bare skin. He knew the smoke would rise, but the fire would need to get him first.

His skin started to ache and turn red. It singed, and he moved out of reflex. But everything was hot. Embers bubbled through the walls. More smoke poured in, filling the space with a haze. He could barely see now. He held his breath still, but his eyes streamed and his head pounded.

He breathed, taking in a heap of smoke and he coughed. *Sigur, end my suffering. Let this cure work! I have done enough!*

He heard a sizzling sound. It was his skin. He writhed, afraid to touch anything, but it all burned, all branded him. He forced his mouth shut—he wouldn't show his fear in the face of this purification. Sigur ordained this. Vetterand was His vessel and acted with His authority. He never should have doubted the Grand Inquisitor, and now he would suffer for it.

The cure would work.

Fire is the only cure for the beast.

A pyre, built to honor Him, caging a man that defied His presence with every unending breath he took.

The cure would work.

He screamed. Dazzling flame burned his eyes and he rammed them closed. It boiled his skin. Pain shot through every pore, a million needles, then deadened. If this was death, he welcomed it. He tried, but every breath came short. Not enough air. Not enough of anything. He swallowed flame and his eyes burned out and his hair caught fire and his tongue tasted it, tasted death, boiled the water in his throat and pitched into his lungs.

It surrounded him. He was barely aware of the transformation taking hold. It did nothing. He still burned. Skin healed and reformed, only to be boiled away. Fur ignited; he could smell it until his sense of smell burned out.

This cycle continued for... he lost track of time. By turns, he lost consciousness. It repeated. Wake up, burn to death, transform, burn to death. Awake, burn, transform, burn. Flashes of orange and white passed in front of his eyes before his corneas scorched out, leaving him in darkness once again. Excruciating darkness.

And his body healed every time, so even the bliss that came when his nerves died only lasted a short time, before agony tore through his skin again. Inescapable agony.

He sat, ignoring the pain, ignoring the chasing of breath and the swallow of fire. The boiling of his lungs. He closed his eyes—not that his eyes worked—and went inward. The agony subsided. No, it never subsided, but he could ignore it.

That was the thing about pain. You could get used to anything given enough time. He had taken his fear and his pain and replaced them with something better: boredom. Or worse, he wasn't sure. Like the waterwheel set into motion by a strong current, each moment he died, and each moment he came back. But what can a waterwheel know of pain? It'll keep going as long as there's momentum.

Desperation wore the skin of faith and wore it well. After all, what was the difference between a faithful man and a man driven to faith?

THE NIGHT SKY WINKED in from the top of the cage as the pyre crumbled around him, burned to embers. A cool breeze washed over him, soothed his singed skin and aching bones, like a whore airing out her nether bits after a vigorous client had finished with her. He lifted his hands up to look at them, unsure of what he'd see. They were lances of pink and gray, ashen. A fingernail fell off, and he trembled. Fear had long subsided, replaced with something approaching excitement, but tasting bad in the mouth.

Staves chopped in at the sides of the cage, stabbing and clearing grayish black ash, what was left of the wood. The crowd dwindled in size compared to when it started, but he saw the emperor and the empress still there. They watched, their mouths open. All of them stood stunned.

Only Vetterand, who walked up to the cage and unlocked it, smiled. Rather looked like he'd just seen a man sit on the inside of a pyre and not die as it burned around him. And was happy about the results.

"Lords and ladies," he said, "honorable members of the court, esteemed colleagues... the cure for lycanthropy is the pyre and the cage."

They clapped and whistled and cheered. Vetterand was practiced enough not to show his thrill, not to gloat over a victory, but Richter knew what the man was feeling inside.

Triumphant.

The inquisitors helped him out of the cage. "Take him to the infirmary," Vetterand ordered. He smiled, only gently, as Richter passed him.

"Don't fuck this up. Keep your fucking mouth shut and keep your fucking secrets to yourself. Teach those lackwit novitiates properly, this time."

"A war is coming," he yelled. "And now we have a weapon to end the menace, once and for all! Praise be to Sigur!"

"Praise be," they cheered.

CHAPTER 8
LAWS
VERNUS, 1045

Laws must be administered fairly and without prejudice. Failing that, they must be brought swiftly and without mercy.

— HANDBOOK OF THE IMPERIAL MAGISTRATE

"I CAN'T HAVE THEM kill that little girl," she said to Leon. "We need to find them."

"Can't say as I thought I'd be chasing kids like a godsdamned governess, but you're right." Leon glowered. "Even if the boys let her go, they could trip and break somethin'."

Selene stepped gingerly over a fallen branch. Her body ached from exhaustion. "Their necks."

She breathed and pushed ahead. Sweat slid from her armpit, trickled down her back. The top of the hill opened out before her. A flat, bald knob of a hill, treeless, but flanked on all sides by furry pines, it reminded her of Frix's cousin. Ahead, shapes flitted through the trees, yellow and brown. Their clothes. She caught her breath for a moment. They wouldn't get far. On the other side of the clearing was a crevasse where the river cut through the mountain. She could've caught them on horseback, but a horse would be a hindrance here.

"Sanna," she yelled. She cupped her mouth with her hand. "Ulie, Mattias!"

Her voice echoed over the shingle, but the forest remained silent and stark. The smell of rot and damp carried on the wind, carrying the undercurrent of a flowery scent, but false. Some poor imitation of a flower. She realized she'd never been up here, in the mountains beyond the keep, where the white sky loomed unbound and only the tops dusted with snow gave any semblance of breaking to the endless forest.

Gregor caught up, puffed.

"Where are they?"

"Must be further in the forest," Leon said. "Ginevra knows this land is turned inside out. They could be anywhere."

"Stupid boys. I've told them again and again."

"You show them discipline?"

"Eme fucking knows it."

"*Sal'brath*. Well, there's nothing for it. We gotta find 'em before the sun sets, otherwise we'll be just as lost as they are."

They passed into the forest and out of the clearing. The sun smeared beyond the dark green needles, and along the roots of the trees dappled spotted mushrooms. Toxic pricks mistaken for real food to the needy and dying. Poisoners in the Order used them to paralyze and kill Althann. There was the belladonna, too, and the foxglove, hemlock, and a million other varied plants that killed or necrotized or itched. For a Continent originally inhabited by werewolves, it sure did mean to harm them.

Gregor stalked ahead. She and Leon pushed through a rough forest floor littered with fallen trees and branches. They'd been hunting the kids for well over an hour, now. Ahead was a river, and more trees. Everywhere you looked, more trees, but she knew well enough that each tree held its own clue.

"Not there," she told Leon. The leaf litter had been disturbed, but not by a child. Little marks, like a deer, and nearby, tufts of hair caught on some bark. Whether the deer had rubbed itself against the tree or brushed there by accident, it didn't matter. If deer had passed this way, the kids wouldn't be there. More like the other way around, but that also didn't matter. All that mattered was finding them.

Ottille would never forgive Gregor, and demand retribution. That did leave the question hanging: how did laws work in a land where the laws of men failed them so often? The Althann had been failed by Sigur's laws, the Empire's laws. Lords often made their own decisions, and now, as lady, would Selene have to make her own?

And what if one of the parties disagreed?

They rounded a large, lumpen trunk of an old yew that had split and reformed over the centuries. It gnarled at the roots and touched jagged, ancient limbs to the sky. She wondered what that yew had seen—whether it was but a seedling when the Althann ruled this Continent. If all its scars came from just holding on, just surviving, as Selene's had.

She looked around.

"Where's Gregor?"

"What's that?"

"Gregor. The smith. He was just here."

"Didn't see him."

"That's what I'm saying."

A branch crunched and something huge splintered and shook. Birds screamed and fled from the canopies, taking off over the top of them. Selene narrowed her eyes and drew her dagger. Leon drew his axe and his sword.

"Bears?"

Leon waved her down. He was silent, and crept along the ground, keeping to the doused leaves that had rotted. *He's stalked a few animals in his time, then.* Hunters knew. Selene knew, and she'd hunted. Man and werewolf. Not for food, but the principle was the same. He wasn't as practiced as Selene, since he didn't notice the deer marks, but he knew a lot more than nothing at all.

Thumping and cracking, a tree fell just ahead. A small pine, it shook as it landed, spewing a cloud of needles. Selene and Leon uncoiled themselves.

"What is going on?"

"Shh. There's something in the trees." Selene came to one knee. "There." She ambled over, careful not to make a noise.

What could bring down a tree? Not a bear, surely. That fallen pine looked young and healthy. But she didn't know much about pines—it wasn't covered in Order poisons and procurement.

Something bigger, then. A werewolf.

She stood.

Leon looked up at her. "What are you doing?"

"It's Gregor. He's transformed since it's easier for him to smell them out."

"Ah. Well, *sal'brath*. I feel bloody useless."

She laughed. "Indeed."

"You get used to it," Leon chuckled. "I don't know what a flock of knights is called, but Tristain, he certainly killed a flock of 'em. All on his lonesome."

Selene murmured. "Hm. I never knew him as a soldier. What was he like? What was Rennes like?"

Leon glanced at his feet like he might find some courage there. "*Sal'brath*." He sniffed back tears. Selene felt for him. He'd loved Tristain like a son, as much as Selene had loved him like a brother. Once a man she thought she might marry and would've been happy to.

She shook her head. *It's all so complicated.* You lived your life and made choices, doing the best you could to survive. When you look back, you're older and have a few more scars, and you hope you're wiser for it.

She knelt at the bottom of a gnarled, moist ash, and picked a mushroom that clung to its roots. She smelled it. They were the right ones. She rifled through the moss, and made a pouch of her jacket, undoing the tabs at the bottom.

There was yew, yarrow, and willow bark, for their healing properties, yes. Certainly, she could pick out her henbane from her belladonna. What was all of it for? Poisons were useful for killing, though she could at least use some of her knowledge to make remedies for pleurisy, cough, and the like. It helped them make it through the frigid bruma months in the mountains.

Poisons made for hidden weapons and worked on man just as well as wolf. And it was unlikely the Order would just let them survive. Just like her, to be as prepared as she could. These spotted black mushrooms, when dried and powdered, then cooked with suet, made a potent hallucinatory drug. If there was some henbane in these mountains, that would be perfect.

"What are you doing now," Leon asked, impatient.

"The Order won't just let us be. Frix and his cousins' mission attests to that. We need to be prepared."

A branch cracked and Selene snapped her head to where it came from. Gregor and the kids stood on the other side of the gully. He had his two sons wrangled by their collars, while his shirt hung off him, stretched at the seams, needing repair. Sanna, the girl, smiled when she saw Selene.

She ran up, bounding through the muck and the creek, getting mud all over her long dress. Actually, she was covered in it. Had she hidden from the boys? Selene threw her arm around the girl and the girl hugged her tight.

"They didn't hurt you, did they?"

Sanna shook her head.

"Well, your mother will be glad to see you safe."

Gregor lifted his head. "You can be assured that my boys will be sweeping out the smithy and the stables until their hands ache. It's high time you learned there's costs to your actions."

"It wasn't our fault! She started it!" they cried.

"Now I'm bloody ending it. Sorry, milady."

Selene nodded. "That's acceptable."

One of them, Ulie she thought, yelled, "Why do *she* get to lord over me? She's not even one of us!"

"Quiet, Ulie," Gregor snapped. "That's enough."

"No!" Ulie shoved off his father. "We lost Mama, we lost Dog, we lost our home! But she gets to tell me what to do? What's she lost?"

"What have I lost?" She tightened her jaw. "Love. Kindness."

"Sel." Leon put his hand on her shoulder. "He's just a child. He doesn't know what he's sayin'."

"You know what it takes to lead, you little shit?"

"That's enough, now," Gregor said.

"Enough? I've given up all chance at anything approaching happiness. I see ghosts at night, and lost lovers in my nightmares, calling to me, telling me to join them. Every day I know I'm damned for what I did, for what I do. There's no escape from the path I was set on, the path that I chose for myself. I don't want there to be a way out. I don't deserve it."

The edges of her words became sharp until all she spoke were shards.

"You ask what did I give up? My future. I could just walk away, but my son, he'll be hunted for the rest of his life. I shred myself so that he might have something he can hold onto, something good. I shred myself to make a future for him, for everyone in Palerme, all the Althann. I shred myself so that you all may have a sunrise that I know I'll never see.

"You ask what did I give up? *Everything.*"

Leon gaped his mouth. "Sel, I had no idea—"

"I'm sorry, milady," Ulie said. He looked as though he might cry.

She turned and marched back to Palerme, still fuming. She thought the outburst would make her feel better, but it only made her feel worse.

Something warm and smooth slid into her hand. Selene frowned down. It was Sanna, the little girl pressing her soft cheek against Selene's sleeve. Selene slowed. No words were said as they walked. There was no need.

Trestinsen waited at the gate for them with that look on his face, like the burden of life was too much to bear. A green hood framed a guardsman's grimace, one she was sure he wore well when delivering bad news to his ex-lord, and one that he wore now for her.

"Milady," he said. "You—we—we did all we could."

Selene stopped. "Were you looking for Senna, too? She's right here."

"I'm right here," the little girl repeated.

"No, milady, she... the old woman. That merchant... weren't a merchant."

Selene grunted in frustration. "Out with it, man."

"You'd best just come with me," he said and knocked a big fist on the wood. For all his grimacing, the man was a good soldier, and one she'd want on her side in a fight.

The postern gate opened, and Gregor and the others came up behind. Felt their eyes on her. She didn't look at them, didn't know if she could face them after that outburst. Yelling at a child... *what was I thinking? I'm supposed to be keeping it together for everyone. They look to me for guidance.*

Best she got on with the task. No one got hurt, this time, and she thanked whatever spirits looked over them for that.

Through the darkened arch of stone, almost too short to stand fully, the yard echoed with roars, shouts, and snarled words. Her heart quickened. In the center of a circle of vicious faces was the merchant, bloody and gashed, his head bleeding. He brandished a knife at them, eyes wild with terror. Ottille in her long and slender lupine form brandished her own weapons, her long claws, circling him like a predator. Like he was a deer with a particularly sharp antler, no sort of resistance for Ottille. So, what was she waiting for?

"What in the hells is going on?"

Tomas turned his head from facing the center, back to her. From the Tri-tipped Spear, he spoke Osbergian with a particularly rustic tune. "This bastard snuck into your rooms when you were gone, tried to kill baby Tristain. Lucia stopped him, but it cost her life. Ottille hunted him out here, waited for your judgment."

Selene's breath caught, a sinking feeling like her throat had been cut and all the blood rushed out, spattered the ground with vital red. "He tried to kill my son? Where is he? Where is Tristain?"

"Yes, milady. Helena's watching him now. We thought he might not want to see this next part."

Selene ground her teeth and drew her long knife, the wood cool in her hand, and the circle broke for her.

"Careful, milady, he's wilier than he looks."

He was crazier than he looked, taking on a castle full of lycans, and a furious mother. "Who are you? Now!"

He wheeled around, faced her with a grimace. "She weren't supposed to be there, but it's no great loss."

His accent had changed. No longer the whimsical Annaltian, it was something more vicious. Ottille snapped at him with sharp teeth, a warning.

He tried to kill my son!

She turned her knife over by the blade and threw it. Order daggers were made with a single bevel, tapered right to the point where it cut. Made them hellishly easy to throw, carved the air around them, and they took all sorts of punishment before losing their edge. This one had taken its fair share, and more than a few lives. It took another one.

The knife planted in his skull, punching through the bone. His eyes rolled back. Roland dropped to the ground in a heap, his knife clattering off the hard-packed earth, his legs twitching. She enjoyed watching the life leave him.

The only sound in the yard was a crow, presumably waiting for them to leave so it could make a meal out of him.

Ottille's big hands slumped, her furry shoulders rounding. She changed back, fur sheathing, face reforming, muscles shrinking to show a tall, pale-skinned woman, freckles across her naked chest. What looked like shame pricked her cheeks, though it wasn't shame at her nakedness. Nakedness was normal among the Althann, or at least the impracticality of keeping clothed kept the embarrassment away. No, it seemed more like it was directed at the swift end of the man that had killed her mother. She looked at Selene, tears welling in her blue eyes like rain.

They looked at her. She had to take charge. Tempers that ran hot often swiftly changed their target. "I am the lady and I made the judgment. This man murdered Lucia while attempting to murder my son. She will be remembered as a hero, while this man will be prey for carrion."

They nodded, murmured their agreement. Ottille looked disappointed but didn't disagree, left the yard by the door to the lord's tower.

"Milady," Leon said. He wore his disapproval openly but she wondered if he might withhold his agreement. Over bruma, she'd had to make hard decisions that were clear as mud to the outcome, but they'd made it. He had learned to trust her decisions, surely.

She bent over and searched his coat, his pockets. A coin pouch at his belt, heavy with gold. Imperial gold, stamped with the emperor's face. *An assassin, bought by the Order.*

They can't just leave us alone! Angry tears forced their way out, like a dam cracking, threatening to drown the next town downstream. She pushed them back inside. She couldn't afford to break down, to stop. *Grief is for the dead and the dying.*

"I must see Tristain. I'll speak to you when I return."

"Of course."

Helena—a yellow-toothed old woman, though not as old as Lucia—sat in the barracks, on a cot of straw, with Tristain in her arms, sleeping soundly. She stood as Selene paced up, saw a frightened face that Selene did an abysmal job of hiding.

"He's fine, milady," she said. A blanket swaddled tight around him, his long, dark eyelashes closed over big eyes, as cozy as he was in the womb, no wiser to the fact he'd just escaped his ultimate fate. She took Tristain, cooed, brushed a finger across his lips.

"What's the world coming to when a babe isn't safe in his crib," Helena said, more for her own benefit.

"My son will never be safe. I brought this upon him, and it's up to me to stop it."

"What will you do, milady?"

A terrible heritage, a horrific crime. She'd brought this on Tristain by destroying the Order in Osbergia and stopping at home. The Grand Inquisitor would never let them live. They went against Sigur's teachings every breath they took, and it was well-known now that werewolves took sanctuary in Palerme. Sanctuary. They violated sanctuary, killed innocent women, targeted children. It was time to end this. Enough with laws, enough with fairness. The only law she needed was the law of the wild. *A death for a death.*

"What I should've done a long time ago. Destroy the Order."

CHAPTER 9
QUESTIONS
VERNUS, 1045

*When they built Istrya on a lake, did they realize that it had
once been the site of an enormous volcano? The lake was the
mouth of the volcano, and the spit of land that the city lies on
was the ash falling to the ground and solidifying once more?*

— GERAINT FALLSTADT, HISTORIAN

RICHTER'S BONES FELT AS heavy as lead and his skin tingled with
every movement. He pushed up to a seated position in the bed in
his quarters slow and groaning. He could still taste the ash on his tongue.
He knew that taste would never go away. Fire flashed in his memory, and
the remnants of pain threatened to consume him as he sat there. He spent
a few hairy moments trying to breathe, remembering to breathe, trying to
remember how to breathe. It was almost like he couldn't get enough air,
no matter how hard he sucked it in, like an alcoholic with his mouth to an
empty barrel—but the barrel felt full.

He threw off his linens, streaming with sweat, and stumbled over to the
window, pitching open the shutters with both hands. The blighted lake
stared back him, this time gray and flensed white with the threat of a storm.

He leaned his head as far as it would go out of the window. Surely there'd be enough air in the world to satisfy his hungry-fucking-lungs?

There was, and he calmed a little. The wind iced his face, dried his lips. He was surprised he had any moisture left, the way it had been cooked out of him. The sun god left an ugly stain on the horizon as he rose.

A new day began, and he wasn't a prisoner. In fact, he wasn't really sure he was anything. Was he still a Sword? Could a werewolf-cured be a holy warrior?

Life and death by turns; all serve Him.

In his case, he'd taken that one a little more literally.

Heavy footsteps shuffled behind the door. The gait of someone wearing armor, or just a particularly heavy-footed person. Richter looked around for a weapon since you never knew. Friend, or foe. There wasn't much difference where he was concerned. He found a silver candlestick on a counter—about the only touch of luxury in the grim, gray-walled room. Just the way he liked it.

The man in dark navy, could've been black, stepped into the room, carting a tray of something as he pushed in. Richter breathed in through his nostrils and dashed the man over the head with the candlestick.

"Auuguh," came the man's noise as he flopped onto the floorboards. The tray of things he was carrying crashed to the ground in a noisy, scattering mess.

Fruit? There were bits of apples and oranges all over the ground. He looked down. The man who'd brought the tray inside looked up through the wild nest of Richter's ball hairs.

"Father Domitus?"

"I see you're as grouchy as ever in the morning," Domitus said. Blood wept between his hair and down his temple.

"Oh, fuck, sorry," Richter said. He helped the priest stand on unsteady feet. "I should take you to the infirmary."

As soon as the priest smiled at him, he knew he was home. He felt the energy from his smile, a tingling in his ears. Domitus had a way of projecting his care for Richter even when Richter didn't show him any back. The streets of Istrya had long ceased to be home for Richter; wherever home was, Domitus was there.

The priest fingered his scalp with meaty, ringed digits. They came away bloody and he wobbled. "I'm bleeding."

"All right, let's take you to the infirmary."

Try as he might, he couldn't ignore the stares as they went down the long stone corridors, festooned with icons. Dark eyes stared. He thought he might pluck out a few, give them something to truly stare at. Most of them were just puzzled, some outright hateful.

"Vetterand has assured everyone that you're cured," Domitus said. "But us Sigurites are a suspicious sort, you know. You are cured, right?"

Richter walked alongside, supporting him by the crook of his elbow. "Yes, I'm cured."

It's likely as not—I haven't tried. He didn't want to try here—a repeat of the pyre didn't appeal. He reached out with his mind, and it tethered to something outside of himself—another part of him, violent and animalistic. Although that might've just been him as well. Hard to know where monster diverged from man.

"That's well. I hate to see you suffering."

Richter rolled his eyes. "Do you ever stop to think that I'm not worth caring about?"

"Not me. I still remember that broken boy from the Gutter."

"Are you sure that's not just your head still addled from the candlestick? I did hit you fairly hard."

Domitus chuckled then grabbed his head, as though a knife plunged into it, groaning. "You did, didn't you?"

"I never liked breakfast."

Domitus laughed.

THE VESTALS WORE WHITE chased with red trim and cared for the injured and the sick, though only a few milled around the yawning hall. A maw of a gallery replete with stained glass through which grayish light filtered. The glasswork wound in figures of emaciated martyrs, slain by demons. Skewered with their claws, torn apart by teeth. Blood and pus leaked from open wounds. Richter didn't know whether to pity the martyrs or hate them for their weakness—the constant talk of suffering got on his nerves, really.

Needless to say, he preferred the passages in the Book on power, the treatises on bringing war to the demon.

If the Order focused on that, maybe they'd get more done. He'd killed more werewolves than every Sword combined. Though that was no feat to be proud of when he had colleagues like Nials, who stood at the foot of a bed, talking with a vestal.

"Can the priest get some fucking help here," Richter said.

Nials glanced at him and smiled. A melted smile like a candle that had been held to the fire.

The vestals rushed over.

"Mother, the priest has hurt his head."

"Your needn't bother yourself, Mother Anna," Domitus said. "I'll be fine with a bit of bed rest. You neither, Inquisitor."

"That's right," Nials interceded. He walked over. "Richter here has somewhere he's meant to be, isn't that true?"

Am I still an inquisitor? Hang on, what the fuck? "Where the fuck am I supposed to be?"

Nials's voice skipped like a song. "Upstairs, teaching a bunch of novitiates how to tie their fucking jacket laces."

"Vetterand still wants me for that?"

"He didn't tell you?"

Richter gave him a baleful look.

"Right. Well, he's expecting you. Think he'd rather forget that whole thing."

Richter glanced at Domitus.

"I'll be fine," Domitus said. "You should move along, too, young Nials. Don't you have duties of your own?"

"I'll be fine, addled old man."

Richter jabbed Nials with a finger. "You'd best keep your mouth shut. Domitus was a Sword when you were still at your mother's tit. Never underestimate the man who lives to an old age in a profession where men die young."

Nials shrugged. "He carry a sword anymore?"

"Carry it better than you, ugly bastard."

"I use a crossbow, lackwit."

"The point isn't the weapon. The imperative demarcates the entire gamut of weapons a Sword might use."

"*Demarcates?* That's an expensive word, Richter. Guess you northerners are very fond of such things—among them irony, cosmetics, and oiling your faces like women."

"You see oil on my face? Cosmetics? Anyway, wouldn't expect a southerner like you to understand. You still fuck goats in Osbergia."

"Enough," Mother Anna said. "I won't have you jackanapes fighting in my hall. Either way, you're both late. I would think you, Richter, wouldn't want to fall foul of Vetterand's wrath again. And you, Nials, saw that pyre as well as I."

Anna's eyes avoided Richter's. You'd think he'd died, or something. *I did, numerous times.*

"Fine. Feel better, Father."

Domitus nodded and Richter set his jaw to the wide doors and strode out. Nials followed, and Richter tried to ignore the bothersome fool nipping at his heels like a little yappy dog.

T HE SECRETS OF KILLING held a special place in Richter's heart. A man could die seven different ways with just a finger, given the right application of force and technique. Eleven, using the arms and the legs. Not to mention the thousand different ways to snap a joint or break a bone.

"Incapacitating the demon works too," he told the assembled novitiates. They gathered around him like a priest at Gebet, ready to hear his holy sermon. "If you knock them out, they transform back to men—never mind that nonsense about 'true forms'." He knew some preceptors and inquisitors liked to perpetuate that falsehood—that the demon's true face was the wolf. Richter knew the wolf was contained inside the man, not the other way around. At least in his experience, and his experience was vast. If the average Sword's experience had the depth of a bucket, Richter's experience held an entire ocean.

He leaned on a pillar. The training hall echoed with their voices. Some of the others sparred as instructed, and he'd gathered the few that he thought showed promise. Karl, the one who'd killed him. A woman named Fahling, and a Salzheimer lad, blond and blue-eyed, his face suited to beauty contests than swordsmanship, but his chest and arms looked as though they'd been stuffed with boulders.

"But I thought strength was useless against them," Fahling said. She had a savage scar across her scalp, cutting through her dark hair, leaving it flopped on either side like some ridiculous house plant. A woman like that knew, like Richter, what it was to fight tooth and nail for survival. A killer.

"I didn't say strength. I said technique. Leverage and weight. If that fails, use a rock suspended from a great height."

They laughed.

"Besides. Your job is to convince them they don't need to transform, that they should feel comfortable with you. Get close to them, then gut them. My favorite role to play is the travelling healer. But if everyone does it, I'll have to find a new way, since every town will be full of fake healers."

They laughed more. He was enjoying himself. Who knew?

"Don't you ever have any doubts?"

Richter pushed down that fleeting happiness. The boy who'd asked was a weedy lad with a sunken chin, who'd stopped sparring to come over.

"No. I can't afford them."

"But you're one of them."

"Not anymore."

"What if the cure didn't work?"

Richter smiled through his teeth. "You ask a lot of questions." *They're just taking anyone these days.* "Do you want your neck stretched? Get back to fighting. If you turn your back on your opponent, you'll get killed."

The boy backed down. About time someone listened to him. He was worried he'd lost his touch.

"You might be wondering how do you make certain a demon is a demon? See, a wukodlak, demon, whatever, they're looking for a reason to mistrust everyone. You might be thinking that means they'll never trust you, never let you get close, but the demon knows someone will come for them eventually. It's as simple as that. Make it clear someone's after them that isn't you, and they'll come running right onto your blade."

He stood upright, pushing up from the pillar. "I find there's nothing better than learning on the job. You three, follow me. The rest of you keep sparring. Kill each other or not, I don't care."

I STRYA WAS ONE OF those places where one could see both the best and the worst of the Continent. Giant palaces of dukes and grandees floated above hovels that housed stinking bodies in their dozens, crammed in, pushing over each other for air like fish in a net. Women in various states of dress plied their bodily trade along the frontage of dirty houses slotted in between avenues of swirling ironwork lanterns and immaculately kept bushes. Istrya kept her gardeners, her ironworkers, and her whores busy.

A redhead woman spilling from her dress snorted a pinch of snuff from a silver box, then walked into a nearby tavern to cheers and whistles. Not all cities on the Continent were like this. In Rhoregia, the king killed the first sons of his nobility, to keep them in line. Richter admired a man with that kind of foresight.

But not in Istrya. This city was run by greedy lackwits, too obsessed with the newest fabrics from Taneria to think about anything other than their mistresses and their powdered whores.

Richter was fine with that. He understood the city, knew the laws, and he sure as hell spoke the violence that passed for language here. What he admired most about Istrya, though, was that you could find anything your heart desired. Including a fresh kill.

His heart beat a mite faster at that thought. The last fortnight had belonged to the wolves, as Domitus often said, with the pyre and his imprisonment. Now it was Richter's turn. The irony wasn't lost on him. He longed to stretch his limbs in the brutal dance of the hunt.

"Where are we going?" the blond, pretty one said.

When Richter didn't answer, the lad gave him the sign of the up-side-down sword, below his belt. The lad was growing on him. *If he's half a fighter as much as he's pulling those sweet women outside that beerhall, well, we might be in for a treat.* He longed to find some capable hands, if only to make his job easier. He couldn't be everywhere in the Continent all at once. A demon ought to slip out of fingers, and he couldn't have that. Yes, a good bunch of killers would suit him nicely.

They walked together but apart. He instructed them as much. Never knew when someone was looking.

A crier stood on a crate ahead, his shouting getting louder as they approached. He waved a knitted cap at anyone that passed, coins disappearing into its depts.

"Franz to make an appearance at the Karlspalast, Highest, 21 Vernus, to commemorate Ginnsday! Word is he'll speak on his sons and the war! The future of the south!"

Richter tossed a coin the boy's way, and he snatched it out of the air with a greedy swipe. "Thank you, grim sir!"

Richter had to keep up appearances, after all. Rewarding the criers that ran a tight racket was a citizen's lot. Istrya being at the center of the empire meant news came whether people liked it or not. Some of it true, much of it false. The criers vetted their sources, kept rumors from spreading on the emperor's orders.

If the emperor really was making an appearance at Lord's Wharf in three days, he had a hell of a task ahead of him. Many were angry when

Reynard laid his claim on Osbergia, and their anger hadn't abated in the interim. This was Franz's first appearance, as far as Richter knew, since the annexation. Istranites sure loved to let their opinions be known. Screamed, more like, with rocks or rotting vegetables to hand.

It was none of Richter's business, anyway, so he kept his mind on his mission.

The Gully District, not to be confused with the Gutter, needed no more introduction than a diseased dog passing across their path, getting chased off by an old woman with a broom. The dog yelped as it limped away. More of the houses here loomed tall, flaking plaster at their edges. Each block tangled with the other, bleeding together, where the people inside nearly lived in each other's pockets. Fetid, stinking water clogged the alleys, where the sun never reached. The old woman gave Richter a leering look.

Living in the Gully meant seeing the sun god for a few hours in the middle of the day, between slits of tenements and leaning, leaking roofs. You could find all manner of scum and violence here, not least at some of the taphouses. The Dripping Bucket, aptly named, was where Richter rolled in some of that scum himself. You had to be honest with yourself, and accept that you *were* scum and violence, not least for a good cause. That cause being his mission—since it was almost guaranteed that if the Dripping Bucket had a man named Vargen inside, he would find his quarry.

Vargen stood precisely where he always did, at the hip of the bar, with a sudsy brown ale in hand. Richter clicked his fingers.

"You, pretty one, what's your name?"

"Bjorn."

"I don't care for your last—" *He never actually said it.* They were learning. Richter smiled and gave him a few emperors. "Go get some ales for us. The rest of you, find a table."

The man couldn't have rolled his eyes further backwards in his head if he tried, almost entirely whites.

The Dripping Bucket, like Istrya herself, was an exercise in contrasts. Walls of the finest Varangian marble gave way to low, rot-ridden beams that Richter had to dip his head under. Gilded mirrors that the barkeep said he bought from glassworkers in Prolia but were almost certainly replicas. Glass bar-tops that he actually bought from Prolia. The price of the Istryan weissbrau kept the street rabble out but wasn't so high that the gangers and the crims had to find elsewhere for their drink and their Fives. A stink that couldn't be placed, and a thick air of the burning snuff that clouded the gambling tables. And the name, of course, came from the perpetual drip that came from a wall that forever wept, like the martyrs themselves for the soul of humanity.

Marchant Vargen was the sort of man that you found in every bar. An exercise in contrasts himself, an ample gut hung over fine, slashed pants one might see on the finest Annaltian knight. He wore a white smocked shirt over it, rolled up at the arms to reveal girthy forearms carpeted thick with black hair. His head was entirely bald, and an interesting, jagged scar split his face in two, as though someone had decided that they liked it better that way. It was one of the few things Richter was curious about in this world, since Vargen kept his pouty, split lips shut about it.

"Vargen," Richter said.

"Shit and fucking damnation, Richter. Got a lot of gall showing your fucking face in the Bucket again." A few nearby patrons scraped chairs as they moved away. Vargen spoke surprisingly well for a man with half his tongue jutting past his lips.

"Two Rigans you gave the turn to came here the other day." *Two guards came here looking for Richter.*

"About what?"

"A cracked vase." *A dead woman.*

Their code. A modified version of the gangers' cant that none of the crims here would know, not if they were only half-listening. Richter wondered if any of them were even quarter listening.

"Did they say when they'd be back?"

"Didn't."

"Give it a gulp. Looking for a friend, actually." *Don't worry about it. Looking for a kill.*

Vargen chewed the inside of his cheek then acquiesced, gesturing to an empty chair.

"You'd better make it worth my while," he said.

Richter clattered a few coins on the table. Passing coins from one man to another didn't draw any strange looks in the Bucket.

The emperor stared back at him between the webbing of his fingers, the likeness striking. He'd seen Franz only once at the pyre, but he never forgot a face. Side profile, the man lived up to his breeding, with a thick neck and a jaw that held up empires. Richter knew most kings and self-important bastards whose titles exceeded their smarts, that the statues and images of them failed at reflecting the reality. But not Franz. His was an emperor that lived up to the look if nothing else. He remembered Melusine's breasts wrapped like a Sigursday gift and felt a little tingle in his hose.

He wasn't sure who he was more jealous of, Franz or Melusine.

"You in a hurry?" Vargen folded his meaty arms and leaned forward. "Stay and have a cold one. I'll have Hoher bring you one from the deep cellar, none of this watered-down tripe."

Richter smirked. He supposed he could stay for one. After all, what was he in such a hurry for? To get back to boring inquisitors and stifling halls full of bleeding martyrs? A cold one would be exactly what he needed right now.

"One, Vargen. Then I have to eat."

The split-mouth man smiled in a murderous grin—though that couldn't be helped. That was just his unfortunate face. "Hoher, two cold weissbraus from the root cellar. None of that swill!"

Hoher the barkeep had two shining coins dangling from his ears, like earrings. Stamped and threaded, with the image of some ancient king on them. Said they resembled his face—it was one of those old jokes that no one but those deeply familiar found funny. He was a strange fellow, and that meant something coming from Richter.

"Aye," he said.

Richter turned to check on his charges. They huddled around three tankards filled with foamy white beer—Istryan weissbrau, the local specialty. Saburrian spices turned bog water into some fruity business that tickled the back of Richter's tongue. It was much more pleasant than any Osbergian shit he had there, and one of the few reasons he enjoyed returning to Istrya. His charges sat silently like they waited for a body to be put in the ground, scanning the room with their eyes. Fehling saw him watching, and smiled strangely, like she half-expected him to kill her if she proper grinned.

"I'm looking for a nightwatchman," he said to Vargen. *Lycan.*

"Not around here, you're not. Not after last time."

"Oh, come on, you fucking coward. How much do you want?"

"I told you, no. Just enjoy your fucking drink."

Richter's chest burned with anger.

Hoher arrived with their drinks. *What's that smell? Oh... Hoher... bodies in the cellar.*

Richter realized two things. One, that he still had his inhuman sense of smell, which left good odds he was still a demon. Two, that Hoher had bodies hidden in his cellar. The stench of death clung to his clothes like a malaise, as if he had vomited bones in Richter's lap.

As Hoher pulled his hands away, Richter snatched one of them and sliced the palm open with his knife. The barkeep yowled in pain, trying to wrench his hand away.

"The fuck are you doing, Richter?" Vargen pushed out from the table. Karl and the others followed.

"A test."

The crims from all different groups got to their feet, scraping chairs on the floor, drawing their battered shortswords and daggers. White hoods of the Conquerors, who idolized Istryan and emulated him in everything they did. Green scarves and olive skin of the Dolorites, men who claimed ancestry from the Dolor Sea in the far southeast. People from there were renowned for their violence. Men from the actual Dolor looked entirely different, but the fiction was far more important than the truth. The red vests of the Sardos weren't to be seen in the taphouse today, which was a surprise.

But they all wanted to kill him, looked like. Good. He was glad he could unite the gangs in his mutual destruction.

"Er, Inquisitor, sir?" Bjorn said. He had a dagger drawn, the blade drifting unsure by his side.

Richter grinned. "I've *really* been wanting to stretch my limbs. What a perfect opportunity."

He opened Hoher's throat. The barkeep made a gurgling noise and flopped forward into Richter's waiting arms. *Not a demon, then. Oh well.* He picked up Hoher and used him as a projectile, sending him blundering into two white hooded Conquerors. They crashed to the ground, clattering weapons.

"Kill these bastards!" one of the big greens yelled.

Chaos strangled the taphouse. Karl killed a green as soon as looked at him, while Fehling shot two whites in quick succession with two hand crossbows that she then did aside with and moved to a dagger for close work.

Four greens and a white rushed Richter, stabbing wildly with their shortswords. Richter dodged, rounded out the arc of a blade, killed one on the counterswing, and went low to trip up another's legs. Stab, thrust, cut. Hand aching happily. Richter punched his dagger into a man's chest but only managed to slap him with his fist. He'd lost his grip on the blade. His hands were coated with blood.

The white turned, cutting nastily across Richter's arm. Richter smashed him in the nose with his elbow. He fell to the ground with a hoot. The other two came in, licking the air with their swords, hissing like snakes. Richter found a chair behind him, raised it. Their blades caught in the legs. He grinned and twisted, and the greens lost their grips. He snatched the hilt of a sword out of the tangle, beat one back with the chair, shoved the end of the blade into the other's undefended shoulder.

The thing about pain was that not only was it fun, but it also kept the recipient on the backfoot if they didn't have any training to block it. These gangers wouldn't know what the word *pain* really meant. Well, Richter could teach them.

He stabbed, again and again, advancing. They breathed, clutching their wounds and groaning. One threw himself over tables on the way out, and Fehling caught him with a bolt between his shoulder blades.

"You gotta know how to use a blade," Richter said. "You think it's all flashy cuts, like swinging your dick in a brothel, thinking now you'll get your end wet. Maybe that works on whores. But not me."

Vargen crawled along the floor, trying to get out. Richter let him go—he had no qualms with the paunchy bastard.

He licked the blood off his fingers, made sure Karl, Fehling, and Bjorn watched. He didn't want them forgetting this lesson, and hells, he was just enjoying himself. Keeping their minds sharp was half the purpose of this adventure. Taking his mind off everything was the other half. He'd earnt it. Flashes of that day cut across his eye like the sharpest knife. His guts churned as he remembered the pyre. Vetterand's grin as he placed Richter in the cage to be purified.

A green shouted in that moment of inattention, slapping out with the tip of his blade. Richter's nose sliced open. He shouted, one hand grasping his nose, the other launching a flurry of stabs. As the green tried to block, Karl came up behind and stomped on the back of his knee. Coming down with his dagger, the wet punching sound rang out the taphouse.

Karl stood, licking his lips. He gave Richter a look that would make even the coldest killer pause. As it was, Richter had to tear his eyes away, nearly fixed to the spot.

He laughed and it turned to a giggle in his mouth as his breath came shallow in his throat. Warm blood flooded his mouth. He tore up a table-cloth—bloodied by the day's undertakings—and plugged his bleeding nose.

"You three," he told his novitiates. "Hold these ones here."

He turned and went to the cellar hatch. *What was Hoher hiding?*

CHAPTER 10
TO VALENTI
VERNUS, 1045

*If you're looking for safety or kindness in the south, you'd be
better off finding a bull to pleasure.*

— Thousand Son Companyman, Thago Versuta

THE FUNERAL FOR LUCIA took place on the last day of Vernus,
when the day was as long as the night and the past reared its head
like a wolf dragging out a skull buried in a shallow grave. Ginnsday, after
Ginevra, and Leon had been in a sour mood all afternoon. He stood among
the pallbearers, face furrowed like an old field. He hadn't spoken to her
since she'd killed that assassin and confined his children to quarters. Barely
looked at her on the parapet of the keep, where she had some words for the
gathered crowd.

She wasn't sure if they were good words. She never imagined being
the lady of a castle involved so much *talking*, everyone's opinion of you
hanging off your *words*, rather than your actions. They still hung off your
actions, just that what you said mattered so much more. A year ago, she'd
let her blades do the talking. Now her blades were in the armory, and she
couldn't exactly go around stabbing people who didn't like her, or the
other way around.

Well, not quite. She'd killed that assassin as quickly as a blundering fool kills a conversation. Didn't give him a chance to explain, which was her one regret. She didn't get any information out of him, but his children might be enough.

His children. A fiction if there ever was one. But then, who were they? They must've known who Roland was, and she'd find out. But later. After the funeral.

Under the clear blue, the sixty—fifty-eight, she corrected herself—of Palerme watched as the pallbearers brought Lucia out, wrapped in white, the bearers wearing black. The old Continental tradition, as far back as she could remember. Some traditions never changed, like Ginnsday, marked by several splotches of water soaking the thirsty yard. She thought maybe it was time to make their own, seeing as they belonged to neither the empire nor any known religion.

But how to start? How does a tradition start? Do you do something long enough and it just sticks around, like an old wound, to be carried on by the next generation? Strange that given enough time and space to think, you start thinking on the next generation, what you're going to leave behind. More than anything, she wanted to leave behind a world without the Order. A world where she and her son and all the Althann would never be hunted, ever again. A world where they could live in peace with humanity.

But then peace was just a brief window of hope between wars. It never lasted. Peace was for the merciful, and she was feeling mighty short on mercy lately.

The hangdog Dober stared at her, and her cheeks rose up in rage. *What does he want?* She gritted her teeth. If he looked much longer, she'd rather like to see his head split open like Roland.

That rage. The same she'd felt in the South Hills, that piss-swill town Essrich, where they'd met people just wanting to live their lives, wanting to survive. Funny how that part was far less important than the burning hate she felt then. She felt now. Did she hate the Althann? Maybe a little. She hated difficult people, that was for sure. Enough to kill them? She'd done it before.

She crunched her teeth again. The past, rearing its head like a skull dug up from a shallow grave.

The pallbearers put Lucia on the stack of wood, the makeshift structure. A pyre. She'd half-expected them to agree to burying her, but Ottille told her that wouldn't do.

"It's just a tool. Would you never pick up a crossbow to fight if a crossbow killed your mother? A dagger? Besides, we can reclaim it from the bastards that use it to scorn us. Use it for their hate. We can use it for our love, to show our gratitude for a long life."

She was the old woman's daughter, so who was Selene to argue? Whatever her mood when Selene had killed Roland, it had dissipated since. The conversation made Selene uncomfortable, so she left it. Grief did horrible things to her, like made her feel weak, made her cry.

Selene cleared her throat. "Lucia touched each of our lives." Her voice echoed, bounced off trees dusted with new leaves, bright and green. That was a good start, surely. They looked up at her expectantly. Expecting more, but at least they weren't ready to throw her from the parapet yet.

"With her wisdom, her kindness, and her candor. Her biting honesty." Selene chuckled. "Always tempered with a laugh or a wink or a grin." A few sniffles. Ottille smiled, thinking on something she'd shared with her mother, perhaps, the torchlight reflected in her eyes.

"But she also knew, like the rest of us, that our existence is something we've fought for, with tooth and nail. Fang and claw, I suppose," she said to a few laughs. "Something they'll never let us have." She pounded the parapet with her fist. "Something worth fighting for, for the next generation. A sanctuary. A safe place for all Althann to live in peace!"

They murmured their agreement, some clapped. It was a funeral, after all. Sanna looked up at her with wide, bright eyes.

Selene's voice cracked. "I need five men, five men that are willing to leave their homes and come to Alania." It was something she should've done, should've said a month ago, before Frix and his cousins left for Valenti. "The duca will help us fight," she lied. Didn't rightly know why she lied, but Sanna smiled and that was enough. "The Order will never let us rest, never let us be safe. We defy their teachings every moment we breathe. But if they see we're capable of fighting, capable of defending ourselves, that we'd give them hell before they see us through, they might hesitate. They will! Then they'll have no choice but to accept us! To fear us!"

"We've always feared them," Tomas yelled. "Now it's time they feared us!"

Enthusiasm spread through them like wildfire, and they applauded her. She smiled, caught Leon staring back, that same grim look across his brow, like a plow had taken to his face.

"It's time they feared us," she repeated. They cheered. Maybe she was good at this whole *words* thing, after all.

Ottille bore the torch to the kindling at the base of the pyre. Fire spread across the wood, curling the bark, sending up drifts of white smoke, pungent with sap. Powerful tannins of cedar and oak, cut from the land. She recalled something Lucia had said on the first day she arrived at Palerme.

"This will be a sanctuary for all of us. Not just for us living, but for our children, and our children's children. We must tend to it like an old lover, an old husband. With care, otherwise the land will reject us just as we have been rejected from other lands. We must care for the trees, the stones, the waters."

A romantic notion. But they had to feed themselves, too. The farms wouldn't irrigate themselves, and livestock needed clear land to feed on. If they wanted to survive through the winter, they needed to clear more of the forest. They could hunt the deer and grouse that lived in these woods, but that couldn't feed a burgeoning community. Maybe there was a compromise?

It would have to wait, either way. For now, they could shore up the defenses in her absence. Rill was a master mason in the outskirts of Invereid before an inquisitor poked too closely at missing livestock in the area. The curtain wall needed repairing, and crumbled at the rear especially, at the base of the lord's tower. A trebuchet would have it in easily, send the whole thing toppling down on top of them. She'd forgive any number of dead sheep if he could fix that, though he reassured her now that his urges were controlled.

Strange thing, their urges. Like wild beasts, hunting and killing. What made them so fearsome, and feared, and why the Order hunted them in the first place. Selene knew the Order was wrong, but if they couldn't control their urges, what was wrong with putting them down?

Count Sebastian. You didn't let the rabid dog loose on the world, you put it down. But she was their protector and would give them the chance. That's what the sanctuary was for. Not only somewhere they could hide, but somewhere they could go through their changes and learn how to control their urges.

The past rearing its head like an unburied grave.

She felt like she should be mourning Lucia, crying like the rest of them as her body burned down to nothing, filling the air with sooty smoke, clinging to their cloaks.

I don't want there to be a way out. I don't deserve it.

That wasn't her. She didn't grieve, she moved on. There were always other fires. Other Althann to save. Other problems to solve. Other people to kill.

"Helena." The old woman went to hand Tristain to Selene before she waved her away with a dismissive hand.

"I'm sorry to do this, but I'm afraid your daughter will have to nurse him for longer."

Selene's milk hadn't come in, despite her trying. It was the hardest thing she'd ever done. Harder than killing Soren, harder than watching Tristain die.

Trist screaming as he sucked at a dry, cracked nipple. Her sobbing.

She would never go through that again. Happily, Galena, Helena's daughter, had a daughter a few months back, who'd just been weaned.

"Milady," she said. Her brows shot up. "Of course, it's no problem. She'll be glad to."

Selene nodded, smiled. "Good. I must go to Valenti."

AFTER ENSURING RILL HAD the stone for his work and having bribed him with a case of Alanian red to be delivered on their return, Selene and Leon departed with Tomas, Gregor, Dubine Schneider, and Alain Jäger at first light. Violet clouds broke over the flat expanse of the Bight like a gutted wineskin, Solni looming over the world, full-faced and angry.

The ancient imperial road rolled out ahead of the six, riven and scattered from centuries of rain and lack of upkeep. Scattered green hills pocked here and there with farmhouses and mills, border villages that neither knew nor cared which country they were part of. The republics, or the empire. The border changed hands so many times by grubby-handed magistrates on both sides it had to be redrawn yearly.

But the fact that the imperial road was the finest one this side of Ostelar spoke to both the sad state of the empire and the republics.

A crisp breeze blew over them, scattered petals of a dandelion dancing across her eyes. The saddle felt good under Selene's thighs, though the chafing left much to be desired. It only spoke to her delay in getting on a horse and dealing with things the way she used to. Girded her enthusiasm to pass the Bight and hit the outskirts of Valenti by sundown.

What would they find in Valenti? Frix and his cousins sent word last that there was no sign of Order activity that they could find, but that the duca's men were watching them. Alberracin didn't believe their claims that the Order plotted something in Alania. Would they find a man willing to believe the threat? Or not, as Frix claimed? It troubled Selene.

Throwing back a mouthful of brown ale, Dubine Schneider drove Lady Melusine, a mule that definitely wasn't female. The animal had been disparagingly—or affectionately—named after the empress. When asked, he just winked and laughed, and Selene didn't care to press the issue. The mule pulled a cart loaded with pig iron and stacks of fresh pine, two things that would sell well in Valenti.

"They'd sell even better in Vallon," Schneider told her, his voice juddering as the cart's wheels bounced over a small rut.

"Is that right? What makes you the expert on trade goods?"

"Been a trader all my life. I could sell anything to anyone."

"Quite a boast." She refrained from rolling her eyes. The man had been a bore of that country folk flavor, and spoke the tallest tales ever heard.

"What's the difference between a trader and a merchant?" Alain said.

"Aye? What's that?"

"A trader and a merchant."

"I suppose it's scale, innit? A trader buys and sells goods, a merchant does business in buying and selling goods."

"All this talk of merchants makes me think of that assassin," Leon said. Selene turned in her saddle and smiled to see him speak his first words to her, other than to volunteer his sword and axe with a distracted grunt.

She looked at the newest addition to the Althann, Alain Jäger. If Schneider was a country bore, the blond Jäger had all the qualities that he lacked. Slight of build, tall, and refined in the chin, he wore a long knife at his belt. An Annaltian make, she thought.

"Is that a messer," she asked.

He gave the hilt a generous slap. It was riveted through the center of two blocks of wood, rounded for comfort. Simple, but looked no less deadly for the bargain. "A lange messer, made by none other than the steelworks of the Bresinger district of Annalt."

"Steelworks, aye," Schneider said, taking another swig of his skin. "The world is moving too fast for me to keep my eye on. It's enough to send a man spinning."

"I doubt you'd have trouble with that, Schneider," Tomas said, his head bobbing up and down as his horse stepped over a pothole. "That skin hasn't left your hand since you took that mule's reins. Are we sure our goods are safe?"

"Ginevra's beard, goodman, my hands are steadier than a barber-surgeon's. I've been driving mules since before—"

"Since before I was born. We know, you've been a trader for all your life."

"That I have, boy, and don't you go forgetting that."

"A utilitarian sword for a utilitarian man," Selene said, drawing the conversation away from the competence of her driver. It was one of those things best left unsaid, lest she be drawn into a lengthy conversation about mules and trading again.

Alain smiled. Selene drew her own blade. He eyed it, steel glinting like cold murder.

"Mine's shorter than the lange messer," she said, "but I don't find I need the range, often. I get in close."

"Milady's talents for getting in close are well known," Leon said. They all looked at him, silent humor in their eyes. The realization hit him, sending words spilling from his lips. "You know I don't mean in that way—it's—she's good at getting it inside. Aye, not that, either! You know what I mean."

Selene laughed. "Do you think of me getting it in close, often?"

They all laughed as Leon's cheeks brightened to an inferno.

Selene enjoyed the ribbing, grinned. A terrible reminder of how much she'd missed being on the road that these six passed for good company. Then a pang of guilt hit her thinking of Trist without a mother.

How would things be different if I was killed by the Order? I have to do this now, while he doesn't remember. Before it's too late, for both of us.

Of course, the guilt didn't go away. All she'd succeeded in doing is ruining her good mood, and she dug her knees hard, several times, into the gray mare. Finally, the beast moved ahead.

She'd left Eda behind in the stables in Ostelar and missed the old girl terribly. This one was a poor substitute, a nag that had once pulled carts, and she had a temper about her.

She heard hoofbeats approach. Leon wrangled his own difficult mare forward, the beast skidding to a halt at the edge of a rut instead of stepping over it. After some cajoling and annoyed shouts, he caught up.

"You know I don't," he said. "I think of you more like a daughter."

"I know." She smiled. A smile from a pretty woman made many men happy again. She knew his mood, needed him undistracted. Valenti contained more than just a stubborn duca on its list of dangers. They were going into the lion's mouth, and she needed him as the Strong if they were going to survive.

He smiled back but only briefly. "Funerals always leave me in my moods. Forgive me. I've been terrible company."

"I hadn't noticed."

"Sure, you have. I was... It was naïve of me to think that no one else would die. And you're right."

"I'm right?"

"The Order won't let us be. Fucking bastards. Sending an assassin after a child. I knew they were depraved, but to think they'd stoop to that level."

Selene swallowed. Something had changed. Killing a baby was beyond the pale for most inquisitors, most orders from on high. Only the truly fanatic would do such a thing, especially to a babe that hadn't been proved a demon.

"It shows how scared they are," Alain said. She'd not heard him approach. "Milady."

He was trying to make her feel better, but she chewed his words. "The scared beast is the most frightening, the most unpredictable. Of all of us, I would've thought you knew that. You're a huntsman by trade?"

"Grouse," he answered quickly. "Pheasant. They're about as frightening as a drunk."

By trade he was a hunter, *Jäger*, and he'd brought his own horse with him when he fled from... wherever he was from.

"Where are you from, Alain? A sword from the Bresinger district of Annalt, but you don't have an Annaltian accent."

"I was a mercenary, milady. Fought with the Thousand Sons, out of Malatesta. When your quartermaster speaks Saburrian and your sergeant curses in Salzheimish, you lose your accent fairly quick."

Leon chuckled. "It's true." *That's right, Leon was a mercenary too.*

"The Thousand Sons. Isn't mercenary warfare the standard in the republics?"

"The ducas hardly inspire loyalty," Tomas said. "No one will follow them into battle, not that they have any interest in leading them. No, they'd much rather let others do the killing for them."

"You seem to mistake the purpose, goodman," Alain replied. "They buy the mercenaries, so they don't have to fight themselves. It's terribly profitable. Show up outside a wall with a few cannons and a couple hundred gruff-looking men and they throw money at you. I fought for Malatesta against Segesta, Segesta against Malatis. Malatis against Malatesta, when they did exactly as I said, paid us off to change sides. After we finished sacking Malatesta the Malatish refused to pay us, so we sacked them, too."

"You sacked your own home," Selene asked.

"Wasn't my home."

"Cravens," Tomas said.

Alain tapped his skull. "Clever."

"As long as you're making a profit, I suppose."

He snorted. "Those days are long behind me. The Thousand Sons would be like to kill me now as welcome me back into their ranks."

They walked along the road for a spell, the only sound the clopping of their horses' hooves and the rattle of the cart, and a noisy songbird in a blooming willow nearby.

"Some drunks are frightening," Leon said, sour look on his face.

"I mislike this idea of treating with the duca," Alain said. "Rumor has it he knows what you eat for breakfast, even when you forget yourself. They even know what lies on the top side of a cloud. Or so the rumors go."

"You know a lot about Alberracin?"

"No. All I know is that he's called the Eyes of the South among the Thousand Sons, and he's said to have troves of information on every important person on the Continent from balmy Saburria to the frozen Geisteschreien. We never fought for him. Never had the stones."

"I see." She hadn't known that. But then, she'd only dealt with him once, and generally stayed away from men in robes as a rule. "Do you think these Thousand Sons would be persuaded to fight for us?"

Alain's eyebrows near shot off his face. "For *us*? For the right price, I suppose. It's the first of Tribuum, so they'd be getting ready to go on campaign for the year."

She sat forward in the saddle, thinking. "If we had the right price?"

"Look, if you're hoping to deal with them, you'd best let me do it. Giustiniani doesn't deal with anyone he doesn't know. If he's still the captain, that is."

"I thought you said they'd kill you."

"I said they'd be as likely to kill me as welcome me back. That's about as good odds as you can ask for when it comes to mercenaries."

Leon laughed. "That's very true."

"More cloud," Schneider yelled. "That's what's on top of a cloud."

Selene just shook her head. "How many do the Thousand Sons number?"

"A thousand, surely," Tomas said.

"Well, no, that's just a name." Alain developed a far-off look in his eye. "Traces back to the origins of the company's noble founding. Although, come to think of it, the story involves a lot of less-than-noble cajoling by Giustiniani, and there were far less than a thousand of them. But last I was involved, we numbered far more than a thousand. Maybe three thousand?" He nodded. "I'll go to Malatesta for you, milady. Aye, I'll do it. If I don't return in a week, you'll know that the poorer outcome prevailed."

"I'd rather not lose a good fighter, but three thousand hardened soldiers would certainly give the emperor pause."

"Hardened is relative, but you're right. Three thousand crossbows pointed in their direction would make anyone think twice."

"Can we trust men who are capable of turning around and attacking their former allies?"

"You can certainly trust their greed. If you can pay them, they'll fight."

Selene rubbed her chin. She didn't much like the idea of inviting three thousand mercenaries into Palerme, having to house and feed them all, wondering if they'd betray them if they got a better offer. But who else was lining up to fight for the Althann?

"I'll see you in a week, Alain."

He pressed his lips and set his jaw to the east, wheeling his horse around. He took off across the field and soon was just a black dot on the horizon, then he was gone.

"We should keep moving," Leon said. "*Wallenda* is still a day's ride from here."

"*Wallenda?*"

He raised his voice. "I don't know! I'm from the South Hills, Sel. My tongue is no good for these damn republic words."

She laughed. "It's Valenti."

He muttered something under his breath.

"Let me guess, I'm a *sal'brath*?"

He folded his arms. "*N*-No. Maybe."

Tomas laughed and Leon shot him a fierce glance, which shut him up.

CHAPTER 11
FASCINATION
VERNUS, 1045

*Worlds beyond worlds exist in the mind; one can only imagine
what concocteries appear behind the eyes of a stranger.*

— APHE, THE MIND

THE CELLAR WAS DARKER than a grave and stunk like a fresh one. Gloomy hands pressed in on a candle that sat on a shelf above the hewn earth, as though attempting to strangle it. Strangled, that's what this place was, and Richter could taste the death on his tongue. How could he have missed it? For how powerful it was here, it was a fucking miracle he didn't smell it outside. Though the Gully District always carried an edge of murder in the air, like cheap perfume.

In a situation like this, he'd have a bracing line or two from the Book to remind himself of his mission, his stalwart faith. But his mission had gotten hazier, fucked up by his mistake the other week, where he'd transformed in front of a troop of werewolf killers, and gotten burned on a pyre for it. His faith was shakier than ever. Like a mountain that, worn away by time and assaulted by the weather, suddenly comes crashing down and buries everyone beneath it.

He stepped deeper into the unwelcoming stench. The taste of ash coated the back of his teeth and he forced down the itch in his brain that made him want to be anywhere other than here. *It's just a fucking cellar, Richter. Sure, there's probably a few dead bodies in it, but since when have you been scared of a few dead bodies?*

He took the candle from the shelf, passed the light around the room. Ghost-like faces stared up at him, two of them, a man and a woman, their eyes still pink around the edges, as though they were only a few days dead. He leant over them. The woman had her fingernails torn up, like she'd struggled with Hoher before she'd succumbed. Their clothes bloomed with dried, black blood, and when he lifted their shirts back revealing pale, cold nakedness underneath, he saw stab wounds, and the woman's quim had been messed around some. With a knife. Nothing could have excited him less. Hoher was a sadist, not a demon.

Still, he undid his hose and took his meat into his hands and, kneeling over their faces, pulled at himself. *Sigur curse me for this disgusting habit.*

He must've listened because Richter couldn't even get half hard. His cock sat there, soft in his hand, like a sad sea cucumber. *Gods curse me.* Could he get it hard anymore? Or was he just a half-man, a eunuch, without seed and life? He got up and turned to find Karl and Fehling staring back at him.

"Inquisitor, sir," Fehling said. Her eyes fixed on his, clearly expending effort trying not to look at his exposed flesh. Karl didn't seem to care either way, and chuckled.

Richter folded himself back into his hose. "Hoher killed these two. What are you doing down here? I told you to watch the gangers."

"Inquisitor, sir, Bjorn's watching them," she replied. Her eyes passed around the room now that there wasn't an ugly one-eyed thumb staring rudely back at her. "They're half dead and disarmed at any rate. Who are the dead ones?"

"Don't know. But they sure as fuck weren't killed by a wukodlak."

"Well, look on the bright side, sir." Karl folded his arms. "At least you killed a murderer. He tried to hide the bodies, proves his guilt."

"A murderer, perhaps, but not a demon."

Atonement for the sinful, for the lost, and for the guilty.

Well, he was two of the three, and it remained to be seen if he was lost or just bloody-minded. But Richter did appreciate that the Book had returned to the forefront of his mind.

"It doesn't matter if Hoher's a murderer, Istrya's full of them. Bitch is built on the back of the biggest one of them all—shit, she's named after him. You never know what's going on inside someone's head. We came here to find a demon, but we didn't. Let the Watch sort out this mess, we're Order. It's time we started fucking acting like it." He didn't know who he was trying to convince more, them or himself.

"Yessir," Fehling said. "What do you want to do with the gangers? What about the watch, sir?"

"A ganger war broke out in the Dripping Bucket, Vargen will attest to that. The barkeep got hit in the carnage. Collateral damage."

"It's a shame about those gangers," Karl said. "Crime runs rife in the Gully, so they say."

Fehling nodded. "Men without faith. Scum and murderers all."

"That's right," Richter said. "Faith is important to a man. And a woman. There's naught but devilry waiting on the other side for those without it."

He knew the root of all his problems now: his lack of faith in recent days. That's what this business with Hoher had taught him, what the pyre had taught him. Why he had felt so godsdamned weak, like a babe. Never had he been so unsure. But faith in the Lightfather was a hard thing, required sacrifice. Blood must be let at His altar, offerings to satiate Him. Richter knew how to take hold of his faith with both hands and wring the old hag for all she was worth.

"We must atone."

"Atone, sir?"

"Pain brings out the best in all of us."

THAT WAS THE THING about pain: it was all in how you used it. Could be the biting, the gnawing ache, caused you stillness, lethargy. Fatigue. Constance of agony often went that way. Richter had a scar across his neck that was like that, pulled and puckered the skin. When demons healed fresh injuries, whatever god or mechanism that transformed them scarred the injuries over. And the scars never faded, never felt like anything other than not enough skin stretched over too much bone.

But pain could also keep you sharp, focused, like a blade, on your mission. An arrow in flight, unwavering from your target.

Richter opened the case of whips and disciplines. Out of the window, black thunderheads on the horizon blotted out the sunset like the claws of a great black beast consuming the world from the west. Further unwelcoming came from the looks of his three killers-in-training. Karl gave him a curious, but inscrutable look. Bjorn darkened, looking as though he might pull a blade on Richter any moment. Fehling gaped her mouth like a fish.

"What is this?" she said.

"An ancient practice. Did you know that from the first century to the fifth century, the empire was ruled jointly by the Sigurian church and the Lion Throne? Well, that's what the books say, anyway. It's funny how certain things can seem so set in stone, so steadfast as to last centuries, that they almost want to continue, to stretch into forever? But they never do."

He handed them each a knotted whip.

"I won't—" Bjorn said.

Karl cut him off. "You will, or I'll have your balls off, Amstadt."

Richter turned. Karl was looking at his favorite whip. It wasn't a whip, really, not by any stretch of the imagination. It was a leather-wrapped wooden handle binding seven thin chains, each a foot long, the ends of which attached to brutal hooks. But whip worked well enough for a name. It was like most things—Richter was a Sword, and Nials was a Sword. But no one with gray between their ears would think Nials could ever match Richter in anything.

"The Screamer, I call it. Because you'll be screaming before you're done with it."

Karl hesitated, then stepped forward, letting his own whip drop by his side. "What were you saying? This lasts forever?"

"Mayhap. The scars should. We failed today, and Sigur demands pain for our sins."

Fehling let out a sob and fell to her knees. She leaned over, her pale face rushing with blood. "Lightfather forgive me!"

The sound of the knotted cord thumped against her back. Twice, three times. She gasped, face beet red. She made a lowing sound, like a dying calf, punctuated by the beating. It was a knell for their silence and their pain. Bjorn stood as he threw his own cord onto his back. Karl reached out for the Screamer, hesitated.

"Can... you?"

Richter's face flushed. He was driven speechless, if only for a moment. *Just when I thought nothing could shock me.* Shock could be like pain, of course, leaving you gasping.

"Of course."

Richter grasped the handle with one hand, draped the chains over the other. Karl turned, one cheek towards Richter, one ice blue eye wide with expectation. Anticipation. Hope, even.

"The prospect of pain is often worse than pain itself." He was giving the full lesson today.

Karl undid his jacket and came down to his dark trousers, revealing a pink, muscled back full of scars. *A squire? Looks as though he carried the entire platoon on his back.* "Soldier."

Karl came to attention, head forward. "I gladly accept my punishment."

"Find pain to be your worthy ally and no one can stand against you."

"Yessir."

Richter let the chains loose, dangled them by his leg. Then he threw the Screamer forward. Hooks bit into flesh like ravenous dogs as Karl fell to his knees. He didn't make a sound. But that wasn't the hard part. Yes, seven hooks in the flesh hurt like a demon. But what came after made you scream. What goes in, must come out.

Richter pulled.

Karl screamed, his throat full of blood and tears. Bits of flesh stuck to metal like a twisted fisherman's bait. Pouring with great, sopping wounds, his back ran fresh and red.

Bjorn turned, retched, brown spilling from his mouth onto the floor.

"Pain!" Richter cried. "Feel it in the fucking air, your nose, your throat, your *veins!* Embrace it. Become *pain.* Know what it is to fight a demon by becoming a demon. The gods will not save you, so you must save yourself!"

Fehling didn't seem to notice, her eyes glazed over in the trance that came with the whip. Karl's body trembled, bent double, trying to come to terms with the brutality.

Richter undid his jacket and stripped. He flung the chains over his shoulder, and grinned as he welcomed the pain. *Don't fight it. It's no use. Pyre or no pyre, Vetterand or no Vetterand, you are pain. Men piss their hose at your approach. Women scream and cry at your tearing fingers. Soldiers, peasants, merchants, gangers. Kings and emperors live their entire lives hoping that your aching grasp will never darken their doors. Pain, the great equalizer, and Sigur, the almighty god that feeds on it. He will feed well when you are done with this world.*

He yanked his arm, tearing strips from his back.

THE NEXT DAY, RICHTER came to the training hall. The echo of his footsteps was drowned out in white stone corridors clogged with soft men and women. Gray-robed notaries carting armfuls of books bigger than their heads, stumbling along to little success. Black-robed novitiates huddled in quiet circles, like mice trying to hide from the owl's talons in larger numbers. Clerics in their pure white floated above the rabble, seemingly one foot in this world, one foot in the next. Or that was how he'd always thought of them. Talking to them often revealed as much, so he never bothered. He already had enough of that in his own life. Never dying gave you a perspective on life that wasn't always realistic.

People avoided his gaze and gave him a wide berth like he was a jagged rock and they a ship. Ready to dash any of them against his churning face. He stepped into the towering rotunda at the heart of the Fortress. Martyrs and Named Warriors blazed with holy fire and brought war to demons across the vast curved walls, sculpture and friezes adorned with gold and green serpentine and black obsidian. High above, one winged man, armed and armored, bathed in light. The god Himself. Richter usually felt tiny and weak by comparison, but not today.

Today it inspired something higher, a renewed certainty. Pain was power was belief. Sigur took his pain and turned him into something frightening in exchange. His dirty linens clung to the wounds on his back like a lover returned after a long parting. The sores itched something fierce, but he'd had worse. He had to sleep on his stomach, of course, but he hadn't even tried to kill himself that morning.

Is this a fresh start?

Father Domitus waited out the front of the training hall. *What does he want?* His arms were folded in a dark blue robe, that of the senior *notarii*, though Domitus's role was largely relegated these days. White strands smeared over his pink scalp, his hair fuzzy on the sides, thinning. His eyes swam with cataracts, and when Richter asked why he never got them fixed, he told him, "What's the point of fixing something when you're going to be in the ground in ten years?"

Better judgment had a few years, but Richter didn't need to tell him that. He could smell the sick on him, hear the creak in his bones, feel the shudder of his lungs. He didn't quite know what he would do when Domitus was gone. Aside from Vetterand, Domitus was the only one that knew of Richter's past. Of the boy that died and came back a monster thirty-something years ago, and of the story of the killer he became. He squeezed his fists. Coming back to Istrya gave him to remember the past like some aging general, whose glory days were behind him and only the bottle laid ahead.

My glory days are in front of me. Faith in Him cannot easily be turned aside, as I have learned.

"Ah, Richter," the old man said, seeing him approach. "What in the four hells did you do to your novitiates? One's come into the infirmary missing half his back, two more missing fingers, and two with bruises all over their body. One's dead, too, but who's counting." He wore an amused look like he was recounting a joke among old friends. Which, Richter supposed, he was. That calmed Richter, and he forced his fists open. He no longer felt like tearing someone's head off, but half odds that would last to the end of the day.

"I was teaching Karl, Fehling, and Bjorn of the *flagellae*. I don't know about the others." Nothing more needed to be said.

Domitus's face was lined with sadness. "Poor things. To bear such brutality at their young age."

"You're too soft, Father."

Richter frowned. A woman's voice. Karl and Fehling approached, showing no sign of the previous day's activities. But no, on second glance they did—Karl walked stiffly, like a palace guard. Fehling had a slight limp and cringed when she walked. "We're ready for training, master. Who's the old man?"

Master? "Father Domitus has killed more men than you've taken shits, girl."

Domitus looked down.

"Then old age has made him soft. Are we training today, or ought we return to our dormitories?"

Richter grinned. He was really beginning to like these two. "Come, then."

T RAINING WENT RATHER WELL. All he had to do was stand in the corner and shout instructions, and the novitiates that remained simply did what he asked. *If only all of life was this easy.* All the soft ones were gone like so many flowers come the frigid bruma. It wasn't until the bells rang for Vespers that he realized they'd been training all day without breaks. Breaks were for ladies and soft folk, anyway.

Karl and Fehling fought like demons. Bjorn was still in the infirmary, but his other killers exploded at each other with such furious violence he wondered if fingers—no, limbs—would fly. Fehling launched a flurry of attacks with a long blade, her dark hair flopping about. Spinning like the most graceful dancer he'd ever seen. Despite her limp, when she had a blade in her hand it was though no god or man could land a hit.

As it was, Karl had to bring his own ferocity, like a tiger. He launched a flurry of hits at the length of an estoc, a thrusting blade, then stepped in, caught hold of Fehling's hand in the crook of his arm, twisted, brought her to the ground. She rolled backwards, slipping out of his grasp as he chipped stone from the floor with his point. It was like a conversation, an argument of the finest words that Richter hadn't seen except in the best of Swords. *If only I could've taught them how to catch a werewolf, how to kill one.*

Richter stood there, smiling. He thought of their killing in the Dripping Bucket, the fun they had. Gangers that once ruled Richter's life in the Gutter, and the lives of so many, getting their faces smashed in. He couldn't deny the satisfaction. Nothing could break his grin, not even when a warden came to him and said Vetterand wished to speak with him after High Hours. No, not even that. *But what does he—*

The smile slipped, but when Karl and Fehling's swords collided in a sparking crash, it made him happy again. Thoughts clashed in his mind. He pressed his back against the wall. Pain twisted up his spine, bit into the base of his skull, left him gritting his teeth, feeling bile at the back teeth.

A novitiate named Jogaila was having his own metal conversation with a twist-nosed giant by the name of Paun. Jogaila had the moon-shaped face you'd see among the Vyahtken, but the paleness of a Rigan, with ice-blue eyes. Ancestry like a dog's breakfast. Skin almost translucent, though it flushed with red blood at the moment. He punctuated an attack with a lash across Paun's hand, and it opened red and recoiled, sending Paun's blade crashing to the floor.

He yowled, clutching at his hand, then kicked Jogaila square in the solar plexus. "Yeh wet bastard. That was my good hand!"

Richter's brows thundered upwards. A hillman. Paun's nose went one way at the top, changed direction halfway down, as though it couldn't decide which way it preferred. These two looked as much fighters as any among his bunch, apart from the other three. They were big men, without the lankiness that tall men sometimes get. Paun was a head taller than Jogaila, and everyone else came to his shoulders. They weren't as quick as Karl and Fehling, but not slow either. Soldiers, maybe, but they understood the game of killing, that was certain. Richter knew it well enough to know other players when he saw them.

"You're a long way from home, southerner. Get to the infirmary."

"Aye, sir." He walked off.

"Jogaila, is it?" he said to the other one. The Vyahtki-Rigan had tied cloth around the sleeves of his robe, keeping them up and away, a fashion common enough in the north. Richter admired the inventiveness.

"Yessir."

"The accent of an Annaltian, the coloring of a Rigan, and the face of an easterner. You got three parents?"

Jogaila chuckled. "No, sir. Just the usual two. Ma came from a village south of the Forest of Rot, Da from the north. But I was born in Westfalen, not far—"

"I know where Westfalen is, boy." Richter had to admit his curiosity was piqued. Being away from Istrya meant travelling, and it was one of his few loves. "I've seen more than my fair share of the world. It's not until you see the Rigan harvest festival that you've lived, I say." To celebrate a good harvest the Rigans sacrificed twenty scores of cattle every year to Ginevra, and twenty virgins to Sigur. In the fury and bloodlust, men and women fucked in the street, no care for modesty for one night. Richter quite enjoyed himself last year.

"You can take anyone you like and no one bats an eye. Too busy doing it themselves."

Jogaila shook his head. "Can't say as I've ever seen it."

"Shame. You might never. Franz has been trying to clamp down on the whole thing, along with Pontiff Gottscheid. 'Not sanctioned worship,' they say. 'Barbarism.'"

"I heard. That is a shame."

Richter didn't know how to feel about it. He'd seen too much of every different kind of worship of the gods, and that of Sigur, to know that the church didn't have monopoly on the thing, as much as they believed they did. Had the right to arbitrate that.

When he was torturing a weaver from Sanarikki, the bastard cursed Richter with the Great Devil's fate.

"Gods consume you in body and spirit just as they did the Great Devil," he had screamed along with a series of loud Sanarik profanities. It wasn't a fate Richter had known of the evil god and at the time, he thought the Sanarik was losing his mind. It was a fair assumption. Richter had been driving nails into the man's knuckles at the time.

Was he right, though? Could gods be killed? Made sense as Sigur slayed the Great Devil, but what did that mean for the other gods? Faith could prove a fragile thing if gods could indeed be killed. Maybe it had something to do with the gods leaving.

But who was he to wonder these sorts of things? Not a cleric, for sure, not one of those bookkeepers, not even the Holy Pontiff's pimply arse. He was just some bastard who was good at killing and couldn't die.

Faith in Him cannot easily be turned aside. He knew his faith was different from most. It involved more violence, even for a Sword. To say that Richter had done his fair share of it would be an understatement.

The man named Jogaila scratched his cheek. "Inquisitor sir."

Richter looked up. "Huh. Oh. Yes, get back to sparring."

"The bells are rung for Vespers."

He heard the clangor at the time but thought it was just the pounding of his flagellation sores firing into his spine, shooting into his ears.

"Fine. Get lost."

CHAPTER 12
THE LION'S MOUTH
TRIBUUM, 1045

The south is wondrous: clear blue skies, gorgeous, sun-kissed women, wine on demand. If only it weren't for all the fucking southerners.

— OLAF TETENBAUM, COUNT OF KALEST

THE CITY OF VALENTI sat like a jewel on the Bright Sea, if that jewel had been cut by a master jeweler, then bashed at by smokeleaf addict with a claw hammer. Thick bands of white stone cut through each haphazardly constructed district, the terraces of ten thousand homes of dubious construction. Towers sprouted from the ground like ryegrass shoots, almost a stride apart in some places. Red tiled houses were sandwiched between high domes, some of old green patina, some the bright-forged bronze of new copper.

Red banners of the duca hung twenty strides down from the walls, the seven gold *As* of Alania stitched into the enormous rolls of cloth. One for each of the duca's mistresses, it was said. Was it just her, or did the banners look longer than the last time she'd visited? Each one was a rank injustice to good taste. But then ducas were to princes were to ostentatious men whose purses far outweighed their senses.

She imagined it stung to the thousands of Osbergian refugees that spilled across the northern wall, clung to the stone like barnacles. The enormous expense poured into lengthening curtains while they starved and drowned in the southern rains. Their cookfires smeared the air, the wood stink covered by the greater stench that cities often develop—that ubiquitous smell of rot and sick, when more than a hundred people lived together in a confined space.

It was noon when they approached the *Porta du Prix*, the Prince's Gate, and saw that it was closed. Guards on the wall leered down at them, not quite leveling their crossbows at them, but close enough.

"This is a colder welcome than I'd anticipated," she said to Leon.

One of the guards came to the parapet. "Ho! *Como sequair?*" He spoke in Alanian, a language that was half-Badonnian and half-dog barking, at least in Selene's experience.

"*Paleer Natali?*" *Do you speak Osbergian?* It was about the only useful phrase she'd learned, apart from several swears from a particularly drunk duca one night. He told her that Natali was the name for Osbergians—the name for the skin that develops on milk when it's left to boil. Milk-skins. That's what the Alanians called them.

The guard spat. "Fernand," he called in a disdainful voice, and waved a man with excessive mustachios drooping down his face. They spoke rapid-fire Alanian at each other.

The one named Fernand threw up his hands, rattling his mail. "Fine." Alanians didn't care for the plate of the knights of the north, preferring mail over jerkin, thinking the stuff weighty and unwieldy. But many people never let truth get in the way of belief.

"What you want?" Fernand yelled.

"Lady Selene Sigurin of Palerme requests to see Duca Alberracin."

"Duca busy. Come back later."

"Busy? I entreat him as a fellow landholder to discuss issues of import, as well as trade. I'd remind you that the duca has a personal stake in all of this." Palerme was the border crossing, and with the Althann, proved a formidable ally. And Selene intended to prove it.

"Fuck off."

Tomas climbed down from his horse, stepped forward, took off his shirt, his pants. Selene cocked an eyebrow while the guardsmen laughed and pointed. Then he bent double, almost curling into a ball. His limbs exploded in size, brown fur bursting from his skin, his face jutting forward into the visage of a wolf and man in one.

The men at the wall jumped back in fright, unslung their crossbows. Tomas bound the height of the wall in one leap, and when he landed next to them, seething and baring his teeth, they screamed and ran. The one named Fernand tripped and fell.

"Open the gate," the Tomas-wolf breathed.

Selene fumed. "Was that truly necessary?"

"Yes."

THE STREETS OF VALENTI stood as barren as a dying man's prospects. Windows had been nailed shut, and scarcely a dog darkened the corners of the lanes and alleyways that spurred off from the main street. Twisting out from behind houses of white lime and stone, the wind carried strange, garbled voices. The middle of the day, but it could've easily been the darkest hour of night for how many were out.

They crossed a canal and Selene caught a glimpse of sails in the harbor. The tops of galleys and barques, and she thought of Chesterfield, and what he might have said about their situation. What company he'd have provided. The last she'd seen of him was when they fled from Ostelar, sailing down the coast to the Bight. Nearly a year ago.

"Fair and farewell, my lady of raven hair," he had said. "Know that you always have a friend on the seas."

"Where will you go now?" she said. Frix and Leon and the others had scrambled together what was left after their flight from the citadel and spilled onto the skiff that he allowed them.

"I'm not sure. Now that I'm free of their bondage, probably as far away from the Order as I can get. There was a Saburrian woman I once crossed paths with, and she was as charming as a gifted cask of Tanerian white." He spoke wistfully. "Perhaps I'll go to Saburria, where it's said that corsairs are hunted with extreme prejudice."

"You'll be safer there?"

He smiled. "No, my dear. Less competition."

I could really use a friend on the seas right now. His cannons wouldn't hurt, either.

The duca's palace straddled the river Valen like an exuberant lover. It extended with parapets and turrets galore, as though the builder was running a discount on gratuitous stonework. Streamers and pennant flags topped each parapet and turret at regular lengths, each a knife's throw from each other. The flag of Alania, seven golden *As* in an inverted red triangle. One for each of the duca's mistresses.

They sent Dubine off to sell the goods and dismounted, the white stone rock hard under her boots. Two guards in kettle hats pointed their halberds at them as they approached the limestone stairs. Men on the walls trained crossbows at them looking graver than the ones at the gate. At least they took their jobs seriously.

"The duca is taking no visitors at this time," one said. Beyond his kettle hat, she saw dark figures inside, obscured by the brightness outside. The duca already had visitors.

"I am Selene of House Sigurin, former ward of Count Oncierran of Invereid, now Lady of Palerme as invested by Duca Alberracin himself. I recognize his need for discretion, but you will—"

"Let them through," he said. The duca. Alberracin pointed his huge, furred eyebrows at the guard. "Now."

He wore red like a cleric of Eme and a small blue biretta made of silk, flattening the wispy gray hairs on his head. He gestured them inside with a small flourish.

Looming over them, all polished plate and butted velvet, came a woman as dark-skinned as any Saburrian. A giant sword as long as she was tall slung over one shoulder, wide quillons almost taking out Alberracin as she walked up. Pursed lips visible through the mouth slot, a withering look in her eyes, as though measuring their worth. That withering look passed over Selene's missing arm, narrowed to scrutinize, as though distrustful of the absence.

Selene ground her teeth, made sure not to do anything reckless. Though she really felt like doing something reckless right there and then.

"Sergeant, take my guests' weapons, and see that their needs are cared for." He smiled and arched his fingers, stepping across the vast vestibule. Returning to the shadowy hall, where his other guests waited.

"Yes, Excellency. Weapons, please." An Osbergian accent? Interesting. It was unlike Saburrians to live on the mainland, beyond the usual slave, and they hardly had a choice in the matter. The daughter of a slave, perhaps? *Now a sergeant in the Alanian Marines.* Selene might not have liked the woman, but she respected her grit.

Selene misliked being unarmed in this place. It felt like missing another limb. She handed over her daggers, her crossbow, the bolts, her belt of poisons and Order flasks. The woman called for a trunk to hold them all—Leon's axe, sword, and backknife; Tomas's duty sword, shield, and bootknife; Gregor's axe and hammer. Between them, the trunk could barely close as the guards carried the hefty load into a side room.

They paced through the cavernous main hall of the palace, frescos of men and women with wings pointing withering looks at them. A beautiful woman poured an unending amphora, another no-less-beautiful woman grew enormous crops with the touch of a hand. A god of rain and lightning brought life-sustaining water to the land. Sigur, Eme, Ginevra, and Veles, in the southern tradition. Much of this would be blasphemy to a Sigur priest in the north. She wondered if the Sigur priests in the south had the same fanaticism dressed up as piety.

But she hadn't seen such majesty since the cathedral in Ostelar, the citadel of the Golden Swords. For a moment, a pang of nostalgia hit her, a feeling that reared its ugly head like yesterday's remembrance. When did the grief go away? The regret? She made her choices, and she wouldn't have chosen any other way. And yet, she still mourned the loss.

"Duca, I demand that you seize these heretics and traitors at once!" Another Osbergian.

The shout came from the shadowy hall at the back, dark as clotted blood. A furious priest strode up, finger aimed at them accusingly.

Selene found herself wishing she'd kept back a hidden knife.

The sergeant moved in front of them, moving both hands to the hilt of her huge longsword. "No one demands the duca do anything, priest." She spat.

"They blaspheme the very name of Sigur every breath they draw. I would see them burned at the stake."

"Father Gothenburg, I would hate to stain the floor with your fallen corpse."

"Your Excellency!"

"You heard my sergeant," the duca said. "These are new Varangian tiles. Beautiful, but they stain terribly. If you have a problem with who I take as my guests, air your concerns with the Count of Fontesani."

"Where is this Count of Fontesani, then?" His face turned bright red, his cheeks exploding with the words.

"The stables."

The sergeant sniggered.

It took a moment for the insult to register. The priest turned as bright as a burning building. "The pontiff shall hear of this," he said. "Alania will regret the day they harbored traitors and heretics!"

He shouldered past Selene and marched out, his jowly chin trembling with the effort of keeping his face fixed on the door.

Alberracin yawned. "What an itinerant bore. He accosts me about restoring an old preceptory outside the city, then insults my guests. No matter. Sergeant, take the lady's companions to the garden. My lady, please come with me."

He offered the crook of his arm and she nodded to Leon, who wore a scowl of disapproval. Old men and their lecherous fingers were well known to Selene, but she could keep her wits about her. He certainly wasn't about to fall for any of his charms, that was certain.

They passed through an arch of fluted stone into a garden of bright flowers and groomed shrubbery. In the center of the garden stood a figure of a naked woman leaping into the air, delicate legs kicking backwards, water pouring from an outstretched jug. Her enormous breasts made her vastly unsuited to the task, of course, but that was artistic license for you.

The smell of lavender filled the air, and she was back in that chair, Mother singing to her, brushing her hair with her fingers.

I let you go so sweetly.

"Northerners. Can never quite let the past go, can they?" The duca's voice brought her back to the present.

"Sorry?" She thought he could read her mind for a moment until she realized he was talking about the priest. "Yes. Let the old empire die, I say. It was dead before my grandfather was born."

The old empire included the republics; the new empire didn't, after they declared independence a century ago.

"The Tanerians are worried that the empire wants to reclaim their old territories. Malatesta wants to form a Greater Union with Vallonia and Badonnia: 'A bulwark against northern aggression,' he says. But you know old men. The closer they are to the grave, the more people they see trying to shove them in there. I'm no exception, of course. But one thing I've learned is that there's a difference between imaginary threats and real threats. And I've learned exactly how to tell the difference."

The garden disappeared behind another arch, the smells fading. Old walls of crumbling limewash gave way to a narrow hallway, a heavy iron door at one end. A single candle burned in a sconce at the entrance.

"Am I about to be tortured?"

Alberracin chuckled. "No, my dear. Believe me, you'd know if you were about to be tortured."

That gave her little comfort. The hairs on the back of her neck stood on end. An old man presented no issue without a weapon, but the two marines in the other room, enormous longswords at the ready—they might present a sizable obstacle to any rapid flight she might need to undertake. Locked doors in dark hallways had that effect on her. Gods knew she'd seen enough of them in her lifetime.

The duca unlocked the door with an iron key he fished out of a pocket. It was suitably ornate, heavy and iron like the door itself. He pushed it open, and it glided, whispering on oiled hinges.

Lanterns of green glass and solid iron hung from chains from the roof, surrounded by weighty glass spheres. Sticky light at regular intervals cast over a room filled with stacks and stacks of papers, scrawled notes in slanted handwriting. Shadows stuck between the pages like congealed blood.

"Every letter that comes from riders to the south or the north must be surrendered to the authorities for examining. This process passes the letter across my desk. I copy their contents since I trust no other person to do this faithfully, and this is the result." He opened his fingers, showing the room off like he expected it to start performing tricks. "I also have documents for every person on the Continent worth knowing. Some have a folder, some have a drawer."

Her mouth gaped a little, at the sheer scale of it. "Shouldn't this, you know... be a secret?"

"Why? I prefer my enemies know that I know their every move, their every message. Keeps them on their best behavior. Besides, people would far rather believe a fantasy than the truth." *Don't I know that.* "What have you heard about me?"

"That you know what I had for breakfast. That you know what's on the top of a cloud."

"More cloud, obviously." He waved a dismissive hand. "But you see, lies and rumors swirl about a thing until it becomes the truth, or at least obscure the truth so greatly that it's impossible to tell the difference. Rumors can be worse than a pillaging army, I've found. Uniting the republics with the two kingdoms will destroy us just as swiftly as the empire would."

Selene shook her head slowly. "Politics give me a headache."

Alberracin chuckled. "You learn to breathe through it."

Curiosity nipped at her like dogs at her heels. "Then, what do I have?"

He smiled, pinched his thumb and forefinger together, about a hair's width apart. "A folder this thick."

She didn't know whether to be flattered or insulted. All she could do was laugh.

He folded his hands in front of him. "How can I help you, my dear?"

My dear? What was she, a child to dangle sweets in front of? She chewed the inside of her cheek. "An assassin went after my son."

"I'm sorry to hear that. Congratulations on your child. A healthy baby boy?" *I hadn't told him that.* "Relax, I'm truly happy for you. Children are a gift from the heavens."

"Then you know how angry I am." She squeezed a fist. "You heard the priest. The Sigurites will never let us live, not as long as Palerme stands in opposition."

"You think it's the Sigurites?"

"Who else would it be? The Order have a million reasons to kill me. Palerme opposes their view of the world. Says that werewolves can coexist with humanity."

"Can they?" Alberracin grimaced. "It's a troubling notion, to be sure. Don't worry, I don't believe in the Order way of dealing with things, of slaying them all."

Selene wrinkled her nose. "That's comforting."

"Nor do I believe in letting them run unfettered, like beasts. Tell me, what do you think? Do you believe we should let them roam free, able to kill and hunt with impunity?"

She clenched her jaw. The line of questioning made her angry. Was he trying to trick her? "I believe just as a man who commits murder should be punished, so should an Althann."

The duca raised an eyebrow. "Althann?"

"The old hillmen word. See, we were the invaders. We conquered them, forced them to the edges of our society. No wonder they're angry."

"Interesting. And how do you know this?"

"It's a theory. I don't know for sure."

He smiled and came to a strongbox, fished out a smaller key from his robe. With a click, it opened to reveal yet more paper. *Seems to be a running theme.*

"One of my agents took this from a historian, in Vallonia. You're right, of course. They had no choice but to fall in line, to integrate. The ones that live today are descendants of humanity and the demons—my apologies, Althann, you said?" He closed the box and handed it to her, key still in the lock. "It's the proof you're looking for. Consider it a gesture of goodwill."

Selene raised her brows, took the box gingerly. "You mean... I didn't quite believe it myself."

"No, you're right. Werewolves were indigenous to the Continent before humanity arrived with Istryan from Tiellieres. At least, the western half was. The empire is built on genocide. But then, what empire isn't?"

She hesitated. "And you're giving me this for nothing?"

"Well, not for nothing. Answer my question: what do you think should be done about them?"

"I think they should have a sanctuary where they can train and learn to control their emotions. They're not wild animals, nor are they cursed. They're like us, just as complex and shitty as the rest of us."

"And if they don't want to learn how to control their urges?"

"Why wouldn't they?"

"It's a fair question. Not every one of them will accept your offer. You're not one of them. They might take issue with the woman who used to hunt them giving them orders."

She hadn't thought of that. Out of everything, she couldn't believe that there would be werewolves perfectly happy to murder and kill, slaves to their urges. "I intend to help them. Why would they take issue with that?"

"Intentions count for very little, I've found." He waved a hand. "No matter. What do you want? What do you think I can give you?"

"Something to keep the empire from attacking us. Soldiers, arms. Cannon, if you've got it. One of us is meeting with the Thousand Sons now, but we need the gold to pay them."

"Thousand Sons, eh?" Alberracin nodded. "Of all of them, they're the most reliable. Though that isn't saying much. All right. I'll give you the mercenaries you're asking for. The Thousand Sons are the largest, and they'll serve as a powerful deterrent to imperial aggression. You shall have them for as long as it's required to keep the Sigurites away."

"I... I don't know what to say." *That was too easy.*

"'Thank you,' might be a good start."

"Thank you. But why?"

"I've long thought to turn Palerme into a border fortress, to keep an eye on imperial movements, in case they ever decide to do what Malatesta constantly worries himself with. But restoring a keep is no small feat, nor is garrisoning it with loyal men. Happily, I have someone willing to do that for me, someone with a name to legitimize it."

On the face of it, she was getting everything she wanted. So, why did it feel like she was getting the short end of the bargain?

"Someone with a vested interest in keeping the empire away from Alania," she added.

"Precisely. With my northern border secure, I can turn my eye to uniting these idiots. See, Malatesta sees enemies in the wrong direction. The empire is as fractured as a sailor's wife. It would take a true Sigur's Day miracle for the northern lords to stop fighting long enough to form an army and reclaim their old territories. If Alania, Taneria, and Prolia stood as one nation, a Grand Republic, we could stand equal to the Vallonians and the Badonnians, instead of squabbling and killing each other every fighting season."

"With you as its grand leader, I suppose." Alania, Taneria, and Prolia. Each were ruled by a duca ostensibly elected by the people. But as was the case with many of these situations, the people swapped one king for another, just with the trappings of fairness. Duca Constantin Furlano de Civitati d'Alberracin, or simply Alberracin, had ruled Alania unopposed for the better part of two decades. It seemed now that he'd decided that wasn't enough.

Alberracin smiled wryly. "Someone must."

She looked back to the door. One way in, one way out. Suddenly she thought that this place would be extremely flammable if one of the lanterns were to fall. Probably why they were suspended from heavy chains and encased in thick glass.

"I know what you did to the previous inhabitants of Palerme."

"An unhappy circumstance. They didn't know their place." His face flashed with anger, the first time she'd seen more than just bored ease from him. "I trust you won't make the same mistake." He smiled, regaining his uninterested mien. "Another bit of advice: don't trust Giustiniani. He's only loyal so far as his coin goes."

"I had no intention of doing so."

"His lieutenant, Rolco, is far more malleable. Some men were made to lead, some to follow. He's the latter. Should he find himself in the captain's chair, we will be all the happier for it."

"Good to know." *Is he suggesting I get rid of Giustiniani for Rolco?* She ground her teeth, trying to ignore the headache building behind her eyes. *Politics.*

"Very well. I believe that covers all matters for discussion." He gestured to the door. A marine stood there, called by some unheard sound. "Mariano will take you to the guest apartments."

"Oh, and Selene." He didn't look at her, thumbing through a stack of half-scrawled pages. "Don't forget who owns you."

CHAPTER 13
UNORTHODOX

Sometimes I wonder what the gods drink, you know? Does Sigur
enjoy an ale now and then?

— Overheard in the training halls of the Order

RICHTER ADMITTED IT WAS unorthodox to have a bunch of novitiates in his room after Vespers. But he wanted to drink, and he didn't want prying eyes. Drinking was forbidden by the tenets, but if every priest or vestal was executed for a tipple now and then, the churches and preceptories would be draftier and emptier than they already were. You could find it if you looked, could get it for the right price. Paun had earned his stay by bringing a barrel of weissbrau along from somewhere. Stolen, most likely since they had to crack through the maker's mark to open it.

"More!" he yelled. They threw back tankards of beer as Luni draped her light through the open window like an expensive whore teasing a potential client. Dull silver graced the knotted, oily boards, left black shadows. A fat tallow candle stunk up the room with its greasy light, flicking huge, monstrous doubles across the peeling walls.

Five men, and a woman. Not the worst company he'd ever kept, and he was even beginning not to hate some of them. He'd often found that the best friends made the worst enemies, and the worst enemies made the best friends, or at least the most trustworthy. You knew what an enemy would do. You never knew what your friends were planning.

He didn't really count any of them as friends, or enemies for that matter. He hadn't known them long enough. Though Karl and Fehling, they seemed a good sort, or at least knew how to kill and how to suffer, and that made them a line higher in his book than most. They lounged together, propped up by a collection of greasy cushions stolen from the neighboring room. In the darkness they pretended as though nobody could see them and looked at each other with the hunger of young lovers about to tear each other's clothes off. The hunger of young lovers with too much seed in their pants and not enough sense. Not that Richter had an issue. He only wanted more drink.

"More!" They did another round, with the hillman Paun doing the honors of pouring the drinks. "If I can see," Richter yelled. "I'm not drunk enough!"

Bjorn finished his cup and set it aside, belching loudly. He smacked his lips and wandered his fingers across his chest, like he couldn't find anything better to do with them.

"Inquisitor, sir," he said. "I've been in a few fights in my life. Few tavern brawls. Never killed a man over it. Never had much cause. See, in Salzheim, I was a mason. Built churches, until my wife was killed by a demon. There, a man fights and you know he'll be your brother by the end of the night."

"What are you saying?"

"How did you know Hoher was a murderer?" he said. "Or a demon? Seemed like you smelled it on him."

Richter smiled. "It's not hard. Most people have something dark in their lives. Their ghosts, their desires. You just have to be honest with yourself as to what can go through someone's mind, what's going on in that strongbox of their head. See, could be Fehling's imagining making me into a eunuch with her knife because she caught me pulling myself over a couple of dead folk." He spoke without looking at her. "She already caught a glimpse of the hell that runs like a gutter, collecting all the feces and the piss and the corpses that pile high in a mind. Me, I'm just more honest about it where that gutter runs to."

The northman Jogaila lounged by a fireplace blackened with old soot. Cushions propped his head up as he downed his fourth ale. He tapped his chest and vented a loud burp. He looked as if he had more than a belch on his tongue, and spoke awkwardly, like a demon had gone away with his words.

"Inquisitor, sir... then why do they call you a hero?"

"Who called this ugly bastard a hero?" Nials roared. Somehow, he'd found himself involved in the proceedings to get absolutely blind drunk without Richter's knowledge.

"The Hero of Ostelar?" Fehling said, her voice a few octaves higher than usual. Richter saw the culprit. Karl had an arm down her unbelted trousers.

"What did you do again? Save a few archivists?"

Richter grumbled and threw back another gulp. He misliked the title. It ate at his shame. He was surprised he had any left. A burning taste hit the back of his tongue, though that might've just been the beer repeating on him.

"Good riddance, I say," Bjorn said. "Those southerners take their cows to bed and put their wives in the field."

They laughed, Richter loudest of all.

"Not that you'd know the difference between a cow and a woman, Salzheimer," Nials spat. "Don't all you northern cockhairs grow them big and ugly up there? Not met a Salzheimess that looked better than a plucked pig."

"Sight better than your ugly mug, you southern spawn of a whore."

"Your mother weren't complaining last time I visited."

"Southern bastard."

"Northern cunt."

"Enough!" Richter threw his cup across the room, seemed like the thing to do. White liquid spattered the boards and the tops of his shoes.

The room spun delightfully as he stood. The fortress was built on solid foundations, more than a foot thick, bigger around than three men linking arms together. The Cataline Hill itself hadn't shifted or weathered in three hundred years, give-or-take, according to the Order's finest surveyors. So, he grinned when he realized that despite his hardy constitution, despite his anger, despite his shame, the floor seemed to wobble out from underneath his feet. As though he stood at the tiller of a ship in the middle of a storm.

"More, Paun!"

"Aye, sir!"

"You a hillman?" Nials laughed. "How the fuck did a hillman find his way to Istrya? Surprised he didn't get lost knee-deep in his sister." He looked around for support, though none was found in their silent, thinning lips.

"You're a lovely man, hangdog," Paun replied. He set down the jug of beer, folded his meaty arms.

The man was enormous, even for a hillman, and that meant he was truly huge. His arms were the size of Richter's waist, and he stood a head taller than Bjorn, who was still taller than anyone else by far. The bandage on Paun's hand didn't lessen the effect.

But Richter knew it wasn't the size, it was what you did with it. Killing a man was very different to intimidating him. Another drink found its way into Richter's hand, and he downed it in one gulp.

"Hangdog?"

"I've seen bloodhounds better lookin' 'an you."

Nials drew a long knife. "I don't have to suffer this shite from a cousin-fucker."

"Is it sister, or cousin?" Karl said. He didn't take his hand out of Fehling's trousers. She was making grunting noises like a mare in heat, her eyes closed tight.

Nials turned, eyes wide and weeping with that foul yellow he sometimes got. Like his tears were poison as well as his words. He looked a right animal, unshaven for weeks, ready for violence at a moment's notice, only delayed by the distraction. "What?"

"Is it knee-deep in his sister, or his cousin?"

The question caused Nials to stutter. "*B*-Both. Who cares!"

"Maybe he's confused from fucking so many cows."

"There's naught honor in anything else, down south," Richter said. They all laughed, except the mangled inquisitor.

"Honor," he said. "That's rich coming from a man that saved a bunch of cowards while a city burned around him. You're no hero."

Richter smiled, a full-faced grin, never feeling so low. He didn't like the smile. Felt like doing violence, instead. Maybe it would make him feel better. He always liked to make himself feel better.

The point of his knee caught the hangdog right in his plums, doubled him over with a breathy woof. He grabbed the back of his sweaty head and put his other knee through the man's nose, heard a thrilling crunch. Taking hold of Nials's jacket, he pulled him forward, towards the window.

The hangdog inquisitor pleaded nasally. To deaf ears. "No, *please!*"

Richter tossed him into the void. His legs clipped the frame, went sprawling, spinning, the open air swallowing him like the maw of a giant beast. Nials's scream faded as he tumbled into darkness. Richter heard an even more thrilling squelch and the screaming stopped.

"No great loss, I say," Bjorn said. "Seems like he's been waiting for someone to come along and do that to him."

"You have no idea how right you are, my friend." Richter's hands started to shake. Weren't guilt, weren't horror. That was the thing about Swords—you didn't have a family, and no one missed you. They'd been drinking near an open window, see, and the inquisitor had a bit of a tumble.

"No one's going to miss that fucker," Karl said.

Richter held up his hands. A spot of blood clung to his palm, where Nials's bloody nose had dripped on him. They trembled as though he was a virgin bride on her wedding night, wrestling with her husband's cock. *At least the female novitiates of the Order have been freed of their burdens.*

"Can we fucking drink in peace," he roared. And slumped down into a pile of cushions while Paun raced to hand him a full cup. "How does a southerner not die of shame with a city of demons on his fucking doorstep, anyway? Gods know what else besides, but that place needs to be burned to the fucking ground."

"Palon?" Jogaila said. "No, what is it, Paloria? What do you call a group of demons, anyway? A hive?"

"Palerme. Not right, there being a city of them. Goes against sense." And every fiber of his being. Here was a man who'd faced death countless times, who'd rid the Continent of more than a hundred werewolves. Who'd led countless hunts and murdered ten days in the Forest of Rot. Now these cunting demons banded together like a pack of wolves, wanted to live in some shitting haven in the balmy south.

"Shit and pox on that," Karl said. His eyes caught a glint of murder in the silvery light. "We ought to go kill them all."

Fehling made a lowing sound, a cow in heat. She had a bout of kicking and spasms, arched her back.

"Fucks' sake, you two," Bjorn said.

Karl extracted his hand from her trousers, fingers glistening in the moonlight, gave them a lick.

Fehling panted as she said, "You jealous?" She crawled over to him. "Karl's still slick with my quim, might go better up your back end."

"Fuck no."

She gave a pouty frown. "Then perhaps you had something else in mind?"

"Maybe I should steal a barrel of weissbrau every day," Paun muttered, half-chuckling.

"You'd better," Bjorn said as Fehling unbuckled his belt, undid the knots. The Salzheimer's cock flipped out, stiff as a spear. She devoted her long fingers to it like it was the finest marble and she a sculptor.

Karl marched over and took one of her hands to his own ready member. They lost themselves in the passion and the fervor that Fehling was affording them. Yes, Richter came to realize, this bunch of killers would do nicely.

H E UNTANGLED HIMSELF FROM their spent bodies just before High Hours. At night, the hall outside his room looked, felt, tasted different. The walls peeled their render, and a damp permeated the air. Like it needed a good draft to get the stink out. Sweat tickled his scalp. The candles spluttered in their cradles in the hall, strangled by the gloom, casting sluggish shadows into every corner. He felt almost like he was back in that cellar.

Why after High Hours? Rooms studded from the sad uniformity, barred with iron and thick wood. He wondered if the debauchery that had occurred mere hours ago went on behind these doors as well. *We're all sick.*

The Order is rotten inside and out. I partake what I can while I can still enjoy it, but I'm not alone. Vetterand commits his crimes behind closed doors, and the Order does nothing, and the demons survive.

What the fuck was he doing here? Maybe he should take Karl and Fehling and the others and ride down to Palerme. It wouldn't take much. Poison in their water supply would do the trick. *Poison is a coward's weapon. I'd much prefer to take them head on.* But a frontal assault would be suicide. He'd never fought more than five werewolves at once, and they didn't know what they were doing, attacking on primal instinct. *I imagine this traitorous cunt has taught them how to make their transformations conscious.* That made things difficult. That made things dangerous. In all likelihood, his new friends would be slaughtered, and Richter captured. *Or maybe they know the secret to keeping a werewolf dead.* He'd thought about doing it himself—setting up someone to cut his head off when he died but before he could transform. But the mission was too important now. He had to see this hive of demons destroyed, at the very least, before he left this world.

Vetterand's door stood ajar. Richter reached out, hesitated, then a voice called from the other side.

"Come, Inquisitor."

He went inside, saw Vetterand sitting by a blazing hearth, swirling a silver cup bedecked with rubies the size of eyes. *If the Order executed everyone who took a tipple now and then...*

Vetterand was not an ugly man. In fact, for a man well into his middle age, hair silvering and black, some might call him handsome. Not Richter though. Those eyes of night blazed with some implacable wisdom, as though he was always measuring up a man, seeing what use he could make of you. He scarcely liked to look in those eyes, Richter. Saw too much of his own, but also the pyre, and the training over the years.

He makes me reminisce like some drunk general. It's him.

"Sit."

Richter sat on the chair opposite. The fireplace was made out of a giant block of stone, carved into the shape of a giant wolf, its yawning mouth filled with flame. Fire licked the roof of the beast's maw, and Richter felt his pits dampen with sweat.

Vetterand stared at the fire. "You and your new underlings seem to be getting on. Drinking and fucking like rabbits. A liberal interpretation of the codes of instruction." He paused to sip his drink. "Do not think there is a single thing in this fortress that I don't know of. In this city. Yes, you've been a very busy boy. Killing gangers in the Gully. It rolls off the tongue, doesn't it. And Nials, too." He sucked his teeth. Frowning, dark eyes locked onto Richter's, standing his neck hairs on end. Disappointment in them, perhaps, or just the cold anger of a killer.

"I had a visit from Gottscheid yesterday. He's upset. Upset with you, Beltrand. 'An uncontrollable dog,' he said. 'A mad bastard,' I believe was also uttered. He's quite angry about what happened in the Gully. He demanded your head, failing that, forthright removal from the Order. Stripped of your rank. I think we know which one he would prefer."

A nasty, icy smile, the kind that killers honed to a point. Richter was familiar with that smile. They stared at each other, the firelight glassy off his eyes. It might've made a pretty picture, but Richter was only an artist with the blade and claw. Vetterand was an artist, too, had many tools in his arsenal.

"Do you want me to scrape and beg for my life," Richter asked. "You would need luck trying to kill me, remember?"

Vetterand swirled the cup and took a sip. He smoothed the skirt of his white and gold-threaded robe, the fabric rasping at his touch.

"It's a good thing I never liked that Annaltian prick. There's one thing the Order of the Golden Lantern are good for, and it's for sitting around arguing the finer points of a martyr's brown hole and whether it's holy or not. There's no one quite like you in the Order, and I'd quite like to keep you. Pox on the pontiff."

"Well then, what did you call me here for?"

Vetterand chuckled. "You're not in trouble, my boy. You know, when I found you on the streets of Istrya, you were likened to a rabid dog. In many ways, I suppose you still are. It took three full-grown men to wrestle you down, and you cut the belly of one of them, nearly killed him."

"I remember." *Domitus.*

"That's the kind of fire I need, I know now."

"Something has changed."

"Something has indeed. You once lamented the fact that we're not doing enough to bring war to the demons—that's why you ventured off on your mission and why I indulged you, despite your... less-than-clean methods."

He leaned forward, put his cup on the side table and pushed out of the chair. Richter flinched when Vetterand put his hand on his shoulder. He never forgot the first time Vetterand had taken to his fingers with pliers, to test the resilience of his claws. It was what make him so acutely aware of how to selectively transform them, so he supposed he had Vetterand to thank. Bastard of a thing to thank him for, though.

"You know, I've always thought of you as the son I never had."

Hell of a family. "Is that so?"

"Yes. And a son would like to make a father proud, right? Well, all things considered, you have."

Richter's eyes went as wide as Luni's face. He felt an ugly swelling of emotion in his chest, a thing he'd spent years trying to stamp down. It came roaring like a panicked crowd, stomping all over each other to get to safety. It would almost have been delicious had he evoked it in someone else. "You're... proud? What were the words you used earlier, rabid dog?"

"Even a rabid dog can have a proud master, and your teeth have been sharpened to a razor point. Tell me, what do you think of the emperor?"

Old handsome bastard, they all say, and the appearance lived up to the rumors. A bit ineffectual in controlling his sons, but you could call that love. I wouldn't, but I've never known love. An old champion in the tournament lists and on the battlefield, and a scholar of war, but like all men at the top rungs, never got his hands dirty. "I don't think of him, sir," Richter said.

"A fine general if there ever was one. He wrote the book on battlefield engagement. But these aren't times for a general. For a soldier, would you agree?"

"No, sir." *These are times for killers.*

Vetterand granted a kinder smile. "He's beloved by the people for his even temper and his fair taxes. More of a reformer, and a sight better than any emperor in recent memory. Better than his sons, that's for sure. A coward, a brigand, and a cripple. I dare say most would prefer none of them inherit. Though to be fair, if I had to live up to their father's reputation, I'd probably choose the coward's way out myself." He went back to his seat and lowered himself with a long groan. He reached for his cup again, gave it a swirl, then a drink.

"I want you to kill him," he said finally.

Richter blinked in surprise, half-convinced he'd imagined the words in his ears. "You want me to do what?"

"I want you to kill the emperor, in your demon form."

"The cure was a ruse."

"Of course. Do you think me a god's fool?" He shook his head in exasperation. "Pay attention, son. If the emperor is killed by a demon, they'll be begging us to wipe out the beasts. We can be rid of that sore on Osbergia's arse-end once and for all."

"You're asking me to... kill the emperor?"

"Yes. Emperor Franz Josef Lorenz Maria von Karstein Saxen und Trestinsen must die. And he must die at the hands of a werewolf. At your hands, my son."

Richter leaned forward with interest. "So, Franz must die. When?"

CHAPTER 14

BONDS OF BLOOD

TRIBUUM, 1045

Never underestimate the number of rituals you perform in a day, just out of habit. Do you put your shoe on starting with the left, always, without even realizing? Try to think about it, next time, and you'll see.

— MERA BRUMAL, PRIESTESS OF EME

THE MARINE LOCKED THE door to the apartments with a soft click. Selene tried the crystal doorknob, and it slipped around her clammy fingers. Not one to leave her grievances unsaid, she bashed on the heavy wood with a deep thumping noise.

"What are you doing," she shouted. "We are guests of the duca!"

She almost thought the guard hadn't heard her when he replied, "Alberracin's orders. You will be free to go in the morning. He doesn't want you wandering the city at night. For your safety."

My safety? Then she recalled the priest, Gothenburg, demanding her be burned at the stake, and thought perhaps being locked in one of the most secure buildings in Valenti was a good thing. A locked door locked both ways, keeping malcontents out. Then what about the malcontents inside?

Locked doors. At least this place wasn't a dingy basement under a cathedral filled with screams.

You're not one of them. They might take issue at a woman who used to hunt them giving them orders instead. Intentions count for very little.

The duca's words stuck with her during her journey to the guest apartments and hadn't shifted since. Like a knife in the guts.

Not having much else to do, she looked around. Maybe she could find some inspiration in the reputedly incredible guest apartments of the duca. If not, then perhaps she could distract herself enough that she forgot.

Walls of white render laid thick with reliefs of men and women, children and animals playing in pools of water. Glass beads a vibrant blue, like the deepest ocean, toyed with the afternoon sun leaping through a high arched window. The shutters were open, letting a cool breeze into the apartment, a refreshing reprieve from the warmth of the south.

To think that only four years ago, her life was different. It wasn't happy, certainly, just different. Tristain was alive, and werewolf attacks were a thing that happened to other people. To the unlucky and the heretic. How wrong she was. On the face of it, she lived a blessed life as the ward daughter to a well-respected count, destined for marriage to another count or a duke, perhaps, to live the rest of her days in luxury. Yes, any marriage arranged by her adoptive father likely would've been just as hard as life with him, but she knew now that people had worse problems than a foul temper to deal with.

The blood of others soaked her hands, her legs, her body. She was neck-deep in it, now. How many people had she killed to get right back to where she was heading—the lady of some castle?

But there was no point lingering on her lot. Life never waited for you to come to terms with it. You had to hold on with your fingernails for all you were worth.

The south was a strange place. Bathed in centuries of Vallonian, Badonnian, and Saburrian influence, it was some syncretism of imperial culture and those southern kingdoms, who at one time or another over the millennia of the empire's existence, had controlled the ancient cities of Valenti, Malatesta, Segesta, and the rest. Those cultures clung to this place like her bloody underlinens after baby Tristain's birth.

There was a lesson in there, maybe. That no matter how hard you tried—the Duca's plans of a Grand Republic, declaring independence from the empire, fighting with each other to be the biggest jewel in a heap of shit—you could never escape your past. It clung to you like bloody underlinens.

"Sel, is that you?" Leon came from a balcony, earthenware goblet in hand. At first, she worried it was wine or some other booze, and he'd gone back on his vows, then she saw the liquid was orange.

"Squeezed oranges," he said quickly, preempting her question. "Quite tasty. We should grow some up in Palerme."

He handed her the cup. It tasted fruity and tangy. Warm, but just the thing she needed to cut her thirst. She downed the cup in one big gulp, wiped her mouth with the back of her sleeve. "Sorry, I was thirstier than I thought."

Leon frowned over the top of the cup. "Uh huh." He snatched it back. "I'll get more. There's a jug outside."

Maybe we should grow oranges. How hard was it to grow a few trees? Much harder than she'd realized. She never quite understood how hard the Invereid estate tenants had it until she'd tried to turn seeds into a crop. Near on half of their planting had died in the frost in the mountains, though what had survived was just enough for bruma. Might not be enough next time, not with added mouths to feed.

Every day in Palerme scraped like a knife on bone. Working from sun-up to sun-down and never feeling like she'd done enough. There were always more things to do, to fix, to plant, to build, and the things that they'd built would start falling apart and they'd have to start the whole cycle all over again.

She'd had her doubts, of course. The duca was right. What made her the right person for the task? But if not her, then who? They would never have Palerme if it wasn't for her, for her name. It legitimized her claim to the land, in everyone's eyes, the duca included. Nobles only recognized nobles, even those with trappings of equality. A grandmother of his had married the archduke some sixty years back, and that made him noble enough in many eyes. It was why the archduke always had a claim here that could be pressed at any moment, which clearly gave the duca pause, even if he hid his feelings about it extremely well.

No one—imperial, republican, Badonnian, Vallonian—nobody would ever accept a demon owning land. If they wanted to find themselves at total war with the entire Continent, that was how to do it. And as far as they'd come, it was a finger's width on a road of a million miles.

If she wanted to save the lycans, she needed to take what was offered. If she wanted peace, she needed to take it for herself.

He smiled at the threshold to the balcony. "Frix and the others are here."

She was pulled out of her reverie when through the open door came singing. She walked onto the balcony. Frix and his cousins lounged on a fat-legged day bed by a stone balustrade, cups of wine in hand. Gregor and Tomas laughed at the noise, pointing over the rail to a courtyard below.

The Saburrian marine sung a ditty, though it sounded more like a dirge of the dead with the way she was wailing.

Bring us no fair maid,
For she did cost me pretty,

Bring us no fair beef,
For there's many bones,
The laughter built as her voice went higher.
Bring us no bacon,
I've had enough of that,
She slapped her metal belly with a clang.
Bring me good fucking ale,
For blessed Eme's sake,
Bring me good fucking ale!

"If you want some good fucking ale, come up here," Frix yelled.

The woman turned, adjusting the longsword over her shoulder instinctively. Her face turned bright red. "You were... you could hear me?"

"I dare say even the emperor in Istrya heard you!"

She looked around. "They'll relieve me soon. Promise you've ale?"

"Aye," said Leon. "They seem to deliver it through the door. Don't know how it gets there."

The woman laughed generously. "The duca wants to keep you happy. Make sure you don't run loose, and we'd have to kill you all."

Selene frowned. *More's a party, I suppose.* She misliked the idea of drinking with one of the duca's loyal marines, but the sergeant could do anything she liked. She would have keys. She could steal into their apartments at night and kill them all in their beds.

You're seeing threats everywhere. The woman just wants a drink, for Eme's sake.

She couldn't blame her for that. Selene needed a drink herself.

The cool jug of sparkling white, perfect for the warming months, poured generously into her cup. A little black bug came flying up, perhaps looking for water, and she waved it away. That was something she noticed in the cracked earth and wilted fields of the south—the place was drier than an old woman's tit.

She smiled. Lucia would've enjoyed that one. She tried not to linger on that thought, feeling the crushing grief threatening to overtake her, tears needling at the back of her eyes. She sighed greatly as she sunk into an empty chair, passing it off as boredom.

The courtyard, she realized, was the same as the one she'd passed on their way to the papers room. The same ludicrously huge-breasted woman pouring an eternal fountain of water from her jug. What she hadn't noticed, though, standing behind a hedge trimmed to a perfect square, were big double doors that led out to a stable and some grounds. She could see over the high stone wall to the grounds beyond, which were far less manicured and absent of any heavy-breasted marble women. A few horses milled about a fenced yard in front of the stable, and a further high wall surrounded the palace grounds proper. For all his claims at equality, for all his easy words, the duca clearly had his issues in his own city.

Leon slung his legs over the top of the balustrade, cup of juice full again. "I could get used to this. You don't know how good a featherdown mattress is until you go without one for a few years."

"Ah, so you've already tried the beds."

"Sel, I already had a damn nap." He stretched out his arms with a pleasant sigh. "The best nap of my whole damn life."

She took a sip and looked at Gregor, Frix, his two cousins, and Tomas playing a game of Fives that they'd hauled out from a small cabinet by the fire. "They seem to be enjoying themselves."

"It's nice to have a break. We've been working our arses raw fixing up Palerme, trying to make it some kind of place to live. Eme knows we've deserved a little relaxation."

She pressed her lips into a weary smile. "I suppose." Something still felt off, made her uneasy. "What happened to..." She didn't want to think of his name. "Our prisoner."

"They sent him back to Palerme under guard," Frix said. "Thought you might like to deal with him yourself."

"I suppose I will." Could she kill a former friend? She could, she supposed. It wasn't like she hadn't done it before.

Leon slapped her knee. "Your mind is too fixed in the future, Sel," he said. "And lingers too long on the past. Enjoy more of what you have, in the now."

Anger flared in her chest. She didn't quite know why. "Is that how you became a drunk? Got your men killed? Nearly got Tristain killed? Enjoyed a little too much ale in the now?"

He retracted his hand. The others went silent. "Alright, then."

"I'm sorry, I didn't—" Guilt and grief in hand tore at her throat, threatened to choke the breath from her.

"It's fine. You're angry, I get it. Meeting with one of the most powerful men in the Continent would do that to you."

Frix looked up from smacking down a chip. He was losing, quite badly. "What did he want, anyway?"

"I met with him. He promised us the Thousand Sons."

Tomas and Gregor clapped their hands. "Happy news," Tomas said.

"We do?" Leon frowned. "But we've scarcely raised the money, yet. Unless—"

"He'll pay. Wants to turn Palerme into a forward keep, to watch any imperial movement on the border."

"And more, likely."

"Those were the terms," she snapped. She took another sip. "He wouldn't go back on them."

Leon sighed. She knew he didn't deserve her scorn, but nothing would shake her mood. "Powerful men and their promises are soon forgotten in the tides of politics."

I know but what can I do? The duca's last words to her stung her ears. *Don't forget who owns you.*

"Don't worry, milady," Frix said. Something warm in his voice reminded her of Mother.

He was a handsome man, no doubt, and had a fair temper. He wore a moustache in the northern style that she deeply disliked, for it reminded her of Father, but that was hardly his fault. He was the opposite of Father in every way there was. If only more lords and powerful men were like him, and less like Duca Alberracin, the world might be a better place. But then, powerful men didn't stay powerful by being fair or even-tempered.

They took what they saw as theirs. That was power, Selene had realized. Men like Aloysius Bugold, who covered his son-in-law's crimes. Men like Alexei, who killed all those women because he could. Men like Alberracin, like Bann, like Grand Inquisitor Vetterand. The powerful didn't care what the less powerful thought, what they wanted, what they needed. They took what they wanted. They enforced their will on others. If the Order had taught her anything, it was how to enforce her will.

But how to make the story? That was as important, if not more. No one *liked* to be controlled, to be ruled over. People chafed for freedom like Vyahtkenese stallions at the bridle. And yet, the Order managed it, Alberracin managed it, the emperor managed it. Stories. That's what bonded people, kept people fettered to their bondage. The power of rituals.

"We'll figure it out," Frix continued. "For now, let's just be happy we have the Thousand Sons."

"Aye, and no lie," Leon shouted. Selene smiled to see him happy again. "Let's see those stinking Sigurites try to come down and kill us with three thousand crossbows pointed right at their faces."

"If only Lucia was here to see it," she said. That left a wistful silence hanging over them like a shroud of the dead. Even the Fives game had paused.

"Where do you think Althann go when they die," Gregor asked, idly picking a sliver of render from the wall he leant on.

"Oye," Tomas said. "We're having a relaxing afternoon at the duca's expense. Talking about death like that ought to bring a dark cloud on us."

"Gregor's thinking of his sons," Frix said.

Gregor looked at him like he was about to cry and all but confirmed that notion.

"Back to the ground," Selene said. "That's what Lucia said. Your body goes back to the ground and becomes part of the land for the next generation to have, renewing the cycle."

"I'm not having them bury me under a fucking field," Tomas shouted. Everyone laughed.

"I don't think it's that. Waters and lands are everything for Althann. Every root, every tree, every river, all ours. What we take from them is given back on our deaths, to help the next generation."

"I see," Gregor said. "What else did she tell you?"

"The folk tales that everyone knows, especially the hillmen, were the rituals of old Althann. Old family traditions, that sort of thing. The South Hills were the last holdout of the Althann against the invading empire. There, they survived the longest. But it was still hundreds of years ago, and the Sigurites covered it up, so all we have left are folk tales."

And the proof. The duca's strongbox, the one with the papers inside. It was sitting just inside the apartment, by the door. She hadn't known what to do with it. What form could proof like that possibly take? And what was it worth, anyway, when the church could just claim it as false?

"Every Ginnsday," Frix said, a sly smile on his lips, "my family would offer part of ourselves to a cup—a drop of blood, usually, mixed with wine. Though Uncle Johannes once cut off his pinky and put it in there. It was disgusting, but we drank anyway—"

"You *ate* a finger?" Tomas retched.

"No, we just drank around it. I was only a child, but we all found it hilarious. Less hilarious when Uncle Johannes died a week later from rot."

Leon spat orange juice onto his lap. They all laughed.

"Anyway, it was a nice way of coming together as a family, and my grandmother said we've done it since the first ones of us came with Istryan. Harmless, really, unless you got the rot. But when my grandmother did it, we never did. She'd put the blade in the fire and let it cool before she cut us."

"I wonder why," Tomas asked.

"Don't know. All I know is Johannes cut himself, and he died. When Gran did it, none of us did."

The power of rituals. The idea poked out from the muck of her thoughts like a dead man's bones from an unearthed grave. "We should—"

Pounding at the door and Tomas nearly tipped off his chair in surprise, letting out a short shout. "Ginevra's tits! Who is that?"

Selene ambled over to the door, feeling a little tipsy. She'd not drunk much since being pregnant, not at all while she was. In fact, this was really the first time she'd had more than a sip of the stuff, not being allowed it much at the Oncierran Estate, except during feasts. She was to be a proper maiden, and ladies who drank were unsightly and improper, or so the wisdom went.

The rituals of the pompous. We're all slaves to rituals, to stories, one way or another.

"I don't have a key," Selene said.

"Ah, Eme's fat arse," the visitor said. A woman. The Saburrian marine, probably. She had thought to make good on that promise of ale. Her voice faded out and muffled shouting followed. Then the lock clicked, and the crystal handle turned.

The woman grinned. A generous smile, revealing rows of full, white teeth. A sight more than Selene expected her to have, considering the monstrous scar on her forehead that she didn't bother to hide with tight, thick curls. She wore her armor, though she'd deigned to leave behind her helmet and longsword. That was cold comfort though. She still looked like she could kill just easily without a weapon.

But so could Selene, though she was a little out of practice.

Selene put her hands on the knobby bits of her hips. Her pregnancy had changed her body beyond recognition, and now her hipbones jutted out like an emaciated corpse, bones that stuck out further with her lack of training and requisite loss of muscle.

"Is this your way of respecting our privacy? Pretending you don't have a key?"

The woman laughed. "Shit on your privacy." She shouldered past Selene and sauntered somewhere between an Ostelarish whore in Lower Market and a stiff-legged soldier. The effect was mildly amusing. She threw a sour look over her shoulder. "Don't have a key. Only the marine watching your room does." A flinty smile. "Don't you trust us?"

"Not really." The marine outside closed the door and the lock clicked.

"If we wanted to kill you, you'd be dead."

Selene followed her outside.

"Though, this big one might survive a touch longer than the rest of you. Good morrow," she said to Gregor, fingering his jacket tabs.

Gregor smiled awkwardly. "Good morrow."

Sigur's fucking lantern, who does this woman think she is?

"Now, where's the—ah!" She snatched the jug on the table and nearly unhinged her jaw to take huge swallows, her thick neck working, frothy suds spilling down the side of her mouth onto the balcony tiles in heavy splats. Having ingested the entire jug, she lowered it and wiped her mouth.

"Ahh," she said, the noise not unlike a stallion finishing in a mare. They stared. "Oh, calm your cocks, I'll get more."

She clapped Frix on the shoulder and slammed him into the wall, nearly punched him through it, and went back to the door. If anything, Frix was happy about the whole thing, laughing like he'd taken a blow to the head. Which he might have.

Selene turned back to them and pulled her knife out. "Then we should do it." This was how she'd get them. Bonds of blood.

"Do what?"

"Your grandmother's sharing of blood. For health and wealth, and because none of us have any families anymore, naught any that haven't followed us. We make our own family. A family of Althann." She snatched up the small knife they'd given them to cut the cheese and opened her finger, ignored the pain. It was only a little scratch, and she'd had far, far worse.

"May our blessings be doubled, and our troubles halved. It's as Lucia wanted it."

"Gods, Sel, you're serious," Leon said, standing.

"Alright," Frix said, offering his cup. She let a few drops fall and handed Frix the knife.

He frowned. "We should clean it, at least." He took the knife and wiped it on his sleeve, rinsed it with wine.

She looked down. *In my rush, I hadn't thought about it. But this is the answer! This is how I control them!* All this talk of control gave her pause. Did it make her a bad person? Better to be a little bad for a lot of good. For Palerme to work, she had to have their loyalty. Gregor's son was just the first one to speak on it. There was bound to be others; those that came after, that hadn't known the flight from the Citadel, her saving them.

How had it come to this? Bleeding herself into a cup. But then, it was no different to many of the Order's rituals, the church's rituals. *We are all slaves to rituals, one way or another.*

"Am I interrupting something?" the Saburrian said, jug of ale in hand. "I can come back."

"Perhaps that would be best," Selene replied, letting her distaste for the woman tinge her words.

"Nonsense," Frix said. "Milady." He smiled wryly. "All Althann are welcome to share." The implication was clear.

"Frix?"

He didn't take his eyes off the woman. "Milady. I can smell it on her."

The Saburrian woman grinned. "I was wondering if you could." There was no mirth, just a mild curiosity in her words. The mild curiosity of the supremely confident. Selene didn't doubt she could have the six of their innards out in as many moments if she was so allowed the opportunity.

The tension in the air stretched out like skin over jagged bone. Selene really did wish she had kept a hidden blade. She eyed the pokers by a fireplace arranged in carved marble. The hearth still burned, kept by the duca's servants. If she was quick enough—

"Relax. I was curious," the woman said. She held out a hand. "Kyrah Al-Lami. What was it you said, Althann? I've heard the name. That's your word for demon, right?"

Selene shook it, nearly double the size of her own. She felt inadequate compared to this tall, muscular, confident woman. The woman that Selene had been, before pregnancy. Kyrah could've crushed Selene's fingers more than likely with those powerful, callused hands, the hands of a warrior. But she didn't. In fact, the touch was gingerly and soft, like she was trying to avoid doing that exact thing.

Shame reddened Selene's cheeks. She tried to push the feeling aside, got about half-way. "We prefer Althann. It's Hillard for friendly spirit."

"The South Hills? I see." She pursed her lips and put the jug on the table, filling each of their cups. Selene could tell she had more questions, the woman trying to contain them like a gutted soldier trying to pull back in his intestines.

"Shall we?" Selene said to Frix, not much caring.

Frix returned from the fire. The blade had that sleek, gray look of heated metal. Not hot enough to glow, just hot enough to burn. He cut his finger with a sizzling sound, and steaming blood dripped into the cup.

He held out the blade. "Anyone else?"

Tomas snatched it, full of the bluster of the unassured and the nervous. Everything Kyrah was, he wasn't. Selene knew that feeling well of late. *You'd think an ex-guardsman would be used to a few cuts.* "Here's to new beginnings." A shallow cut and blood dripped off the end of his finger with a *plink-plink*. He handed it to his cousin, the tonsured one.

"Fuck it," he said. *Plink-plink.*

The other cousin. "Here's to any god that takes pity on us heretics, demons, and witches." He made a seething, squealing noise. *Plink-plink.*

Leon was offered the knife. "Oh Ginevra, no. I ain't Althann."

"You mightn't be a wolf but you're as Althann as the rest of us, *sal'brath*. Shit, more. I ain't a hillman. None of us are." Frix socked him in the mail of his shoulder. "Just fucking cut yourself, Sir Strong. May our blessings be doubled, and our troubles halved." He glanced only briefly at Selene's disbelieving eyes.

She found it hard to believe it was this easy to convince them all. She'd prepared more arguments, thinking to leverage Lucia's death and their guilt for not doing more to protect her son, but happily she hadn't needed them. Good thing, that. The lie already spoken—that Lucia would've wanted it—plucked at her vocal cords like a harpist with blades for fingers.

"Ain't a knight no more." Leon eyed the knife then Selene. "Better do it before someone thinks me a coward."

"I don't think you're a coward," Selene said, voice breaking a little.

A plaintive smile. "Was talking about me," he said, voice thin. *Plink-plink*.

Something about him had changed. The last few months had made him weary, like an old man seeing his grave yawning down at him. He was hopeful enough when they first arrived in Palerme, and threw himself into work, but maybe he was ignoring his own grief as well. He'd loved Tristain like his own son, and he'd lost both. That would take its toll on any person.

As long as his grief didn't get in the way of his sword and axe. It might've been calloused to say, but she only thought it. Thought it well enough of herself, as well. Grief was only so useful as long as it didn't get in the way of the things that needed doing.

Gregor was the last. He took the blade without question and added his blood to the cup.

"Alright then," Selene said. She took the cup. It half seemed a mystical object now, and she held it like Rotersand—Bann—had, when he'd offered her the blood of the werewolf she'd slain. Strange that of all things, that came full circle.

The Saburrian woman barked a laugh. "What is this? It reminds me of the Sigur crap the priests bang on about. Holy fucking arse blood."

"I don't tell you how to be an Alanian marine, *kalb*." Maybe that was a step too far, but it was like the woman had taken a file to Selene's teeth from the unpleasant moment of their meeting and hadn't done much to shift her disposition since. Salim had used the word often enough in training that she knew it was an insult of sorts.

By Kyrah's reaction, it was as though she'd kicked her in the mouth. "*Kalb*," she spat. She growled like a ferocious wildcat. Pulled back a fist to throw a blow, her face scrunched tight in rage. "You fucking northern cu—"

"*Fouco*," someone bellowed below. Some Alanian word, though the bellower's panic was well clear. "*Fouco! Fouco!*"

The noise pulled their eye. Kyrah's blow stopped at the draw and her arm went limp. "Fire?"

"Wait, don't!" Selene shouted.

Two guards in the courtyard unbarred the doors to the palace grounds. From the other side of the wall, doused in twilit shadows and carved with sneers, metal glinting and torches sizzling in the dark, a mob charged.

CHAPTER 15

DETAILS

TRIBUUM, 1045

The most important details are hiding in plain sight.

— GRAND INQUISITOR ULRICH VETTERAND

DETAILS MATTERED. WHEN A crowd thrummed with that enticing cocktail of excitement and fear, anger and dread, you needed to capture the details of the scene. The right application of a blade left a man bleeding or left a man dead. Or a claw, in some cases. There was nothing in between. He needed to get it right. To not miss any details.

Details were that the naming of a new member of the Merovian Guard drew an enormous crowd. Ascension of a pompous idiot, if Richter was asked, but it made a terribly big deal of things. People rarely had occasions to celebrate anymore, not with Prince Reynard's war and the springing up of that hive of lycans, like an ugly wart needing removal. But it drew a crowd. Good for this black work.

Best of all, it drew the emperor out of his palace and in front of a large crowd.

The sky over the Palatine Hill clogged with clouds, carrying the stink of smoke from the stacks and the manufactories, cloying the air, wrinkling Richter's nose. The stench of the glassworks drifted up from the lake.

Damp clung to peeling whitewash, cracking masonry, like the buildings themselves were sweating. Stuck his jacket to his skin, too, though he'd be free of that soon enough.

He shouldered past a woman in a gray kirtle, pushed through a pair of lookalikes, their resemblance uncanny in matching red doublets. Moseyed past a group of men and their wives, little children lost in the press of shuffling feet, screaming about not being able to see. Men brought their wives, their mistresses, their children. A family affair. Gangers stayed as far away from the Merovians as they could get, but he recognized their easy eyes and slimy grins among the crowd. The entire city had come. Grimy and stinking, just like the weather.

He wondered who among them would survive if it came to a panic. But that was how he worked. A blunt instrument that crushed more than you intended to hit. Details mattered.

A woman in a giant hat blocked a vast portion of the crowd's sight of the Martyrerplatz. He meant to shove her out of his way, but someone took care of that for him, sending her on her arse and stealing her hat for good measure. The commotion allowed him to get closer, right to the boundary. Crossed halberds blocked his path. They shone with polish, wielded by men in particolored doublets and scalloped plate. Merovians. The best fighters in all the Continent, or so it was said. Richter knew all that metal did little against a well-placed blade.

He'd watched them for a time, staked out their routes as they assembled in the morning. Details. Given enough time, a man can plan for anything. If Richter wanted his crusade, Franz had to die. And Richter wanted his crusade, as much as a drowning man wanted breath.

Behind the Martyrerplatz, the immense Karlspalast loomed, all columns and towers, a motley of parapets and turrets, as though two architects with egos matched only by the size of the building itself competed with each other to see who could erect the tallest one. Jutting out from the black stonework, statues of great fathers and emperors of old lurked over them, watching the proceedings. Istryan, Jovian, Luthan. He wondered if they realized they would welcome a new member among their ranks soon enough.

Black, the color of martyrs. Martyrerplatz. It struck Richter as something of a joke that no matter where you came from, no matter whether you were a frozen Rigan or a sweating Saburrian, black was the color of the dead. Black stone, black tiles, black statues, run through with a red stone, like old wounds.

The gods saw fit to add to the jolly sight by sending a black cloud over them, dropping the pressure in his ears and coating all with earthy, rot-stinking rain. If nothing else, it eased the heat a touch. He looked at the roofs. Merovians in those motley, puffed doublets guarded the tops, gray steel running with water. Unmoving, like statues, with halberds unpolished. Used. Like they expected them to be used, and consequently didn't need polishing.

The rain broke as quickly as it arrived, saturated their clothes then left the heat to dry them out again. A throng of grandees like worms after rain sprung up from the dais, ready for the raven's clutches. The procession filed out of the Karlspalast's small door at the big double-door's base. The empress counted thirty ladies-in-waiting, countesses and duchesses among them. Crowned with feather hats next to them like preening peacocks stood forty-two men.

He never missed a detail. Armed with expensive, giltwork swords, the kind you'd be hesitant to draw if it came to a real fight. These fools likely hadn't handled a proper sword in their entire lives. They murmured with anticipation, facing the Karlspalast, where the emperor would emerge.

Richter left the front of the crowd and shouldered through the mass. Someone or something slapped his back and made him cringe. The wounds from the Screamer still had yet to heal fully and now pained him as he pushed through the bodies. That was the thing about both pain and details. You could ignore them until they were right in front of you—or in this case, behind.

He made it to the foot of a jeweler's, thick with pillars and brickwork in meagre imitation of the Karlspalast, along with half the other buildings on the avenue. A few Merovians imposed themselves on the walkway on the second floor, and a few Wall Guards besides. The flame of Martyr Brigida, a giant pyre, blazed on the front of the Guards' blue tabards.

Two of them sat behind the shop throwing dice and shot to attention when they saw Richter approach.

"Shit, fucker. We thought you were the captain."

Richter kept walking.

The taller one frowned, put his hand out to stop Richter. "Fuck off, no visitors allowed. This is a—"

A knife slid under the man's chin, cut off his braying. His friend's face spattered with drops of blood. Again, came the knife, and again, quick work so he was dead. Before the second one could blink, Richter punched his throat with a fist. It made a squelching sound. His mouth moved in a scream, but nothing came. As he stumbled around, eyes wide and face turning purple, Richter lowered the dead one to the ground, careful not to make noise. You never knew who was listening, who could hear.

Still clutching his throat, the guard got his sword out a handspan from its scabbard before Richter slammed it back home with a palm, headbutted him, sent him sprawling backwards, gasping noiselessly. Richter caught him with the knife between the breastplate and backplate. Lowered him slowly. It wasn't often he was trying to be silent but needs must. If they caught wind of an assassin, who knew what kind of stupidity they might attempt. Franz would be snatched out of reach, that was for sure. Richter could probably find him in the Imperial Palace and kill him, but the murder needed to be visceral, to stir anger, to stir violence. Most of all, it needed to be public, so there was no mistaking.

He dragged their bodies away, out of sight. Put them behind a stack of crates in a nearby alley filled with refuse. *More to add to the pile.* He thought about stripping one and wearing the armor, but a noise drew his attention away. A patrol was heading his direction, their boot heels clicking on the cobbles.

Applause rang out from the crowd, muffled by the stone. *Shit. I'm running out of time.* He doubted his ability to sneak up and gain access to the dais in Wall Guard armor, and he wasn't exactly inconspicuous. His neck was scarred with repeated suicide attempts, and these men didn't have helmets or gorgets. Whatever the quality of a soldier, whatever the look, Richter knew he didn't have it. He was a crazed killer.

He spotted the dice by the back of the jewelers. Blood spotting the ground. *Shit-shit-shit.* He walked to the edge of the alley. What was he thinking? *Sorry, lads, spot of trouble with the game, got into a bit of a fight. Killed them. Sorry.* He pressed himself up to the wall, peeking around the corner. The two guards turned, going down another lane parallel to Richter's. They didn't seem to notice their missing compatriots, or the dice.

He quickly pocketed the dice and threw off his cloak, grinding it into the fast-drying blood. With any luck, it would look like a damp stain. Dripping water from a gutter above, perhaps.

Then he remembered with some dumb luck that the patrol didn't go this far along, turning at that lane instead. Then, with the movement, he felt his back wounds, the pain present in his mind. Annoying now, not satisfying.

Details mattered, and the difference between a sharp, focusing pain and a mind-numbing ache was a thin line. And time was not on his side. He beat back anger and pushed himself up, reaching for a handhold in the frame of a window.

Cheers rang from the crowd again.

He planted his feet and up he went, higher, higher, pulling up-up, scaling the building's side. Shocking pain froze his muscles and he muttered swears, in Annaltian and Osbergian and any language that came to hand. At least twelve of them. A man needs to know a few if he's to kill his way across the Continent.

He grunted and pushed higher. Two more floors before he was on the roof.

He slipped. The rot of a window frame gave way to his boot, sent bits of wood and render clattering to the ground. He looked down. Over the lip of the next building, he saw the patrol head his way again. *Fuck-fuck—*

They'd decided to change the routes at the last minute. Twenty fucking times they'd patrolled up-and-back all the way to the other side of the lane, but now it seemed they'd changed their plans halfway. *Lazy fucking bastards.*

He twisted his hand to try to get a grip again, and pushed himself on, back protesting. Panic, a long-forgotten taste, rose like bile in his mouth. He was easy pickings for a crossbow, sprawled out on the side of a fucking imitation-Karlspalast. What would it mean if he failed here? If he was killed again? Vetterand's plans—his plans—would go up in smoke. No crusade. Order disgraced. Richter would be thrown in chains to the bottom of the darkest prison, or the deepest depths of the lake, trapped there for all eternity. Maybe he deserved it, maybe he didn't. But he sure as hell wasn't going to find out.

"Excuse me!" A woman's voice. Behind the patrol, in the lane. He looked over to the source. The woman wore a tight dress, green, silvered in the gray day, her thin shift pushing upwards from her bodice enticingly. The men were certainly enticed, leaning forward over each other like she was a mare in heat and they were stallions. Her black hair fell limp like a houseplant, split in two.

Fehling! What was she doing here?

"You must help," she said. Their eyes met for the briefest moment, as if to say, *climb, now! The fuck are you waiting for?*

The fuck am I waiting for?

He reached up for the side of an unfinished gargoyle. Unfinished, as though since it faced a back alley, the architect hadn't put much thought into it. Heaving, mouth moving breathlessly, uselessly, he hooked his leg up and sat on the creature, a gargoyle of his own making.

Richter's heart was in his throat. An odd feeling. Novel, exciting. A different sort of excitement to murder, and not unwelcome.

"Mistress, sorry," the one on the left told Fehling. "We're on emperor's business. Don't have time for the likes of you."

"Would love to make time," the other one said.

"No, Bors. Sorry, mistress."

They started to turn back.

Fehling's eyes darted upwards. Then she called out, "Yoohoo!"

She unfastened the hooks and eyes at the front of her dress. Her shift spilled out, wet from the earlier deluge, and she undid the strings on the front. Even from here, Richter could see her pink nipples, like little roses. He felt something stir in his trousers. It had an even greater effect on the patrol, where they could see it all the better from their vantage.

"This bitch want it?" one said.

"Happy to oblige," said the other. And they were off, following Fehling like a couple of dogs after a hare, drawn by the promise of an easy meal.

"They might find her tougher to eat than they think," he murmured.

Steady, even words bounced off the walls of the surrounding buildings, but garbled all their meaning before they reached Richter's ears. The emperor or someone else important besides. He only had a few more moments before the ceremony would be over. Opportunities needed to be seized while they were in grasp, he long knew that. He knew it from the moment he'd pickpocketed that magistrate in the Gutter, knew it now.

He turned, brought his feet up to perch on the gargoyle's severed stump of a neck, and reached up to the eaves. He breathed, bracing his stomach. If he fell from here, four, five stories up, he'd make a hell of a sound and likely break his neck otherwise. Death, if he was lucky. Paralysis, if he wasn't. Lying there, broken and paralyzed, praying for death. Didn't appeal. He could turn, but he wondered if he'd lost the knack now that he thought about it.

He heaved up. The roof sloped and he had to reach high, his fingers sliding. A horrid scratching noise rang out as his nails bit into the tile. He fumbled a knee, then a leg over the lip, rolled up, held himself there with an outstretched arm. Breath coming fast, he climbed up, careful not to make noise. Crouched, he came to the top of the gable, to the roof-cap. Peered over it.

At the center of the dais, a man in a black tunic and gold armor adorned with gold lions shone even in the gray. Shone brighter for it, like a sunflower in a field of muck. His white hair slicked back behind his ears, short white beard groomed to a point below his chin. He really did match the images on the coins. It struck Richter almost as a pity that he had to die.

Franz called a man in a white cloak who knelt below his armored legs. Another man in a long, red robe, the chamberlain perhaps, handed him a greatsword, the sword nearly dwarfing the both of them. Franz leaned down to hand the new Merovian the blade with some effort. Richter thought the opportunity was as good as any.

He closed his eyes and focused on the sharpness of his fury. All edges, bleeding at the touch. The roughness of a woman, his mother perhaps, an early memory. Stumped arms where they'd been cut. A thief. It ran in his blood, so it made sense that Richter fell into it. That was what they did in the Gutter. You stole from the Palatine, you stole from the rich, or you stole from just the plain unlucky. Stole from the dead in the street. Or you starved. That magistrate was just one more in the long line of easy marks for Richter and his friends. Or so he thought.

The sheriff brought the mace down on young Johannes' head, sending pink mush and shards of bone flying outwards. Some of his friend landed on Richter's cheek. The sheriff made them watch. Richter thought the pain couldn't get any worse, until the mace came for him.

Fur unsheathed itself from every pore. His eyes sharpened, focused like a predator's. Smells of the stinking crowd below poured into his nose like the finest Alanian white. Tiles loosened as his bones shifted, pushed downwards across the slope of the roof, as he gained weight and size, his clothes ripping at the seams. He wasn't an idiot. They weren't his inquisitor's vestments. Plain homespun, something belonging to a comfortably wealthy peasant, perhaps. He cast them aside onto the roof as they fell from his body. Details mattered.

He drew in a deep breath and jumped, tiles cracking under the strain. Air rushed past his snout. Soaring over the square, he came down like a fast shadow, like a giant bird on wing, diving on its prey. Screams drawn from below, shouts from further along, gasps rippling through the crowd. The stink of fear.

Richter came down on the dais with a loud bellow, careful to draw as much attention as he could. The emperor stumbled backwards. The Merovian recently ascended brought the greatsword around, but it was too clumsy, too close quarters for such a huge blade. Richter slapped the hilt down and reached his claws inside the man, pulled the contents out. The Merovian died, falling to the side, dead eyes staring.

As Richter advanced, steel rang out, the drawing of swords. Turned out he was wrong about the grandees' hesitation.

He pounced on Franz. The emperor managed to extend an arm, avoiding the swipe of claws but the arm snapped the other way, bending and lolling not like an arm should. Steel blocked the first swipe but the next ripped his breastplate open at the straps, the buckles snapping open. Opened like some shellfish, revealed soft innards.

He brought a club-like fist down on the emperor's beautiful face. Teeth and bits went flying. His jaw lolling, raw meat sucking in air with a whistle. Shrill screams pierced the air, the empress, and her entourage, fleeing. One of them tripped down the steps, stepped on by her companions as they fled.

Blades punched his hide. The crossbows wouldn't fire on him for fear of harming the emperor, though he scarcely noticed. He would not be finished with Franz until he was dead.

It was irritating how long it was taking. Franz put his unbroken arm up to guard his face, somehow still able to think, to survive. Richter admired the man's tenacity. He held down one arm, raked claws across Franz's face with his other. More steel entered his hide. Two big Merovians shoved him off Franz, fearless, heedless of their own survival. One stumbled down the steps, lost his footing. That was all Richter needed. He rather enjoyed opening that one's throat, causing him to lose more footing and flop onto the steps in a crash of metal.

Hate, hate. That was all he felt. All he could feel. He would bring ruin to Franz, whether or not he deserved it. It didn't matter. Some details mattered and some didn't.

Richter shoved the other one aside and went to charge Franz again when he saw life leave the man's eyes. Even in the carnage, Richter tuned his hearing, heard the last rattle of the emperor's breath as though it stamped on his ear like a panicked crowd.

He flicked his prehensile ears. There was a gap in the wall of advancing Merovians, in the trouble brewing for him. He swept his thick arms around, once, twice, beating aside halberd heads and sword blades. It was almost a game, how outmatched these men were against the might of a demon. It almost made Richter pity them.

Rumbling from the Karlspalast, over the screaming and the panic. The giant doors burst open. Out of its yawning mouth, glinting murder in the gray, a giant, four-pronged arrow cut the air towards him. *A ballista!* He twisted, the bottom edge of it scraping the back of his thigh. The force of the impact dragged his leg out from underneath him. The bolt itself careened off into the crowd, punched a ragged hole in the wall of terrified, wobbling flesh.

Richter landed on his snout, smacking his face against the stone. He could hear the ballista loaded again, the team cranking away at the wheel. Rage abated as the wall of Merovians surrounded him. That was the purpose of their gap, he now realized. They knew the ballista was coming. Halberd points pushed him down, bristled into him like a porcupine.

He roared and gathered himself, then jumped over the guards, cutting himself along the way, and darted down the steps, through the crowd. They seethed around him like thick muck, a fleshy obstacle to his freedom and his crusade. Well, he'd get his crusade now. He couldn't have been more successful if he tried.

He crouched, then on the push, the twinge in his leg troubled him. He twisted in the air, coming crashing down not onto the roof, falling short, but into the third-story window of the building ahead. He skittered onto floorboards, breathed, caught his breath, panting. He looked around, sniffed the air. No one came with blades—no one came. He counted his blessings.

He giveth, though he also taketh. I can slip out of here, but I have to be quick. He set aside his rage and it gave way to overwhelming numbness, palpable in his skin, his sweat, his bones. The calm of a shopkeeper sweeping up in the quiet after a vigorous rush on his vegetables. His monstrous form folded up inside of him with all the ceremony of a stopper on a poison bottle—the sealing away of a dangerous object always at hand.

Details mattered, he knew, and so he snuck away in the man of the house's robe, careful not to wear something too garish.

"You're not my father."

The boy stood at the doorway. He was five or six, maybe. Come to investigate the crashing noise upstairs. Richter didn't feel like killing a child, today, so all he did was walk up and brush his fingers through the boy's hair, gave it a tousle. "I'm your uncle. Just borrowing your father's clothes."

The kid grinned. "Ah, you're playing a trick."

"Something like that. Hide from anyone who comes in after me, alright?"

He nodded. "I will."

He left the house and dropped into the churning crowd like a fish thrown into a stream. Just as a few Wall Guards went in after him, crashed in through the door. "Spread out and find that bastard," he heard.

Richter grinned now. He would have his crusade, and live free long enough to see it, to lead it, Sigur willing. A detail he wouldn't do without.

INTERLUDE
EVA

*Man's monster lurks in even that which looks the most inno-
cent.*

— Sabrast Vercurian, Saburrian Royal Guard

That bitch Kasia wouldn't have survived the sack if it weren't for Eva, and she knew it. When the blacks came and lined up the women and girls, taking the best pickings for themselves, who was it that hid her in the false bottom of her dray? When her house was burned to the ground by a soldier looking for valuables, who had taken her in? When her brother and father were run down in the street, knights' blades sweeping their heads off to the shoulder bone, like the butcher's knife to well-bred cattle, who was it that arranged her marriage to a master-at-arms, letting her come out of the dreck with her dignity and lifestyle intact?

And she had the fucking gall to associate with that Ginevran priestess, Valya. She was a Rigan, of all people, as pale as a ghost and practically a savage. It was a tribute to the goddess's sect that she spoke Osbergian and had any measure of comportment.

As it was, Valya had Kasia thinking of taking the cloth, and where would that leave Eva? Having to explain to an Annaltian master-at-arms that his marriage was now annulled? She may as well slit her own throat now and be done with it.

Only Kasia couldn't be blamed. The Ginevrans had come out of the woodwork like so many lice after the sack, feeding the poor and the orphaned, offering shelter in their temples. Temples that had, miraculously, gone unburned by the besiegers. Offering a beacon of hope in such a dark time... *blah, blah, blah.* Kasia had been taken in. But then, not every woman was as world-weary and clever as Eva. It was like blaming a dog for eating a piece of meat left on the ground. She would guide Kasia back to the right path.

A Ginnsday mess. The crowd gathered at the front of the temple doors as Valya offered her hands to the people at the front. They clung to her like she cured diseases and sundry other misfortunes, and she wasn't just a charlatan in blue robes and raven hair.

"People of Ostelar," she said. Her voice sounded as smooth as poured honey, poured right into the crowd's ears. "We have been brought low in these last few months and have suffered under the yoke of a tyrant."

The crowd cheered.

That surprised her. Two guards at the edge of the square shifted their hands to draw weapons but, wary of the size of the still-growing crowd, didn't move to disperse them. The sack had made people angry, and she knew riots could be deadly. When Albrecht had brought in tariffs on serfs ten years back, some ill-guided attempt at reform, her husband had arranged roughs to burn down the granaries. That led to hunger which led to riots, and Albrecht was forced to roll back his misguided notions of equality.

These people had far more grievances than a spot of hunger. The prince's armies had taken everything not nailed down and set fire to anything that was. The granaries had long burned down, and the grain was rationed out by the Annaltians at whatever was apportioned for that day. Which invariably in these situations never turned out to be enough.

Funny that she still thought of the archduke as Albrecht. They only briefly touched each other's circles, the slightest of fingertips brushing—she a very successful merchant's widow, he an archduke. But everyone that knew him called him Albrecht. Last she heard, the coward had fled to Vallonia, terrified of his youngest brother's armies.

Kasia lifted up on her tiptoes. "She's wondrous, isn't she?" Eyes like a lovestruck girl.

Eva chewed her cheek. "She has a way with a crowd, certainly."

They cheered again at something Eva had not heard while Kasia prattled on.

"Oh, people of Ostelar!" Valya's voice carried over them again, kissing their ears, teasing their hearts with empty sentiments. "Dry your tears. Your mothers and fathers and daughters and sons now rest in the bosom of the mother. They have found their peace, and their names will be carved in her chalice to carry on for a million years. It is up to us that are left to carry on, to make them proud. The Sigurites and the Annaltians both, they dishonor their memory! I know, I know... friends, you may disagree, but let me convince you." Someone shoved to the front, shouting. Others clamored to stop him. "No, please, no—let him talk. Speak, friend."

"What horseshit," the man yelled. Eva couldn't help but crack a smile. Someone else that saw through her lies. "Sigur's the only one who can save us!"

"It's alright, we must all be free to speak our minds. The goddess tells us that the depth of her mercy is unrestrained, and yes, it is all well and good to think that the god of death and strength and war and justice will save us, but I ask, not to you, my friend, but to the god Himself! What lives will we have if everything is handed to us? Oh, Sigur, strike me where I stand if I am wrong!"

The crowd rippled with horrified gasps. Eva found herself aghast, gaping her mouth. To invoke such bald-faced violence from the god was to speak heresy right there and then. Where were the guards? Where was the Order?

"Why is this woman allowed to speak free," she hissed. "She'll get us killed!"

"I would rather die on my feet than kneel to a god that never saved us," Kasia said.

Eva clipped the girl round the ear. Kasia shouted in shock, grimaced in pain, a look of betrayal in her eyes.

"I saved you, child. What thanks do I get for saving you from those raping knights? They would've filled you with babe and then where would we be?"

Kasia pursed her lips together, her face red with rage. "Just because they didn't want to hump an old widow doesn't mean you did anything for me! You stuck me with a fucking Annaltian! A northern beast!" She threw her hands up.

Eva shook her head. The girl had notions that would only bring her harm in the long run. "Marrying Master Radomir and giving him children will be the one good thing you'll amount to in all your life. He might be gruff, but he's far better than you deserve. He'll keep you fed and wealthy, and that's a sight better than most people get these days."

Why couldn't she see this? What kind of hold did Valya have on her?

"Yes," the priestess continued, walking forward into the crowd. People parted before her, brushing their hands against her outstretched arms like she was some holy martyr given flesh. "Sigur will not save us. We must find it in ourselves to save ourselves. Ginevra gives us that strength, and it flows through all of us."

Sighs of admiration. Eva hocked a ball of spit and it flicked off a man's leg in front.

Valya made their way to them. To them? Why was she coming this way? Well, let her. Eva had never been one to miss an opportunity.

When her husband was despondent at the archduke's serf reforms, she told him to buck up and force Albrecht's hand. That old prick owed most of his fortunes to her—he wasn't much more than a warehouse owner before she met him. Eva had forged him into a titan of industry, head of the merchant's guild. Before he'd died, of course, but she'd secured her fortunes from her inheritance. Now she was the head of the merchant's guild. Until, of course, the guild's leadership was killed in the sack of the city.

Except for her. She'd rebuild the guild from the ground up and get richer than ever. Sacked cities needed rebuilders, after all. That was one thing she learned. Nothing was ever static. One day you could be hiding your gold in Alanian banks—if there was one thing the southerners did well, it was count money—and one day you could be rebuilding a city. Eva was the hero this city needed, not this false priestess.

The woman came to Kasia, cupped her face in her hands. The girl's eyes blubbered with tears, a wellspring of falsities. Eva's words died in her throat, she wasn't quite sure why. Maybe it was the turning tide—she too, knew how deadly an angry crowd could be, and they were not on her side.

"Ginevra gives us strength," Valya repeated. "Gives you strength, my child." She let her hands fall and turned to the crowd. "I call on all of us to denounce the words of the Sigurites, the words of Pontiff Gottscheid, as he peers down from his roost, knowing nothing of the struggles of the common people. Worse yet, they try to enforce their will upon the people. Not all of us worship Sigur, and for good reason. War and death do not satisfy us in our souls!"

The crowd cheered. They were lost now. Eva faded back. There was nothing she could do for them. Nothing she could do for Kasia, now. Radomir would just have to be satisfied without a wife, for now. Her plans to turn the Annaltians to her side hit a small snag, but there were opportunities in this. She had a keen eye for them, after all.

"It is as Ginevra says," Valya continued, her voice fading out from behind the mass of bodies in the square. The temple stood behind them, all soft arches and pale limestone. Around, the burned-out husks of a dozen timber houses, their frames poking up like the blackened ribs of a charred corpse.

"We must help the weak, the broken, the shunned."

A corpse of a city, that would one day—soon, if she had anything to do with it—grow anew out of the ground. But first she'd have to take care of some malcontents.

"We lowborn folk have more in common with the demons than we do with the tyrants who take cities and seek to rule."

Demons? Eva's eyes near fell out of her skull she opened them that wide. She scoffed, hard, so hard she coughed a fit and the guards nearby looked her over.

"Don't tell me you've got the plague," he said in his best Osbergian, which wasn't much, admittedly.

Eva stared. "Don't be ridiculous."

"Aye, that's all we need," the other one said.

"*Pest. Plage frau.*" He drew his sword with a ringing of steel. "Pale. Looks pale."

The other one joined in menacing her with his blade. Anger licked at her chest with hot tongues. "Don't you have anything better to do, like rape little girls? Bastard northerners. *Schwein.*" She knew that much Annaltian.

But why had she said it? She said it with the bluster of the firebrand she'd been in her youth, before her husband, before everything.

The guard slapped her with a gauntlet across the mouth, her vision went white and then black and blood sprayed from her cheek. She tumbled and found herself on the ground, pain wracking her skull, acrid metal on her tongue.

She raised her hands, her eyes spinning and her ears pounding. Breathing pained her, the roar of the crowd carved her mind like a knife gutting a fish.

"I'm sorry! Sorry! I didn't mean it," she pleaded, but they were already moving in. One raised his sword. "You bastards," she shrieked. "Don't you know who I am?"

Something like a blue sheet of cloth moved across her blurry vision. "Wha—" she began, but an ear-splitting shriek cut her off.

"You will not harm this woman!"

The priestess?

"She is protected by the goddess, as are we all," Valya shouted. "Do not strike her, for you shall incur the wrath of the Mother goddess. Food will turn to ash in your mouths, drink will never satiate, and you shall wander the Continent as the *hungry*, forever cursed, unable to die, unable to fill your bottomless stomachs!"

The guards hesitated, looked at each other. She'd thrown herself in front of their swords. Eva tried to wipe off the blood but all she succeeded in doing is smearing it across her inglorious face.

The guards backed up as people started jostling to see, spilling out of the square into the road.

A pale hand draped with soft cloth extended down to her. Long fingers, graceful but firm in Eva's hand. The priestess pulled her to her feet, wiped her face with a length of linen with one hand, kept her from reeling backward with her other hand.

Eva frowned, her eyes still fuzzy. "Why did you do that?"

A sad smile. "Every life is precious."

Her naivety about the world was refreshing, like a flower growing from a mound of shit. Eva couldn't help but bark a laugh, then she realized everyone was watching. The entire crowd, those guards, Kasia. The girl's bright face in the crowd. Eva's cheeks burned with embarrassment.

"Come, you're hurt." She gestured Eva to the temple. Spots of light blared across Eva's brow like there were a hundred suns instead of just one. "You need healing."

She planted her feet. "What I need is not to be treated by a charlatan."

"Eva," Kasia admonished, as though she was the adult and Eva the child and not the other way around.

"I cannot force her to come," Valya said. "That is not the goddess's way."

People broke from the crowd, either bored or respecting the priestess's position and her work. Not that Eva cared a whit, but she was clever enough to know that Valya commanded a modicum of respect among the rabble.

Kasia clutched Eva's arm. "Please," she said, batting her eyelashes like a young girl might. That made Eva smile, a little bit, and the pounding in her head faded a touch. But her jaw was still as stiff as iron. "Valya knows what she's doing. She's healed so many wounded from the sack already."

That was true enough. The woman had scarcely slept, Eva knew, passing among the bodies and doing *something* to them. Healing was an art far out of reach of Eva's understanding, though most of the people Valya had treated recovered, so she had to admit that much defeat.

Eva sighed. "Fine, I'll try."

"You are a true treasure, Mistress Kasia," she said in her strange Rigan accent. "And if it please you, Mistress Eva, if you do not feel comfortable or my remedies don't work for you, you may go at any time, with the goddess's blessing."

"I suppose that's acceptable."

Under the fluted archway of the great stone doors, she entered an unlikely marriage of a dingy cavern of carved stone and a greenhouse, with enough candles to light a bonfire across the back wall. A shaft of light reached down from a hole in the roof to gleam off a heavy altar of the goddess, a beautiful woman in loose robes holding a basket of freshly picked apples. In her other hand, she would have held the chalice of her insignia, dripping fresh blood, but her arm had been severed at the elbow and the only remnants of the piece a few chunks of chalk on the black slate floor.

So, the temple hadn't gone as miraculously unmarred as I'd thought.

As she looked around now, she saw that settings for gemstones stood empty, their contents prized out. Gold had been cut from runnels along the walls, only a few fragments remaining, where chisel marks completed the story.

The priestess must've seen her peeking around. "We've done all we can to fix the violation of this sacred place. While donations have been generous, we can only—" She interrupted herself, a touch of anger in her voice. Not the righteous anger, the anger of an orator, out the front of the temple. But true anger, anger capable of violence. She took a long inhale, held it for a few moments, then vented it over a few more moments. "I should be grateful. The people have truly looked to the temple in their time of need and offered what they have as thanks."

"People often look for false hope in their time of greatest need. Truly the tragedy of humanity." As Eva sat down on a side bench, the priestess drew a short knife from her robe, cut various herbs and flowers from pots on a table by the wall.

"Eva, please—"

The priestess raised a hand to interrupt Kasia. "Mistress Eva is entitled to her opinions, as I am entitled to mine, as is everyone."

"Not an opinion." She was regaining her smirk, perhaps a little worse for wear, but just as useful as before she'd put it down. "A fact. I've been through two sacks, four riots, a plague, and a bout of dysentery in my life. And you know what I'd discovered over all that? That you have to bite down and take what you deserve, not put your hope in a god or a goddess that everything will be alright."

Valya ground up the herbs in a mortar and pestle, scratched and tapped, sprinkling all sorts of little flowers into the mix—yellow, blue, green. "That sounds like an unhappy existence."

Eva scoffed. *Unhappy? Who does this woman think she is?* She looked down at her furs and voluminous brocade dresses, as if to say, I haven't known hard in my life. Her clothes were scuffed from her fall, but it was nothing a tailor couldn't mend.

"After the city recovers, I will be wealthier than ever."

Tap, tap, tap. "I am not talking about wealth."

"What, then?"

"Happiness."

"Happiness is for god-touched fools," Eva spat. "It's a fleeting emotion, clouds the mind."

"And yet, you pursue it."

Eva couldn't help but laugh. "*I* pursue it?"

Valya came over, cloth in one hand, pestle of green paste in the other. She approached with the cloth and Eva flinched, then let her do her work.

The priestess's warm breath tickled her cheek. "Kasia told me you helped her during the sack and secured a marriage for her."

"And? Marriages are rarely happy." She remembered her husband on her wedding night, haggard and old to her young eyes, and how he climbed on top of her with his stinking breath and sagging belly. He'd given her two babes, but they'd both not lived beyond the cradle. Blessedly, not long after, he reached the age where things that should've been hard were suitably soft.

"Your interest in Kasia goes beyond a mere selfishness, does it not? Sir Radomir is rumored to be a merciful man, possibly the only one among the occupiers." She applied some of the cold paste on Eva's jaw and rubbed it into her scalp. "Mind, this will be cold and tingle a bit."

"He's also the richest among the unmarried men in the garrison. The archduke's plundered treasures have made him rich indeed."

"So, you saved Kasia at no small risk to yourself, sheltered her like she was your family, took her in and looked out for her, secured a marriage where she will be wealthy and treated with mercy, which is far more than most women will ever have in this life."

"You think I should marry him?" Kasia gaped her mouth, appalled. "He's a northern brute!"

Valya turned. "I've talked with the master-at-arms myself, mistress, and he's actually quite learned. He speaks fluent Osbergian, since his grandfather was the Count of Calw, and taught him when he was young."

Eva hadn't known that. Valya was more than just a priestess, it seemed. She had her own ambitions, perhaps? But no matter, the conversation was straying into territory she didn't want to cross.

"This conversation is absurd. Kasia is not my daughter, and I do not care a shit what happens to her, whether she's treated with kindness or not." Eva gave vent to a growl. That irrepressible firebrand of her youth reared its ugly head again. "Sir Radomir can rape her every night, beat her within an inch of her life for all I care." She stabbed the bench with a finger. "As long as I get what I want out of the bargain."

Kasia squeaked, her eyes welling with tears. "I thought—"

"You thought I cared for you?" She stood. "You thought of me like a mother? You're only as useful as your beauty, and even that will fade. If you won't marry Radomir, I'll find another who will. And then what will be left for you? You should just kill yourself now, save yourself the trouble."

Valya placed a hand against her chest. "Mistress Eva, that's quite enough—"

Eva shoved down her arm. Her breath burned in her lungs. "And you, you charlatan. Speaking about hope and love. 'War and death do not satisfy us in our souls,' as though war and death are not the natural state of the world." *We deserve everything we get, and have to take the rest with bloody, scraping fingers.*

"If that is what you believe," Valya said, as calm as ever. Was that a little smirk worming its way across her face?

She's baiting me. Wants me to react, so she can point to the ills of the world and say, "Here's another fallen that must be saved by the goddess."

"It's not your fault your daughter died, Eva."

The words slapped harder than the guard's gauntlet across her face. "*How dare you,*" she seethed. Eva ground her teeth. "Call for your goddess!" She shoved her, hard.

Valya shouted, tumbled, pestle tossed from her hand and scattered across the floor in smears of green paste and broken stone. Her hands flailed out, head hit the edge of the bench, snapped forwards with a great *crunch.* Blood poured out from behind her dark hair, all tangled now, and welled into a crack in the slate. Her light eyes stared up at Eva, unblinking.

"Eva!" Kasia rushed over, scooted forward on her knees, cradled Valya's head in her hands. Just as she'd done in the square outside, offering the goddess's strength. "What did you do?"

"I... I didn't mean to." Her hands were shaking. Like someone reached down and pulled her guts inside out, she felt hideous, empty, cavernous. She stumbled back, generous arse bouncing against a stone table laden with donations of food and drink. For a priestess that would never use them.

Visions of something came, an emaciated figure, bones poking from loose, sagging skin, white hair falling out, eyes sunken pits of black, tongue rotted in its mouth. Then she saw the figure had her nose and her brows and it became all too clear. Food was all she wanted, and horrible, horrible hunger ripped through the pit of her stomach.

Her hands scrabbled across the table, snatching up a loaf of bread in one hand, an apple in the other. She shoved the apple in her mouth, the juice running down her chin. It tasted like nothing, like eating hardtack, just cud, nothing sustaining. Pulp. She bit a huge chunk out of the bread. The same. Sweat prickled the skin behind her ears.

Food will turn to ash in your mouths, drink will never satiate, and you shall wander the Continent as the hungry, *forever cursed, unable to die, unable to fill your bottomless stomachs.*

Kasia lifted eyes heavy with tears. "What... what is wrong with you? What are you doing?"

Between mouthfuls, Eva groaned. "Eating... hungry...what she did..." She couldn't formulate words. All she wanted to do was eat. She started hiccupping, eating too fast. More food followed the bread—dried meats, pastries. A fish, bones and all. People saved the best for their piety. Eva was all too happy to relieve the dead of their burdens.

Kasia locked an arm around Eva's. "Stop! That's for the temple!"

Eva shoved her aside with a scream. She wouldn't allow anyone to take the food from her. They'd have to kill her first. Kasia slipped on a hunk of bread Eva had dropped in her frenzy but caught herself on the table.

"You've lost it," she said, and marched from the temple.

Where are you going? Eva meant to ask, but her mouth was full, and she found she cared very little, anyway. All that mattered was the next bite, the next taste, *something* to fill her fucking belly. Deep, yawning pain radiated from her stomach even though it was bloated now, stuffed, and she should've been full, more than full, from how much she'd just eaten.

She took care of the contents of the entire table. Three dried lengths of sausage, four loaves of bread, that fish, several pies. A basket of apples. Her stomach distended out from her dress, but the pain deepened. She needed food. But where was she to get it?

She looked back. The herbs. She didn't think she'd be stuffing her face with whole green shoots and healing flowers at the start of the day but it was looking more appealing as she came to its end. Still, it didn't satisfy.

She took handfuls of the herbaceous dirt, stuffed her mouth. A great whine came from her guts, and pressure built up under her ribs. Bile pushed its way out of her throat, heaving glossy, dirty sick and great disgusting chunks of half-digested meat and bread and other, unnamable things.

She coughed, falling to her hands and knees in the muck. She wanted to retch again. Still, hunger clawed its vicious knives at her guts. Still, she needed to eat, more than she wanted life itself. What kind of life was this, anyway? What did she have to live for, now, that Kasia was and hated her for a murderer. That's what she was. A murderer. The cursed. The demons weren't the only cursed in this world. Ginevra had her own tricks.

Eva stood. Not for the first time, she'd take something for herself. Death. She took the knife from Valya's robe and ran it across her throat. Black blood splashed across the slate, hot and thick. Lowering to a crawl on her side, her legs numb, she accepted that probably she shouldn't have struck that priestess. She was never a charlatan, and only tried to help, in her own way.

And she was right, after all. That little girl in that grave behind the house, the one wrapped in the shawl Eva had knitted herself, the shawl that was supposed to be her cot cover, she was long gone. Kasia was gone, too, and Eva had nothing left.

The world faded. In the unending darkness, a woman's gentle voice called out to her.

VOLUME FIVE

HIGHEST IN CONFIDENCE

Maxime Sancta et Venerande

Grand Inquisitor Ulrich Vetterand

The Sword that Pierces the Dark

The Head of the Order of the Golden Sword

The Grand Holy-Fortress

Istrya

30 Tribuum, anno 1045

de: Stratagem for Maximum Effect

Altissimi Grandmaster,

Your masterstroke that was the Terror of the Palatine was premonitory. The result of said action has decisively placed our Order to seize control. The empress will be placed in regency, in lieu of her coward son Albrecht taking the throne. The Istryan Empire is ours for the taking, and I have assurances from the clerics that the populace will welcome this news with open arms.

All that remains is Annalt. That backwater of prideful muck farmers should feel the wrath of the Order of the Golden Sword if they do not submit, but I have proposals to avoid such an occasion. To their credit, the folk are fearful of the rampant and raging lycanthrope army of the so-called Demon, who is nothing more than a minion of Veles. But the Annaltians are frozen to inaction through their own prince's indecision. There also remains the issue that Osbergia endures as a hotbed of recruitment for the demon.

My humble offering of a stratagem to defeat this menace, once and for all in the south, is triple-pronged:

Primo, we relocate Prince Reynard and his heirs to a more suitable location for safekeeping and to ensure the line of Osterlin continues. Without the line of Osterlin, the populace will lose their resolve. We have spies and infiltrators within his palace guard that would ensure this takes place.

Secundo, the Pontiff calls for an army of the faithful to defeat the menace in Palerme. The slavering fanatic would need very little convincing in this regard. The only fetter is that the empress would not assent to this plan, but if the first step is followed, we need only apply pressure until she agrees. The prince's eldest son is a prime target for this, if needs must.

Tertia, we replicate the Prolian Strategy, but on a much larger scale. We utilize the antipathy towards the lycanthrope, driven by the army of the faithful.

Omne recte, we choke the skies with the ash of the demon's brethren. Just as in Prolia, the populace will turn on each other given a modicum of fear. The brotherhood of clerics informs me that fear of the werewolf has already started to spread. I would see every city in our empire painted with lycanthropic blood and ash. It is the hope that the Great Devil will show himself at the sight of so much of his kin now dead, and we will be ready for him.

I humbly request that this stratagem be executed forthwith, with your illustrious blessing, and the lycanthrope menace will be driven from the Continent once and for all, completing the great work that the Lightfather started.

Oratio pro victoria

Most Reverend Konrad Steppenwolf

Lord Inquisitor of Salzheim

ex Citadel Lorquem

Salz

CHAPTER 16

THE WOLVES AT THE DOOR

TRIBUUM, 1045

What is known is that the demon infects and like an infection must be scoured.

— HIGH NOTARIUS GIAN ADALLA

FIGHTING TORE THROUGH EVERY level of the palace. Dead men in hallways, corpses to step over. Men leaking from the head, their innards on the outside, limbs broken, severed hands and arms and legs. Running down the walls was black blood and pink stuff that could've been brains. You knew friend from foe just as easily as frenzied sharks in chum. Except everyone was a shark.

If they ran at her, she killed them. She wasn't about to ask whether they were the duca's men or the mob or Frix or any of the rest of them. One ran at her, hadn't learned the lesson from the last four, and she swept out with the sword she'd taken off the first man's corpse. His head came clean off, rolled along the ground, and came to rest at the foot of a floor-length painting. Maybe she recognized his face. The one from the *Porta du Prix*, the Prince's Gate, when she arrived at the city. It didn't matter at all now

200

what his name was. Dead men had no need for names. All the living could do was mark their memory and move on.

Plus, he tried to kill them, so she spat on his cheek and promptly forgot his name.

She breathed, flinched, as ahead shouting echoed down the dim hallway. Leon crept along, broadsword pointed forwards, axe held behind. Selene stepped over a severed hand, its owner nowhere near, since all the dead nearby still had all their bits.

She hadn't seen a massacre like this since Ostelar, but even that she'd not seen the worst of. The city burned for six nights, it was said. She wondered if Valenti would be the same by the time they were done here.

"The duca has far less control over his people than he makes it seem," Leon said.

"That priest is responsible for this. If he'd just left it, we would've returned home and none of these people needed to have died."

"That's priests for you—*quiet!*"

Another crash and a roar from ahead. The distinct roar of an angry werewolf. Selene had to admit the noise still gave her skin goosepimples, fear like a spike slamming through her chest, even though she knew they were on their side. Fear learned is not fear easily forgotten.

The priest, Gothenburg, had drummed up a bout of religious fervor the people were all too ready to throw themselves into, like an addict into a pile of smokeleaf. A mob of peasants armed with handaxes and bills had attacked the palace. Nothing more than farming equipment and, even zealous as they were, they were no match for hardened marines armed with crossbows and longswords. It wouldn't have been enough, but Gothenburg had taken advantage of a lapse in pay of the gate garrison.

You can always count on a Valentish to get their pay.

"Do you see the others?" She was worried. They had been separated in the assault, when the firebombs descended on the garden and their rooms, the mob forcing their way into the guest apartments.

All the Althann—Frix and his cousins, as well as Gregor and Tomas, tore through the hallways with abandon. They weren't likely to stop and wait for two humans, even if they happened to be allies. Is that how she thought of them all? Just allies? She was ready to drink their blood only that afternoon. They had to be more than that.

"I tell you what, if I see them, I'll let you know," Leon said, tension in his voice. "For now, let's just focus on getting out of here alive."

A black shadow flitted crossways just ahead, at the junction of hallways. Candles snuffed out with the cutting wind that followed, plunging them into darkness.

Selene clenched her jaw and moved ahead, sword point extended to feel around the space. "Where are you, Leon," she said. It wasn't the black of night, where eyes adjusted in the gloom, in the light of the moon, the faintest of reflections and scatterings from the stars. It was the darkness of a cave, of the deepest pits of hell, where only the lessening of the stench of death was some indication that she was heading anywhere brighter.

Her foot clipped something soft, her ankle rolled, and she fell, jarring her bones against the floor. The sword clattered out of her hand. Cracking noises. Her breath came short and sharp. A presence, something huge, stinking, and warm, loomed down on her. Then it left her, and she nearly voided her bladder.

A door crashed open, and she rolled over, searching for her sword. Her hand thumbing along the ground. Wetness. Not her. Blood. "Leon?"

Light splashed across her face, and she narrowed her eyes, squinting in the sudden glare.

"Selene, it's me." A deep voice.

"Frix?" Her eyes adjusted. He was stark naked, the glow of his lantern dancing across his body. She felt a halt in her breath at the sight, she couldn't lie, but there were other things on her mind. "Where is everyone else?"

"Where are your cousins?" Leon asked, moving into the light now. It was still a pit, the long corridor. Eyes stared at her, goggled in their skulls, dark blood pouring from wounds. Feet, fingers, limbs, all like a forest of horrors doused in shadows. The noisome stink of early rot and shit and vomit and metal, where men had vented their stomachs, some upon death, some after.

Selene wondered if that was the moment the spirit left the body. When the god that person worshipped came down and took them, the body had no reason to hold onto anything, and let go. A morbid thought, but then it was a morbid night.

"They're up ahead," he said. There was sadness in his eyes, though that might've been the lantern throwing waxy shadows across his face. "We got cut off from you." He looked around. "But it doesn't look like you needed our help."

Leon pulled off a dead man's shirt. Homespun, might've belonged to a farmer. Didn't belong to anyone, now, and he handed it to Frix.

Frix led them down the left hallway, past looming tapestries of people playing by a river. Images of happiness had been cast dark and violent in the gloom. A woman throwing her baby in the air looked as though she might drop him, dashing his brains on the stone. Two men cornered a woman by the water, ill intent in their eyes.

The duca's palace had been turned into a charnel house, the people of Valenti making it their final resting place. It couldn't have felt satisfying, though. The scale of the death only brought bile to burn her mouth. But she would not shed tears over the dead. The mob attacked them, first, and would've killed them given half the chance.

"It was the priest," she said. "I saw him, at the head of the mob. He did this."

Luni was just a bone sickle in the sky, casting a wan glow over the garden. Smoke cast a heavy pall over things, the bushes still smoldering from the fires, an acrid taste on her tongue. Three werewolves lurked in the center, the black one sniffing the air. She didn't recognize that one, but the other two—a gray and a brown—snapped around when they entered.

A wrinkle came over the gray's snout, then she saw the dead man at their feet, great bloody gashes across his body.

"They surrounded him," Frix said.

"Tomas," Selene said. She walked over, her hand loose around the hilt of the sword, but ready to be used at any moment. She couldn't help being prepared. She was only too aware of her own weakness compared to these monsters.

Monsters. It was terrible that she still thought of them as such but even in the sad face of the gray, who she knew to be Frix's cousin, Sefinn, she saw only teeth and the flash of murder in those limpid, yellow eyes. His pupils were wide, taking in the night.

No one stood a chance. Men were levered out of their mail, rings broken and snapped, scattered across the ashen yard. Clusters of gutted bodies, intestines still steaming, sat under smoldering trees and blackened bushes. People wound up by fervor, given false hope by their belief in Sigur. Tomas wasn't the only dead among the smoke and ash.

"Here!"

They fixed their heads to the arch that led to the throne room and vestibule. She wondered morbidly what kind of horror could be seen in there, if only to see the destruction wrought by rampaging werewolves. Werewolves, amusingly, that were on her side. That novelty still made her chuckle.

Two marines emerged from the archway, but between all the blood on their tabards and armor, it was a wonder she could tell who they were at all. The only sign was their enormous swords, doused with red of course, and their charge. The Duca Alberracin, untouched, still in his red silk robe, trimmed with gold.

And behind them, another marine, pulling a balding man clad in white. "Gothenberg," Selene seethed. The werewolves in front set up their hackles, the fur on their haunches standing on end, their teeth bared in deep growls. Growls like the grinding of mountains.

Gothenburg screamed, tried to run, but the marine threw him down and he hit the dirt with a girlish grunt. Selene smiled to see it.

The black werewolf turned. She, Selene realized, shrank into the muscular form of that Saburrian woman, bare skin as dark as the night sky. She was powerfully built, with shoulders almost as large as Gregor's, and muscles that seemed to form the shape of a pine tree across her lower back, tensed now. She appeared to be holding quarter, though.

"No, heathens! Heretics! Cursed woman. Sigur shield me from this demonic form!"

Kyrah walked up to him and grabbed his chin, forcing him to stare at her naked body, grinning. He tried to pull away, but she was too strong, his face turned red from the effort. He settled for a sideways glance, then the others changed back as well, finding clothes among the dead.

"You steal from the dead, too?" Gothenburg spat. "It is no surprise, I suppose."

"And you rile up ordinary, hard-working folk and lead them to their deaths," Selene hissed back.

He lifted his eyes, looking as proud as he could, given the circumstances. "They gladly gave their lives to fight you. The only tragedy that one of you died." He laughed as he looked at Tomas's bloody corpse. "Too bad it was not more."

Selene marched up to him and shoved her thumb in his eye. He screamed, clutching his face, and reeled onto his back with a grunt.

She didn't wait for them to stop her. She brought the sword down on his head, dashed the edge through his eye and upper jaw with a thunking noise. He bayed like a dying dog and clawed at his bleeding face. She brought it down again on the backswing, the force breaking his wrist, snapping noise ringing out, his arm spasming in pain. His cries got quieter, but he said in a low voice, *"Sigur take me into the Golden Halls, bless my soul, curse these demons, I will bring no quarter if you save—"*

"Save your prayers for a god that listens," she shouted, lifting her sword high. The blade cleaved his eye socket in two, cut a great pink gash across the meat of his nose and cheek, left him gasping bloody for air, making popping and gurgling noises. Once, twice, three times. Rage spilled with each blow, like a tide that filled her higher and higher, drowning her in it. *Thunk, thunk, thunk.* The gurgling became quieter. She brought the blade down a fourth time, jarred her hand, tried to pull it free, but it was stuck fast. His head lolled to the side as the weight of the sword pushed it down, and a low, inhuman noise came from his throat. His remaining eye rolled around in its sockets, blood gushing black across his gaping face.

Gods, he was still alive. And she still had that rage, but now it was mixed with sick at her back teeth. Killing Bann, killing Alexei, that had felt good, if only for a little while. Revenge had satisfied her in the past, so why did this leave her hollower than ever?

In the end, no one stopped her. Gothenburg's chest ceased moving.

She breathed, lifted her face, breath hot against her nose, felt a cool breeze as the heat of the day finally broke, well into the night. Luni still hung above, a bone-white rib in the sky.

"Well," the duca said, breaking the silence. "I believe I speak for all of us when I say that I'd be glad to see an end to this day. Kyrah, get organized. You're leaving with them in the morning."

"Me?"

"I need an agent to make sure my money is used satisfactorily, and by the looks of things, they need you to fight as well. The Lady Selene will be your commander in my stead."

Her hand still hurt. She became aware of it again and flexed it as she stared down at the duca. Tired, uncertain, but unwilling to argue, she just agreed. "Very well."

"The city of Valenti thanks you for your service in defending its law and order."

The city of Valenti lies dead at our feet, she thought, but was too exhausted to say. She nodded.

The duca raised a finger. "I will arrange for your man with the cart to return at once, with victuals and provender from my stores, as well as arms, and..." His gaze passed over the naked Althann. "Some clothes, too. Spares from my servants." He sighed. "Who are likely all dead now."

"In exchange?" Selene asked. She didn't care about the weariness in her voice. She just wanted to leave this city already, get back to Tristain. To see that little smile again.

"You saved Valenti, you and your men. The palace might've been razed to the ground had not you noble demons here saved it." *By slaughtering hundreds of Valentish.*

"Your Excellency," Leon said. "There'll be reprisals when the families of the men dead here find out what happened."

"Let me deal with that, Sir Strong. That is Valentish business, and Valentish business only. You need not concern yourself with that. But needless to say, you should leave and not return. Not ever."

Selene thought of nothing more than turning her back on Valenti. She tried a perfunctory bow, her hand still jarred and hurting. Gothenburg still leaked out on the dirt, stunk of shit now, his spirit giving up and going. She wondered if he'd be taken to Sigur's embrace for his piety.

Piety that led to the massacre of innocents. But then, nothing more could be expected of Sigurite worship. She'd done as much.

Vomit forced its way up her throat and nose, spilling on the ground, and she doubled over. Leon's hand found its way to her back. "Are you alright?"

"Fine," she said. "Let's just get the fuck out of here."

CHAPTER 17

THE SIGURITE STANDARD

LEVITUM, 1045

The Sigurite Standard is a reminder of a more brutal, animistic, baleful past of sacrificial worship and dedications of blood and bone. After all, if you can't give your body and soul to the God of Strength and War, who can you give it to?

— HIGH INQUISITOR KONRAD STEPPENWOLF

THE GIANT STANDARD LIKE a giant corpse lumbered south. Skulls adorned the top of the creature, many heads and hollowed eyes casting a watchful gaze over the gathered thousands. Two lengths of shining white linen blazing with fiery golden swords draped the beast's spine like a stole, while swinging from the hulking creature's underside were reliquaries and ribbons, gold pennants and giltwork swords like exposed innards, pulled out and glistening. Four tireless oxen urged it onwards, themselves urged by oxen-faced men flailing black whips.

The Sigurite Standard was many things to many people, but for the pontiff and the others, it was a reminder of their purpose. The reason they assembled. For Richter, it was a mark of his success, of the renewal of his faith, of the power he commanded. He toppled empires in the name of

Sigur. Well, had done an emperor in anyway, and now the Order all but commanded the greatest army in the history of mankind. He saw Franz's raw meat face trying in vain to suck air in a wave of the gold cloth, the sun warping over the pate of the skulls, the play of light across the reliquaries. It made him smile.

Since they'd left Istrya twenty thousand strong, two thousand more had joined them. They weren't yet to Annalt, where another thirty thousand were said to be waiting. Prior to his death, Franz was thought of as a sober, sensible ruler, if a bit ineffectual, with a couple rebellious sons. Now you'd think he was a bloody martyr by the way people talked about him, swept to the army's side like vultures on a carcass.

"He was the greatest since Istryan," a tearful woman, some wife of a general, had said to Richter. She detained him over duck liver at the officer's banquet the night before.

"Mm," he said, neither agreeing nor disagreeing. He didn't care a shit, he only wanted the food. He looked around for someone to redirect the woman onto, but no one was at hand. How was it he could face down a dozen Merovians armed to the hilt, or a family of werewolves in the Forest of Rot, but a high society dinner, even one on the road as they were, made his hands clammy with sweat?

The woman careened on regardless. She was taller than Richter, loomed annoyingly in his eyeline. "Empress Melusine is a wreck, of course, and it's only right that the pontiff and the Lord Council should direct her army at a time like this. This is about our eternal souls. Damn the demon, and it's high time we did it, lest we all end up like Franz, Lightfather rest his soul. Sigur wills this crusade. Let us hope our listening does not come too late, Sigur willing."

That had been a new addition. The high classes were never particularly pious, but the brutal death of an emperor at the hands of a demon made many into believers overnight. Even if the one who had done it fattened himself on the duck liver they so generously left out for him.

It's not my fault they just leave it on the tables. He plopped a chunk in his mouth, hoping its size would relieve him of his duty to answer her.

It didn't matter anyway. She could talk the ear off a dead man. "Perhaps it is our punishment for not heeding the warning. Prince Reynard thought to save Ostelar from the demon, but it was too late for him, as well."

Richter swallowed. That was new as well. "What?"

"Oh, hadn't you heard? I do suppose not everyone in the church is so familiar with politics. It is good that you should leave that sort of thing to your betters."

He could've punched the woman in the nose, stoved it in. "What the fuck are you talking about?"

She tutted. "Prince Reynard," she said, exasperated, "committed Ostelar and its surrounds to the torch, to save it from its own impiety. *Extermina-tus*, I believe your clerical phrase goes."

"I was there, cunt, and I didn't see him burning anything other than innocent folk and their homes. Folk who just happened to live on the wrong side of a wall and couldn't swim."

"Excuse you," she said, huffing. She walked off, cutting through the powdered crowd.

He took another bite of the duck liver, the fat sopping his fingers and running down his palm. *If I knew all it took was a little insult...*

But what was this business with Reynard? Revision of history went hand-in-hand with victory, Richter supposed. He hadn't gone so far as to try to save any of the people, couldn't. The defenders folded like paper, the defense lasting only half a day after the walls were breached, and all he had time for was to get the clerics out, and the archives with them.

"Making friends already?" Vetterand's voice. He'd hear that voice in the dead of night sometimes, and snap to attention, only to find it was a dream. A nightmare, maybe. But this time, the voice was very, very real.

"Not my fault she's taken in by lies."

Vetterand kept his eyes fixed on the crowd, didn't look at Richter. "People are taken in by whatever makes them sleep easier at night. If it makes her feel better to think that Albrecht was harboring demons in Ostelar, and his god-fearing brother sought to right that sin by embarking on his own crusade, then let her."

Richter felt Vetterand's hand creep up his shoulder, tried not to flinch. "Even if it's not the truth?"

Three women cackled, throwing their heads back like crows fighting over a tasty worm.

"What is the truth, anyway?" He leaned in. "Franz was a decent man, but no one worth dying for. He barely inspired loyalty in his own sons." He lifted an outstretched hand to the gathered officers, men wearing enough fancy fabric to upholster a palatial lounge room. Swords and armor ready for wear. A few of them Richter recognized among the emperor's entourage at the Karlspalast, which made him snort. Dukes and counts of the empire, in command of thousands. Many nodded to Vetterand as he gestured to them. "Aren't we glad that his death could be so useful?"

Richter smiled. The first time he'd smiled all night.

But that had been last night, and this morning the march moved ever onwards, south. Well, southwest, precisely. Solni at their backs in the morning, roasting Richter's neck. The Schwarze braced the left of them, the emperor's road taking them right up until the stink of rot and moss was in their noses. Thick trees and darkness blocked the guts of the forest from view. Nothing could wipe the smile from his face.

The Schwarze gapped the boundary between the Nistrian mountains to the east, pale, snow-capped peaks cutting the underside of the horizon, and Annalt herself. She was hidden by the hills, but a telltale black smog lingered to the west. It was a small wonder the air smelled fresh, and not stinking of the foundries that pumped out the finest steel in the empire.

He wondered if he might pick up a new blade there. A man always needed good steel.

Three towns along the road had added more to the army's numbers, and the host sprawled along the road like a freshly fucked lover across sheets. Green stags of the Hornstags, singing songs so pious the pontiff would be proud. Red coins of the Gelderlings, the yellow circlets of the Amstadts, reaching for old glories. The brown Paulings, and the shit brown Bedestins.

You'd almost think a tourney was on.

The Sigurite Standard lumbered slowly along at the front of the army, but it moved. The heat left an imprint on his skin, made his back stream with so much sweat it felt like he floated face up in a river, like a corpse. The smell of leather, oiled metal, the touch of other men's clammy bodies, the jostle to keep position. At least the army was moving; at least the crusade was underway; at least he'd be there to kill Palerme. Hold the blade himself, maybe. Might even get to kill that traitor bitch, the one everyone had started calling the Lady of Wolves. The Cunt of Dogs, the Bitch in Heat, maybe. He laughed, kept that one in his pocket in case anyone brought it up.

He imagined gutting her, killing her for her betrayal of the Order, for her betrayal of humanity. The gall of it.

"Makes me furious," he said out loud.

Fehling looked to the side. The newly confirmed warden's black jacket sat open to the chest, tabs flapping in the breeze. "What does?"

Gravel crunched under their horses' hooves, the ground pitted already with the feet, cloven and otherwise, of hundreds ahead, with thousands more to come. The emperor's road would be left a beggar's road by the time this army was done with it.

"That woman, the traitor." Spittle flew down his chin. "Makes my blood boil that she'd have a single moment of safety."

"Don't worry, Inquisitor. You'll teach her what it means to betray the Order."

"That's right," Karl said. He'd overheard them. "The bitch'll eat my knife before she's done."

"What?" Jogaila frowned over them. The gathered thousands left a din in the air, a pall over their words. Their voices came as a shout and no other way.

"Palerme, you know. Where we're marching."

"I thought we marched to Annalt," Fehling shot back. Jogaila opened his mouth to correct her when he saw the smirk on her face, and he grimaced. They laughed.

"To Annalt first, then Ostelar, to pick the cream from the prince's army."

Bjorn snorted. "The cream of a turd is still a turd, present company excluded. The Craving Count, they call him. Always envied his older brothers their larger holdings."

Karl fixed a glare on Bjorn. "Whatever he is, he's still my liege lord, and I was still born in Annaltia." He turned his gaze upwards, like a man searching for the right words to say to a friend with an arrow through his guts. "Annaltians are a proud bunch, won't like serving under foreign lords."

Bjorn nearly choked on his words. "Foreign lords?"

"Annaltia is a part of the empire as much as Riga, or the republics. In name, yes, but the emperor hasn't set foot in Annalt in twenty years, and for good reason."

"Won't, now," Richter said.

They laughed. Fehling gave Richter a knowing glance. He thought about killing her, pondered it for a long time. She'd helped him, and that left him indebted. But no secret had been revealed. Had it been this crusade wouldn't have been coming for Palerme, it would've been coming for the Cataline Hill. He was left to conclude the worst: she was loyal.

Who knew a man like him could inspire loyalty?

Hanging limp over the walls of the fort were the banners of some march lord who'd set to decorating every thrusting parapet and crumbling crenellation within reach. A stag piercing the side of a wolf with its antlers, lifting the creature triumphantly into the air. Hopeful, if nothing else. In Richter's experience, the wolf was far too canny for such a trick. But march lords had to reach for hopefulness, since there wasn't much else in the Cisnistrian marches.

The marches formed a crescent in the shadow of the mountains, a chain of miserable villages slumped and moldy, joined by an equally miserable chain of roads that wound through bog and muck. The bulk of the army avoided the marches, going on to Annalt, but Richter had been charged with recruiting from the towns in this part of the country. Several other inquisitors and a count by the name of Toland joined him. Enthralled by the hopes and dreams of a crusade, several hundred men of fighting age joined them on the road. It was either that or spend the rest of their lives eking out miserable existences in the mud. Richter wasn't the only one on a mission.

The years hadn't been kind to the march lord, where half of the wattle-and-daub outbuildings and thatched roofs sagged. One great side of the castle had given way, rubble down the cliffside. Something about the shiftlessness of the march lord himself, coming to greet them, told Richter that he expected unkindness in his future. *Smart man.* In all his years, he'd never found men that held a little bit of power over another to be kind, far less so an army. In the republics, war was a business, the sacking of cities practically a tradition. Northerners considered killing to be far too personal for Richter's liking.

The march lord stepped up to a gap between the merlons, like a gap between the flat teeth of an oxen. He had the swagger of a man whose great-grandfather had been born to the position. His pale head shone through thinning gray hair, a pocked mouth crowned by a huge moustache, white stubble around it.

Count Toland stepped forward, his own moustache dueling the march lords' in size, feathered helm in the crook of his arm.

"Well met, I am Toland, Count of Magberg," he said, speaking up to the marcher, his voice taking files to Richter's teeth. A grating voice for a grating man, he was flaxen-haired and in his mid-thirties. His gilded breastplate sat so tightly around his neck that it was a wonder his head hadn't popped from the pressure.

Richter never liked aristocrats fat on gold and safety. But he really didn't like Toland, who spoke through a scented kerchief, careful not to breathe the march air. The effect wasn't lost on the lord.

"I'll meet you well when you withdraw your army from my gates," the lord said, eyes narrowing over the band. Karl gave Richter a meaningful look, the sort of look that preceded trouble, the same sort of look he wore in the Dripping Bucket. "Your army of peasants gives me no pause, Magberg, but I've not made it to my age by taking risks."

Toland clicked his fingers. His squire rode forward with a scroll, the end of it flapping and torn. "We have dispensation from the Most Holy to conscript men from every lordhold from Istrya to Avercarn—"

"Show me that, boy." The march lord waved his arm, his own charge lowering a bucket on a long arm. The squire put the scroll in the bucket, and the long pole was wound up, nearly tipping on the way.

"The dance of squires and underlings," Richter said. Karl and Fehling laughed.

Jogaila frowned up at the negotiators. "Dance of counts and their cocks."

Bjorn picked the dirt from his fingernails. "Cocking counts."

"It's better to pretend at fighting than actually fighting, all said."

"Northerners and their preening, eh?" Bjorn looked at Paun, waited for a response. The monstrously tall hillman didn't bother to look and nodded.

"All's well, then. I cannot refuse an envoy of the pontiff. You may enter, but your army must remain outside the walls." Then the march lord turned on his heel and disappeared behind the merlons, and shouts sounded from beyond the wall.

"Very well," Toland said to himself, perhaps insulted at the short reception. He turned as scratching noises came from behind the gates, and the two solid doors at the top of the rise creaked open slowly, heavily.

"Inquisitors Hildebrand, Amherst." The two in black at the other side of the party. Two Richter knew as the usual Order functionaries. Good at their killing, good at their politics. He'd been godawful at the politics, much better at the killing.

"Go see to the heriot. Take Sergeant Rasberg with you, and his men. You've been charged to my duty, so I want no disagreements."

They nodded and half the party left, along with a great chunk of their new recruits. Crusades took many bodies, and many mouths. Mouths that needed to eat, and all that food had to come from somewhere. It was theft on such a massive scale that a pontiff basically had to ordain it. As it was, they had to make do with the meagre offerings of the Cisnistrian marches.

"Sigur wept," Richter overheard one of the men say. "When can we kill some goddamn demons, already?"

Soon, Richter kept to himself.

"Inquisitor Beltrand, take your..." He stared at Paun, lifting his eyes, realizing the sheer scale of the man, standing a head taller than some, and a chest taller than the rest. "Men, and scout for us. If the enemy comes for us while we're spread across the farms with our hands in the dirt, we'll—"

"Die with our cocks in our hands," Richter said.

Toland lifted the kerchief from his face, revealing thinned lips. "Quite."

"I'll outride for you, but I want a guarantee."

After a lengthy pause, Toland said, "What do you want?"

"Make sure the marcher gives us everything. No holdouts. No excuses."

"Oh, I'll guarantee that for free. I suppose suspicion comes with the territory of an inquisitor."

"Not if you don't have something to hide."

Richter whistled and turned his horse away from the keep and towards a set of equally sagging stone walls sagged a millhouse at the run of a narrow stream. The stream cut away at the land, leaving a motley of ragged farmhouses on the other side, mounted on stilts. A stand of choked mangroves, roots exposed to the air. Come aestas, this part of the country would be submerged in a foot of water.

"Counts and their cocks," Richter muttered under his breath, gave his horse the heels of his boots.

CHAPTER 18
LIONS
Tribuum, 1045

One should think, given the ever-presence of wolves through-out the Continent, and the lycanthropic menace, that the wolf should be the symbol of imperial power, not the lion. It does make one wonder if Tiellieres, where Istryan sailed from, had an ever-presence of lions, rather than wolves. Equally troubling is the notion that perhaps there were man-lions on that prog-enitor continent, instead of man-wolves. Was that why Istryan left in the first place?

— Apostate Loristin

THE HUMID DAY GAVE way to a humid night. The bone finger of Luni hung high, suspended as though from strings, in the black sky, marked High Hours. She had to correct herself. Outside of the Order, they never called it High Hours. To everyone else, they were still asleep, though they might've called it the middle of the night.

They walked along the emperor's road, from Valenti to Palerme. She thought she could still hear the groans of the dying on the wind, a nause-ating dirge in her mind. Those men in Valenti earned their deaths, so why did they haunt her?

Gothenburg's leaking corpse, bashed brains spilling across the yard. Tomas's shredded body, where a dozen men had surrounded him and given him enough cuts that he couldn't heal from. Spots of exposed innards, ribs, opened bodies. Ripe and stinking. She'd taken part in her fair share of the murder, and knew it was right. They were trying to kill her, and so she had to kill them first. Guilt weighed heaviest on the clouded mind, perhaps. And her mind had been deeply clouded, ever since the sack of Ostelar.

A small and wrenching thing. How long before she bowed under the weight of such guilt? Before her back snapped with the load, her shoulders ground into dust. That gave her shoulders a roll, almost without effort. The knotted flesh that was the remnant of her left arm clenched and rivulets of sweat ran down her neck. She ground her teeth to ignore the pain.

Her hand still ached.

Leon rode beside her. "Night marches are slow going," he said. They weren't on a march, they were travelling, but they might as well have been, for their flight from Valenti bade them travel at some speed. Dubine's mule could barely keep up. "These roads shouldn't be dangerous, but it's hard to see any ruts or holes as we go. And the road wasn't easy to travel at the best of times."

"And these aren't the best of times," Selene mused.

As the cart lumbered over the ruts and rough ground, Tomas's body shook, his wrappings coming loose around his feet. A foot stuck out like a sign of death, dappled orange and waxen in the torchlight. Selene saw dark shapes above, birds of carrion predating above, waiting for their chance to get at his corpse. It was already starting to stink.

"I rather think any robbers wanting a try," Kyrah said, leaning over the horn of her saddle, "are going to find we're more than equipped to handle them." She tapped the sword tucked into the bag at her side, wrapped in linen, sticking out behind the horse's rump.

"Indulge me, marine. Why do you fight with a sword?"

She smiled. "Why do you fight with one?"

"Because I don't have claws."

"Could've fooled me," Frix said. "Gothenburg underestimated you to his peril."

Selene pressed her lips together. A split-open head, pink and white mottled flesh. She gritted her teeth.

"You look like want to about kill your friend, too," Kyrah said, then nodded. "I fight with a sword for the same reason I fuck." She eyed Gregor and he returned the look with a sheepish grin. "Because it's fun."

The woman surprised her. She wasn't what Selene expected from a Saburrian, nor a slave, or the child of a slave. "How did you get your freedom?"

"Freedom?" She looked at Selene like the question slapped her across the mouth. "Do you think I'm—Sigur on a fucking pole, I'm not a slave."

Selene's cheeks burned. "I'm sorry—I didn't mean to—"

"I'm a free woman, just like you." She rode up and stared down Selene. The hairs on Selene's neck stood on end at the vicious look. She was still cowed by her previous embarrassment to speak.

"You saw me naked, a privilege only few women have ever managed."

Selene's face burned brighter. She could feel the warmth spreading, hot and quick like spilled blood from an opened vein. "Yes."

"And my skin, was it different from yours?"

Was this a trick? "No, apart from the color."

"The color, aye." She snatched Selene's hand and placed it on her forearm, made her brush the skin. She didn't wear her marine arms now, just a baldric for a shortsword and a spaulder on her left shoulder. Her forward arm, in the stances of the south. "Feels the same as yours, don't it." She let Selene's hand go.

"Yes."

"Does it look like I've ever worn chains?"

"No."

"Exactly. Just because I'm Saburrian don't mean I'm a slave. There're lots of us, free and otherwise, across the Continent."

"I didn't mean to—"

"Assume? Yes, you did. You'd think you would know a thing or two about people assuming things. I don't need your pity, nor your congratulations. I achieved what I achieved with my own hands."

Selene still had her pride. This woman would not take that from her. "And so have I, just with one fewer. I've scraped and scratched out every fucking morsel for myself and for Althann like you. And what have I got? Nothing but grief."

Kyrah groaned. "Fuck your grief. No one asked you to do that."

"Tell Sanna that, you'll see." She remembered the little girl, Ottille's daughter. The soft, small hand that wormed its way between her fingers, cooled her temper. "You may not appreciate it, but everything we're fighting for is to make a better world for werewolves. A better world for their children. Everything I'm fighting for. Even if a dog like you can't see it."

"Selene," Frix admonished.

"Ah, that's right." Her eyes flashed with malice. "You called me *kalb*, before. I let that slide because I was feeling generous." She pulled back her lips in a sneer. "I'm not feeling so fucking generous, now. Call me that again and I'll cut out your tongue."

Anger shuddered her chest, mixing with fear like a heady cocktail, made her eyes swim. She brought her hand to the dagger at her hip. "Try it."

"Both of you, shut up," Leon said. She hadn't noticed it before, but he held his side, winced a little. "Tomas's body ain't even cold. Pack your fuckin' attitude, we're all on the same side."

Selene grunted, gave her horse knees, and sped off down the road. *Ungrateful bitch. Why is it so hard?* If only they respected her more! She liked to think that she was hard, but fair. The Saburrian didn't know a fucking thing, and she'd had done a hell of a lot more than that woman had to help the Althann. Selene lost everything to get this far.

What if she just let it go? Let the Althann fall to the Lion, get swept aside by the imperials? The Sigurites? That thought gave her pause as she barreled into the night, and full gallop.

The road moved or gave way. A rut. Riding full gallop at night, how stupid. Her horse fell out from under her, something snapped, a cracking noise in the blackness. The lantern on the mare's saddle threw off, crashed against the ground, broke into a flare of fire, glass, and metal. Selene screamed, rolled, felt something break in her side, her leg. She rolled to rest against a rock.

Pain bit into her flesh like dogs tearing at her. Her breath came sharp, shuddered. Dazed, she laid back, let her head rest against soft dirt, looked at the sky. Her leg burned with pain. She looked down. Sharp bones poked from her calf, dark blood gushing across the ground. But above, splashed across the sky, a painter's sprinkling of white ink against a canvas, came the stars. The heavens. She could've died, brained herself on the rock she rolled near to, if she'd only been a little further along when she fell. *What kind of god watches over me?* Fate or a god ordained her survival, surely. Was it a god from there that saved her? Or a worldlier god—like Althann?

A troubling thought occurred to her. Why would Althann care for her? She wasn't one of them, nor did she descend from them, as far as she knew.

The duca's strongbox would have the answer, perhaps, though she didn't know if she could bring herself to read it.

Her horse dragged itself up, one leg lagging behind the others. Broken, lolling. White bone pointed at Selene, pale in the silvery gloom. It grunted, pulling itself toward her.

She gave the beast a sad smile. "Why are you coming to me? I'm just as broken as you are."

It laid its head in her lap, deeply confused as to why it couldn't move like it used to. She brushed her fingers across its snout. "Both of us are used up, aren't we?" Tears stung like nettle behind her eyes. "The world has no use for either of us."

She wondered, in the back of her mind, though now the thought was moving forward to settle closer to the front, whether they would find her. She'd gone far off the road without even realizing, and her lantern was a wreck near her, its flame long gone out. They might not find her until the morning, and by then she'd have bled out, more than likely.

She stroked the beast's ears. It tried again, to stand, but its broken leg gave out. The mare twisted its head awkwardly to avoid coming down on Selene's own broken leg, grunting softly. Tears ran down her face. "I'm sorry. This is it for you." *And for me, too.*

It looked up at her with squarish eyes, silvery in the starlight. Selene felt bad that she ever mistreated it, thought it was somehow less than the mare she'd left in Ostelar.

"Eda," she said, and blinked back the wet in her eyes. She drew the dagger at her hip. The dagger that had taken her through so much, been with her since the beginning. It would've been terrible to leave it at the palace, after all.

She shoved the point in the horse's throat. The mare spasmed, kicked its legs, groaned, whined, then its movements dulled, and it breathed out a great sigh. Selene breathed, pulled out the blade, dropped it through bloody fingers and cried. She sobbed, sobbed until it was though all the terror and the fear and the bloody ache of a thousand horrible years threatened to leak out of her, threatened to kill her with the pain in her chest. Tristain was dead, Sorenius was dead, and she'd killed him. Dear, dear Soren. The man she'd loved. She wouldn't deny that now, not to herself. All she was left with was a boy she couldn't even breastfeed. She couldn't do that *one* thing, after failing everything else.

And now she was dead of a broken leg.

"Sel! Selene!" Leon. Lights danced into view across the expanse, black figures on blacker horizon. Came closer, and Leon's face like a bright sun at rise moved into view. "You're hurt!"

"Leon," she said. "Just leave it."

He came to her side, eyes flicking over her leg, the dead horse, her eyes. Back and forth, as though he couldn't decide how to process the chaos before him.

"How could you be so stupid, Sel?" He tutted. "Riding off like that. Don't let that woman get under your skin. You're better than that."

"Why do you care?" Selene frowned. "I'm nothing to you. All I wanted to do was kill Tristain until you changed my mind. But if you hadn't, I'd have not changed my ways."

He pursed his lips but didn't answer, his eyes focused on the task in front of him. He fetched out his knife and cut a length of cloth from his shirt, passed it under Selene's leg and tied it higher than the exposed bone, just above the knee. The old army commander, the old mercenary, spurred into action like an old draft horse, doing what he's always done.

"You care," she realized. "It's what you do."

Leon nodded, tying the cloth off, tight. "That'll stop the bleeding, for now. But you'll need a barber to set the bone, make sure it heals right."

"And we just left the only place for a hundred miles in any direction that might have one."

He grimaced. "Might be there's one on the road. If needs must, we can pay one to come from Invereid or Valenti. I still have some coin left from selling my holdings."

Selene bit her lip until it hurt. "How do I do it, Leon?" Her voice broke. "How do I make it so that every day isn't a fucking struggle? How do you keep going? I want to give up." She couldn't rightly say the next words, but she tried anyway, looked away, didn't know if she could face his eyes when he heard the words. They shattered in her mouth, cut her tongue and cheeks. "Sometimes I wish I never had Tristain."

He didn't say anything for a long time. But he didn't move, didn't shout in horror. Didn't call her a bad mother, just sat there, sat on his feet.

"One time," he said, after a long while. "Erken was being a real prick. He called me every name under the sun, and you know us hillmen, we can shout new and varied profanities you've never heard." He smiled. "I wanted to smash his brains in. Smash his brains in for being a stupid cunt, and I even said to him, 'I wish you were never born.'" He shook his head. "And I meant it."

"What did he do?"

"He wanted to fight a losing battle. I knew he would die, and I told him as much. But he still wanted to fight, to prove himself." He took off the pendant around his neck. The chalice pendant he was never without. "I carved this for him, to give him luck. So, the goddess would smile down on him. Silly me. Most fathers make swords for their sons, wanting Sigur to give them strength. But I wanted him to be merciful, to show strength in the face of horror, and make his conscience right with the world." He looked down. "Maybe I should've carved him a sword. He died before I could give it to him."

"I'm sorry."

"Don't be sorry. It was my stupidity that pushed him away. But you do the best you can, and hope that it's enough." He handed her the pendant, winced. "That's all you can do."

She frowned at his flinch. "What is it?"

"Give this to your son." He grabbed her hand and placed the pendant on her palm, closed her fingers around it. "Let it be his luck."

She leaned forward, lifted his arm. Blood pooled around a jagged tear in his mail, just below his ribs. A wound taken from the attack. "Leon, you're hurt."

"It's nothing. I've had worse shaving." He winced again as he stood.

"Stomach wounds kill slow, but they kill just the same."

"Let's get going. We'll have to load you on the cart. Sit with Dubine, make sure you don't move that leg too much. There—there we go."

Leon put her weight over his shoulder, helping her to walk on her good leg. She grimaced. *Dubine.* The thought of a journey sitting next to that braggart wheat-thresher pained her almost as much as the standing.

There was something in Leon's eye as the others arrived soon after, Frix leaping down from his horse to rush over. The sadness had lifted, it seemed, and as she saw that and looked into herself, she saw a little of the heart-crushing pain lift to a numbness that spread through her chest, warming her.

She wondered if she should tell them Leon was hurt, but it seemed like needless worry for them. They were already in a panic at her state.

"Sefinn, Olaf, clear room on the cart," Frix ordered, and his cousins snapped to attention. His voice broke when he saw her, and he turned away, wincing. They started to take the crates off, undid the ropes. "We'll have to leave some of this behind."

"It's fine, Frix," Selene said. "It's more important that we take every-thing."

"With respect, milady, no, it isn't."

"Enough, I've already decided. I'll ride up front with Dubine."

CHAPTER 19
THE LADY OF PALERME
TRIBUUM, 1045

The Six Years War? Does that come before or after the Seven Years War?

— A MERCENARY

THE MULE ROLLED THE wagon into the yard of the ostler's as the sun broke the eastern mountains, light spilled like bright blood in the haze coming off the snow tops. Her leg didn't ache anymore, only felt numb, and though the bleeding had stopped, bones still poked gruesomely through the broken skin and muscle. She turned away. It was likely she'd lose the leg. Maybe she'd end up with a pegleg like Chesterfield's bosun. She smiled fondly remembering him and Estelle and the others. Privateering across the Bright Sea and the Cape of Knives, she'd probably never see them again.

Dubine wasn't bothered by her leg, or if he was, he didn't show it. Blessedly to Althann and all the gods, he hadn't said a word on their journey, only to say that their flight from Valenti was a rushed one, and that it was improper to travel at night, worried that his mule might throw a shoe.

Selene vented a huge yawn, her eyes whirring from tiredness. "It'll be good to get some sleep," she said, mostly to herself.

Dubine just nodded. "Been on the road most me life. A spot of sleep is good when you can get it."

The groom came from the horses and led the wagon into a covered shed, out of the drizzle that had picked up in the morning. He didn't ask questions about her state or the cloth-wrapped body on the top of the wagon, and Selene handed him a bag of the duca's coin to keep it that way.

"Boy," she said, leaning down. "Is there a surgeon around? I need my leg set and my friend needs his stomach patched up." She looked back. Leon was unsteady on his horse now, pale in the bloody sunrise.

The groom was no older than twelve, wisps of a light beard across his mouth, and curly black hair. The features of an Alanian, most like, though if the man emerging from the ostelry proper—a squat, thatched building, tarred to keep the rain out—was anything to go by, the boy's mother was the southerner.

"Aye, there's Muselio," the boy said. "Lives on the other side of the hill, where he makes his business for traveling folk like yourselves. I can—"

"Sesar," the ostler warned. "Come inside."

The boy hesitated, then ran inside, the man fetching the coinpurse from his hand as he passed.

"I heard there were travelers on the road from Valenti, come at night," he said. His huge arms folded after weighing the coinpurse in his hand. A milk-skinned Osbergian of the country variety with meaty brow and forearms coated in a thick layer of black hair, like a fur coat. "Didn't think they'd be in such shambles."

The question looked to be on his lips. *Who are you, and why are you traveling at night? Running from something?* Word would've spread quickly of the riot in Valenti, though Selene hoped they could be ahead of the rumors, leaving as quick as they did. Not quick enough, apparently.

"We're just traveling through, looking for a barber-surgeon. If you like, we can move on."

He chewed those words, looked them over, measuring them as much as he measured the bag in his hand. "Gold is gold. We've three cots available, and they're free of lice, which is a sight better than you'll see between here and Invereid. You'll have to share some, of course."

Selene looked around. They'd had far worse, all of them. Except maybe the Saburrian, but she gave an unruffled look, as though sleeping in a cot was much better than most options open to her throughout her life. *She's had a hard life. She scraped for everything she had, just like me.*

"That's fine by us."

"Good. We've ale and soup by the fire. Goat stew. Thought that might be of interest to some."

Selene frowned. *Why would it be?* A strange comment from a strange man. "And the surgeon?"

"Sesar'll run and get Muselio as soon your horses are stabled," he said, and suddenly the boy appeared, guided Frix and Leon's horses to the stables as they dismounted.

The man gave a small bow. "I hope you'll find everything to your liking, milady."

That's what the comment was about. He knows who we are. He would well within his rights to refuse them, cast them out as demons and heretics. But gold was gold, like he said.

The boy approached Kyrah and she swung a foot at him, made him duck. "Piss off boy, I'll stable my own horse," she said, and hooked her leg over the saddle, hopped down.

Selene shook her head as Frix helped her inside. Maybe the woman irked Selene so much because they were so similar. Headstrong, stubborn, violent, charismatic. All qualities of good leaders, she realized. That was what made them butt heads. There was one too many leaders in this small group, each dancing that preening dance to maintain control, like a couple of bright-feathered cocks. She'd seen it in the Order, seen it here.

She trusted the others to follow her lead, though. Althann were a naturally suspicious bunch, and she could count on that. Behavior bred by years of learned survival; trust didn't come easy. She'd earned that if nothing else.

She smiled at Frix as he helped her over the threshold, and he smiled back. The crushing pit in her stomach hadn't felt so bad, felt better than it had since even before Ostelar. Lighter, so even the prospect of never walking properly again didn't seem so bad. Felt like she could take each day as it came. Maybe that was hope talking, but that was a feeling she hadn't suffered in a long time, neither. Couldn't rightly remember if she ever had.

It was nice.

The ostler's was quiet and warm, with three men sitting at a table by the fire. They acknowledged her as she entered. The small fire cracked and popped, sent wisps of heady smoke through the smoke hole at the top. A fresh log curled at the edges with new flame, and above the fire hung a black cauldron half-full of brown stew, bits floating inside that she could only assume were hunks of goat and cut-up vegetables. Hearty peasant fare, enough to get you through a day of travel or a day of farming. Two fat loaves of bread, fresh from the oven, sat covered in coals to keep them warm. The place was fine, though not quite worth the ten pieces of gold he'd given the ostler. No, she paid that for discretion, an understanding.

"Well met," one of the men said.

Selene nudged Frix to let go and she sidled into the table opposite the men. Her leg shot with bone-crunching pain as she sat down, and she grimaced. Frix sat across from her.

"That's a nasty fall, mistress." One had his head tilted sideways, face shaped like an egg, long chin covered in brown scraggle. "You fall off a horse?"

She opted not to engage and let the moment pass. They'd return to their conversation soon enough, and by their muted voices, they hadn't been drinking all night. That boded well for them minding their own business. She warned Frix's cousin, Sefinn, with her eyes when he entered. Olaf, Dubine, and Gregor joined them soon after, and Leon and Kyrah after that.

The three men's eyes didn't move from the table after the Saburrian entered. "What news from the sandy south?" the egg-headed man said.

"I've never been south," Kyrah said, as though it was a point of pride. *I've scraped for everything I've got.*

"No need to be rude, dog. Just askin' a question."

"*Dog?*"

Selene shook her head. "Can we just enjoy our mornings in peace, and go our separate ways when we're done?"

"Aye, that's no problem." The egg-headed man sat back. His friends had sneers on their faces, laughter on their lips.

She looked at Kyrah. She must've known they were goading her. The woman's jaw worked its powerful muscles, but she nodded. "Yes, can do," she forced out.

Gregor returned with bowls for the seven of them and a loaf of the fresh bread, letting Selene have the first try. "Thank you, Gregor."

"Only right, milady." The bread was better than she expected, only a little chalky, like they had used mostly actual flour, and not sawdust that peasants were known to cut their flour with. *Ostlers must do better than I thought, on these roads.* Though the roads were quiet when she'd traveled them lately, she supposed a lot of trade came through here, being the borderlands.

The soup was hearty, as expected, and had an aniseed bite. It was warming and pleasant as it slid down her throat, and the goat was perfectly cooked.

"We've not a farrier here," the ostler said, walking inside, brushing his meaty hands over his apron. "But I can call one. The mule needs new shoes on his front, and the bay mare has got a rock lodged in her back left hoof." *Frix's horse.* "I can't get it out, and it's liable to throw a shoe or fester if I leave it."

Selene um-ed. She hadn't asked him to do that, though she was glad for it, she supposed. But was he trying to get more money out of them? "Dubine, your mule needs new shoes?"

"Aye, milady. I didn't say none 'cause I knew we"—he glanced at the three men—"needed all the coin we could spare."

"The mule is important. He pulls the cart, and I don't fancy our chances without..." She was about to say, *without the arms and goods going up the mountain,* but she stopped herself. She didn't want to give the three men any clues.

"Aye, milady. Too right."

What's going on with him? He's been quieter than ever since we came back from Valenti. Normally she couldn't have got him to shut his mouth, but now his lips barely opened, like a vestal's legs.

"Alright, good ostler," she said. "Call the farrier. We have to wait for the surgeon, anyhow," she said to the others. They nodded.

Leon cleared his throat. He looked pale as ever, almost ghostly in the firelight. As he sat there, he swayed a little, eyes blinking independently of each other. "Too right, Sel."

Selene chewed her lip. *I hope that's soon.* The ostler nodded and left through the door again, calling for his son.

Selene frowned. "The boy hasn't left, yet?" She was more worried about Leon than her leg, but even so.

"It's a damn tragedy," the egg-headed man said, to himself, mostly. He appeared to be their leader, the others' heads bobbing along like buoys in a thunderstorm. "Franz was a hero."

Franz? A friend of theirs?

"Aye," the other one said, ratty moustache the only hair across his pock-marked face, his woolen hood over his head. "'Tis a damn shame. The Terror of the Palatine, they're callin' it."

The Palatine? Isn't that in the capital? Selene watched them, their mood shifting darker.

Frix waved his hand. "Hm?" she said, looking at him.

"You going to eat that?" Her bowl, still steaming and full, almost, had all their eyes on it. They'd scoffed theirs down, except Leon, whose bowl was being finished off by Gregor. She shook her head, didn't quite find it amusing that they were so starving.

She put another coin on the table. "Good ostler," she said, "another serve for all my friends, enough for them to be satiated. Do you have baths, too?" The duca had given them new, blood-free clothes, but they would've had the reek of death and sweat on them still. Selene longed for one, after her leg was set, of course.

He stood by the fire, stoking it with another log. "Aye. Ain't warm, though."

"Good enough. Where's that surgeon?"

"Sesar'll be back soon."

Selene sighed. Leon touched her wrist. "It's alright, Sel."

"It's not alright—"

"Where'd'ya get that coin, mistress?" The third man, this one with a scar across his nose that cleft it in two, left one half chasing the other down a sinuous curve. Their eyes were sharp, the eyes of those accustomed to fighting. Soldiers, maybe. *Deserters?*

Word had it that the archduke's men, those that had survived, anyway, deserted his army by the score after hearing that Ostelar had been taken. Were these some of them? They were persistent, Selene gave them that. But then there were two paths open to the deserting soldier. Sell your sword or go into brigandage. Which path had these three taken? Based on the state of their clothes and the swords at their hips, likely the latter. Although if these three were an advance party of a mercenary company, she and the others would be knee-deep in a mountain of shit when the company came looking for their men. She opted to be friendly, but firm. What she'd learned in her inquisitor days—engage with the rabble, but don't indulge them.

The man continued. "That's Alanian, right? You don't look like a southerner."

"I do business in the south," Selene said.

"You don't have to answer them," Frix whispered. "Let's just wait for this surgeon, then be on our way."

"We can get a farrier to come to Palerme," Sefinn said.

"What's that, lad?"

Selene's stomach sank.

The one with the moustache leaned over, his hand on his sword. "Did I hear you speak the name of that heretical place?"

"You're mistaken." She leaned over the table, extending a coin their way. "How about another few rounds of ale, for all of you. Gold is gold."

"Gold ain't fucking gold if it comes from a demon, wench." He stood, chair scraping on the boards. Kyrah and Leon shot up, Leon wincing. They both had their hands on their weapons.

Selene raised her hand in conciliation. *These idiots are going to get themselves killed.* "Please, we're all friends here—"

The egg-headed one stood slowly, followed by the scarred one, and rusty arming swords slid from their scabbards, metal scraping. The ostler disappeared behind the bar at the back of the room, rummaged around.

"Pride'll be the fuckin' death of you, idiots," Leon said, swaying on his feet, his voice firm despite that.

"Ain't pride, hillman. This is righteous retribution. They killed the fuckin' emperor."

The emperor? Selene's eyes nearly bulged out of her head. She wasn't alone. "The *emperor?*" she shouted. "What are you lackwits on about?"

"Emperor Franz, you dog—" His eyes narrowed to slits. "I see. This bitch sleeps with 'em. She's the cunting Lady of Wolves! That's why they call her milady. See," he said, pointing to her missing arm. "She ain't got a left arm, just like they say."

"Ah, the traitorous cunt," the hooded, mustached one said. "How does it feel to betray your kind? Not as good as wolf cock in your quim, I suppose."

She groaned, put her hand on Frix's wrist to stop him from drawing his sword. He bared his teeth at them. "Sit before you get yourselves killed." She was talking to all of them.

"I agree with Lady Selene, there," the ostler said, leveled a crossbow in the men's direction. "There'll be no blood spilled in my inn."

"Anyone who takes the side of the demons'll be burned right along with 'em."

"You still have a choice," Selene said, finding she'd lost her appetite for blood tonight. Or perhaps she'd already had it filled, and she became sick as it overflowed. "You could walk away."

The one with the scar tugged at his comrade's sleeve, the hooded one. "Jakob," he said. "We should go. They outnumber us, anyway."

"One of 'em's a walking corpse," the hooded one, Jakob, replied, not moving his eyes from Selene. *Leon.* "And one of 'em's a cripple. A twice cripple, by the looks. The other one's a Saburrian dog."

"That still leaves four, though."

"Five," the ostler said. "I was a crossbowman for the Duca of Malatesta during the Six Years War." Selene looked at him. *The Six Years War.* One of the constant southern wars between Vallonia, Badonnia, and the republics. That must've been the source of Sesar's parentage. He'd met a southern woman and had a child; bought or built this inn with the proceeds of his army days.

"Believe me," he continued, "when I say that I'll drop one of you before you make it over to me. Maybe even two, depending on how quick you are."

"Fuck this," the scarred one said, and backed up. "I'm getting out—"

"Shut up," Jakob yelled, placing the end of his sword against the scarred one's padded jacket. "Don't you fucking move, Elias."

"Sigur'll give us the strength of ten men." The egg-headed one leaned on the point of his sword, smiled. "I like my chances there. What's that... thirty to six?"

Kyrah grinned. "If you want to meet Sigur so badly, who am I to deny you?" She drew her blade and stepped past the egg-headed man's pitiful guard and split him open, from navel to breast. He reeled, and there was a twanging noise as Jakob raised his sword, bellowed.

"Fucking wolf cu—" A bolt thumped into his back, sent him stumbling sideways, and he slipped over the fresh log on the fire, crashed headfirst into the table at Selene's waist, forehead bouncing against the wood with a hollow *clonk*. His sword flew out of his hands, scattered across the boards.

Elias raised his hands as his friends groaned, leaking blood onto the boards. The ostler had his crossbow leveled on them again, as practiced a hand at reloading as he was at firing. *We could use a man like him on our walls*, she thought.

"Stop! I won't fight!" His sword clattered on the wood as he threw it down. "Just don't kill me!"

Kyrah pointed the end of her blooded sword over at Selene. "It's up to her," she said. "She's the one you insulted. As the Lady of Palerme, she has the authority here, as much as any other lord does. Speaking of: who's the lord of these parts?"

"There ain't none," the ostler said, not lowering his crossbow. "Or if there is, he ain't bother us in years. Not since I've been here."

"Then it falls to her authority."

Selene's surprise was tempered by the sickness she felt in her guts as Jakob's groans turned to screams, and he started rolling side to side, pushing the bolt deeper in his back. The egg-headed man wasn't moving, dark blood pouring from the great open gash across his torso.

"Don't kill them," Selene said. "We'll take them back to Palerme to meet justice." The words spilled from her mouth. It made sense, though. Lords and ladies settled disputes and judged the guilty of capital crimes. Murder, rape, kidnapping, brigandage. Petty crimes were resolved by the local sheriffs or magistrates, but this was a capital crime. Attempted murder and waylaying most definitely fell within the purview of an imperial lady of a castle, especially one that was so near.

"If they don't die on the journey. Does this satisfy?" she said to the ostler and Elias.

Elias's head bounced up and down as quick as a jackrabbit. "Sorry, milady. I weren't lookin' to kill anyone. Just take a bit of coin, threaten an assault if they didn't hand it over, that sort of thing."

"Fine, I'll not judge you as harshly. But you must be held to account. And you?"

The ostler nodded and lowered his crossbow. "Aye," he said. "Call me Casimir. I'm happy."

Kyrah wiped her sword of blood and sheathed it, while Jakob's screams changed to moans, bloody smears worked into the boards beneath him.

"That surgeon's gonna have his work cut out for him," Dubine said while Kyrah laughed.

Selene was in no laughing mood.

CHAPTER 20
OF RATS AND WOLVES
TRIBUUM, 1045

No, the empire is more like a collection of independent states bound together by shared culture and somewhat-shared language, that was once united under the banner of a conqueror, and has since been ruled by bureaucrats and the effete.

— TOMAS VERDUN, HISTORICAL ACCOUNTS OF THE PRE-IMPERIAL PERIOD

RICHTER'S WHETSTONE SCRAPED OUT with every swipe. There was something honest in the work, something about the *scrape-scrape*, the spit that went into making the edge shine. Like a little bit of himself went into the blade. And when it sliced through skin and muscle and bone with the ease of cutting through an apple, a bit of himself was entering his enemy. That made him smile, reminded him everyone was just a bag of meat in the end, even him. He was just a bag of meat that proved mightily hard to keep down.

At the height of the day, they shaded themselves in the canopy of a pine. They had to walk with their horses, over the thickets and between the twisted, gnarled trees. The forest teemed with life, practically seethed with it. Dragonflies buzzed over an uprooted tree covered in moss, chasing each other. Over the next ridge, the sound of a stream. A babble, a garble of words, as though the trees themselves were talking to him. The cool breeze pushed flaxen hair into his face, and he scraped it back with muddy fingers.

"You look ready to drop," Bjorn said, laughing at the hillman.

Paun had turned white, not his usual healthy pink. His mountainous voice grated but seemed deadened by the closeness of the forest. "There's witches in this forest. And demons besides, and—"

"Mothers' tales?" Fehling said as she brushed her horse's coat with a stiff comb.

Karl handed out a knob of bread to each of them, while pleasant smells came from the roasting pheasant he'd hunted that morning. "My mother told me little men would cut my neck in my sleep and make necklaces out of my teeth if I didn't eat my supper."

Jogaila scratched his cheek. "If every stand of trees had a witch or a demon or little men inside, it'd make our jobs a sight easier."

Richter ran his blade over the whetstone. "Just do your fucking job, hillman, and I won't string your guts up on the nearest tree." Scrape, scrape.

That put a pall of awkward silence over them. He hadn't really meant for it to come out like that—since they'd all kept silent Nials's death he felt a touch of friendship about them, and certainly what came after had bonded them further. Richter never had any brothers, but the boys in the Gutter had been something like family. He was beginning to think of his new charges as family, too, as close as scum like him could get to some, anyway.

But it was something about this place made him feel itchy. The sounds of the wind rustling the leaves washing over them. He went to sit up, felt a tug on his jacket. Caught on a branch. He undid the thing and took it off, let it fall by his waist.

Something tugged at his mind, made him feel something he'd long forgotten. Made him feel at peace. He hated it. Felt like shoving his hand into a too-small glove. He didn't deserve peace, but what you get and what you deserve are never the same. Couldn't have been, surely. Just his imagination. This world was dead, full of the dying. Some of it was just taking longer than the rest.

Now, Istrya, that place was dead. Annalt, dead and burning. In the Schwarze, in all forests, he couldn't quite find it, but they were surely dying too. They smelled enough of rot and decay. It wasn't the rot of dead bodies, though, and even those had their place here. Carcasses fed the trees, fed the ground. Rats fed the foxes fed the wolves that feasted on them. Each had its place.

"Besides, I've crossed the Vyahtken wastes. Witches don't exist." Each word came out punctuated with a scrape. He waved the blade toward Jogaila's face. "It troubles me you think on fighting imaginary enemies when real ones are easily within grasp, in every village from here to the Geisteschreien. Before long, you'll face your first. One's that trying to kill you, anyhow." He looked meaningfully at Karl. Karl said nothing and returned the glance with his usual friendly stare.

"Too right," Bjorn said. "With the rush on this crusade and all, we've not had our *Velitore*. Before long, we'll face our first."

"What's it like?" Jogaila asked. He poked at the ground with the end of his sword, digging around a root with the point.

"It's like nothing else." Karl never took his eyes off Richter. "It's like death incarnate, moving so quick you can scarcely breathe, think, let alone move before it's on you."

Richter nodded, baring his teeth a little.

"How do you kill a thing like that?"

"You don't. Not on your own," Richter said. Scrape, scrape. "You trap it, corner it. A poisoned bolt to the neck usually does it." *Though I have my own ways.* "But most of all, kill it before it transforms, and have off the head. Some of them have an uncanny knack of seeming dead when they aren't quite."

"Bloody business we've chosen, isn't it?" Bjorn tongued a scrap of bread between his teeth. Sucked it back into his mouth, kept chewing. "But I figure there's not much else I'm good for. I was a ship's guard, for a while. Went trading up and down the coast and when the trading turned sour, we stole. Turned out pirating was more profitable than trading, so that's what we did, all across the Sea of Martyrs."

Karl cut bits of pheasant flesh, handed them around.

"But Reynard's navy got us eventually, and the captain was killed, along with half the crew. The other half were taken as slaves."

Richter lifted his eyes. "You were a slave?"

"That I was. It was go into the Order or work in the prince's foundries until the day I died."

"I know what I'd choose."

"It's not just that, though." He looked at his hands, covered in dark bits of pheasant meat. "I'm good at killing. There's not many better in a trice."

"That I saw in the Bucket," Karl said. He turned to Fehling, grin on his face. "But where does a girl like you—"

A cracking noise rang out, came from over the ridge of their little gully. Two figures imposed themselves on the ridgeline, then four, then eight, hooded and shaded by the sun. Surrounded them, thirty in all. Karl drew his blade on instinct, and an arrow thudded into the meat next to his shoulder, went right through the leather jerkin. A war bow, drawn by a practiced hand. He dropped with a shout, but none of them moved to help him.

"Little rats in the forest," one of the archers said.

Richter threw away his long knife ahead of him and stood slowly, putting his hands out in regard. "Now, now, there's no need for that. We're from the Order, representing the authority of Pontiff Gottscheid."

"We know."

"Then you know that assaulting an inquisitor or his retinue is a crime punishable by death." He grinned. "Not just any death. You'll be hung until not-quite-dead, stretched over a rack, and then burned at the stake."

"I've always wanted to be stretched," one of the marauders said. They weren't just any raiders, though. They spoke perfect Annaltian and were heavily armed. *A count's men? But they wouldn't dare.* "Always thought it would fix the ache my back has of a morning." They laughed.

"I would know who our would-be killers are before our untimely demises."

One of them stepped forward, lowered his hood. Perfect jaw, bright green eyes, wavy black hair. A beauty, if there ever was one, and Richter found himself staring longer than he meant to.

"I am Count August of Tolsberg, son of Reynard, and heir to the Lion Throne. This crusade is a farce. My grandfather was murdered."

Richter raised one eyebrow in a practiced way. He was far too remorseless to feel any kind of guilt for killing this young man's grandfather. Cross-bows and war bows stood at the ready, nocked. He wondered if he might kill the lordling and all his men before they got Fehling and Karl and the others. But that would be a long chance, one that didn't appeal.

"Yes, he was murdered by a demon," he said.

"A demon, yes, there's no doubt. But one sent by the Grand Inquisitor, to lock the Order's wretched arms to the throne."

"So, you attack outriding parties instead of the host?"

It was the handsome prince's turn to smile. "You'll see, master inquisitor. You know, I've heard of a demon hunter described as heavily scarred"—he drifted a finger towards his neck—"around his neck, as though someone tried to cut his throat and failed at the endeavor every time."

"I'm happy to see my reputation precedes me. What will you do with us?"

"That's up to my father."

I guess we'll be going to Annalt sooner rather than later.

CHAPTER 21
TO BEAR
TRIBUUM, 1045

The Saburrian physician would find his services much maligned on the mainland. Centuries of poor treatment by men with saws and unsteady, drunkard hands, has given the barber-surgeon a poor reputation on the Continent. Then it is up to the noble physician to comport themselves in such a way to counter this belief.

— MASTER AL-FARUK OF THE BAUSHAR ACADEMY

SELENE SCREAMED AS HER bones scraped against each other, the noise like taking files to her jaw. Pain shot through every fiber of her body. Spots of white burst like suns across the inside of her eyelids. Only childbirth was more painful, though this was a close fucking second. Frix and Gregor held her tighter, braced their bodies against the table, bashed around as she thrashed in pain.

"Hold her tighter," the surgeon said.

She barely heard the words. Fixed on the ridiculous southern accent, she shrieked, "Republican bastard, I bet your mother fucks any man she comes across!" The pain lessened, and he leaned back. Then he came close again with a small needle, stitching the skin, bolts of pain like lightning jolting up her leg.

"Ah, fuck you. Fuck. Arsehole. Bastard. Prick. Fatherless cunt."

"There, done," Muselio huffed, getting up from the bench. He lifted his eyeglasses up, dark features gathered in a frown. "I'll wrap and bind the leg, then we're finished. It was a clean break."

"What does that mean?" Frix said.

"It means I might walk, after all," Selene said, shaking off her shoulders, and sitting up.

"If she keeps off it for a few months," he said. "You are her husband, yes? Make sure she does." He stepped close to him. "Women don't listen to you unless you... you know." He gestured with the back of his hand.

Frix's eyes widened. "I'm not—"

"Piss off, you drunk," Selene shouted.

"Northern women," the surgeon yelled, throwing up his hands.

Leon bellowed with laughter, watching from the shadows with Kyrah and the others. She was glad Leon was feeling better. For a moment, or many, she worried that his wound had festered, but Muselio packed the wound with linen to stop the bleeding, which he said was the cause of his torpor. He sewed it up, and a few bowls of stew later, Leon had already regained his healthy pink color. And his laugh. He'd have to get the packing removed in a week, but that was better than an agonizing end by afternoon.

Elias sat in the corner, hand resting on a propped-up knee, while his friends shuddered in and out of consciousness, scarcely looked up at Muselio as he went over to the fire.

Muselio glanced at Selene. "Did you kill these men with your tongue as well?"

"They're not dead," Frix said.

The surgeon took his tongs to a bandage from a plate sitting above a boiling pot of water. Boiled linen. The surgeons in the Order did the same thing. Supposed to help with the rot.

"In all my years, I've seen many dead," he said. "Believe me when I say that these men are dead."

He returned with the linen and two lengths of wood, cut to size by the ostler, and wrapped the linen around the wound, being purposeful about it. It was tight, but not so that it numbed her foot. Then he arranged the lengths of wood, and another set of bandages, fixed her leg in a loose, extended position, but so she couldn't bend it. He poked her toe with the sewing needle.

"You feel that?"

"Fucking yes," she yowled.

"Good, then I've not wrapped it too tight. Do this, every day for two weeks, with a length of boiled cloth like I do. Come back then and I'll remove the stitches. It won't fester, you can be sure of that, as long as you keep it clean and always wrap it with boiled cloth."

"You certainly know your craft," Frix said. "How did you learn?"

"The finest school in the world, in Segesta. Master Al-Faruk's school, the greatest physician the Continent has ever known."

"A Saburrian?" Kyrah leaned forward, her dark skin dappled with the reflection of the dancing fire, half-empty bottle of dark red in her hand, wine sloshing around.

"*Si,* mistress." He rattled off a sentence of quick Saburrian, something like a breathy murder. They went back and forth, laughing and shouting, angry at each other while smiling and laughing. Thoroughly a strange interaction. Selene rolled her eyes and let them have it as Gregor returned with a green bottle. He pulled the cork with a *thwop* and handed it to her.

"Thanks, Gregor."

"Aye." He leaned against the table as though he meant to say something more.

"What is it?" She closed her lips around the bottle and took a few labored gulps. It was a dark, tart red, and she suddenly had the smarting realization that they never did get the case of Alanian red that was Rill the mason's payment.

"Ulie was wrong for what he said." Gregor's face was downcast. "He'd lost his mother, and he was acting out."

What's she given up? Ulie's words echoed.

"He was right, in a way," she said. "Everyone's given up something to get this far." She took another swig. The warming feeling in her belly was helping the pain in her leg. Helping to numb it if nothing else.

I see ghosts at night, and lost lovers in my nightmares. I don't want there to be a way out. I don't deserve it. She didn't seem like the same woman that spoke those words. Maybe there was a way out, and maybe she wanted it. Maybe Palerme could be it, baby Tristain.

"We've all ghosts in our past," Gregor said. A sad smile spread on his face. "Doesn't mean he was right to say that."

"He's your son, he'll come good, I know. If he's anything like his father." She offered him the bottle.

"Thank you, milady." He smiled generously now and took a swig, strong neck muscles working under thick beard. "We've lots of work to do when we return, and you can be sure my sons will be helping. I won't have them causing mischief."

"I appreciate that." *That's right. Rill's work was only the beginning.*

"There's *what?*" Kyrah shouted. "It's not true, it can't be."

They looked over. "What is it?" Selene said.

Kyrah's face had flushed pink, her eyes wide. "There's... Muselio says there's a holy army coming to Palerme."

A shocked sigh rippled across the room. Selene blinked. "Truly?"

"From the capital," he answered. "My brother in Istrya tells me they number twenty thousand or more."

"Twenty thousand," she repeated. That didn't seem real. It was the population of Invereid, a huge town on the banks of the Inver river, a big trading town. *That many people, taking up arms against us?* "Because of the emperor."

"Because of the emperor, *si*."

"But we'd never do that," Olaf said. "I don't even know who the emperor is."

"Whoever did it, we've been blamed for it." She laughed at the absurdity of it. "They'll never let us just live. There can never be a sanctuary for lycans while the Order exists. It's just not possible. It goes against everything they've been indoctrinated to believe."

Leon wiped his face. "Sel... what do we do? Even three thousand cross-bowmen are no match for twenty thousand imperial soldiers."

"We draw it out. We know this forest, they don't. And the Order may know how to fight us, but the imperial armies don't. They're used to fighting each other, with knightly charges, and all that. We can use that. We know they're coming, and we'll be ready for them."

"You'd be better off running," Kyrah said. "You of all people should know how fearsome a person is when they believe they're fighting a righteous cause."

"No." She put down the bottle, pressed a finger into the table to punctuate her point. "I'm done running. We'll be ready." The others nodded, their fear as plain as the bloody sunrise that broke over the eastern mountains. But they nodded anyway.

"Where would I go?" Frix said, shrugging. "I've nothing else. If I can take down a few imperial bastards before I die, more's the better."

Selene gave a firm nod. Frix's bravery set the tone for them, and they all nodded. "I'll fight for a better world for my sons," Gregor said.

"I'll fight just to kill a few bastards, settle a few scores with the Order." Sefinn.

"Oh yeah, if I kill an inquisitor, I'll die happy." Olaf, with a grin.

Selene smiled, smile turning to a knitted frown of worry as she turned to her friend, her adoptive brother's—her love's—knight and mentor. The man whose opinion she valued above all others. "Leon?"

"How long until they arrive," he said. His heavy frown darkened his face in the firelight.

"Three months," Muselio replied. "Give or take. He says in the letter they go to Annalt first."

"To get more men?"

Muselio gave a weak shrug.

"Makes sense. The Annaltian knights are fearsome, and well-equipped. And Reynard will be a wily opponent. He got us in the back in Rennes, wiped out the entire Osbergian army."

"Who leads them?" Selene asked. "If there's anything you can count on, it's that imperial lords don't like taking orders from other lords."

"He says the pontiff has formed a Lord Council, with all the dukes. Said the Order leader is part of it too."

"Grand Inquisitor Vetterand," she said. "Bastard. I shouldn't be surprised. He's notorious for his brutality. It's said he's got a loyal dog that has a hundred werewolf heads under his belt."

"I think I'm gonna be sick," Dubine said. "I'm just a farmer."

"You'll be a soldier before the aestas is through," Leon said. "Don't worry, Sel." He nodded. "We'll be ready."

"Then we should return to Palerme as soon as we're ready."

Casimir clattered his crossbow onto the table next to her. "I'm coming with you." He preempted her objection. "No. I won't hear it. You think soldiers are going to stop at Palerme once they're done? A single castle satisfying twenty thousand men or more? I don't think so."

The Six Years War. He'd seen his fair share of death, likely given it as well.

"You're fighting for the wrong side, surely," she said. "We're demons and demon-lovers, didn't you hear?"

"I've fought for worthy causes and not-so-worthy causes. I'll fight to defend my home, and if I can put a wall between them and me," he said, twirling a bolt between his fingers, "I'm happy."

"Me too," Muselio said. "My oath is to protect the injured, protect my patients. If I must travel to Palerme if only to make sure your leg heals properly."

Selene nodded. "Very well."

"I'll fight too," Elias said. "If you'll have me." Everyone looked at him. "I've been wantin' my revenge on those northern bastards since Ostelar. And I think we stand half a chance if you demons are as strong as they say."

"I think your math is off a little on that," Muselio said.

"But we'll try," said Selene, before the conversation went too far into despondence. "We know the forest, and I know a few things about how the Order fights. We'll surround the forest with traps and pits, and let's see them bring their twenty thousand to bear."

.

CHAPTER 22
BEAST

TRIBUUM, 1045

Beasts only respond to aggression. You must meet tooth with
tooth, claw with claw.

— MASTER OF THE GROOM SCHOOL IN ISTRYA

T HE STALLION LOOKED READY to mount the nearest post, shaking its head, snorting, stomping, its engorged cock flopping about like an arm divorced of all its bones. Men struggled at the bridle, the reins, trying to keep the beast from bolting from the yard. Looked ready to kill, elsewise drag the men off their feet and jump off the castle walls looking for a mare to stab. There was a lesson in that, maybe. Don't want something so bad it costs you your life, perhaps. Or maybe there were things worth wanting more than your own life.

Richter liked to see the lesson in events—there wasn't much point elsewise. That was one detail he never forgot. Except his mission, of course. The lesson to be had in that was *the strongest will wins*. And his would be left the strongest, no matter what. He would make it so.

The air stank of beast, but beyond that stone and damp. On three sides of the yard, walls of thick gray blocks and limewash sweated in the lank air, sticking Richter's flaxen hair to his cheeks and neck. On the east side, through a grid of salt-crusted iron, splayed the city and its walls, and beyond that, a seething mass of men. The crusaders.

Looming down like a god removed from his subjects, the fortress had an enviable view and a vastly defensible position were the negotiations to break down. Whether it was a siege or not depended on Reynard's charity. But it looked like the city, with its unfettered access to the sea, could last a very long time. Perhaps longer than the patience of the crusaders.

It swelled Richter's chest with rage. Rage at the prince's reticence. How could he not see the point, even if his father wasn't really killed by a Palerme demon? Rage at the need. Surely, they could just take Palerme with the men they had? Though Richter found it easier to control his anger, easier than ever. Sigur had helped, the Screamer had helped more. Fixing on his mission, even further.

A slight delay. If needs must, he could slay the prince and throw open the gate for the pontiff, claiming the city in Sigur's name. Considering they were all too gleeful to use the emperor's death to their advantage, what was one prince?

A man of average height with salt-and-pepper hair stood at the rear of the yard, flanked by two guards in black and red, watching the proceedings. The prince, presumably. The Craving Count. Prince Reynard. A man whose ambitions reached beyond his station, even beyond the heights he stood already.

Four men in red surcoats and black jackets urged Richter onwards, halberds by their sides. As the two at the front spread out, the prince's eyes were drawn over and he clicked at a boy in a tight coif, who raced off. Red silk patterned with the gold lion of the imperial family draped over a well-muscled frame. What was it his son, Count August had said? *Prince of the Lion Throne?* Albrecht was still alive, just in exile. He was the heir.

The Craving Count.

These headaches of aristocracy sent his head pounding, his mouth dry. He nearly ran from the yard in terror of what the prince might have in store for him. Richter shuddered on the thought that perhaps he might ask him for the worst: a favor.

Politics, he thought, feeling like a buttermaid had churned his insides, and the rage left him through numb fingers.

"Inquisitor, well met," Prince Reynard said.

Richter bowed his head deeper than perhaps was serious, nearly bending double. "My prince."

Prince Reynard nodded, ignoring the exaggeration, or perhaps enjoying it. Either way, he kept a serious look about him. "I have many important meetings today, inquisitor, and I would appreciate some brevity. What should I call you?"

"Richter."

"Richter, Your August Highness," snapped a tall man behind Reynard who had seemingly appeared from nowhere. High forehead, broad nose, black hair oiled to the point of absurdity, to the point it almost dripped down his ears. Something about him was familiar, and he spoke with a republican accent.

"It's quite all right, Galeaz," the prince said. "I see you met my son, August. How did he treat you? Well, I trust?"

"Much better than I would treat a prisoner," he said. If August were a prisoner of his, he'd be lucky to walk away with all his limbs, if he walked away at all. "But I thought you wanted brevity?"

"*Some* brevity." He lifted a finger to punctuate the word. "I won't forgo the nourishing provender of conversation. I'm not some impatient hunting dog slavering after a pheasant."

No, you just prefer to test everyone else's patience.

Their conversation, what provender could be found, was dashed when the black stallion made a sound not unlike a roar and shoved over a groom. It pulled the remaining grooms onto their faces, skinned against the dirt, made them lose their grips on the ropes.

Reynard groaned as the beast ran for the portcullis. "Get that bloody beast under control!"

Two guards headed it off with their halberds, and the creature snorted violently, rearing, and brandishing its hooves. It turned, doubled back on the grooms. One of them was unlucky enough to be in the creature's path, and caught a hoof right in the face, turned the man's nose and jaw into pink mist.

Galeaz made a sound that could almost have been called gleeful.

The grooms caught the beast's ropes, bringing it bucking and snorting under control. Another man was brought forward, and at the pointy end of a halberd, ordered to take hold of the dead man's rope. Two of the guards dragged the corpse out of the yard.

Reynard worked his temple with a thumb and forefinger. "Vyahtkenese. Wonderous in a battle, deadly in combat. Equally as likely to kill the rider as the rider's opponent."

"Breaking a beast requires the strongest of wills," Richter said.

"Quite. You know this is but one of several scores of the creatures? My Alanian advisor found them in Avercarn, had them brought here once we returned from our glorious campaign in Ostelar."

Richter glanced at the Alanian, Galeaz. The man's vicious stare hadn't moved, hadn't broken, he realized, through the stallion's temper. He wondered if the stare would have the same effect if they sat plucked on the man's breathless chest or plopped in his mouth.

"Speaking of dogs," he said, "does your Alanian dog hold your chamberpot when you shit?"

The republican stepped forward and jabbed a finger into Richter's chest. "Ugly rat man, I should have you hanged."

"Step back, Galeaz," the prince said. He didn't seem like one to raise his voice, and the man stepped back, lowered his finger, cowed.

"Apologies, August Highness."

"It is the inquisitor's job to rile the interlocutor, let him spill his own secrets, correct?"

Silence, apart from the snorting, bucking stallion.

Reynard smirked. "Yes, I'm sure of it, now. But I see your point. Privacy is expeditious to good conversation. Galeaz, see to this. We will repair to a more private setting."

"But, my prince," he stuttered.

"Thank you, Galeaz." Reynard was already walking.

Richter followed. The cacophony of the yard faded through an archway revealing a close hallway marked with tapestries, so quiet he heard his heart pumping in his ears. Like a secret passage, a secret that if told could upset more than a few folk's ideas of the world. Candles in gold cradles cast deep orange light, and deeper shadows. Scenes of serene violence played out on the tapestries. A demon tore through a bored man, wolfen jaws tearing him in half. A king in full mail and a golden crown lanced an unbothered were-wolf through the heart. Everything was wildly exaggerated in proportion. Men were the size of castles, horses the size of three men, werewolves the size of five men. All dull-eyed, as though getting speared through the chest or getting eaten alive was just another afternoon's work.

"*Tabula Morgenensis*," he said in High Istryan. *Morning Tablet.* "Copied by Raphael from the original at the megalith in Prolia."

Richter shrugged. He never saw the appeal of a giant obelisk in the middle of nowhere and had even less desire to know what was carved into its surface. History was best left to stuffy clerics, but he did know that the Tablet was heresy, possessing it punishable by death.

As they walked along, he noticed the prince had an odd gait about him, a slight limp. An old injury, perhaps. Nothing that seemed to trouble him much, though. They came to the end of the hallway, and the dark stone opened out to a large alcove lined with tall, blazing candles burning high and bright. They illumed an enormous, unhinged mouth, demons, men, women, and children all falling into it as it swallowed the world and the sky.

Richter stared into the dark maw, a prickling feeling dancing across his neck. Felt like something evil, eviler than even his darkest actions, was staring back at him.

"The Great Devil, if you believe it," he said to the tapestry, then smiled. "I suppose you'll have me detained now for heresy."

"It's tempting, and I've done more for less."

"But you won't?" Silence. "Interesting. Why?"

"Because I would be a fool to think I would make it out of your castle, and because, I'm rather annoyingly attached to my companions, whom you still hold in your dungeons."

"They're not in my dungeons, Inquisitor," he said. "Do you think I'm a tyrant who throws his enemies in the deepest pits?" He smirked. "I'm no Sigurian."

"That, I could have you burned as a heretic for."

The prince seemed to understand his humor and laughed. "You are quite right. Let us begin, shall we?" He proceeded through a doorway at the other end of the alcove.

It opened out to a balcony, the sea breeze buffeting them as soon as they stepped outside. Brown seabirds wheeled across the sky in a great circle, the sound of waves plunging into the cliffside below, sending a spray of mist across the gray horizon. A black cloud lingered in the distance, like a predator biding its time.

Reynard came to the parapet, gestured over the wall. Richter leaned over. Nestled into small shelves in the cliffside were speckled shells poking out from kelpy nests. Among some of the nests, hatchlings lifted their shivering, weak necks, looking for food that didn't seem to be coming.

"Frost-tipped sealark," he said. "Native to the Sea of Martyrs. See their blue beaks?"

He sharpened his eyes on one and saw indeed that the birds had blue tips to their beaks, as though a crazed painter with a bird obsession had taken to them with a brush tip. They were remarkable in that they were completely unremarkably brown save for their beaks.

"There are only two nesting spots in the entire coastline. Here, and two miles north, or so my gamekeeper says."

"Is this a plea for clemency? You won't have the pontiff declare *Exterminatus* and attack the city because you're worried some birds might die? I've heard some calls for it, but this one takes the winner."

He laughed. "Eme's tits, no. The sealark leaves its young to fend for itself. The chicks become so hungry they usually eat each other, and the largest chick generally survives. I have a theory." He lifted a finger. "They do this because on the side of a cliff, with pounding waves and picky nesting habits, there's not much to be gained by having more competition, but there must be enough to continue the population."

Richter nodded, thoughts joining to each other. "They self-cull."

"Exactly." He grinned, showing rows of perfect white teeth. "We self-cull in our own way. The Order, the pontiff. But who should declare the judgment? Who holds the judge's staff?"

"I'm inclined to say whoever has the bigger staff."

"Then we agree." He sighed, looked out across the water. "I ask myself, was my father just another chick to be left in the cold, to be eaten by the bigger, to be broken by the stronger will, the bigger staff, as you said. By the Order."

Richter leaned on cold stone heavy with salt crust and dried bird shit. "I don't know what you mean."

"Come now. Why would a demon travel more than a thousand miles, surely knowing that if they just kept to themselves everyone would probably just forget about them, and kill the emperor? What did he ever do to them? If you're going to kill someone, why not the Grand Inquisitor? Pontiff Gottscheid?"

"You assume they're intelligent. They're not," he lied. In his experience, he'd met demons that were as crafty as an old general, as sly as a courtier, or as sharp as a swordsman. In fact, he'd hunted demons that held those very positions, and it had taken all his tenacity just to kill them.

"Still a detriment to your best bet of just being ignored, but they would at least be more sensible targets. My father was a Sigurite and was crowned by the pontiff but that's where the connection ends, in accordance with the Council of 322. And they are intelligent," he said with a lengthy pause and turned to Richter. "I'm aware of just how intelligent they are, firsthand."

"Is that so?"

"I know for a fact that the lady who leads them is as sharp as an Annaltian blade, and as shrewd as a republican dagger in the dark. She's no demon."

"You know her?" This piqued Richter's interest. He'd heard many stories about the woman, the inquisitor Diana who'd turned hide and betrayed her own kind. His neck itched at the mention of her.

"I met her once. Just before Ostelar fell. The Lady of Beasts." He sighed, wistful and reminiscent. "Charming woman. You remind me a lot of her. Ambitious, misguided. As it is, I don't think a person ever goes into the

Order if they're looking to get ahead in the world. Survive, maybe, but that's what they prey on. Vetterand and Gottscheid. The whole apparatus, perhaps."

For some untold reason, Richter felt his heart thump like a carpenter's hammer to an outstretched finger. "You're wrong. What's the point of this? *Brevity.* When can we go?"

"Fine, I'll cut to the quick. Stand beside me against my father's murderers, support my claim to the throne."

Richter barked out a laugh, nothing approaching mirth. "The Craving Count. Your brother is still alive, you realize. Your campaign in Osbergia failed."

"Did it, indeed? I own the conqueror's port, the landing that Istryan made on the Continent when he arrived more than a thousand years ago. Albrecht is a coward and a craven and will live the rest of his days in a bathhouse in Vallonia—if someone doesn't stab him in his guts before then. Heinrich has sired no boys, and all the barbers and healers in the world cannot make wood out of a wet noodle. Whereas I have three boys, one a very accomplished fighter already. I am the only sensible choice as heir. Alas, I cannot stand alone against this crusade, even with the might of Annaltian knights, not without a senior voice in the Order bringing the truth of things to light."

He paused. "I know, I know. I'm asking a lot, but think on it. If I am the emperor, I would have a great say in appointing the next pontiff. Do you want to be pontiff? Or Grand Inquisitor, perhaps? I can make that happen, even easier. What is your loyalty to them, anyway? You are the demon he sacrificed to the pyre, are you not? *Cured?*" He punctuated that last word like it was a crossbow bolt and it struck Richter in his soft bits.

"I— He—"

"I know not if there's a cure, and I know not how you survived. I'll leave that to the alchemists and the barber-surgeons to reckon. All I can say is that if a man I'm loyal to buried me in a pyre and burned me alive, I'd be burning for blood. If I'd survived, I'd want his head, his wife's head, his children's heads."

Silence. Richter burned inside, felt the same as when he burned for Vetterand and all those sycophants on the balcony in the Holy Fortress. Was that the lesson to be had from this? Loyalty was repaid with betrayal?

Richter extended a finger, pressed it against Reynard's chest. The prince winced. "He's secured this crusade. Because of him, there will be nothing left of Palerme. There will be nothing left of the demon, nothing substantial, anyway. The ground will be burned, soiled, and salted, so nothing ever grows. And anyone or anything that stands against him will be swept aside just as easily."

"Who, Vetterand?"

"Yes."

The prince's eyes sparkled with something like realization. "I suppose so, but we'll see who has the strongest will in the end. But it doesn't matter what I think. It matters what people believe. See, if I believe in anything, it's the power of the sword. You said it. The man with the bigger staff makes the rules. Might makes a man right, and this crusade will prove itself right in the end, I think. The victors name the tales, write the stories, and compose the songs, after all."

"That it will. Palerme will be nothing but a distant memory, until it's all forgotten."

"That's a shame, truly. But I do wonder if the Lady of Beasts will prove a worthy adversary. She knows all your secrets, all your tactics. She was a fine inquisitor if I ever saw one." He gave Richter a nod. "Among the best." He gestured to the doorway that took them back through the hall with the tapestries and smiled in conciliation. Near made Richter ill. "Stay a night. You don't have to give me your answer now. Dine with me."

"Do I have a choice?"

"Not if you don't want you and your fellows to get thrown into a dungeon and have hot pokers shoved under your tongues as spies."

"I thought you said that wasn't your thing?"

Reynard smiled. "I never said that. Just that I don't resort to that as the first course of action. I prefer the more refined way of... charming my enemies. I can retrieve the hot pokers if you wish?"

Richter sighed. "When's supper, then?" *Politics*, he thought, acid taste in his throat.

CHAPTER 23
POWER
TRIBUUM, 1045

*Dreams are often where the secret world emerges. Care what
you say there, for it may be used against you later.*

— APHE, THE MIND

S HE TOSSED AND TURNED restlessly when she returned to Palerme,
her broken leg splinted and placed on a pillow, the dark walls swelter-
ing with heat that seemed to follow their flight from Valenti. Just when she
felt a touch of hope, Tristain was there to haunt her again.

In the castle where he always haunted her. The castle where she lived,
from before she could remember. Until she ran. There, the paneled walls
sweated like lovers reunited, perspiration streaming into her eyes. Wood
creaked with her every breath, expanding to fill an outer space, then
shrinking inwards to fill the inner. Breathing with her. Flickering candles
bounced off the boards, off their faces, struck the plaster with a wan glow.

Tristain stood in the hallway where he'd always chased her as a demon.
He wasn't a demon now.

"I haven't seen you in a while," he said.

"I haven't thought of you in a while."

"That's a lie. I'm all wrapped up in your guilt about what happened, aren't I?"

Selene sighed. "Yes."

"It still seems to be that you're throwing yourself into this mess with the werewolves because of me."

"Maybe I am. Why do you care? You're dead."

"You can't change what happened. I chose my path and there's nothing you could've done about it."

He wore a fine doublet, like the day of the tournament, that same handsome young man she always remembered. But now there was a rigid confidence in the way he stood, the way he spoke. Like he knew he was right, and there was nothing Selene could do but accept his truth.

"You ought to do the best thing you can for yourself, and for your son. Let it go. The Order will forget about you eventually."

"You want me to run forever?"

"You know the werewolves don't stand a chance. Palerme is nothing compared to the might of the entire empire."

Selene sat on the enormous, carpeted stairs. They turned into the lee of the hill where she overlooked the field of tents earlier that day, outside the walls, the image falling into place. Tristain put his hand on the grass to balance himself as he sat next to her.

"You have to forgive yourself someday."

Selene didn't say anything, eyes on the field. Shining knights battled against each other in the lists, spurting with blood as they struck blow after blow against each other, though neither of them fell.

"The werewolves need someone to bind them. Someone who can lead them. Someone they can stand behind. I might not be the best choice, but I'm all they have. I'm the only one they all trust. Maybe one day, I can stand aside, let someone else take over. But not now. Not now. They'll all be killed. And I need vengeance. The Order took someone I loved, and they nearly took my son."

He exhaled happily and smiled, looked down as though remembering something. "Leon has taken you under his wing, you realize. You're the new me."

She laughed. "Yes, I noticed that." They laughed, and held hands, though it felt like nothing. Felt like touching air.

"Thank you," he said.

"What for?"

"For naming your son after me."

S ELENE WOKE, HER FACE wet from her pillow. She'd been crying. The dream faded as quickly as it seemed to arrive, and by the time she slid out to the edge of the bed, the details were fuzzy. She was careful not to hurt her leg or move it much, failing spectacularly. Wincing with pain, she picked the leg up and let it fall over the side of the bed, then sat up. She scraped together the semblance of a smile and called out for Ottille.

The woman entered with Trist in her arms, wrapped up in a bonnet and little linen shift, precious gray eyes staring back at her. His moon-like face, chubby with milk, deepened her smile.

"Hello," she cooed. "How are you, little one?"

The boy simply stared, his eyes quietly studying her. She'd missed him last night—he was asleep when she returned, though she visited him at his cot.

"At his age," Ottille said, "they can't tell people apart. Don't worry if he's not smiling. He knows his mother."

"I know." *He probably doesn't.* "Mind you, he probably thinks Galena is his mother. How is she finding it, anyway? I hope it's too much of a burden."

"It's alright. She's happy to do it, truly."

She grabbed the underside of one breast idly, thinking, hoping perhaps, that she might make something of them in response to his presence. But they were drier than a desert. "I don't know what I'd do without her." Tears nettled her eyes. She sniffed and turned back to them, held her arms out for him. Ottille handed him over and Selene stared deeply into his eyes.

"I love you," she said. "I love you more than anything. More than life itself."

Was that the hint of a smile at the corner of his mouth? Selene chuckled, the overwhelming urge to laugh and cry taking over, just an impossible love breaking over her like a vast ocean, unknowable yet familiar. "I will never let anything happen to you."

"He knows," Ottille said. She was quiet, and that moment of mother and son stretched out for a long time. A long look at each other. A calm understanding, a soft moment.

It wouldn't last. She looked up at Ottille, hearing now the murmurs of morning through the open shutters—sawing wood, crunching boots, idle chatter to start the day. Six hundred miles stood between Annalt and Palerme, about three months before the crusaders arrived.

"There's much to do today," Selene said. "Please, bring me my crutch."

Ottille gave Selene the length of wood, a cradle for her armpit, thick quilted layers of wool as cushioning. Selene put Tristain down on the bed and leaned, almost fell forward, and pushed up on her good leg to take the weight. It was intuitive enough for her to use, and relieved the issue of how she was going to not be bedridden for two months while the break healed.

"That barber's a sight better than most," the woman said. "If it happened in Triburg, you'd never walk again."

"Trained with some Saburrian master, the best on the Continent, apparently. I've learned much about Saburria in my time with him and Kyrah. How is our Alanian attachment, anyway?"

"She's... something." Ottille breathed out her nose. "I thought I was an early riser, but she was up before dawn, training with that sword of hers. She's quick. Quicker than someone using a sword of that size has any right to be. She's Althann, though, so maybe that helps."

"Maybe so. Did I tell you about Manus?"

"Your brother's experiment? The giant?"

Bann had done something with the Order's vast array of poisons and potions to Manus, turned him into a creature of superhuman strength. "I'm thinking now he might've been Althann, too. Bann only inhibited the transformation partially, unlocked some hidden potential."

Ottille shook her head, picked up Tristain as he started to fuss, and Selene reached out to stroke his cheek. She wondered if he might understand what they were saying. "Disgusting. It's not natural."

"No, it's not. The Order have much to answer for, and I will have my revenge, you can be sure of that. My brother had his own designs, but the Order let him do it. Vetterand knew what he was doing. He must've."

"The more I hear about this Vetterand, the more I hate him. And what about this rabid dog he has working for him?"

"He goes by many names, but I only know a few. Richter. The inquisitors spoke of him like he was a secret."

"Which tells you how vile he is."

Selene nodded. "As long as we keep our wits about us, and these promised mercenaries arrive, we'll be alright."

Ottille nodded and studied the babe. "Do you believe that?"

Yes. Maybe. It doesn't matter. It can't hurt to be prepared. "Do you promise not to tell a soul?"

"Yes, milady, of course."

"I had the miners dig a tunnel out from the mines, take them out the other side of the mountain. I told them it was just in case of cave-ins, but it's not just that. It's our escape. I knew at some point the Order might attack, just like they did to the people who lived here before. And this time, they would erase everything. They'd tear the castle to the ground, brick by brick. There'd be no quarter given. So, if it looks like we're going to lose the castle, we flee through the tunnel, and collapse it behind us."

Ottille laughed. "Practical as always, milady." Tristain giggled and Selene laughed.

"Did you just laugh? Did you just laugh?" The boy giggled again, the sound like music to Selene's ears.

E VEN IN THE LATE morning, with the sun over the mountaintops and breaking higher and higher as they spoke, the forest in front of the keep screened the light, cast them in perpetual twilight. Two hundred yards through tough ground to the castle walls, another four hundred from the road. An old path that swerved uphill and around trees, overgrown with ivy and sedge, was the only access to Palerme. It cut double, of course, screening any approach from the defenders.

"To properly assault the walls, though," Leon said, trailing an outstretched finger across the trees, "they'd have to advance through six hundred yards of old growth. And that's where Lady Selene comes in."

She moved forward, leaning on a trunk for support. The others leaned to hear her over the roar of cicadas in the trees. The forest stunk with life—fresh sap, new leaves, that heady, woody smell of old and new growth. She liked this place, from the moment she arrived. Giving up Palerme was the last resort. She'd do everything she could to save this place, everything to fight the empire.

"Pits with spikes, slathered in excrement. It's an old trick the Order uses—the fall breaks the leg, and the wound festers. Kills within days. We should dig trenches all across the approach to the keep. Felled trees, placed so battle lines can't be formed, and ladders can't easily be brought in front. It's too bad I don't have many poisons—they would've been perfect to put on bolt traps and spring traps. But we'll build them anyway, and I'll show you how."

She noted Gregor shifted uncomfortably. "What is it, Gregor?"

"Did you ever use them against werewolves?"

She saw no point in lying. Uncomfortable truths were better than comforting lies. "Yes. And I'm sorry for that, but I was only doing what I thought was right."

Some of them gave her sad looks. "Then I suppose it's good," Frix said, "that you're on the right side, now."

"I am." She adjusted the crutch. "Many of you would still be rotting in the Gray Citadel had I not saved you."

"Too right, Sel," Leon said. He gave her a firm nod.

"If it's all the same," Kyrah said, swiveling her sword by the pommel, the point on the ground, twisting up dead leaves with each turn. "I'll do my own thing."

Selene scraped her tongue against her teeth. "What would you suggest?"

"The Order might be fanatics, but lords are just as likely to kill each other as march alongside each other. Their spines would break at the slightest pressure. I suggest we assault them on the road, sneak attacks at night. A few of us can get in, kill a few, set fire to their wagons and supplies. An army that size needs lots of food." This drew many nods and murmurs of agreement.

"That's..." She couldn't rightly come up with a reason that wouldn't work. "It'll be dangerous though. If they catch you—"

A flinty smile. "They won't."

"Still, only those that volunteer, and only three of you."

All of them shot up their hands. Even Ottille. "I want some payback," she said. "The Order killed my mother. It's time they knew fear."

"You know the risks, Ottille. What about Sanna?"

This gave her pause. Selene didn't mean to use the girl against her, it just came out that way. She had a tendency of putting her foot in her mouth. Selene looked up. Bright finches flitted between branches, rustled leaves. Ants made their home in the bark of the old oak she leaned on. A hummingbird hovered around a nearby pine, getting at the different angles of attack for the best insects. This place teemed with life, and she wondered if any of the animals here would even notice their absence.

Ottille slowly lowered her hand, looked down in shame. "You're right."

Gregor and a few more, those that had children in the castle, put their hands down. The cook, Dunstad, lowered his hand as well.

"Dunstad?"

"We need food, milady. Someone needs to cook. And I won't leave Rani," he said, squeezing the woman tight. They were a pair, nearly inseparable, worked in the kitchens together. If there ever was an example of opposites attracting, it was them. He was short and squat, while Rani, on the other hand, was tall and lean, with a rounded chin and bright blue eyes that seemed to be looking past them all at some secret hidden behind the world.

"I appreciate that," Selene said. "Well, I've no desire to argue because your plan is sound, Kyrah. I'm placing a lot of trust in you, though, and you've only just met us. If anyone trusts Kyrah's plan that much, then I'm happy for her to decide who she should take."

Most of them nodded. "She's just another target for the Order," Frix said. "That mob at the duca's palace wasn't asking questions."

Selene's stomach sank. *Not you, Frix.* Of all of them, she wanted him to go the least, but it seemed to be heading that way.

"I'd take Sefinn and Olaf," Kyrah said. "They fought well in Valenti. And Frix, too, if he'll come. I won't take anyone that has children or a wife. No, no one'll miss us when we die."

"I'll stay," Frix said.

"No," Selene said. "Go. It makes sense. The three of you are our best fighters."

"Wouldn't it make sense to keep one of 'em back, milady? If they're so good?" Gregor raised a good point.

"Am I not wrong, marine, that the better the fighter the better the chance of success?"

Kyrah nodded. "Aye. Us four can bring chaos to the army." She elbowed Sefinn. "I'll have to teach you how to be sneaky. And when to keep your mouth shut."

Sefinn laughed. Already they were getting along, the three cousins and the Saburrian. It was nice to see, though Selene had her doubts that Kyrah's best options were all their best options, that she had their best interests at heart. *I've scraped for everything I have.* Someone like that, with a past like hers, often ran at odds with others when it came to her survival. Selene knew everything about that. From her first werewolf kill, at the *Velitore*, where she'd sacrificed that novitiate to take the beast by surprise, and since then.

Until now. Now she had everything to live for, everything to keep safe. It wasn't just her she had to look out for anymore.

"Alright. Leave by sundown," she said. "Take the back roads and cut across fields. The Order has spies everywhere."

"Yes, milady," Frix said, a hint of something wistful in his voice. If she didn't know better, she thought maybe he was having doubts about leaving. *Maybe I ought to see him before he goes.*

She adjusted herself in the crutch. Her good leg got stiff sometimes from supporting her entire weight for so long. "The rest of you start digging. We have three months, and I'd rather not rely on skirmishes to destroy them. Even if nine-tenths of their army was to desert, that's still far more than I would like to come against unprepared."

CASIMIR PLACED THE CRATE of red on Rill's drawing table, on a spare space that wasn't taken up by rolls of scrawled-on paper. Measurements, diagrams, some metal instruments, a length of charcoal and white chalk dust piled on almost every inch of the trestle table. Rill himself chipped away at a block of gray stone with a hammer and chisel, leaving it perfectly flat on all sides. Selene hadn't a clue how he did that, but the effect was uncanny, and left her feeling a bit untalented for the comparison.

"A case of Alanian red, as promised," she said.

"Aye, very well, good lady," he said. He had the accent of an Ostelarish, she now realized, though a lowborn one. "The build is well, though I wish I had my old crane. I've had to make do with Trestinsen and Gregor's sons while the father was in Valenti, and a few old boards."

"Those blocks must be heavy."

He slapped the top with a solid *thwap*. "Takes three men just to lift her, and if she falls on your foot, you're not walking for a while, if ever again." He turned. "Ah, apologies, milady. Perhaps a touch soon for jests."

She chuckled. "Not at all."

His brows knitted. "There was one thing. I found there was a slide of the lord's tower, at some point in its history. Part of the tower's given in, and they've fixed her, but she's a touch unstable. I'll have to reinforce the base again, otherwise she's liable to fall in on us all, bury milady in a mountain of stone."

"Very well. What does that mean for the repairs?"

"Nothing, milady. It'll just take another few weeks. There'll be a weakness on one part of the wall, as well."

"A weakness?"

"Not a structural one, but a... what do they call it, a military one?" He stroked the thick white moustache hanging over his lips. Pulled it hard enough it looked like it might rip out if he did it much longer. "There's a pile of rubble that's fallen over the wall. Anyone could climb it and get into the lord's tower."

"That's not good."

"Yes, milady. No, it's not. It'll take months to clear since it's all stone and mortar and the mortar's calcified in the rains."

"What can we do about it?"

He offered a light shrug. "Hope the soldiers don't find it?"

"That's hardly reassuring. And we need everyone at the front, where they're likely to advance from. We could post a detachment of the Thousand Sons there. Could we build the walls higher?"

He screwed up his mouth. "Perhaps a wall out of stakes, but stone is only as good as its foundation. That pile of rubble is too misshapen and unstable to build anything on." He ran his palm along the flat of the freshly carved stone, the dust covering the floor in waves. "I won't do it. Get another mason if you must, but you'd be puttin' your faith in something that's likely to crumble at the lightest sneeze, let alone a cannon stone."

"How do you get them so flat?" It looked impossible, and yet masons had been doing it ever since there was stone and chisels.

He raised gray, bushy brows, surprised that Selene had taken an interest. She surprised herself, but when survival depended on the stability of their walls, it wasn't such a stretch.

"Years and years of practice. I was apprentice to my father, who taught me everything I knew." He stroked the block with a lover's caress. "It's all about finding the right angle, hitting the right grain, breaking it just right. It's all about the right amount of force, too. Too much, and it'll shatter. Too little, and it won't break right. It'll crumble, and you don't want that."

"There's probably a lesson in that for us all," she said. "Have Trestinsen and the others build the palisade, and we'll have to just keep them occupied at the front, so they don't get the chance to look around the back."

"Yes, milady."

She turned to the ostler as they left and grimaced. "How do you fancy your chances? Regret putting your faith in us?"

He leaned on the wall. The mason's hut stood at the rim of the bailey, the sounds of hammering from the forge ringing out. Frix and the others splashed mud under their shoes. It rained the night before and the yard milled with so many people that it flecked at the edges with foam. She'd have to ask Rill how to fix that, so someone didn't slip. One broken limb among them was bad enough.

"I told you I fought in the Six Years War, right?"

Selene nodded.

"In Prolia, there's a fort—disused now—called the Throat Cutter. The duca posted our platoon there as a skeleton garrison since we were on the back lines of the fighting. But the Vallonians went around the Badonnians and the Malatestans, heading straight for Malatesta. The Throat Cutter was the only thing standing between five thousand men and the sack of the city. See, there's a pass that takes you through the Cartenusia, funnels you right into the path of the Throat Cutter. Twenty of us held it against the Vallonians for three weeks, in harder conditions than this. During bruma, so it was nonstop rain. The cannons wouldn't light, so they were forced to bring up ladders. I must've killed… oh, five hundred men by myself." He snorted, rubbed his nose. "Worst part was, they were just things to kill by the end. Weren't even human."

"So, you're saying that we'll be fine?"

"I'm saying that by the end, you won't even recognize yourself."

Selene glanced around. The others were returning from the forest, many of them covered in dirt, shovels in hand. By bruma, they'd have much more than mud on their clothes. How many of them would balk against those odds? The coming odds? Would she cower and run, too?

"How did you keep your nerve? Five thousand must've looked like the entire world had come against you few."

He raised a hand, meaty fingers thick with hair. It trembled. "Who says I did? I'm scared now, and I was scared then. But it was fight or die. There was no escape. Now I fight for Sesar and Delia. Don't underestimate that. If a man sees no other way out, he'll fight like a rabid dog to survive."

She was curious, now. *Delia must be his wife.* "And how many of you survived the Throat Cutter?"

"Only me."

A SLICK SHEEN OF exhaustion stuck her hair to her face as she made her way to the storeroom under the keep. It was cooler down here, for all the mercy that was worth, but her state meant Ottille had to help her everywhere, propped under her good arm. The serving woman had her narrow face fixed forward, shoulders bunched, taking great care with each step. It took all their effort to balance with three good legs on the smooth stone, like some skittery, lumpen creature. It was then that Selene summoned the courage to speak, and after everything, didn't feel so hesitant in doing so.

"Ottille," she said, "how are you?"

"I'm... alright." Her eyes didn't fall on Selene's, so it was hard to tell. Her voice was level. "It's interesting. I should be scared, but truly, I've never felt better. After what they did to my mother, it's finally a chance to settle the debt."

"Good, I'm glad." Selene breathed. "You mean the Order, right? I think the kids didn't know anything about their father. If he even is their father."

"Of course." She chuckled. "I'm not a child murderer. Not like their father."

At the bottom of the stairs, the wall pulled back to reveal a small chamber lit but dim and claustrophobic, and it was behind the iron door at the back that they kept the children. Selene took a moment to reflect, and felt as though iron determination pushed her now, and not vengeance. As though she knew she was the only one that could do this.

"Open the door."

Ottille nodded and Selene plodded closer. The iron door swung back with a creak. Inside, the young boy, Roland, sat on his sister Lorela's lap. They looked up as she entered, their eyes watchful and cautious, ending their chatter. They were playing some game, by the looks. A wooden figure that belonged to Roland, a knight on horseback. A common kid's toy.

A crate sat next to the door, stuffed with jars of preserved fruits and lamb meats. Their one victory from the last harvest. Selene lowered herself with her good leg, pushing out with the splinted one, the wood scraping across the smooth stone floor. The effort bunched up her hip, turned them into a cluster of raw nerves nearly to match her knotted shoulder, worse than ever. It took all her might not to wince.

"Are you well?" she asked, speaking calmly like one would approach a wounded dog. "Have you eaten enough?"

The girl, Lorela, nodded. She'd put on some weight, Selene realized. Her hips had rounded out and her cheeks were broader, lips fuller, hair darker and thicker. A woman, by all regard except her age. A target, if Palerme were to be sacked. Selene thanked all the gods that Sanna was too young yet for that.

"My father—"

"We're sorry," the boy said. He still had the high-pitched voice of the young, though he'd be in his changes soon, a man in no time at all. Tristain would be like him soon enough, on the cusp of manhood. "To us, he was just our father. But he wasn't our real father."

"He wasn't a merchant, was he?"

"No."

"Why didn't you tell us?"

"We were scared," Lorela said. "He said he would hurt us if we told the truth."

"So, you would let a baby die instead?"

"We had no idea! He just told us we were going to Palerme, so we listened."

"Truly?"

Ottille said, "Selene, they're scared, but they're telling the truth."

"I know." She drew a knife. Even now, she carried them, though she would've been next to useless in a fight. Maybe that was why she carried them. She offered it to them. Lorela put her brother aside and walked up, took the hilt in gentle fingers.

"Next time someone promises to hurt you," Selene said, "hurt them right back. Power comes from the cowardice of others. If you stand against them, and you come armed, they might back down."

Lorela nodded.

"If they don't, you can't be afraid. Don't be afraid to kill, and then no one will ever have power over you again. Power is simply indomitable will: the strength to see your vision of the world and make it a reality." She wasn't sure if she was saying it for herself more than them.

The children looked at each other. "I can do that," Roland said, bunching his fists. "I will kill when it's time. We don't have to be afraid anymore, sister."

CHAPTER 24
HEART OF FIRE
TRIBUUM, 1045

Very little is known of the many subforms the lycanthrope can take, but what is often the case is that the lycanthrope's primal form takes on qualities of emergent personality of the lycanthrope in human form. A blacksmith I tortured, for instance, had much tougher and thicker arms than I'd seen in others, and used them as weapons more so than his claws or teeth.

— GRAND INQUISITOR ULRICH VETTERAND

FRIX AND KYRAH, AND his two cousins, stood at the open gates, the threshold to the wilderness and the winding, ivy covered road that led to the coast road, and a boundless Continent after that. But here, Palerme was their mountain home, a sanctuary in the forest, and Selene thought it would be a tragedy if she didn't farewell them. Leon and the others came to watch.

They talked and laughed as Selene hobbled over. Frix unlaced his jerkin, Kyrah doing the laces at his sleeve. She said something Selene couldn't hear, and they both chuckled. Frix wasn't hers, of course, but the thrusting of this fair, confident woman into their midst drove like a wedge into her lungs. A wedge of jealousy. She was everything Selene wasn't. Had been, once, but not anymore. That stung more than if she hadn't ever been a match in the first place.

They bowed their heads. "Milady," Frix said.

"Lady Selene," Kyrah said.

It was nearly nightfall. Setting out now gave any spies in the woods hard task of seeing their departure, and their Althann form had no issue seeing in the dark. "How goes the preparations?"

It was strange to see them undress. She expected to see soldiers going off to battle, armoring themselves in mail and plate and helmets, but in a way, they still were. Armoring and arming themselves, just in their primal way.

Frix snorted. "Truth be told, I've prepared more to go to the privy."

Kyrah stripped down to her shift. She slung a satchel of rations over her head—the preserved meats from the storeroom, along with some goods that the duca had given them. The satchel hung low around her, down to her calves.

"If we're lucky, we can find game to eat along the way. But we shouldn't be gone that long. Maybe two weeks." She grinned evilly. "As long as these pricks here can keep up with me."

Frix raised a brow. "Oh, you think you can keep up with me?"

A war consumed Selene's heart. Part of her still remained the hunter, the woman driven by vengeance, but now another part of her wanted to build something for Baby Tristain, since the entirety of her life had been fraught with so much destruction. Funny that it took a broken leg to realize the extent of her longing. Maybe Frix could be part of that when he returned.

After they defeated the empire's army. If.

She touched Frix's arm, then took her hand away awkwardly when he looked. "Please be safe. All of you. You know what the Order will do if they catch you."

"Aye, milady." This darkened their mood. "We'll take it seriously. I'll keep my cousins in line, don't you fret."

"If he doesn't," Kyrah said, "I will." She slapped Olaf around the neck as he scratched his bearded chin.

"What was that for?" he shouted.

"You were thinking," she said. "Leave the thinking to me."

"Aye, sir. Shit…"

Perhaps Olaf didn't realize just how hard a taskmaster Kyrah would be or was just realizing it now. But there was still the problem of her loyalties. "I need to speak to Frix alone," Selene said gently. "Don't worry, I won't keep him long."

"Aye, milady."

They went behind the stable, the horses softly nickering; Roland, now the groomsboy, settling them for bed. The patter of feet and hooves muffled their conversation. "What is it, milady?"

"You can call me Selene, please."

"Of course. Selene." He tried the word, let it fill his mouth.

"What do you think of Kyrah's plan?"

"It's sound, mi—Selene. If we can get in and out without detection, which Kyrah seems to think we can do, and cause havoc, it'll be a boon to our efforts. If she's to be believed, the army might even disband."

"I think that's hopeful, and we should be ready, regardless. I'll feel better when the mercenaries arrive." She leaned on the fresh-hewn logs of the stable's rudimentary construction. Solid, nothing fancy, it served its purpose well, and would stand for many more years. *Something for all of us.*

She looked in his eyes, now. They were bright and green, even in the twilight. "Do you trust her?"

He chuckled. "Are you jealous?"

Her cheeks flushed with embarrassment, and she hoped to all the gods that he couldn't see it in the evening light. "No—I..." She looked away quickly. "She's loyal to Alberracin."

"The duca might pay her wages but she's Althann, through and through. That's not a bond you can easily forget. It's... almost been forgotten that she works for the duca. She seems as committed to the defense of Palerme as any of us." He touched her shoulder, her good one. "I feel an affinity for her, a kinship. Nothing more."

"Please..." A feeling she'd long strangled burst to life, like a heart of fire in her chest. It scared her, and she wouldn't stoke it. She smothered the feeling as soon as it came, shrugged his hand off. "Try not to get killed. I need all the soldiers I can get in the coming fight."

"I won't." A look of concern flashed across his face, disappeared as soon as it arrived.

She took a shallow breath in, held it for a few moments, then breathed out. "Good luck."

They went back out to the gates, and Kyrah laughed. "Were you two fucking back there?"

"No!" they both cried. They looked at each other, red embarrassment bright on their faces.

"Too bad. I need clear heads."

She closed her eyes and took off her shift, hunched over, groaned, then her change took hold. Her midnight skin erupted with fur, and she turned tall and broad—even taller and broader than usual, her breasts flattening into huge mounds of muscle and hair. The satchel around her neck pulled tight. Her strongly curled hair shot back into a mane as black as the deepest pits of hell. It reminded her of Tristain—when she'd hunted him, he'd been as black. But Kyrah had a different gait about her, now that her limbs changed into forms better suited for an apex predator, hanging low about her powerful thighs. She had a confidence, an agility contained in her firmly bound muscles. Something primal.

The others transformed, but none of them looked nearly as fearsome for the comparison.

Something in Selene believed now that whatever Kyrah set her mind to would be done, no way around it. It made her believe they'd all make it home.

ON THE FOURTH DAY after their flight from Valenti, and two days from Frix's departure, the two men, Jakob and Rudi, died from their wounds. No one, not even Elias missed them, but Selene gave them a proper burial anyway. The pyres burned the stench of charred meat over the castle, the easterly wind blowing the smoke back over them. It hung heavy with the question of what to do with Elias, their friend.

What she'd mistaken as the sharp eyes of a killer were the eyes of a scared man, at heart. Colored by the violence she expected, they were nothing but the watchful, needling eyes of a coward. But a coward and an opportunist, and by his own admission, he'd done nothing and sat by as his friends killed Osbergian refugees on the road, for their gold, their jewels, or just for fun.

"I've done my fair share of killing," he said. He leaned on the wall at the bottom of the oubliette, that shaft in the ground, looking up, while Selene looked down on him. Their other prisoner lingered somewhere in the black, that space yawning with the decision of what was to be done with that one. The air chilled her neck, sent shivers down her spine. She didn't like being down here, much. "There's only so many times you can make excuses to men like Jakob and Rudi."

His eyes stared far off, as though remembering every person he'd ever killed or seen killed.

"The punishment for murder and brigandage is death," Selene said, unsatisfied at the prospect. Revenge sat well for her, and she'd imagined bringing ruin to the Order for what they'd done, killing every single one of them. But this man seemed hardly deserving of that rage, that deep core feeling that she held in her heart, had made her heart. A heart of fire, burning all that came near. Even Baby Tristain would be burned eventually, she knew.

"I know." The brigand looked down in shame. "I didn't feel good about any of it, if that helps."

She let his words linger and Leon lowered a rope to him, looped it around his waist. She approached the stairs and let Ottille hold her about the underarms, readied herself to climb these cursed stairs again. Readied herself to experience pain. After all, it was a reminder that she was still alive.

It was strange. Given everything, how could she forget that pain and blood and loss were a part of her, just as much as the Althann. Werewolves split their flesh where it wasn't meant to be split, just like her. She was as unnatural as them—by human standards, anyway. Perhaps it was ordained—this was the blessing of the werewolf god that blessed them all. The awful pain experienced during Trist's birth was only one part of it, while the placenta was another, one that meant consuming what sustained him in the womb. That meant a speedier recovery from his birth, but it was just more blood for her to endure. The loss of her arm, a lesson in pain taught by her father. Not her real father, of course, but that hardly mattered. Family, pain, and vengeance. Three things present always in her life, in her heart. It was a mark of her life.

She didn't deserve to bring Frix into that. Little Trist hardly deserved it either.

"YOU HAVE CONFESSED TO murder and brigandage, grave crimes that deserve the gravest of penalties. Though we do not recognize the law of the empire here," Selene said in front of them all, in front of the makeshift gibbet, "these are things we cannot abide."

She turned to Elias. Leon looped the rope around his neck, while Roland readied the gray mare, now reshod. The rope had been thrown over a beam of the stable, the only place in the center of the castle where his punishment would be seen by all. All the groomsboy would need to do was give the horse a shove, and the man would be lifted into the air.

Selene's guts churned. Another man's death on her hands, one that felt remorse for his actions. But he had to answer for everything he'd done. And then, deeper than all of that, Selene had to make it clear what the punishment was for such grievous crimes. Make it clear to them.

She looked at him. A resigned sadness in his dark eyes, but there was nothing more to his face. No fear, no shame. It was as though everything in his life had come to this point, and he'd been at peace with that. "Do you have any last words?"

"If I can ask one last favor: give my ashes to my mother. She lives in Invereid, on Rosin Street."

Selene nodded. "Alright." She glanced at Roland, who gave the horse a push, and Elias's feet were lifted into the air.

He bobbed and swayed, his face turning red, his mouth reaching for air that could never get to his lungs. Selene held her breath in turn, as though she couldn't breathe while he swung there, like a beautiful marionette. Silence plunged on the yard, the only sounds his labored grunts. He turned bright purple, then, and jerked out with his legs a few more times, then stopped.

"It is done—"

A whistle pierced the gloom, shattering the silence as easily as thin glass. Trestinsen, shouting from the curtain wall. "Men! Coming! Thousands of them!"

Selene looked at Leon and Ottille in turn. Lungs punched by fear, her voice came weak. "Prepare arms!" She cleared her throat. "Prepare arms!"

Althann transformed, their clothes tearing to make way for monstrous forms, Gregor and Ottille among them. They raced off, scaled the stairs, and mounted the walls. Selene hobbled over to Leon as he ran over to her. "Here? Now?"

"It can't be. They're months away. Wouldn't Frix and Kyrah have returned?"

"Unless—"

"No, it's not possible. Surely, we would've had some warning. What of the traps?"

How is this possible? How did they avoid our traps?

"Doesn't matter," she said. "Just get everyone to the walls and direct the defense. Go, now."

She climbed the steps, one by one, excruciatingly slowly. Casimir and Sesar passed her on the left, the loading winch hanging off the father's belt clattering with each stride. The crossbow had earned a new oiling, and new furnishings, by the looks of it, the metal glinting in the morning light.

She breathed hard as she made it to the top. Looking down on the small clearing at the front of the gate, she saw now that an army had indeed arrived, but it wasn't the army they expected. It was, in fact, the army there to help them.

The broad man at the front wore a huge, fur-trimmed cloak that trailed far behind him. He stroked his long auburn mustache as he peered up at her, giving him the look of a statue of an old general. His cloak draped over a breastplate, while a wide, floppy hat fell over his eyes, bright cock feather sticking from its top. He drew the hat from his head and bowed with a flourish, revealing short-cropped red hair.

"Captain-General Salvio Giustiniani de Regia," he said, accent so strong it threatened to knock her from the wall. "You are Lady Selene, are you not?"

"Yes, I am."

"My *campanero* here has told me of the locations of your little... presents." He waved at one of them still preparing the traps out by the road. He looked a little worse for wear, bleeding from the mouth. "He didn't want to tell us. But I can be very charming, as you will find out, my lady."

She couldn't deny a little thrill zip up her spine. This man was more dangerous than he appeared at first glance, and she needed to be careful.

"Will you invite me inside your walls, my lady? Or shall I be forced to keep shaking in my boots at the sight of your defenders?"

She noted he didn't balk at the sight of twenty Althann, brandishing claws and teeth sharper than any blade.

"Well met, General Giustiniani. Our holdings will not serve all of your men, I'm afraid. Our walls will explode should we invite all of you inside." Men disappeared into the trees, stoic faces and stoic weapons winking murder through the canopy.

"As though a cannon had done with it," he said broadly and laughed generously. *Ominous.* "Of course. Only me and my fellow captains will meet with you, and we will discuss our arrangement."

CHAPTER 25
MARROW AND BONE
TRIBUUM, 1045

*Impalement is among the worst of the punishments that the
Order of the Golden Sword levies on heretics and apostates. A
skilled impaler can keep the punished alive, in immense pain,
for weeks. I have performed such a feat myself.*

— APOSTATE LORISTIN

RICHTER SLURPED THE MARROW of a bone, sucked the meat from
a thigh, chewed the gristle from a hoof. He was eating it too fast
to really take it all in. Didn't matter much if it was pig, cow, sheep, horse,
or even dog. He didn't care. All he knew is that it tasted better than the
hard salted meat, unsalted hunted pheasant, and moldy bread he'd had for
the last month. Soups, pastries, pastries in soups, and sad heads of various
animals floated around, a furious dance of plates. They knew how to eat as
the city stood on the edge of burning.

And didn't they know it. There was that sharpness he'd noticed, where
men talked too loudly, women laughed too loudly, and all around the
wine flowed as easily as the debauchery. *Nothing like imminent death to
lower one's standards.* A woman in red silk danced her way across the floor,
spilling wine from her cup as she twirled to the applause of a group of

nobles. Even the guards took part in the festivities, though what they were celebrating slipped Richter's mind. Almost as though they celebrated their own grisly demises at the end of a spike or a pyre.

He finished one plate, and another took its place. Wine filled his cup, though he didn't partake. Drinking in the company of companions just as likely to be excommunicated and burned as you were, was one thing. These people had no loyalty, or at least their share of equal danger should they drink. In fact, Richter wasn't sure these people had even heard of the word *loyalty*, or the word *danger*, for the matter.

"You know they're going to burn you all," he said, fingering a chicken pie. They didn't bother to listen, not that they could over the blare of the longhorns of the Annaltian tradition. Longer than a man, each string of blasts, indistinguishable from the rest, rang out for… everything, it seemed. Firsts, seconds, thirds, between meals. Start of the meal, end of the meal. Someone farting. Someone shouting. Richter had heard better noise from pigs squealing as they emptied their balls. Just when he'd thought he couldn't be surprised, that he'd seen everything the world had to offer, a fucking longhorn does him in.

Aside from the noise, the room was pleasant. A great dining hall of some note, it was all gilded edging, carved stone, fine carpet. Portraits of important people, or at least people rich enough to have their portraits done, hung from the walls. Richter didn't quite know what it was about rich people and shiny things, but they were drawn to them like crows, or idiots. *I suppose we all are, in a way. But it is as the Book says, 'take possession of your worldly gifts, for you cannot take them beyond.'* That was it. They were all pious here. *My mistake.*

He sat near the middle of the table at the head of the room, on a raised dais, Count August to his right, some soft-fingered arsehole to his left. He wondered who the man seated lower in importance to an Order inquisitor

was, then decided he didn't care. These people had no idea what was waiting behind the façade of nobility and high breeding. No idea of brutality,
of murder. It was true, they'd probably had some blood on their hands,
but none of them truly knew what it was to scrape and claw their way to
survival. He wondered if that would change in the coming days.

Richter's companions sat at the other end of the hall, at the end of the
long table, behind a sea of swimming faces. Fehling caught his eye and
smiled. She wore her hair differently, some fashion that covered the curved
scar across her scalp. She didn't look so sickly pale, either. *Is she wearing
makeup?*

As the earsplitting horn blasts eased, the soft-fingered asshole in black
silk made the mistake of engaging him in conversation.

"Gracious inquisitor, I wondered if you might intercede on my behalf,"
he said.

He'd been to enough dinners and sat at enough fine tables to know that
most people dreaded a conversation with him. A man who judged every
word, held it to the light of scrutiny, made sure it was pious, didn't make
for a great dinner companion.

"Are you sure about that?" Richter replied.

"Quite sure. See, the comtessa here has my balls in a bind."

"Comtessa?" *A southern title, here?*

An elegant woman, the man's younger by half, had turned to face them
in her chair. She wore a collar of lace that parted around her tanned chest,
skin like poured honey, and as smooth moreover. Her fingers danced along
the table, long and slender. She extended her hand, for Richter to shake it,
presumably.

"Comtessa Alana de Legíon," she said in a thick republican accent. "A
pleasure."

He took her hand. "A Prolian, in Annalt? You picked a shitty time to visit." He held her hand a moment longer than was proper, noticed the ring on her index finger. It could hardly be missed. A sapphire the size of her thumbnail and as fat sat on top of it, probably cost more than the entire set of jewels hanging from the princess consort, who snoozed to the left of the prince, despite the noise. She was as still as a rock when the horns blasted to thunderous cheers.

"*Si*, I have some business I must attend to, then I will return." Her Annaltian was perfect.

Finalizing her business in Annaltia before the city is put to the torch? Clever.

The man in black silk leaned forward. "A woman of high education, high breeding, and she handles her own business? You are a dove among pigeons."

"You flatter me," she said, cheeks pinking. Richter had heard enough honeyed words to know when someone was lying. And to force her cheeks to blush on command? That took skill. *She'd be a good agent.* Agents of the Order embedded themselves in high courts across the land, and were unknown even to most inquisitors, since their jobs might require them to intercede in ways that might be considered damaging to the Order or the church, at least in the short term. They all reported to High Notarius Gian Adalla, a grim man who at least had the good grace not to join the crusade.

"And what do they call you, Inquisitor? Or can you not tell me?"

Demon. Killer. Monster. "Richter."

The man clapped his hands like a trained monkey you might find in the markets of Valenti. "Then answer me this, Inquisitor Richter. I believe that the division of body and soul is essential to life after death. Whether it's the Golden Halls or unity or bliss or whatever the Veles worshippers believe, whichever god graces you, must take something from you when you die. I believe that's the soul."

"Where I believe," the comtessa said, pointing a finger to the heavens, or at least the gilded plasterwork on the ceiling, "that the body is no agent of its own, and there is no division, because the body is just a case for the mind—the soul—to inhabit."

"I've no doubt that the comtessa is right in some regard, as am I. I am willing to consider a third option, though?"

"I see your problem," Richter said. "You're confusing me with someone who cares. These are cleric problems."

"Cleric problems? These are questions for our time. We may never know until the day we reach our ultimate fate, but isn't it fun to question?"

He stabbed the table with his eating knife. "Fun? You want to know what I think? I think I've seen enough dead bodies in my lifetime to know that there's no such fucking thing as the soul. The gods don't care a shit about the Comtessa de Legíon nor you, nor me. How's that for fucking fun." He hadn't meant to yell that bit. Gods, his head was aching. *Politics*, he thought with a groan.

"Excuse us, Inquisitor," the man said. "We didn't mean to disturb you."

"Yes, excuse us," the comtessa said, then, "*arse-tonguing goat-fucker*," she whispered in Prolian.

He slumped forward, cracked his neck, then got to eating again. The younger version of the prince whispered next to him, to the true article.

"Does he have to sit with us?" Count August said, sneering. Lamb shanks dripped brown sauce onto a trencher before him, though he'd barely touched them. The wine had no trouble going down though, Richter noticed. He was younger than he seemed in the forest, at the head of a band of murderers, and visibly swayed in his chair. Funny that a man can project strength among his fellows but look weedy and unprepossessing on his own. Well, a boy, really, in his teens.

"And why did you give him a knife? He's just as likely to use it on the duke as the piled meat on his plate."

"I prefer to use my fingers," Richter replied, waving a greasy digit in their direction. He didn't specify whether it was for the duke or the meat.

"Come now," the prince said. "We must find common cause on a day like today. May Eme herself shine down on us for our conciliation and friendship."

"Gods know you need all the help you can get. Because when that army comes crashing through your walls, and they will, you'll wish you had a god on your side."

August snorted and stood, threw his chair back. "I demand justice for that remark!" The prince scowled at his son.

The duke, the one Richter had insulted, laughed. "Can an Order inquisitor even be challenged to a duel?"

Richter spoke low. "I take all comers."

"Sit down," Reynard said. The prince went to say more but was interrupted when the republican Galeaz reached over the table on the prince's left and said something in his ear. He nodded.

"Very well." The color had rushed from his face, leaving him as white as a ghost.

His son sat back down. "What is it, Father?"

"His Most Holy Pontiff Gottscheid will meet with us on the morrow." Reynard swiveled the point of his eating knife and fixed his eyes on the room. Jaw set hard. "To talk terms."

August deflated visibly. "I see. What terms?"

"All our knights must swear fealty to the Lord Council and their holy army, otherwise they'll declare us enemies of Sigur and pronounce *exterminatus* on Annalt."

"Lord Council? What tripe. *Exterminatus?*"

"They'll kill every one of you," Richter said. "Not just that. They'll impale you on spikes and burn you alive on pyres. Then they'll take your charred corpses and mount them on the walls as a warning. I take no pleasure in imagining it," he lied. If it were up to him, he'd start with the longhorn player.

"Then your presence is paramount, Inquisitor," Reynard said, the usual bluster in his voice faded. His eyes were glassy with concern. Richter thought he'd feel some thrill seeing a prince broken in this way, a noble arsehole brought low, staring down the nasty end of a spike, but he only felt pity. It made him want to void his stomach, or maybe it was just the sheer amount he ate, leaving him ill.

"The Lord Council," August said through gritted teeth. "Bastards and murderous scum."

He looked around for his companions. Fehling gave him another affirming smile.

"I repeat my previous offer of the highest holy chair in the land," the prince said. "There must be a way to turn the army against this corrupt council."

Change had a funny way of coming all at once. He'd felt it a little since before the pyre. The doubts. The creeping thoughts that his mission was endless and pointless. For every demon on the Continent, three more sprung up in its place. He thought he'd be happy with a crusade, but the crusaders seemed more concerned with burning unrelated cities on their way down the Continent rather than actually killing any lycans. Vetterand himself saw him as just a tool, really. Richter had no doubt that the moment he stopped being useful, Vetterand would get rid of him forever. Seal him in a dark pit somewhere. It was what Richter would do in his shoes.

Then the pyre, and the betrayal. Prince Reynard had only brought those thoughts to the fore, and the hot, burning anger he'd felt made the thoughts all the stronger. But more than all that, his companions. Fehling's unflinching kindness for him, Karl's unblinking bravery, Paun's love for all things beer. Bjorn's relaxed repose in the face of death, even knowing that his life would end. Jogaila's... something. He didn't know much about Jogaila now that he thought about it. But he still felt that affinity, as though two kindred souls found each other at last. There was no coming back for anyone but Richter, and demons like him. Even Nials had offered his own lesson in his way, which was that people abhor difference. The Order took you in but never really made you feel at home. It just made you a killer, and the difference between the two was like an ocean.

He didn't want to be pontiff. Ambition had never been his strong suit. But he could right the wrongs he'd been dealt, right the wrongs the Order had gotten away with. Then they could get on with the business of destroying Palerme. If Richter had an army at his disposal, he might not be able to root out every single demon, but it'd be a sight better than trying to cover a whole Continent by himself.

"There is a chance."

"Oh?" The air filled with a pregnant pause. Their expectant faces looked on with hope. He had them by the short hairs. That he of all people should decide the fate of a city... *Sigur, they really are desperate.*

"Promise me you won't disband the holy army, and that you'll name me commander and allow me to use them as I see fit."

The prince looked around, eyes flitting over the tables. He stood. "Come with me, Inquisitor. Count August and Duke Roburg, too." Richter followed, and they left the comtessa and the sleeping princess at the table. A foreign lady, regardless of her business, had no business in the room behind the great hall.

Carpeted and furnished with plush couches, it was blessedly quiet. The pressure in his ears had dropped, and he no longer felt like strangling someone. Draped on the walls were tapestries that deadened the noise further. Candles burned low, and a fire burning in a stone fireplace filled the room with heat. At a desk setting, filled with neatly stacked papers and quills of all shapes and sizes, sat the Alanian, Galeaz. Black hair drooped over his eyes as he scribbled furiously on a parchment.

He heard them enter, stood, smeared his hair back, and bowed. "Your Highness," he said to Reynard. "Your Grace, my lord," to Roburg and August. "Inquisitor." His lips barely contained the bile in his voice.

Richter looked at the man. The murderous desire came flooding back, and he looked away, passing his eyes over the fire. Flames danced, mesmerizing in the gloom.

"We are discussing our response to the pontiff, Galeaz, should you wish to offer input."

"Yes, my prince. It is said in the camp that there is some doubt as to the leadership of the army. Many of the lords believe they should sit on the high council, not just the pontiff and his leashed dog."

Vetterand? A leashed dog? Surely, it's the other way around. But that would be what Vetterand would want others to think.

"Who told you this?" The prince put his hands on the back of a chair, leaned on it. He looked exhausted, dark circles under his eyes giving away his feelings about the situation. *Imminent invasion and brutal murder would make even the most unbothered man restless.*

"I trust my sources." Richter snorted. Galeaz struck him as the sort of man that would sell his own mother if it gained him an advantage. *Trust.*

"Very well."

"Father, why don't we flee? Two of our ships wait in the harbor, and the navy has been recalled. The ocean is ours, should we wish it."

Reynard shook his head. "I am no craven like your uncle." A year ago, he'd put his brother in this very situation, and Albrecht had broken and fled to Vallonia, seeking refuge. "And I will not live in exile while my city burns, and my people are punished for a crime they didn't commit."

"A valiant defense of the city, then?" Duke Roburg thumped down unceremoniously into the chair opposite Reynard. "Best we hope for a quick death at the end of a spear or an arrow than one at the end of a spike."

"They'll kill us, first, surely," August said.

"They keep you alive," Richter answered the question that was on all their lips. "There's a cut between the balls and the brown end. Two men give it a push, and it slides right through. It doesn't take much. People are very soft inside. The most you can hope for is that the two doing it don't know what they're doing and nick the heart as it goes through. If they do know, well, if they sew you up you can live for days, slowly bleeding out on the inside. I've seen one that lasted two weeks."

All of them had turned pale, fire dancing across their clammy skin. Duke Roburg gulped audibly.

It took Reynard a few moments to gather his words. "What did you want? Command of the crusaders? You have it. When I'm emperor, I'll name you their general."

Richter had already worked out a few contingencies and was in the middle of saying them. "If you don't like that idea, then—what? You don't want to know what I'll use them for?"

"If you can stop my people from being spitted and mounted on the battlements, I don't care."

Richter swallowed, his hands needling with fear. He'd felt it facing the pyre, facing the sheriff's mace, felt it now. "Then you must trust me."

"Trust you?" August said, laughing. "You'll betray us the first chance you get."

"You're already betrayed and the pontiff knows it."

"It's rumored Gottscheid wants Annalt to answer for their tolerance of the other gods, especially Veles," Duke Roburg said. "He won't rest until Annalt is brought to heel, and now he has his chance."

Richter felt sick. His molars throbbed. It took only a month for the crusade to be used to settle a personal, petty vendetta.

"That damn temple." Reynard's voice couldn't even muster anger anymore. Just tiredness. "I should've kicked out the embalmers when they arrived."

Embalmers? Richter spared him a glance. He hadn't known this.

"And there's reports that the crusaders have killed people in the outlying villages because they won't hand over their cattle or their grain."

"Pillaging, in other words."

"Regardless," Richter said, "there are twenty thousand soldiers and six hundred Golden Swords waiting outside your walls for an answer. You'd best give them what they want."

"I cannot."

"Then your pride will seal the end of your city."

"How many defenders do we have, Father?"

"Six thousand men-at-arms, three hundred knights."

The duke rubbed his chin. "What if we armed the people? If they knew they would meet this grisly end unless we won, they'd fight."

Reynard nodded. "I hadn't thought of that."

"It won't work," Galeaz said. He hadn't said a word since they'd barged in. Richter had forgotten the republican even stood there, listened, like a man with the talent for it. "The foundries are run short since Ostelar, and the armories are empty. And the number of defenders is the nominal count—most of our men-at-arms and knights are away in Osbergia, raiding. At last count, we have two thousand defenders, including Duke Roburg's men."

The duke nodded. "My prudence has finally reaped a reward." The duke and the prince shared a dry smile. It was a remark with a history behind it, one Richter didn't reckon or care.

"Could the men in Osbergia attack from the rear if we get word to them?"

"They could, but it would take days for them to arrive. And they would still outnumber us three to one."

"The crusaders have cannon," Richter said. "The walls won't last."

"Cannon." Reynard slapped his fist on the table. "Cursed invention. What's the point of building walls?"

"You used them to great effect in Ostelar. I heard."

"What is your plan, Inquisitor?" The duke turned to him, waited for Richter's answer. All hostility had been forgotten, swept aside in the wind of imminent death.

"We must convince the lords that the pontiff is corrupt. Discredit them." The wheels turned, like gears that, having trapped a finger, turned until they crushed the skin, the knuckles, the bones, left them all a mangled ruin. He had a talent for that. He never created, only destroyed. It was the only thing he was good at, really.

If I revealed myself, if I revealed that the cure didn't work, then Vetterand would be discredited and the man that so eagerly promotes his prowess would be as well. But it would be risky. And how was he to manage the generalship if everyone knew he was still a demon?

"Just trust me. You can't give anything away." Richter couldn't believe his ears. Was he really doing this? Gods, he needed a drink. Gods, he needed the Screamer, just to take the edge off. It was scraping against the underside of his brain, like a file. But he'd left the whip in Istrya, thinking he wouldn't need it.

He was getting what he wanted, after all. And it had gone all so very wrong.

"We come to the problem of trust," Duke Roburg said, cutting off August's protests before they could start. "You have yet to give us any reason to trust you."

"You don't have a choice."

"That we don't," sighed August.

He wasn't going to open any veins without spilling a bit of himself on the blade. There was a quote from the Book that would seem to come to mind, but it faded in the raging torrent of his thoughts. Those words would seem to come less and less of late.

"Vetterand found me in the slums of Istrya. My mother had her hands cut off so she didn't work. She would beat me and get me to steal for her, so I left." He was surprised how little emotion he felt when he recounted that. The men listened on regardless. Maybe they could sense the truth in his words. Sigur knew he didn't like to share this part. "My friends and I stole from a magistrate, who set his sheriff on us like an attack dog. Made me watch as he smashed my friends' skulls in." He lifted a thumb and forefinger, made the width of an eye. "Squished one of their eyes in front of my face. I doubt I'll ever forget that sound. Vetterand... saved me and took me into the Order." It was more or less the truth, with a few details left out, of course.

"But he was no better." Richter undid his jacket down to the underlinens, lifted his shirt over his head. Roburg and August gaped their mouths. The prince leaned forward on the chair, green eyes scrutinizing. The republican just watched with mild amusement. Was all right, Richter didn't much care what the bastard thought.

"He took knives to my body, taught me the lesson of pain, again and again. He visited me in my bed when I was younger, taught me that lesson, too." *Whatever lesson can come from draining your balls into a child.* "I have more reason than most to see the cunt destroyed, and his lackey, too. You're wrong, advisor," he said to Galeaz. The pitch-haired man lifted a brow. "Gottscheid is the leashed dog, not the Grand Inquisitor. Trust me on that." Richter dressed himself, lacing back up his jacket.

August looked like he might be sick, a green color forming on his cheeks. Roburg just shook his head. "You poor man."

"Everyone has a tragedy," Galeaz said, sucking his teeth. "But I fail to see how this should make us trust you, still. Only yesterday were you a loyal inquisitor of the Order, were you in the Schwarze because they ordered you there." He turned to the prince. "An outrider so that the crusaders could pillage unmolested."

The men argued. Richter spoke through gritted teeth. "But—"

"The inquisitor is right." Reynard spoke over them. "He has more reason than most to see the leadership of the church destroyed. Men follow orders, but we cannot fault them for choosing the easy road. What recourse did he have?"

"I don't like it."

"Then it is a good thing I'm the prince, and not you, Galeaz."

Richter couldn't conceal his smile. The republican dog had been beaten to heel.

"Then I must have my protest noted." He marched from the room like a stroppy child.

"It is noted," Count August said. "What a shit."

"He's only concerned for the wellbeing of the city."

"A republican," Richter asked. "Why would he care about a northern city? Besides, why isn't he on the nearest boat, escaping back to the Bright Sea?"

"Because I pay him enough to care. I'm sure when it comes to it, and the city is burning and the walls have fallen, he'll make a miraculous escape on some secret ship. He was in Ostelar before it burned, you know. He came to me before the assault and told me of how many men my brother fielded for the defense, and where they were posted. I knew the number would be pitiful, but it was good to have reassurance. He saved many of my men's lives that day by doing that." *At the grave cost of the Ostelar garrison, of course.* "I was grateful to him for that, offered him a position in my service."

The prince paused. "Then it is decided. We place our lives in your capable hands, Inquisitor Beltrand."

"Your scarred ones, at least," Roburg added, and their chuckles lightened the mood.

"But if you fail, if you give the city up, I will make it my mission before I die to kill you, brutally and slowly."

"I wouldn't expect it any other way. We'll ride out tomorrow and meet with the pontiff. Vetterand is bound to be there. I'll handle it from there."

CHAPTER 26
PREPARED FOR ANYTHING
TRIBUUM, 1045

Grand Inquisitor Ulrich Vetterand's ascension to the highest position in the Order is perhaps the most ordinary story: he was and remains a competent functionary, whose slavish devotion to the church and the word of the emperor and the pontiff is admirable. It is as though he has no mind of his own—and is thus better suited than anyone else for the task.

— IMPERIAL CHAMBERLAIN LUCAS GROZDANY

WHAT WAS HE THINKING?

All that certainty he'd felt in the room with the prince melted away given half a chance to think about it, his mind flailing in a sea of doubts. *Doubts...* That was new. His stomach turned as he climbed the stairs to his room, passed by a series of hunting trophies in a little hall of four rooms. The guest apartments, or so the palace chamberlain had told him. He paused at the door where Karl and the others were staying, thought about going in. Reached out, touched the latch. If nothing else, he could destroy his mind with some famous Annalt barley spirit. He saw a few cases at the dinner. It wouldn't be so hard to secure some from the kitchens, where they'd probably end up. Or maybe they'd still be downstairs in the great hall.

But he didn't. He didn't rightly know what he would say to them, and they'd ask. *You were with the prince for a long time. What did he say to you? What did you say to him?*

I promised to destroy Gottscheid and Vetterand, betray the Order, and more than likely get you all killed.

He withdrew his hand. Went to his room instead.

There were a few things he expected to see in the guest apartments of a lord. He'd stayed in a couple over the years. Fine carpeting, gilded trim, sturdy four-poster bed. Windows looking out into the gaping night. A hearth burning, a lantern above the bed casting all kinds of tasteful shadows. They all largely looked the same. Nicer than staying in an inn, inoffensive to the senses. Entirely predictable, he supposed. Nothing that would shock a visiting lord or lady, nor be so expensive as to be garish.

He did not expect the naked woman lying on his bed, however.

"I almost fell asleep waiting for you," Fehling said. She rested her head on a propped-up arm and extended a pale, smooth leg in his direction, toes pointed. All muscles and curves, like a dancer. "My sister always told me that the best thing to do after drinking was fuck. I think that goes double when we're all about to die."

Richter tried to think of something smart to say, but the only head doing anything was the one in his pants, his cock swelling against his legs, against the fabric of his trousers. "I—"

"As much as I like the staring, wouldn't you rather come here?"

He didn't need telling twice. He strode over, unbuckled his pants, danced across the floor as he tried to take off his boots at the same time. He tripped and flopped onto the bed with the grace of a newborn pup, while Fehling stretched her long limbs over the covers. She crawled over to him, helped him with his boots, then a hand frolicked under his trousers, warm fingers curling around his hardness. It evoked a sound not unlike a cat's purr.

"What was that?"

"Sorry."

"I... liked it." She climbed on top of him, pressed her lips into his. Wine and flowers, berries, and salt. Sweet and savory and bitter and acidic all at the same time. She kept going with her hand, didn't think one was enough, and shoved the other inside his trousers as well. With one hand she danced her fingers along his shaft, with the other she played with his orbs, massaging them softly, then harder. Soft then hard, gave them a bit of a tug.

It made him jump. She did it again and he jumped less.

He noticed the other hand disappear somewhere, if only because he missed the feeling on his cock like he missed a long-gone lover. Something flashed in the light of the fire and cold steel pressed against his neck. He blinked.

Fehling had a grin on her face, eyes of bright blue making his knees weak. But the knife at his throat distracted him. Then she offered him the handle. "I want you to hurt me."

"Hurt you?" He'd heard a certain Saburrian sect of whores were trained how to bring pleasure from pain. But a blade? The idea intrigued him, if nothing else, and he certainly hadn't wilted.

"I've been thinking about that day in your room for months. The pain cleared my head, made all the thoughts that tug at me so violently just... fade. I want you to do it while you fuck me."

She looked at him with such eyes that his cock nearly exploded right there and then. She laid back on the bed as he took the blade, and he pressed into her, her wetness slathered up from her quim to her thighs so that it barely took any effort. Her legs folded around his thighs, pulled him deeper. Air puffed from his lungs at the same moment, about the only sound he could manage.

He looked at the cold steel, the hearth's light dancing across its length like bodies in the throes of passion, or violence. He supposed there wasn't much difference, at the end of things.

He sliced a shallow cut across her chest. Her eyes widened and she yelped, perhaps at the shock rather the pain. He hadn't gone very deep. Her freckled chest blushed, blood trickled from the wound. She arched her back, everything tightening around him, so much so that he felt his seed rise up and nearly burst.

He did it again, and she shuddered, her legs bucking, pulling him even deeper, right to the hilt. "Come on, you fucker," she screamed. "Are you a craven?"

Again, and again. Blood formed drops across her perfect, pale breasts. It ran like tears across her belly, pooled in her bellybutton. He pistoned into her at the same time, and she nearly bucked him off. It was like riding the prince's stallion, the one he was trying to break in the yard.

"One more, just one more," she pleaded, like a smokeleaf addict begging for just one more puff.

He sliced a long line down her stomach, and it glistened with bright red blood. She curled up, pulled him tight with her arms and her legs, made a loud lowing sound like a cow and tightened up her hot cunt all at once, practically forcing him to apex. He grunted as he burst inside her, spasming, blood and hot cunt and seed and all the other fluids mixing to a great wetness below, a flood across his stomach and his thighs. She bit into his lip, drawing blood. It nearly made him burst again. Pain and pleasure as one. *Maybe those Saburrians are onto something.*

They lay entangled with each other, hot breaths filling the quiet, something hard pressing against his rib, until the wetness started to turn cold. He rolled off her, the knife leaving an imprint against his skin as it fell from his sweaty, sticky body. It dropped onto the bed with a soft thump, edge gleaming with red. His stomach was slick with red, too, and his bush flattened and wet.

"I needed that," she said, lying back and stretching out. She curled her feet in circles, ankles cracked, made a sighing noise. The cuts had been shallow enough that they already stopped bleeding, but he tore a bit of the sheet with the knife and pressed it against her.

"Thank you," she said. Her fingers danced along the rim of his ear. She wiped herself off with the other hand. "I know it's probably not what you had in mind, so thank you for indulging me."

"No, it was... fine."

"Just fine?" She pouted. "Good to know I'm barely passable."

"That's not—not what I meant."

She smiled, humor in her eyes. "I know." She laid her head back on interlocked fingers. "I'm fucking amazing."

"I'm just surprised, is all. I thought you and Karl..."

"Karl and I have an understanding. Just like you and I have an understanding. An understanding that goes far beyond the bedroom, I thought." She hinted at something deeper than sex.

Shit, was he feeling something stupid? He had an early memory, felt a brush on his cheek. *Mother.* He'd loved her once, and she'd loved him. He'd nearly forgotten what that was like.

"Why me? When you could have Karl, or Bjorn, or Jogaila? Handsome men. I'm a scarred old cunt, who's done some awful fucking things in his life, and enjoyed them."

"Because I want you. My sister always told me that women love dangerous men, too. Maybe that's it... but I all I know is that I don't want anything else. Karl was a bit of fun, and so were the others in your room in the fortress, but you're... like nothing else."

He gave another look at the blood smearing her breasts. It had already lost its fresh luster and was starting to dry. "So are you." *Fuck.* His heart was fluttering, and he felt like a boy after his first kiss. He settled for a sigh. "I meant to ask but in all the chaos of the last few months, I never had a chance. Why did you help me in Istrya? How did you even know I was going there to do that?"

"You're not the only one with tricks."

She followed me that night when I thought they were all sleeping. "You eavesdropped? Vetterand would kill you if he found out."

"It's a good thing I wasn't caught, then."

"You still haven't answered my question. Why did you help me?"

She reached out and stroked his cheek. "Because you helped me with my dark thoughts. I also figured a senior inquisitor owing me was a good thing."

"Then you know?"

"Yes."

"Why aren't you trying to kill me, then?"

She frowned. "Why would I? It's not like I could, anyway. You'd see me coming a mile off, and even if I succeeded, it's not like it would take."

Richter's chest felt cold, like he'd plunged into an icy lake. "You know that, too?"

"Of course, I do. I figure a man that can get put in a cage and set on fire, burn for hours, and still survive... it's going to be something of a trick to kill him."

Richter laughed. "What a fucking joke. Inquisitor Beltrand, the famed hunter of demons, an unkillable demon himself."

"It's something, all right. What do you think it is? Some god keeps you alive?"

"Maybe. Keeps me alive for his amusement. Can't think of anything else, and I've seen a lot. Impenetrable mists in the Forest of Rot, disembodied screams on the wind in the Geisteschreien. Screams so loud it's though they're right in your ear, then when you look, there's nothing there."

She blinked with surprise. "You've been that far north?"

He nodded. "There's not a place on the Continent I haven't been, except maybe the eastern kingdoms. But it's said there are no demons there, so I haven't bothered. Bit far to go to confirm or deny a rumor."

"Dare I ask..."

"What?"

"What did you and the prince talk about? You were gone for hours."

"The plan for tomorrow." *Dare I tell her?* Maybe it was the bloodlust, the pain and pleasure mixing as one, the lightness in his head, but he trusted her. And she'd only ever been loyal to him. She kept his darkest secret, even when she had the chance to tell everyone.

"I'm going to change my skin in front of the generals, make it clear that Vetterand's cure didn't work. He'll be shamed, and the man who sings his praises will have to lose face. Hopefully, it'll be enough to turn the army against them, and back onto their actual mission."

"Vetterand's not likely to give up that easily. He might order the Swords to attack."

"If he does, they'll be slaughtered."

"Along with us." She sighed, sat up, a distant look in her eyes. "They're not likely to distinguish the Swords on their side from the ones who turned against them, and they'll be angry at being used."

"That's why I'll kill Vetterand after I transform. He won't see it coming. He still thinks I'm loyal. The Swords will surrender, but I doubt any of them will be killed." *Because I'll be the Grand Inquisitor, and the new emperor will name me supreme general.* He could free all the Swords as he saw he fit.

Her eyes widened almost imperceptibly. "That would be quite the trick. I've heard he's prepared for anything."

"I won't let everyone die. I must admit, I've grown fond of you all."

She pouted again. "Just fond?"

They laughed.

It was his turn to pout. "I didn't see you coming a mile off. You almost got me with the knife, just before."

"You of all people should know that just because you cut a man's neck doesn't mean they die."

She sighed, laid back on her side. The cleft of her arse where it met her leg, freckled and pink, made him want another go. She must've seen the intentions in his eyes, or his rapidly hardening cock. He wasn't exactly subtle.

"Well?" she said. "Morning can wait. We're going to die tomorrow, after all. Well, maybe not you."

RICHTER RODE OUT WITH the prince at dawn. He took a hundred men with him, all clad in black plate, the finest Annaltian knights in all the land, shining and bristling with lances. Well, the finest Annaltian knights they could still find in the city brothels and taverns, drowning their sorrows in drink and cunt. So about what Richter would do in the same situation—what he had done, really.

He had untangled from Fehling some time just before dawn, when the sharp rap came at the door. They were leaving. That was fine with him. He had too much on his mind to sleep, anyway.

The curve of the land followed a small copse, a trickling stream, a simple smithy with a watermill. Small stone walls broke the terrain, separated golden fields ripe with grain, tiny farmhouses in the distance. Those lucky enough to be close to the city, lucky enough to escape the pillaging. A tickle filled his throat, the telltale tickle of burning on monstrous scale, and indeed in the distance, a thousand smoke trails rose into the eastern sky. Bright red in the blazing early sun like a thousand bleeding wounds. *What a crusade.* Intended to be the largest army in the empire since Istryan a thousand years ago, united in a single holy purpose, and all they'd done was part scores of farmers from their lands and their lives.

The prince had managed to break his Vyahtkenese warhorse in and rode the enormous black beast. His black helmet had been made into the shape of a lion, the morning sun dancing across its bared teeth. He looked every part a king, an emperor. Richter supposed that was the point.

The crusaders reportedly camped at the outskirts of a nearby village, Turingen, though twenty thousand men shouldn't have been hard to miss. He was no general, but he imagined if they wanted to attack the city they'd have to advance over miles of flat, open country, the defenders having ample warning of their arrival. And Annalt's wall still punched its gray, unyielding face into the sky, miles out, the great trebuchet towers likely being readied in case of the worst.

But cannons. They changed everything. It came from the Vallonians, originally, hence the name. The terrifying power of chemistry. Rotersand's carrack *Iustitia*, loaded with the things, was the reason he'd been sent to Ostelar, but it was gone by the time he got there. Strange that he should now be on the prince's side, after everything, riding out to destroy the Order. Or Vetterand and Gottscheid, at least.

Strange or not, he felt good about that. Revenge had only ever been on his mind when he was young, when Vetterand first took him in. Those memories came reeling, stabbed up now like nails into his eyes. When the object of your torture can't die, you get creative.

He looked forward to tearing Vetterand apart. Gods knew the man had earned a longer death, but it was all Richter could do to stop him from ordering the Swords to attack the crusaders. Six hundred stood no chance against twenty thousand, but it might offer enough distraction for Vetterand to get away. There was no way that was happening, not while Richter was alive. And dying never stuck to him.

"I should ask you, Inquisitor," Roburg said. He shouted over the din of the hooves, rode on Richter's left. Half a pale face and dark eyes shone out from the black helmet. He talked, though his mouth was covered by the Annaltian design gorget, that extended up to cover the neck and jaw. "Do you believe in a soul?"

"Not this nonsense again."

"It's not that—my daughter is back in the city. Will I see her again?"

"Later today, as soon as we're done here."

He gave Richter a sharp nod. "I hope so." He turned a hard face back to the front.

The prince's son, August gave him a nod behind, must've overheard their conversation. Or perhaps he didn't hear a thing, and he just followed his elder's lead like most lordlings. *Idiot.*

Colors splashed across the valley like a vast motley of flowers, if those flowers had been trodden on and covered in muck. Twenty thousand men, all arrayed across the field, encamped, and thousands more, and more floating between them and around them. Camp followers. Many taken from the farms along the road, he guessed, because none looked happy to be there. Though if he had to clean a soldier's soiled underlinens, he'd not be thrilled either.

And at the front of the camp, in an absence of color, like a void that sapped the life around it, was the black of the Order. Vetterand and Gottscheid and a hundred attendants, all inquisitors with their gold pins, sat on horseback waiting for them. He spotted a few among them he recognized. The two who'd taken him to the pyre, next to Vetterand. His cheeks felt like they had been slapped, his stomach did somersaults. *What were their names?* Jonas, he thought was the flaxen-haired. He couldn't remember the other one's name, wasn't rightly sure if he'd caught it.

Not that it mattered. At the end of the day, he'd be their master, and regardless of his ill will towards them, or theirs to him, he'd have them on the road to Palerme. He smiled. He was beginning to warm to the idea of running the Order. Why hadn't he been running it from the beginning? What was the use of someone like Vetterand, who balked at the things that needed to be done? It was only right that the new emperor appointed someone like him, someone who could end the demonic terror once and for all and bring glory to Sigur. Bring a little glory his way, as well. It was only what he deserved, after all. He'd suffered enough for the Order. Time something good came his way.

Vetterand wore a smirk when they arrived, like he knew something the prince didn't. Well, he'd see.

One hundred knights did the opposite of what knights were meant to do and stopped at a gallop. It took a bit of managing, and some of the knights shot forward of the line, nearly barreled into the other side. Some of them were probably still drunk, which didn't help. But no one seemed to care, as though it was expected. The competence of the prince's army, on show.

Richter tasted bile. They'd see, soon enough.

The pontiff's horse pulled forward as the old man dug his knees into the beast's side, and they met five strides distant. His horse stared dumbly at the others, unconcerned for the battle that was coming. *Horses... stupid beasts.* The distance wasn't much for a well-placed knife throw, and certainly nothing for Richter to cover, especially in his changed form. Even if he moved not an inch closer, he'd have the pontiff, Vetterand, and ten inquisitors dead in as many moments.

But he knew Vetterand wasn't stupid. He'd be prepared for anything, and often was.

"Well met, Prince Reynard," Gottscheid said. Topped with a white, pointed hat and a stole of purple silk around his thin, sagging neck. Sweat dripped across his brow from the weight of robes on him. The stole was embroidered with the golden lantern of Sigur, crossed with the golden sword. Both His symbols, it was almost a joke that the God of Strength was represented bodily on the Continent by a sickly old man. An old, frail man, a stiff breeze as likely to kill him as anything else.

Reynard's stallion gave a loud grunt, shoved Richter's horse. He swore quietly, smacked the beast around the ears with his gauntlet.

"Your Holiness," he said. "I wish I could say it is well to see you, but I find myself wondering if you do not mean to steal my home out from under me, bringing such a large army to bear, along with a supply of cannons."

On the next hill, over the sea of motley bodies, were forty fat black bodies of cannons. Not pointing toward them, thankfully, not mounted on racks, ready to fire. He'd seen the force of the iron balls and the black powder firsthand and didn't fancy facing them down even in his changed form. Castle walls were as much protection against them as paper, let alone armored skin.

"My father's killers were not satisfied with his death, and seek to kill his son and claim his city? And they call *me* Craving?"

Gottscheid bristled, his saggy neck wobbling as his cheeks turned red. Vetterand continued to smirk.

That bastard... what's he planned?

Before the pontiff could respond, Reynard's horse roared again, reared, and the prince was forced to smack him down, hard. The beast nearly seemed to foam at the mouth.

"Galeaz, what's wrong with my horse? I thought you broke it yesterday?"

"I did, my prince," the Alanian said. He looked as surprised as Reynard.

Reynard gave the creature another smack on the ears, and it seemed to calm. "Bring forth the men responsible for my father's murder and I will hand over my knights for your crusade."

"Our crusade," Gottscheid corrected. "It is the responsibility of all of Sigur's creations to bring war to the demons."

"Last I heard, the demons lived in Palerme, not Annalt."

Gottscheid smiled a gapped grin. Almost certainly he'd lost a few teeth to age, though a rumored smokeleaf habit could've taken its toll, as well. "The lives of your people are entirely at the whims of the prince of Annalt."

"You have my bargain," he answered. "Bring me the heads of my father's killers, and I will hand you my knights for you to do with." He turned to the assembled soldiers, not the Order. Clever.

"You see the justice of the church on full show! They cannot even answer the charge of my father's death!"

Some murmurs in the crowd pulled Gottscheid's attention away. "The prince's insinuations are troubling! This crusade *brings* justice to the emperor's murderers!"

Richter caught Vetterand's eyes. Something like amusement flashed behind them. He winked.

Richter's breath caught in his throat. It was going all wrong. "He's done something," he murmured.

Reynard looked at him, his eyes wide. "What?"

"Give me the signal—"

Roaring escaped the Vyahtken stallion's throat and he bucked and surged in Vetterand's direction, but it was nothing a practiced rider like Reynard couldn't handle. It bucked again, turning, trying to mount Vetterand's mare from the front, shove the arm-like cock in its face. They shouted in surprise.

Snapping rang out. Richter wondered if he imagined the sound. No one reacted. Then the prince tumbled from his horse, gauntlet slipped from the saddle horn. He screamed in terror. It was a long way to fall. He landed crooked on his helmet, his neck turning one way, his body going the other in a great crash of metal.

Silence. The silence of the dead.

The prince's eyes stared into the now bright, blue sky, the shade of his eyes and their glassiness turned the same color. Dead. Reynard dead.

Dead. Reynard is dead. All of Richter's planning had come to the same abrupt end. Richter leapt down from his horse, whispered to all the gods that he wasn't dead, that Richter was just mistaken. That the fall hadn't been fatal. That some hope could be scraped from the remnants of the prince's promises.

It wasn't to be. "He's dead," Richter said to no one in particular.

Men raced to the stallion, pulled it under control, pulled it off Vetterand's horse. The beast kicked, caving in one man's chest, a great puffing sound leaving his throat. He dropped dead as the prince had. The duke rode over to the beast, great mace in hand and brought it down on the creature's huge head, snarling fury. It reared, half its skull caved in, then realized it was dead, and its legs slipped out from underneath. As it collapsed in a heap of stinking horse flesh, a great fart left its arse and shit exploded from its hole, covered the corpse of the prince in a heap of dung. Richter jumped back to avoid it.

Through all of this, he realized, Vetterand had been smiling.

"Prince August," Roburg yelled. The new prince looked lethargically at the duke, like he'd just been dreaming. Like he'd imagined the whole fucking mess in front of him. "What is your command?"

August cleared his throat, fixed hard eyes on the knights behind him through tears. "My father would not want this fighting to continue," he shouted. "Our knights are at your disposal, Your Holiness, and our city is open to your army for as long as they need to rest and enjoy the hospitality of Annalt."

That was quick. Almost like he'd prepared the whole thing.

Richter looked at the Grand Inquisitor. Vetterand winked at him again. "Fucking murdering bastard," he yelled. "You killed the prince!" He roared, lunged at the mare, drove his blade through the beast's eye before Vetterand could react.

The mare reeled, snorting wildly, collapsed under the Grand Inquisitor, but ten inquisitors were on Richter shoving him down, disarming him, pushing him into the muck. He nearly transformed then and there, but something stopped him. It was like a locked portcullis formed in his mind, one he'd never noticed before. He writhed in the muddy ground, forced a breath, felt the air squeezed out of his lungs, more bodies heaped on top of him.

"Apologies, Prince August," Gottscheid said. "This mad dog must be brought to heel."

"Of course."

Richter's eyes tried to focus on the new prince, but they were blurry. He seethed through gritted teeth.

"This is an internal Order matter and must be handled as such."

Has he been working for the Order this whole time? "Bastard. Craven," Richter roared between snatched breaths. "Coward."

"Rest assured, Your Highness, Inquisitor Beltrand will be punished to the highest degree."

Silence, one where you were only left to assume the boy prince nodded. Richter grunted as they pulled him upright, his arms nearly forced to breaking behind his back as he squirmed. Bellowing, heaving, they only pulled tighter.

He was done. He was angry, angry at the boy prince, angry at the old prince for falling off a fucking horse and dying, angry at the pontiff, angry at the Grand Inquisitor. Angry at himself, most of all, for showing his hand. There was no way Vetterand would keep him around now. He'd outlived his usefulness, showed his loyalty to the prince—or at least showed his ambitions.

CHAPTER 27
TO THE VICTOR
TRIBUUM, 1045

*It is amusing to think that maybe, just maybe, the gods never
left the world. What would they think of this shithole that we've
turned their world into?*

— PRINCE REYNARD OF ANNALTIA

THE DINING HALL KEPT none of its secrets. Built on the second
level of the lord's tower, it overlooked the muddy yard, and was all
polished stone and knotted boards, fresh and oiled. Selene was quite proud
of the fact they had a functioning hall to entertain guests, though you
wouldn't know the gratitude of those guests from their reactions to the
furnishings. Captains Giustiniani, Arno, and Rolco.

Captain Arno had a permanent sneer on his face, sniffed the air as though
the long trestle table in the middle had a corpse lying on it. A knee-length
doublet of silk pushed out the bottom of a fluted breastplate. He seemed
the sort of man to kill someone then complain about the blood staining
his sword.

Being a Thousand Son must pay well. Though if mercenary reputation in
the republics was anything to go by, they took pay from all comers—from
both sides sometimes.

Rolco was Arno's complete foil, a no-nonsense short beard to match thinning, close-cropped brown hair. Lamellar armor formed the man's hide, polished but worn. It had seen some fighting, unlike Arno's breastplate.

The two men tramped into the hall, their boots clanking on the wood, almost in time, and came to opposite sides of the long table.

As far as she understood it, the captains united under a single general, but each of them were largely independent, responsible for the pay and upkeep of their own men that they brought into the Thousand Sons. And their orders, though they fell in line under the general's command.

Or so Giustiniani told her, as they made their way into the hall. Selene hopped double-time to keep up. "They run their ships as sturdy and leal as their preference and pay their crew how they like. There is, of course, the matter of payment." He stopped at the head of the table and turned his head to face her. "The Duca of Valenti is funding the voyage?"

"Yes," Selene replied. "I trust you'll find everything to your liking."

Arno tutted, clicked his fingers a few times at Leon and Ottille. "Do all northerners live like ascetics, or is it just you demons?"

"Ignore him," Giustiniani said. "He's irritated because his wife left him for a minstrel."

"Bitch was sleeping with him for months." Arno's accent colored everything with a humorous tone. "They had a fucking kid! So, I killed him and his fucking friends. How do you say it in *Natali?* I don't know—*pattana de catzo!*"

Selene hid her humor at his ridiculous accent, the absurdity of his outrage, and covered her mouth. He was like a child that had his toy taken away, only murderous. Which made it all the funnier.

"Truly a tragedy," she said, pushing down the laughter. "For it to be so fresh, then to have to go on campaign."

"It happened six years ago." Giustiniani rapped the top of the head chair with his knuckles twice. He leaned over to Selene as she hobbled up. "But you should welcome guests with music and refreshment."

"What are we to think?" Arno said. "That you demons are savages?"

"We're not demons," Ottille said, eyes narrowed with anger.

"Just savages, then?"

Ottille huffed and marched from the room. Sanna had stuck her head through the doorway behind them to see the guests. Her mother chided her as she passed, picking her up and placing her on her hip as she went down the hallway.

Selene spoke through grinding teeth. An insult expected, but no less acidic. "Leon, find someone who can sing a tune or has a vielle or something. Dunstad plays a basso. Find him, and have Rani bring bread and ale for our guests."

"Yes, milady." He left, and Selene was reminded of Mother's skill in hosting. *A guest must feel as though the entire night has been effortless for the host. If he forgets, you can be sure he will forget his place, and let secrets fall from his lips that might otherwise stay locked away.*

She didn't forget what Duca Alberracin told her, of course. *Don't trust Giustiniani. He's only loyal so far as his coin goes. Should Rolco find himself in the captain's chair, we will be all the happier for it.*

Selene took a breath, held it for a moment, and breathed out, smiled broadly. "Please, sit. We will have refreshments brought to you." She offered an open palm to them, hopped over to the head chair while Giustiniani pulled it out for her.

"Thank you, General. I hear you've led quite the campaign in recent years." A bit of flattery wouldn't hurt. "Chivalrous in the dining hall and on the battlefield."

He pushed the chair in and she slid up to the table.

"Chivalry is the last thing on the general's mind," Arno said with a wry chuckle. "In the both places."

"The lady has invited us here as her guests," Rolco said. He hadn't said much since they arrived, if anything at all. Selene looked at him. "We shouldn't be so demanding and thank her for her hospitality."

"For her money, you mean," Arno said, skidding into a chair and kicking his feet up onto the table. He took a silver spoon from the table and turned it in his fingers. "Well, the duca's money."

"Yes, for that too."

"Rolco is right," Giustiniani said with a great sigh, as though it pained him to admit. He sat just a chair down from Selene, far from his fellow captains. He turned to her. "We thank you for your hospitality. Before we start, let me tell you that Alain is alive, but he is our prisoner."

Selene was surprised. "Your prisoner?"

"He fled with something precious to me when he left us, and I could not let that stand. But since he is your servant, I will let you decide what to do with him. Should you hang him like that man in the yard?"

"I should like to know what he stole from you, before I was to hang him."

"That, I am afraid, you cannot know."

"It must be terribly precious, but also embarrassing, then."

Giustiniani skimmed his eyes across the surface of the table, avoided hers, and gave a heavy breath. "Hang him or not, it makes no difference to me. But he stays my prisoner." He gained her eyes again, the previous falter forgotten. She kept his gaze, though she knew she was looking into the eyes of someone who had killed many and would kill many more before he was done. She'd seen them in the lord's mirror upstairs.

"Either way, we have business to discuss." He slid a battered flask from his jacket and took a swig. He wiped his face, all serious now. "You've made powerful enemies you'd be better off running from. You could say there are none more powerful than the ones you've made."

Selene matched his eye. It was just them in the room, Arno and Rolco faded into the background. "The pontiff has taken everything from us. We won't run."

"I've no doubt of your conviction. I only wanted to see if you knew the score."

"I know the score."

"Good, then we are clear. To name our material: Rolco."

She looked over as the no-nonsense captain lifted out a ledger from his cloak and thumbed through it, his mouth moving as his finger drifted over the pages. "Two hundred horsemen, nine-hundred and sixty crossbow-men, seven-hundred and ten infantrymen, sixty handgonne, six ten-pound cannon, and three twenty-pound cannon."

Selene leaned forward. "I was told you had more than three thousand."

Rolco turned up his nose as though her words were a stain on his records.

"Last bruma was especially hard for us. Mercenaries are a fickle sort." He tapped the table and stood. "The Thousand Sons will camp by the Bight until the imperial army arrives. We have no need for you to provide us provisions or shelter. The duca's money will suffice in this regard."

"We can't eat money, Salvio," Arno said.

"No, you idiot. We'll send someone to bring a few wagons from Segesta—we'll have to go around Valenti." He passed his eyes over Selene's body. Selene tried not to show her displeasure. It was a relief at least that they wouldn't camp nearby. "I've no doubt you know the troubles the duca has had. The city has been shut, all gates closed and no one is allowed in or out, not for love or money."

"I see." She pushed herself up to stand just as Rani and Dunstad raced inside, the former with a basketful of heavily salted bread and a jug of ale, the latter clattering his oversized lute through the door after.

"Ah, our food and entertainment arrive," Arno said, standing and holding his hands out like a mummer's herald. "It's too bad we're to decamp. I should like to hear what demonic music sounds like."

"We have drills to prepare, my lady," Giustiniani added. "If you would permit us, our men must have access to the walls to train in the defense."

"Of course. Whatever you need."

He bowed his head, and the three captains were gone, the other two leaving without so much as a grunt.

"Well," Selene said. "That was... interesting."

Dunstad breathed hard. "So... I raced all the way up here for nothing?"

"It appears so," Rani said, puffing.

S ELENE WANTED TO SHOVE a blade through the neck of the man that invented stairs. She counted twelve from the yard to the curtain wall, three to the hallway that led to the dining hall, twelve more from the stairwell to the armory, another twelve to the servants' quarters, and, suitably, another twelve to the lords' chambers. If she ever had an inkling she would break her leg and would be forced to hobble up and down each one of them every day for the next six weeks, she would've knocked the whole castle flat, turn the lords' tower into the lords' longhouse.

It was during one of those great long treks to the yard that she overheard two little voices in the dining hall, feet pattering over the boards, and laughing.

"Stop," one of them whined. *Sanna?*

She hopped over the threshold of the door, which wasn't technically a step but still required some thought to get over. "Sanna?" asked Selene.

"You got your father killed," a girl said. The voice was familiar. "Go to hell."

"No! It's not true." Sanna's voice again, thready with tears. She was arguing with an older girl, but Selene couldn't see them.

"Sanna?"

The little girl came running, face wet, bearing down into her forearm to hide her face. She nearly bowled into Selene. "Hang on, girl!"

"Ah!" She stumbled back and landed on her backside. Her face turned bright red, the color of a tomato. "Lady Selene, I'm sorry!" She sniffed back tears and looked up into Selene's face.

Selene frowned. "What's wrong? What happened?"

"Those girls... I..." Sanna tumbled to her feet and turned towards the back of the hall.

"What is it?"

"Lady Selene," Lorela said, curtseying as she emerged from the small storeroom to the rear of the hall. Behind her came that mute girl, the one Rani had working in the kitchens, her apron dusted with flour. Lorela herself was supposed to be with Ottille, running the spinning wheel and carding the wool.

The mute young woman, who everyone had taken to calling Blauna, for her ocean-blue eyes, had fixed her hair in a ponytail and didn't look so wild-eyed, like a bull ready to escape its enclosure and gore someone. Her work had given her happiness, it seemed, or at least some measure of peace. Whatever she'd been through must've been terrible.

"What were you three doing back there?"

"They were—not doing—their jobs," Sanna said, stamping her feet. "I found them." She sounded intensely proud.

"She's lying," Lorela said. Sanna said from behind Selene's leg. "Don't hide behind the lady. Come out and tell the truth."

"I'm not lying. You two were…" She made a kissy face with her mouth, smacking her lips together and running her hands all over her body.

"Shut up!" Lorela ran forward and raised her hand to slap Sanna across the face.

Selene caught the girl's wrist with the end of her crutch, balanced on her good leg.

Lorela stepped back, clutching her wrist in pain. "I… I'm sorry, milady. But she's lying. We never—"

"You're a bit young for such things, aren't you? And you," she said sternly to the mute girl. She wasn't much younger than Selene. "You should know better."

Blauna looked down in shame and nodded.

"It wasn't her," Lorela said. "It was me. I started it—I was curious."

"Curiosity or not," Selene said, "you're both not doing your jobs." She sighed. *Fuck, it's like having fifty children, all with their own temperaments and tantrums.* "We need to prepare as much as we can for the defense, and we need everyone at their jobs. Entertain such things when you're older and have a bit more understanding of what you're doing. I don't want to catch you ever doing it again, is that clear? And that goes double for you, Blauna," she said through clenched teeth. Whatever Blauna had been through, it didn't give her an excuse for touching a sixteen-year-old. "Yes? Otherwise, you're gone, and you can fend for yourselves when the empire arrives." She was deadly serious.

Lorela and Blauna nodded vigorously. "Yes, milady," Lorela added, curtseying again as they both passed Selene and left.

Sanna tugged on Selene's sleeve. "What were they doing? They looked like they were hurting each other, but they were laughing like it was fun."

"Nothing you need worry about," Selene said. "Not for a very long time. Ask your mother if you must." She bent down and stroked Sanna's cheek. *Not for a very, very long time.* She loved Sanna, she realized, like her own child. *My own child.*

"Go see to the horses, Sanna. There's a good girl."

The girl smiled and raced off, legs powered under the spell of youthful excitement. Selene envied that.

S ELENE FELT THAT WHEN it came time for him to remember, to have memories, her son would love her, would recognize her as his mother. But not now. He squalled, pushing at her, his frail, untrained neck unable to stop his own head from wobbling. Awful agony inflected his every cry. She grunted in frustration as he nearly toppled out of her arm and dashed himself on the stone of his chamber.

The woman grimaced a little and took him, and he calmed immediately. "That's alright," she said to Tristain. "Your mother'll figure it out. She's learning too."

Selene shook her head and laughed. "Tell me, how is it possible that he settles in the arms of a stranger but not his own mother?" It came out angry, and maybe she'd meant it to be.

"Galena feeds him, that's all he cares about right now," Ottille said. She stood by the door, arms folded but offering a palm with one hand. "When he's old enough, he'll recognize you."

Recognize me as only as the woman that birthed him. The thought echoed in her mind. She ground her teeth, irritated at what Galena had said. Tristain whined a little, and Galena shushed him. *So, it's not all perfection.* Selene bore a satisfied smile at that as she hobbled over to the window.

The torches in their cradles popped as the sun set outside and a night chill took hold. Behind the room was plunged into a dull orange that lapped their skin.

"No," Galena said. "No. I've seen this before. Mothers in our village who couldn't breastfeed helped in other ways."

She pursed her lips. *I've seen wounds past counting. The fact I can't even settle my own son cuts deeper than them all.* It ached greater than her leg, shredded her more than having her arm split open by her adoptive father's claws.

Ottille thought better than to continue in that vein. "I'm troubled by this holy crusade. How are we to defend against that many? The castle walls can hold a thousand, at the most."

"The Thousand Sons," Selene said. "Our advantage is our size—or lack of, rather." She sighed, looked out on the forest that went to the Bight. Cast in purple, the tents of the Thousand Sons became a bloated corpse spilled across the countryside where men the size of ants teemed within. They weren't three thousand, they were scarcely two thousand, but they still looked like a small town on the horizon, just over the canopy.

How much would twenty thousand look like? They'd block out the entire land. She turned back. "The empire's numbers won't count for much when they can't bring them all to bear. They'll have to clear the forest to get to us." *And doing so would require a huge cost.*

Galena sighed, bouncing the sleepy Tristain as she stared at Selene. The tension in her face started to build. "I'm afeared for my daughter, for all the little ones. The victor takes what they want. I've seen it before."

"I'm starting to think there's nothing you haven't seen," Selene said, offhand. Ottille chuckled.

The woman plowed on. "When the black ones came to our village, I knew what they would do. Rape and kill us, they would. So, afeared for us I was, I took my daughter, and I held a knife to her. I'd do myself as well, after. But my mother said it wasn't hopeless, after all. There was a sanctuary for us. Palerme was that sanctuary, milady. And now it's going as well, just like anything else happy in this world. That army'll kill us all." She held Tristain tighter, maybe without realizing, and the tightness in her eyes made them small and slitted.

Selene rubbed her bodice, the silk smooth as blood running over her fingertips. "Or Frix'll burn their supplies and they'll have no choice but to disperse."

"Either way, we'll do what we can," Ottille offered. "We're Althann. We've fought for everything we have. I'll tell you, I didn't walk for thirty days to keep walking. Sanna and I've built a life here." There was a sense of pain in that statement, as though losing Lucia was everything. This was where she'd been given back to the land, after all. "If you want to run, Galena, then run."

Built a life?

Galena's face relaxed. "Sorry, milady. Sorry, mistress," she said to Ottille. "Just scared, is all."

"Aren't we all," Selene said. "But if we keep our nerve, we'll survive. We're Althann—survivors. The Order have tried to destroy us before, but we survived then, and we'll survive now."

She turned back to the window. A cool breeze broke the heat of the day, the faint gray of smoke and the stink of cookfires blowing over them. The vestiges of Solni fading behind the horizon. Come victory or defeat, come life or death, she'd be ready. She'd been ready for a year now, and it felt like something she'd been working her whole life towards.

She wondered whether Frix would now be looking at the same sunset, days of travel distant. Days in werewolf form were of course far different to days walking. They were likely already to Ostelar, and the sunset there would be different enough. Would it be a sunset full of hope? Or a sunset like dark blood, spilling across a bruising sky.

"May I speak to you, my lady?"

Selene turned. Ottille looked at her with hopeful, wide eyes. "Of course."

"In private."

"Galena?"

"Yes, milady." The woman left with baby Tristain after swaddling him, and he went to sleep immediately. Selene had a pang of jealousy—she'd never even been able to swaddle him or get him to sleep. *Why are ladies never taught to be mothers?* But of course, this was no different. Ladies often had wet nurses and nursemaids to look after their children, to keep them out of sight. So why did Selene feel so guilty about it?

Maybe it was for the same reason that she didn't feel like a lady, not really.

Galena closed the door behind her with a *click*. Selene leaned on the windowsill, the draft at her back chilling her, making her neck all bumpy.

"Milady," she said, playing with her hands. "I'd... I'd like your blessing."

"My blessing? What for?"

"I'd like to marry Gregor."

Selene pulled back her face in happy shock. "Marry—oh, this is wonderful. I had no idea you two were close."

"We've become closer over the last couple months. That's why our children don't get along, they see how close we are. I think his twins are upset at me for trying to replace their mother."

"And that's why they take it out on poor Sanna."

Ottille nodded. "They're coming around. Gregor is on them like a taskmaster these days, and the defense seems to have given them renewed purpose."

"They'll come around, I'm sure." Selene sighed happily and limped over to Ottille, stroked her arm. "Of course, you have my blessing."

A sigh of relief and Ottille opened her arms then hesitated. "May I?"

Selene leaned in and passed her hand around Ottille's back, tried to keep her weight on her good leg but failed, and she hopped, crutch clattering off the ground. Ottille caught her and they hugged and laughed. "Apologies, in all the excitement, I—"

"I should like you to be my officiant, if you'll accept. Not that it'll be official, since no magistrate will marry two demons, of course—"

"I'd be honored." As Selene felt a tear worm its way out of her eye, she realized she'd never had a friend like this before. Not even her servants had been so close, back in Invereid. She felt something inside her mend a little, like a piece of her shattered heart was glued back on.

"Sorry," she said, wiping her face.

Ottille's wet cheek met her own. "It's quite alright, milady."

"A bit of happiness will do us well. Shall we set the wedding for tomorrow?"

"Yes, let's do it."

"We'll have to invite the captains," Selene said, stepping back a little. Ottille bent down and handed her the crutch. "They're our guests."

Ottille bared her teeth in a smile. "That's well, milady. It'll be a fine opportunity to show them a little Althann hospitality."

Selene laughed. "Indeed. Oh," she said, starting, "I almost forgot. Your daughter might ask some questions about sex. Blauna and Lorela were... kissing in the storeroom in the dining hall."

Ottille gaped her mouth. "She's—"

"Half her age, nearly. I know. I made it clear that if she did it again, she'd be gone."

"Good. Sigur's fucking balls," she swore.

"Don't worry. Just... be prepared."

Laughing, Ottille brought her hand up to her chest. "Oh, don't you worry. Sanna's already had the talk about where babies come from. This will be a breeze by comparison."

CHAPTER 28
THE SPOILS
TRIBUUM, 1045

What is the megalith? Why does an enormous tower of black, smooth stone with no entrances or windows, an edifice of night, like a stain on the world exist? Who built it? Steel tools cannot make a dent; therefore who carved the Tabula Morgenensis into its face?

— TOMAS VERDUN, HISTORICAL ACCOUNTS OF THE PRE-IMPERIAL PERIOD

THE FIST RATTLED RICHTER's jaw, sent teeth flying, bits of teeth flying. He was sure he'd bit his tongue. The chains caught him, swung him back, his naked, bleeding body dangling over dank stone wet with his blood.

"Again?" he said. His voice was strange, full of blood. He spat a glob of it on the floor. "You taught me how to resist more pain than this, Ulrich." He looked at the wire-mouth torturer and laughed. "You'll have to try harder than that, Sallust. Are you getting old?"

Sallust returned a savage look, about all he could manage, since Vetterand wired his mouth shut years ago. Richter was well acquainted with that look, as well as that fist.

Vetterand chuckled. "Indeed, I did. This is just the appetizer, my boy."

Richter chest burned with anger. "You truly think yourself a father?" His voice boomed in the small chamber. "You buggered me like a common bedwife, turned me into a killer, destroyed me. What kind of father does that?"

"A loving one. One that sees the truth of what you are, of what you could be. Sallust, leave us, but bring the brazier in from the outside before you do."

The big inquisitor nodded, since it was about all he could do. Richter frowned. What did he mean to do if he sent away the torturer?

"What will you do with me?"

Vetterand stroked Richter's cheek. He flinched and the Grand Inquisitor frowned. "What have I done to make you hate me so?"

"You know what you fucking did." He shouted, thrashed against the chains, wanted to slip free and close his fingers around Vetterand's frail neck until he turned purple and glass-eyed. "How did you do it? How did you make the prince's horse throw him?"

"Simple. On a hunch that he would take the opportunity to claim the Vyahtkenese herd outside Avercarn, I bought a mare in heat from a nearby ostler. The beasts really are as stupid as their reputations maintain, like knights, only charging forward, no thought for the consequences. Happily, I didn't have to leave it to a hunch. Count August"—he put his hand to his chest in mock apology—"sorry, Prince August, was all too happy to claim his father's seat. He met with the pontiff two nights ago, and I arranged it all. He even put an old, worn buckle on his father's saddle, like I told him to, knowing it would snap and seal the prince's fate."

Richter shook his head. "And they called his father the Craving Count."

"Like father like son."

Sallust opened the door, the brazier scraping its iron feet across the stone, sparks and fire casting dancing shadows across the mossy walls. They were in the base of the Annalt castle, in some old storeroom, but it was suited to purpose. That purpose being that no one could hear his screams. Wouldn't want to ruin the new prince's celebrations, after all.

The door closed with a *thunk* as Sallust left again. Vetterand put a long knife into the fire, jabbed at the burning wood inside, shooting sparks up.

"Did you think you could trick me? Deceive me? Kill *me*?" The last word turned to a shout.

Richter didn't answer. Maybe he did, maybe he didn't. He was full of bluster only that morning, but now it all seemed so fuzzy, the confidence he felt had fled him like the tide of a filthy ocean going out, leaving only wet muck in its wake.

"What was it you said... 'you'll have to try harder than that'?" Vetterand sighed. "It is the folly of the father to believe that his son is without fault. I am as much to blame as you are. No: more. You know, I would've given you the leadership eventually."

Richter swallowed. Vetterand lifted the long knife out of the fire and it glowed red hot.

"How did—" Richter's breath caught in his throat. "Did I fail?"

"Do you think it was a coincidence that Fehling followed you that day, helped you?"

"Her?"

Vetterand waved the blade in front of Richter's eyes as he talked. He felt the heat pour from the metal, sweat pouring down his cheeks, his brow. He blinked, the salt entering his eyes, making them itch. He blinked harder.

"I bade her follow you, help you, make you love her. I thought she might prove a tempering influence, or failing that: she could watch you, made sure I knew whether you were doing anything stupid. And she did—"

"How? She was with me, all night."

"No, she wasn't."

Richter wracked his memory. She'd been with him, all night! There was a moment he'd slipped into sleep, maybe, but that had only been a moment. Surely. When he woke, she had laid his head in her lap, stroking his scalp. *No...* But he knew it in his heart, the sharp point of his neck working up and down with a difficult swallow.

"She sent a message. The fucking Alanian."

"Alanian? What Alanian?"

"Galeaz, the prince's chamberlain or advisor or buttwiper. Whatever he was."

"Oh, him. He's been executed. Ex-Order agent, and all that. The information he had couldn't be allowed to be freely repeated, so I corrected an oversight left by the Ostelar Lord Inquisitor."

"Ex-agent." He knew it. The man clearly had some skill in subterfuge, some training far beyond a regular prince's chamberlain. But Richter had bigger problems in front of him.

Vetterand looked down at the blade. It had cooled to a dull sheen. "Damn it. You left me talking too long." He shoved the knife back into the fire with a clunk.

"Sigur knows you don't need my help to do that. You love the sound of your own—"

Vetterand's knuckles cracked against Richter's mouth in a sharp backhand.

Richter spat blood. "Come on, then. Do your worst. Sigur fucking knows you've had me spent for years. What more could you do to me?"

"Oh, plenty." He grabbed the blade and placed it ever-so-slowly against the top of Richter's left ear, where it met his skull. Flesh melted, hair burned, the stink filling the room, making him retch, the pain keeping him from retching, and he screamed. Vetterand took his time, sawing back and forth, making a meal of it. Richter howled, felt the sudden urge to change.

Worst of all, he only had himself to blame. If he'd been quicker, smarter, less obvious, Vetterand wouldn't have got away with it. It was so clear in hindsight. Of course, Vetterand would come prepared, would see the prince as a needless obstacle to be flattened. Richter would've done the same thing in his shoes.

He whimpered and shuddered as Vetterand stepped away. The noise was coming from someone else. Somewhere else.

Again and again, Richter found himself realizing that he'd never learned the lessons Vetterand had taught him, for all his ruthlessness, his fury, his brutality. It was always an equation to Vetterand, always impersonal, always business. Getting involved, falling in love. Who was he? What had he become? He needed to be cleverer, more thoughtful, *prepared*.

"Interesting," Vetterand said, though it sounded like was coming from the bottom of a well. Or maybe Richter was the one in the well, and Vetterand was looking down on him, watching as he thrashed around in the water, trying to find a foothold.

"I wondered if it might grow back, like when your body heals upon transforming. It seems not."

Richter realized it wasn't that Vetterand's voice came like at the bottom of a well. It was muted compared to the rest of the noise from above them. Shuffling of feet, the murmur of voices. He looked down, fur covered his body. He'd slipped into his other form without realizing. It was so easy, like flipping a switch in his head.

"Why couldn't I do it before?" he meant to say, though it came out all garbled. His wolfen mouth wasn't made for the syllables of Low Istryan.

"Do what?"

"Change."

Vetterand leaned close, a scrutinizing eye trained on the side of his face. Richter seized the moment, lashed out with his teeth, grabbed hold of Vetterand's cheek and pulled. Flesh ripped and he screamed.

Sallust burst inside, must've been waiting at the door, blade drawn. His eyes widened when he saw what waited him. Richter's form. Vetterand's blooming crimson across his cheek. Panting, Vetterand pressed a rag to the side of his face. Blood soaked the fabric, a blooming rose.

"I'm fine," he said, and waved a dismissive hand. Sallust nodded and sheathed his sword, closed the door again.

Richter smiled. That would leave a great hollow on his face, if it ever healed properly.

"Beeest finddd aah heaaler," he garbled. Then he relaxed and changed back, as easy as setting a heavy cloak down after a long day. "Or a barber-surgeon. Nasty wound like that is bound to get infected, especially with my demon blood."

Vetterand raised a brow as though none of this would ever occur to him. Like his body didn't work like anyone else's. He closed his eyes.

With a crunch, six horns shot outwards from his skull, three on each side, a giant, glowing head, and thick neck formed, eyes silvered in the light, a primal head on a man's body. Something out of a nightmare. His color split perfectly down the middle, his left half white, his right half black. Highest and High Hours. The sun and the moon.

From the measure of it, his head more than double the size of Richter's in his wolf form, Vetterand would be truly monstrous in his full glory. As it was, the horns scraped the underside of the stone ceiling. It might've been comical had it not chased the laughter from his mouth, sent fear to his tongue, needled his fingertips.

"You... what are you?"

A giant, toothy grin spread across his mouth. Or at least bared his sharp, pointed teeth in some resemblance of a grin. It was something primal, something not like a wolfman or anything he'd ever seen. But he wasn't human, that was certain.

On some deeper plane of thought, it made complete sense. Why Vetterand was prepared for everything, why he could sense Richter at the door before he'd even knocked, why he'd helped Richter in the first place.

"There's a secret war out there you haven't begun to grasp." He spoke perfect Low Istryan, his voice like the depths of a mountain.

"I indulged you because I knew that you would never succeed. Your mission was bound to failure, but it molded you, turned you into the killer I needed you to be."

Richter also noticed that the wound was completely gone, healed over into golden cheek.

Vetterand followed his eyes, answered the question on Richter's lips. "You're just a shadow. A low thing that I fancy only as my pet. But when you're thousands of years old, that's all mortals are."

Richter gaped his mouth. "Who... who are you?"

"What are we all? Slaves to our baser instincts. You tried to be a good man in saving the city, but in the end, you resorted to violence to get your way. You failed, but not for lack of trying. Though, I suppose you didn't fail, in a roundabout way. August will keep his city alive and get what he wants. We're all selfish, even gods."

"You're a—"

The door clicked open. An inquisitor, not Sallust, stepped a foot inside, dark eyes moving around the lip of the old, knotted wood. He opened his mouth to say something.

Vetterand faded, left a stain on Richter's periphery. The inquisitor suddenly exploded, gore coating the room in a grisly coat, splashing Richter's face and body in bits of bone, pink bits of muscle, brain, unidentifiable in the mess. It clung to his skin, made him cough with the sudden shock of it, and he blinked.

An enormous golden-skinned man stood behind the inquisitor, or behind where the inquisitor would've been had he not been mush on the walls. Monstrous, bright silver eyes shining, shoulders and back bunched against the low ceiling. His six horns seemed to have grown even larger in stature. None of the blood reached him at all, as though he'd been invisible to it. Gold skin lustrous and shining, even in the dank light of the brazier and the torches on the wall. Like he glowed from within. It hurt Richter's eyes to look on him directly, for some reason. Like looking at the sun.

Richter saw there was a hole in the god's stomach, where he could see gray stone behind. Just nothing there, the wound yawning like a pit.

"Sallust, we are not to be disturbed."

Silence. The only sound was the *drip-drip* of blood falling from the ceiling. Vetterand shut the door with a giant hand, each finger the size of Richter's arm. The gesture was so human, so out of place for what he expected a god to do—just shut the door with his mind, or create a new, closed door in its place—that he could only laugh.

Could he read his thoughts? There was no limit to what a god could do. He wasn't a demon—he was the fully realized form of which Richter was just a shadow. Night and day. The difference between a puddle and an ocean. Maybe that meant that Fehling hadn't betrayed him. All Vetterand would have to do is read Richter's innermost thoughts, of seeking the Grand Inquisitorship. Wait for Richter to stab himself, kill his own plan. Resort to baser instincts.

Maybe Fehling loved him as he loved her. Maybe she hadn't betrayed him after all. Could a god lie? It seemed likely.

He laughed like a maniac. Vetterand loomed down on him.

"You're not Vetterand, are you?"

"Oh, Ulrich Vetterand is me," he answered. *He? Do gods have genders?* "And I am Ulrich Vetterand. I have had countless other names over the ages. It has suited me to have human identities. But we must all do things we dislike, now and then. At least I didn't have to pretend to be one of my brother's *dogs*." He spat the last word, like it tasted bad on his tongue. "But enough about me. I know what kind of soldier you can be in the coming war. You could be my closest sergeant, but I can see that I've been too merciful, too lenient."

Richter recoiled as Vetterand extended one of his huge fingers, a long nail, over his face, his mouth. His head whipped back. He was looking up, and he only felt the absence of something, and he tried rolling his tongue around his mouth, but couldn't. It was gone. Then the pain hit.

Richter screamed, thrashed, writhed. It was the loss of it, more than anything. It was incredible what you could take for granted before you lost it. Speech.

Vetterand held Richter's tongue in an outstretched hand, the strange muscle dwarfed by the enormous palm. Richter whimpered like a beaten dog, the noise foreign in his mouth, the remnant of his tongue filling his mouth with blood. A tiny, wet thing, it seemed absurd that it had once sat in Richter's head. The giant palm closed, making a wet crunch.

"That ends, now."

CHAPTER 29
MARRIAGE AND OTHER DEATHS
TRIBUUM, 1045

*We know that it existed when Istryan arrived on the Continent.
We are only left to assume that the original inhabitants of the
Continent erected the structure. But even the finest imperial
engineers cannot understand its construction. It seems to defy
sense, changing its measurements seemingly at will. It is as
though it defies our attempts at understanding it.*

— TOMAS VERDUN, HISTORICAL ACCOUNTS OF THE
PRE-IMPERIAL PERIOD

THEY WOKE BEFORE DAWN and stole Ottille from her bed. Selene watched Dunstad cart her over his shoulder as she screamed and thrashed around. Rani laughed, the tall, lean woman carrying a viperous look in her eye, like she might lash out and open a wound at any moment. Selene could only watch from the balcony as the cook put her on the cart and shouted, "Save your wife, Gregor! She's going to die if you don't."

The bride screeched with laughter, stepped around Dunstad and almost got free when Trestinsen snatched her up again by her kicking legs and threw her back onto the cart.

"Someone help," she yelled, tongue-in-cheek.

Rani leaned forward, took hold of Ottille's shift and tore it open, the tearing noise echoing across the yard. Everyone watched and laughed. The gray-blue of early morning marred the wildflower bouquets hanging from the walls, splashes of color in the guttering light.

Ottille clutched at her bare chest and shrieked, "They're going to ravish me, husband!"

Gregor stepped out from under the eaves of the dorms where everyone slept. "Unhand her, now," he shouted. "Or I'll have you beasts in my stew this evening!"

Selene chuckled as Gregor leapt forward and chased the two men around with his hammer, swinging half-heartedly in their direction, just missing. Missing on purpose, really.

We're all slaves to rituals, in one way or another. This one was an imperial custom, and a particularly evocative one. Perhaps it was a remnant of a more violent past, where bands of men used to claim brides and ransom them to the groom.

A question came to mind: how were they to be wholly Althann when they were tied to these Istryanish customs? Or maybe they were something new. Althann and human—something unseen on the Continent for centuries.

It was all in the strongbox. Whoever collected the journals and the records had been thorough: it proved it. Althann had children with humans, when Istryan first landed. It was for peace. An impossible, shredding truth, and yet made perfect sense. Nearly everyone here were the descendants of those noble families that thought to make peace with the werewolves, and the werewolves who thought to make peace with the humans.

Someone had betrayed them, and time had erased them from knowledge. No, not time. The Sigurians. The new gods, real or not, had turned humanity against them. Or maybe it was never gods, and they just became excuses.

But here could be something new! Ottille and Gregor's marriage was only the beginning. The beginning of an idea long thought impossible since the beginning of the empire. All they had to do was defend it. But if they *won*—imagine the possibilities! Wolf and man, living alongside each other. Selene allowed herself something she rarely ever felt, and it filled her heart like a hollow filling with water.

Hope.

Leon rushed out of his sleeping quarters, arse-naked, axe and sword in hand. All pale and freckled, powerful back muscles flexing. "Where's the fight?" he roared, ropy veins dancing across his thick neck.

They stopped the game and looked at him. Then they laughed and his chest and face splotched with red.

"Are you..." The weapons fell by his side. Then he roared with laughter, cocking his head back and throat pumping.

"We've got the decorations out already," Trestinsen yelled, pointing at Leon. "Don't need more!"

"Not sure we'll get much yardage out of that," Rani said, shading her face in embarrassment.

Leon covered himself with the hilt of his axe. "It's cold, alright?"

"Just care you don't lop it off," Selene shouted.

They looked up and laughed, Ottille smiling, her face twisting in apology. *Sorry you can't join us.*

Trestinsen slapped Gregor on the shoulder. "Alright, groom. It's time for us to leave the women to it."

I T WAS LIKE WELL-OILED forge, each part working in unison. Blauna and Lorela did the bride's hair in a high up-do, a courtly style. As they took a thread and needle through her light brown hair, Selene instructed them like a master tailor. Precise strokes, up, down, in, out. Finally, it was all pulled out, and secured with a bow. It was a strange kind of loss, for her, like the passing of a long sick animal.

Selene would've worn her hair in the same style if she were to ever be married. But she'd long given up on marriage. In the eyes of society, she'd be ruined, and she knew how people spoke of her. *The Whore of Dogs. The Bitch of Hounds.* She didn't rightly know if she cared, either. Marriage had been driven into her and expected of her from an early age. Maybe she'd dreamed of being married, once. *That's true. I might've married Tristain.* But now—now she had other dreams.

Below, Sanna and Rani threaded flowers to the bride's dress. Well, the little girl did her best, while the cook's wife followed up with a quick needle, fixing the girl's mistakes. Helena washed the bride's feet in ale, scrubbing between her toes with a brush, then applied pig fat to them to make them shine.

Ottille made a sound, a half-laugh. "I could get used to this kind of attention."

They laughed. Outside the window, the deep sound of a lute rang out, the quick tune drifting into the chamber.

"What's that playing," Lorela asked, and ran to the window, skirts flowing around her skinny legs. Helena had taken up the hem so the long dress—once her mother's—didn't drag on the ground and fray. The girl gasped. "Blauna! Come, look!"

Selene looked out and down. Dunstad sat cross-legged on the cart and plucked at the basso, his fingers moving effortlessly over the huge belly. The strings mixed with the strands of his long blonde hair as it hung over his face. He spoke without looking at them.

"What would the bride like to hear? Glamis of the Tower? Istryan's Flight? To Each The Stone?"

They ran to the window and shouted.

"Ooh! To Each The Stone," Lorela yelled. It was a famous love song about Ginevra's love of Veles, and how she saved his life during the great wars in the Age of Light.

"The fixing of the moon and the sun!" Sanna cried, having snuck over to the window underneath Selene's gaze.

"Althann Walk!"

"I'd like to hear Stone," Ottille said. Everyone went silent.

"The bride has spoken." Dunstad brushed his hands across the instrument's face for the first chord, his eyes tightened, and his brows knitted as he gave himself entirely to the music, losing himself in throes of the song. "*Spires and stones, waiting,*" he sung.

The black earth is yawning,
Hungry and fading,
Fighting until the dawning,
Yet none of us knew,
The god of storms,
Gave to the old and new,
His power and forms,
With all might,
The abomination fought,
Brought the storm low,
Took frightful sport,

The goddess of children and mercy,
Looking on his face,
Took pity on this creature,
Dead and dying of wounds unmade,
The goddess for his hand,
By taking blood to throne,
Spared his life,
To each the stone."

Dunstad finished with a flourish of his fingers and a low note sustained on *stone*.

Lorela sighed. "He's marvelous, isn't he?"

Blauna nodded. She tugged her hand and pointed. Men tramped into the yard, crunching new gravel under their feet put there by Rill, crossbows slung over their shoulder, and the others gasped. At their head, the three captains, frowning up at them.

"I thought we heard music," Arno said. "Looks like I lost, Salvio."

The captain-general laughed generously and Selene gritted her teeth. There was something hateful in their faces, something biting sharper than a sword through the guts. "Five ducats, thank you very much."

Arno slapped a handful of coins into his waiting hand, made that clinking noise only gold can. "Damn you, Salvio. Who was I to know demons don't just sound like screaming dogs."

Selene gritted her teeth. Rani stiffened next to her, tossed her hair behind her shoulders.

"Welcome, captains," Selene said. "You are our honored guests. You are early, however, so Dunstad will entertain you until the ceremony commences."

This drew some sniggers among the men. "Of course," Giustiniani said.

"Please, Rani, see to our guests. That they have all the refreshment and entertainment they could ask for."

"Yes, milady," she said through clenched mouth.

"It'll happen," Ottille said, sighing. She put a hand on Rani's arm. "When my husband was killed, we were called much worse."

"I know. I just... I simply thought for a moment that living far enough from men meant that we could live in peace, live without horrid names that speak of violence." She left the room in long strides, closed the door behind her.

"I should see to our guests, as well," Selene said. The anger had waned some now that Dunstad started playing again and the captains blessedly meant to talk amongst themselves, no doubt making hateful asides.

Why do we need these pricks again?

Because twenty thousand imperial soldiers are coming to kill us and erase us from history.

Selene sighed and braced herself on the crutch, hobbling out the door.

OUT OF THE MUCK and shit of the last years, when Ottille stepped from the arch into the main yard, Selene decided this was something worth holding onto. Her dress wreathed her with a motley of colorful flowers, each like a beautiful butterfly taking flight as she walked, the figure of the Mother Ginevra in her hands, a pretty, carved thing that Gregor had made. Silence descended on the yard as the castle looked on, its walls thick with bright ribbons and smiling faces. The sticky sweetness of burning pine needles and yarrow breezed over them, and Selene thought she could even hear the ocean from here, a low melody that seemed to breathe with them.

Gregor clutched his hand to his face and made a choked sound, his eyes wet. Leaning forward on the crutch, Selene rubbed his arm. "She's beautiful," he said.

Like a door opening to a hidden garden full of gentle flowers and maple and lavender, her heart awed at the sight. All the shit and the blood and the violence faded as she stepped through that door, and into something like hope. She fought it, but like the fierce aestas sun in Highest above her, it beat aside any shield she put up against it.

Ottille was crying, too. Wet streaked the powders she'd had on, but no one cared. Everyone else was too busy streaking their own faces.

Laughing came from above. It was Giustiniani. She narrowed her eyes, then she saw that he wasn't laughing, he was wailing. He'd cracked. A deluge ran down into his mouth, snot exploded from his face, a huge bubble forming under one nostril, grew to the size of his blubbery eyes and popped, soaking his fellows.

It took all her will just to keep it together as they all broke down in laughter. She smiled to see them getting along, if only for a moment.

Before Arno opened his mouth again.

"Come *ragasa*, when we get to the ah—the *consummatio*—the sex?" He wiped his slick hair back with fat fingers.

They sneered up at them. Selene opened her mouth to order them out, appalled they should disrupt this, but the feeling inside more than anything else. It was as though they were making fun of the very notion of hope. "Get—"

"Arno," Giustiniani yelled. "If you don't shut that latrine you call a mouth, I'll tie you to a stone and fire you out of a cannon, *cazza*."

"Is a joke, captain," the lieutenant said.

"Do you see me laughing? Shut up, or I'll throw you off the wall."

Arno huffed, folded his arms like a spoilt child, turned his back on the captain. Was a division there that Selene could take advantage of? Perhaps.

That thought was pushed to the back of her mind for safe-keeping as the bride continued her walk to the foot of the wall. Everyone looked on with adoring eyes, Sanna laughing as she threw flower crowns at Ottille's rear, an Osbergian tradition. Selene wondered if her own wedding that her father had always planned would look something like this, and felt a longing somewhere, that maybe, just maybe, in another life, if things had been different, that she would be walking to Tristain standing there, and then that man standing there blended into Soren, a flash of white hair, and she dispelled that vision as quickly as it came. *I pine for two men long dead.* Maybe there was time for something new.

She caught her eye on Frix. He looked at her, his cheeks pinking, and she smiled. Handsome, in a country sort-of-way, nothing like Tristain or Soren of course, but he was strong, and could do the hard things as they needed. But then, why did she feel that need? Why not be satisfied with herself? It had been drilled into her since she was a little girl that her only worth was as a wife and mother, but why not try something different?

For now, she left the loving to the bride and the groom and looked back to them. Ottille handed the figure of the mother goddess to Gregor, who put it at Selene's feet. Another tradition. "With the binding of these two souls, under the watchful eyes of the Goddess of Mercy," Selene said, "do the Althann walk together into the forest, and the waters and lands will provide, and hold their union fast." She found the words easier to speak than she thought. The idea of officiating their marriage in front of the entire castle made her pits drip, but now she simply let the words come, as she'd heard before among some of the smallfolk on the estate. It felt right to make her own changes, too, and though Ottille looked at her, she nodded appreciatively.

Her own mother had said some of those very words.

"Speak, Ottille, to the ears of the goddess, what this union means to you."

"When I met you, Gregor," she said, her eyes glassy and her breath coming short, "I thought you were too much like my father for me to love, though you looked nothing like him—thankfully." Gentle laughter. "Too stubborn, too argumentative, too dedicated to your work to make time for anyone else." The hint of a smile in his eyes. "Then I met your twins, and I knew that all you were trying to do was forge a world for them, a new world, where we could all be safe. That's why I want to marry you."

Gregor grinned broadly, then swallowed. It was a touching look on the tall, broad-shouldered man, a look that showed a side of him Selene had never seen.

"And you, Gregor?"

"Ottille, you're fierce, and wonderful, and fight for what you believe in—your family. I'm sorry Lucia couldn't be here to see this, but I know she's looking on from wherever Althann go when they die, with a smile on her face."

"She is, I know," Ottille said.

"Family: there's nothing more important to me. You know Sanna means the world to me, and when you said you want a safe world for the children, and you were willing to fight for it, fight for them, I knew I'd met the woman I wanted to share the rest of my life with."

Giustiniani started wailing again, yelling out, "It's just too wonderful!"

"Here, here," Frix yelled. More laughter.

They looked at Selene, and she realized with a little catch in her throat, that all of this had united them in a bond deeper than any ritual of cups or sharing blood. That was all they needed: hope. Hope for the future. Hope that their children might inherit a better world than they grew up in.

Dare I allow myself the same for Tristain? That same belief? She felt it now, and it was hot to the touch, burned her fingers, but salved at the same time. Hope was a pyre. It could offer warmth, but hold it too close, and it scorched. Let them have this gasp of hope, the fire bursting to life, if it gave them strength in the coming battle. They would need it.

"Then have it heard by the goddess, and the lands, and the waters. Ottille and Gregor, you are now bound in sacred union, that none, not even the gods themselves shall break."

Everyone cheered, clapped, whooped, whistled. Dunstad flicked his fingers over the strings and the castle yard rang out with their mirth until the sun dipped below the horizon.

"IT WOULD SEEM YOU have changed my mind, Lady Sigurin," Giustiniani said, bowing his head. His eyes spun a little in their sockets. Drunk on the stores, his men had drained a cask between them already.

Lively conversation stilled, the faces turning to the head of the long table, across plates of roasted meat, greens, and pastries, wafting their delicious scent into the air. Selene's eyes fixed on the general's, two seats down, and she raised her brows in surprise. As far as his capacity to change, she had her doubts, but maybe the drink had lowered his guard. He'd just been handed another goblet by Arno, who sat further down.

"You invited us into what we thought was a den of wolves, a jagged maw. And yet, we have found love can exist in the most unlikely of places, and it brings us great delight. Love is the axis upon which the world turns." The world turned on violence and power and death, but pretty words made pretty feelings. Unrealistic feelings, of course, but one indulged the unrealistic when it came to marriage.

He pushed up his cup, spilled a bit of wine across the table. "Here's to a feast of wolves, and the marriage of Ottille and Gregor. May you have many pups," he said, in a light-hearted, knowing way. Selene found herself smiling. "*Saluti.* To long life!"

"*Saluti!*" they answered, clashing their cups together, spilling their drinks. It was an old tradition—meant to mix drinks so poisoning wasn't a worry. Not that it would be, here. Sharp blades and crossbow bolts were much more the Thousand Sons' style.

Maybe they weren't all so bad, after all.

She drank as they all did. And smiled as Ottille smiled at her. Maybe there was something to this ladyship, after all. That was what she realized—no matter the situation, she'd try to make the best of it. Palerme would work. She would make it work, no matter what.

Arno lifted a leg of lamb to his face and started talking with his mouth shoved into it, leaned forward over the table.

"Mm, yeah, it's got to be said, demons can put on a feast." He chewed with his mouth open and turned to his fellow. "*Ili peggiora kanno a kelor kea nona vatti.*"

The mercenaries laughed. Giustiniani turned to him. "*Cazzo ili re mangiano.* Sorry, Lady Sigurin."

"What did he say?"

He laughed awkwardly. "Hah. I would not repeat it."

"The worst dog is the one you don't beat," one of them said, lacking any such discretion. The other mercenaries lowered their spoons, the brown sauce soaking into their stale bread trenchers.

Leon leaned forward, put his hand on her wrist. "Sel?" She looked down. Her hand reached for the knife used to pare flesh from bone. The sharpest knife on the table. She let it go.

Giustiniani coughed along with one of his underlings who sat next to him. Paulo, maybe.

"It's well, my lady," he said, then spluttered a series of coughs across her, spraying her with spit. She wiped her face. "I'm sorry, I..." His eyes went unfocused like he forgot where he was.

The coughing was contagious, spread to Ottille, who sat next to Giustiniani—afforded the head of the table as the guest of honor.

"Ille, are you alright?" Gregor asked. Her face turned purple. She made guttural coughs, wet and scraping, but nothing worked. She stumbled back out of her chair, her dress caught on the leg, tearing across, a ripping noise ringing out.

"Ille?" Gregor said, sterner now.

"I..." Ottille scraped at her throat. "Can't. Breathe."

Sanna screamed, "Mama!" and kept screaming, the horrible shriek of a child not knowing whether their parent was still alive or just stumbling. Anger leaked out of Selene's skin, and she snatched up the knife. This wasn't food. They'd only been drinking the wine, wine that splashed across the table. Splashed into their cups.

Giustiniani pushed up from his chair and coughed frantically, his eyes turning bloodshot, while Gregor smacked at his wife's back, thinking she was choking.

Rolco matched her movement, flipping out his beltknife. He eyed towards the door: their crossbows and swords leaning against the wall. He seemed unaffected by whatever affliction had suddenly taken hold. But she knew exactly what it was. She'd seen it a hundred times, in the Order.

"Poison," Selene shouted.

The hall erupted into chaos. Althann transformed, bursting chairs apart and rocking the table, sending food soaring across the room. Leon roared, tangled with his own opponent, as one of the mercenaries punched him across the jaw. Pulling him close, he made his beltknife saw against the mercenaries neck, opened him up like a Sigursday gift.

Just her luck—to be attacked on a wedding night when they'd all let their guards down. When her leg was broken. But that was the thing: the world didn't wait for you to be ready to fight. You had to fight with nail and tooth and bone, and sometimes, even that wasn't enough. You had to make it enough.

She pushed up from the table, put the blade between her teeth, and snatched her crutch. A coal-haired mercenary slammed into her, pain shooting up her broken leg. She struggled with the grip on the handle and her balance. She turned, let him move past, his face slitted with fury back at her. Dropped the knife into her hand and planted it to the hilt between his ribs, three, four times. He grimaced, clutched at his chest, then fell over, brought a chair with him with a crash of wood and limbs.

A wolf's howl and bodies clashed, wet smacking sounds of fists and kicks slamming home.

Selene clutched her leg as pain rooted her to the spot. She looked up at a flash of movement and brandished the blade as not Rolco but Arno advanced. In his arms, a crossbow. He lifted the bow high and lashed out with his boot, struck her right in the stomach. She gasped as the kick impacted and again when her head hit the boards, something in her leg twinging. White flared across her vision and her head spun.

"*Tu?*" someone screamed. A ridiculous accent. *Giustiniani?* As the white across her eyes faded, the captain-general made a gagging noise, looked like some fat, swollen beet as his leg gave out from under him and he fell, face first, into the table. A plate of gravy and seasonal vegetables flung upwards over him, and his eyes fixed open as he slid to the ground, splotched and veiny.

The table rocked as a light-tan werewolf jumped on top, stalked towards the mercenaries. Arno stepped back, cautious, pointed his crossbow towards the beast.

"Tell him to stop, lady *cagna*," Arno spat. She didn't know the word, but the meaning was clear.

The werewolf bared its teeth, the form slender and tall, more powerful in the legs than in the arms, though those were no less deadly. Thinner, though no less strong.

"I'd have a care," she said. "She's the bride whose night you ruined."

Ottille peeled back her lips, her teeth dripping with knots of saliva. Arno squeaked. "*Pattana*," he shouted and rattled off a bolt. It sliced across Ottille's shoulder and skidded upwards, thudded harmlessly into the ceiling.

The Ottille-wolf grabbed him around the neck with one huge hand, pulled him high. She shoved the other hand into his chest, and he screamed breathlessly, as squelching sounds filled the hall. Steaming blood spilled across the boards. Someone behind groaned. Arno's arms and legs went slack, crossbow clattering to the ground. Ottille let him fall in a heap. She'd shoved her hand inside, turned his lungs to mush. Made him feel what she felt, by the looks of it.

Selene couldn't deny a pin of terror stabbing the inside of her neck. *Maybe they are ready. The empire's not going to know what hit them. I doubt even the Order knows what they're in for.* A feral werewolf was uncontrollable rage, acting on pure instinct alone. That was what made them so frightening, yes, but also predictable. They lashed out at the nearest warm body.

A conscious werewolf, now that... that was something else. A werewolf that could think, could plan? Selene could think of nothing more terrifying. And she ruled a whole castle of them.

Selene fixed her eyes on Rolco, who dropped his knife. Ottille turned her body to face him, powerful form curling up, the wood groaning underneath her weight. Leon came up behind, blood dripping from his hands, and shoved the captain to the ground.

Rolco rolled over, face up. "I know just as much as you do," he said. "Less. Because I have no idea why I'm not being eaten, right now. Not that I'm complaining."

"We don't kill needlessly, unlike you mercenaries," Gregor said, frowning. All that tension released as he looked at his wife.

Leon lowered his hand. It was slippery with blood, but he pulled her upright, and then helped her stand, the hall seesawing wildly. She looked around. All the mercenaries were dead, leaking from holes in their necks or their chests. Sanna's eyes met hers as Helena held her behind her leg. They were full of terror, and it made Selene grimace.

"What do you want?" Rolco narrowed his eyes on her.

"A reason I shouldn't kill you, too. What in the four hells was that about?"

He laid back, his hands clasped under his head. "Ah... my guess is, Arno wanted the general's chair. Maybe he figured he could blame Salvio's death on you werewolves." He flinched as the Ottille-wolf brought a long leg down from the table and sidled close to him. He scrambled back on his elbows to meet Leon's leg.

"He was an idiot, clearly," he said when Ottille relaxed. As much as two hundred stones of muscle and primal fury could relax; less relaxed, more ready to pounce. "A dead idiot."

No laughter went through them. Selene felt the tension as thick as congealed blood. "What will you say happened today?"

"That they killed each other. It was bound to happen at some point."

"And you'll be left to claim the general's chair."

"Naturally."

"Well, hang on," Gregor said. "How can we trust them now? We're back where we started, without help."

The duca's words drifted into her ears. *Some men were made to lead, some to follow. He's the latter.* The rest needed to be convinced of it, though. Gregor and Leon looked like they wanted to kill every single one of the mercenaries camped by the Bight, as well. She understood revenge well. It was hardly ever a *want*, but a *need*.

"We need the soldiers." Selene leaned forward. "And the Thousand Sons have a new general. I don't think he'll be betraying us anytime soon."

"Weee couuuuld make himmm scccreaaam," Ottille said, the words garbling on her wolfen tongue. "Ifff eeee beetraayys us." She snorted, a glob of saliva splatting across his cheek.

"True enough," Selene said. "I don't think the new general overestimates his position."

Rolco shook his head spiritedly. Selene thought she could smell piss, saw a wet patch spread across his trousers. It was amusing to think only a few days ago, they were full of pride. Now two of them were dead, and the other had been brought to heel like a scared dog.

"Will they listen to him?" Leon said.

"They'll listen to coin."

"I still don't trust him," Gregor said, folding his meaty arms.

"I... I can give you your man. Alain, right?" Rolco swiveled his head around, hoping to find mercy in someone's eyes. His life was still quite low on their priorities, and he knew it.

She was curious. "You'll let him go?"

"I don't care about him, it was Giustiniani. They buggered each other, everyone knew it. Then Alain took off after Malatesta, and you can bet Salvio wasn't happy with that."

"A… a bugger?" Selene was confused.

"Fucks men," he replied.

"I know what a bugger is," she snapped, her cheeks heating up. "I just didn't realize Alain was one. Or Giustiniani."

He laughed. "Giustiniani would hump anything with a warm hole."

For some reason, she found herself embarrassed and angered by the implication. "Fine. Release Alain. We need all the fighters we can get. I'm not disabused of the notion that the empire's army will be here in a couple of months."

"And you'll let me live?"

She looked at Gregor, who nodded. Ottille, and she nodded as well, turned back to human form, covered herself with a cloak handed to her by Helena. She leaned down to hug Sanna, and the little girl sobbed, smacking at her mother's shoulders with furious whacks.

"It's alright, Sanna, I'm well," she said, between her daughter's cries.

Gregor turned to Selene. "But how?"

She smiled. "Many, many poisons that kill men just debilitate or take a toll on werewolves, but don't kill them. This was no Order poison. Probably just a foxglove or a hemlock." She turned to Rolco. "Leon and Gregor are going to watch you to make sure you do what you're told. Take him."

INTERLUDE

FERVUM, 1045

The basic premise is questionable. If Sigur truly created the
curse of lycanthropy, why did he make them as strong as ten of
his creations, that being man? With their healing powers, their
nigh-impenetrable skin, and their enhanced senses, they would
seem to be the ultimate predator. It is only a matter of time
before the predator turns on its prey, and the hunter becomes
the hunted.

— APOSTATE LORISTIN

THE CRUSADERS' CAMP WAS a stain on the black, greasing the air with cookfires, leaving behind that noisome spoor of oil, leather, and horse that only armies could produce. It made her think of home. She'd lived on battlefields and in camps for most of her life, and some of her happiest memories had been made in those places. Some of her worst, too, but who was counting? Baba would likely say she was being sentimental, and sentimentality was a quick road to death.

But Baba had drunk himself to death over his wife leaving, so what the fuck did he know?

Frix came up behind, sniffed at the air. He reached out with a claw and pointed at the skyline, where the night breached a gap in the torches, flooding in like a marauding army. She shook her head.

She sensed Olaf drifting towards her, sniffed him out. Not that it was hard to miss. He stunk like a wet dog, ever since he'd traipsed through the upper reaches of the Tibor two days past. He'd insisted on the jaunt, even though they'd be stuck with a wet, stinking furball for the rest of the trip.

Though she could hardly blame him. It was fourteen days of hard running from Palerme, only stopping to sleep. Their inhuman stamina meant they could run for twelve hours at a stretch, quicker than a horse at a gallop, but Palerme was a long, long way from the empire's army.

She'd taken her enjoyment from Frix. He was handsome enough, though a little lean for her taste. She certainly wasn't one for the tonsured Sefinn, nor the pockmarked Olaf. Of the three, Frix provided enough entertainment. One night or two she had the idea of inviting all three into her bed, but decided it was better not to complicate things. Orgies often left one party or another jilted.

It wasn't her fault, not really. The transformation, though conscious, still turned her into a primal beast, something close to instinctual and rabid, only wanting to fight and only wanting to fuck. Some nights, she'd sensed a hesitation in Frix. Not enough to stop him, at any rate. That same animality came as easily to Frix as it did Kyrah.

That was the interesting thing, though: it was only in their human form that they found compatibility. She hadn't realized it before, but her quim actually disappeared when she transformed. Same for Frix—his cock disappeared under a layer of fur, like a turtle into its shell. It was as though, strangely, whatever god had made them hadn't wanted them to reproduce in their wolf form.

But those nights when they stopped to rest—they could scarcely keep their hands off each other. Fucking, writhing, biting, wrapped around each other in the dirt and leaves. She got hers and she made sure he got his. And she didn't leave a wet furball stench wherever she went.

She shoved her hand into Olaf's side, made him yelp. "Lackwit."

"I can't fucking see you," he said. All the syllables were stretched out in his mouth, but they'd grown to understand each other over the last couple of weeks. "Or smell you. You're like a fucking ghost."

"Use your eyes, idiot." She pointed over the vegetation on the dark plain. To the blue distance, and the winking lights and tall, pale walls of Annalt. "There's nothing there. Not a thing. Not even scouts, as far as I can smell. That's where we'll get in."

"What are we waiting for, then?"

Lights winked out in the middle of the camp. Cookfires, doused for the night. No army had its unique rituals. At the core of all the pulsing, beating shit, they were all the same. A crusader army was no exception.

"That."

She inhaled. And tumbled forward, pouncing across the plain on all fours. Pitch-black wheat brushed the side of her ears, her arms, her stomach. Her hands scraped up earth dry without rain, set them flying in clods behind her as she ran. She leapt over a trickling stream, and the smell of piss blew into her nose. Over the flat farms, a man pissing upwind. A soldier, stinking and unwashed. No one important, though. No one worth killing would be voiding themselves into a field in the dead of night.

The others followed, catching up to her as she slowed at the edge of the camp. Someone barked a laugh in the middle distance, while the scent shapes of five men hung close to the floor. Sleeping. Some were still awake, but most were asleep.

Boots stomped the dirt, fifty strides away. She flattened herself. A torch waved across the tops of the wheat, two sentries talked with each other. Frix came alongside her, the other two close behind.

"...know why we're here," one said in Low Istryan, his voice slurred with drink.

"You saw what happened to the prince?" the other one asked, this one less drunk. He had a voice like taking files to the back teeth, though.

"Just another demon attack. About time we killed 'em all."

"He fell off his horse, how's that a demon attack?"

"Demons spook horses, hadn't you known?"

"But there was no demon, I'm telling you." The first one's voice became exasperated. "He's just fallen off his horse, is all. It was a Vyahtken threw him."

"There's horse demons, now? Sigur wept, what's this world coming to?"

The sound of a forehead being slapped. "No, you lackwit. No demon."

"Eh? Then what killed him?"

"His horse."

"Aye. What's that have to do with demons?"

"Nothing!"

They moved past, out of earshot. She looked back, her mind swimming with troubled thoughts. *The prince... Prince Reynard?* Was that why they camped here?

Oh well. They could be camping on Luni for all she cared.

She jerked her head in the direction of the camp, further inside. "Silence," she hissed. She didn't doubt her ability to run when the time came to it. It wasn't about running—it was about inflicting as much damage as possible without being detected.

Troublingly, she'd developed an affinity for the lost souls behind her. That's what they all were, under that ex-Order woman. Lost. No one to lead them, not really. She tried her best, but they needed an Althann. Someone to step up.

Wouldn't be her, though, not for Eme's bounteous arse or Sigur's big sword. You can be sure of that. Once the crusaders were dealt with, she was back to Alania. Cracking skulls and skolling ale, just as she liked it. And there were no shortages of skulls to crack in Valenti. Or ale, for that matter.

She was here because it was a matter of pride. Could she allow Sigurites to wipe out her—dare she say—her kin? No. It would be like asking a battlefield corpse half-eaten by dogs to rise again. She mightn't have had much after Ammercy, but she still had her pride. Ulrich, of course, had gone back to his family once the duca offered her employment. The weak-chinned bastard. She hated him for that. She thought they'd always die together on a rotten battlefield surrounded by the innumerable corpses of their enemies.

She lowered her body to the ground and sniffed out a ring of tents, surrounding a pen of sleeping pigs. All curled up with each other. The men in the tents, and the pigs in the pen. Adorable, really. Almost seemed a pity to slaughter them all.

But that would have to wait. Slaughtering pigs—and soldiers—made a right mess, and wasn't exactly quiet, either. No, she needed something big, and targeted.

Her father had a saying, matched by a story he always told her. The pigs brought it to mind. It was a story of Ansulfiq, the first royal guard. She smiled a wolf's grin as she remembered that aweing feeling of hearing his stories. That way he'd do the voices for each of the characters. Deep and sonorous for the witch—there was always a witch in these stories. Then her smile dropped when she realized she'd never hear those stories again. Not from him.

"We need some pitch," she growled low, sniffing the air. There was none around here, but the faint, acrid smell of black wafted over from the east, towards the middle of the camp. An army this size had need of a huge amount of pitch for their torches.

"I'll go alone." They nodded their understanding. Good—she didn't need them questioning her orders, now. Not when they were in the mouth of the enemy.

She kept low along the black grass, avoiding the sentries and the cookfires. Some were still awake, singing songs and drinking sour ale. Camp followers sung along with them in various stages of undress, pink with merry making. She could smell the stench of debauchery on their breaths.

Are they celebrating the prince's death? There's no love lost between the provinces of the empire. It was a wonder the Lion Throne ever held anything together. They were a bunch of children griping and grabbing at each other's toys, just to see who had the biggest pile. Only with swords and arrows and cannonstones. Maybe it was just impetus, a groaning mountain that didn't collapse out of sheer stubbornness.

A woman stumbled across her path and Kyrah flattened herself against the side of a black tent. There were too many scents to keep track of in this place. The woman was so close, Kyrah could see the whites of her eyes. They were bloodshot, like she'd been crying. From the stink on her, she'd just been done with a group of soldiers. Kyrah was well familiar with that stench. Or maybe they'd just been done with the woman.

She had red hair, and Kyrah noticed now that she wore it down and mussed up, a patch missing from the top. Where it had been pulled. Torn out.

Kyrah's neck bristled with anger, but she breathed. Instead of hunting down and pulling off the cocks of the men that had done this, she unfixed herself from the tent's form and kept going. There was nothing could be done for the woman, now.

Pressure built in her head as she got closer to the center of the camp. An unnerving sort of pressure, like her eyes were being tugged out from the inside of her skull. Like a loop of wire held around the root, and simply tugged a little—like the god or the person holding them wasn't quite committed to having them out, just yet. Every step closer churned her guts, her fur standing on end, waves of repulsion soaring through her stomach.

What is going on?

A yard broke the wheat stalks, cut the field in two. Maybe once it had been a horse yard, but now it had been given over to the mud and metal of drills. Two sentries yawned at their posts, leaning on the shafts of their spears to keep them upright. The sounds of snoring behind them—hundreds of men in makeshift barracks and lean-tos—was like the grinding of a mountain in Kyrah's sensitive ears.

She put down her feeling to a sense of heightened danger—her body realizing she was dead if they saw her. Dead at any moment. She kept low as she followed the length of the fence, more bodily smells drifting into her nose, and the gaps between them, the gaps in bunks. That moment stretched, her heart hammering like a horseman's mace on a man's skull.

On the other side of the yard, she found solace in the gap between the makeshift barracks and a farmhouse. Damp slithered up the farmhouse's wooden walls, the constant rains in this part of the country leaving the timber wet to the touch. Any sign of the previous inhabitants had been washed away by the flood of soldiers, the shelves stripped bare as she looked through a high window. Men slept on the ground around a smoldering fire, dark smoke pouring out of the smoke hole. The acrid taste of ash filled her mouth.

She remembered passing what felt like centuries around a fire just like this, telling each other tales. Istryan's Landing, and songs about the gods. Pandomir knew every single one, and she could hear him now, strumming his lute. Ulrich, Ludi, and her singing along. Her closest companions, and yet in the end, she'd lost them too. The duca's marines hadn't been nearly as close, but if she cared about that, it would mean admitting weakness. Weakness led to liability led to death. She kept moving. There was nothing here, nothing but bad memories and ash.

Around the side of the farmhouse, further rings of tents and If before, she felt like the tugging behind her eyes was gentle, now the bastard who had hold of the wires decided to yank. Pain split her head. Spilled it open, threatening to reveal the pink inside. She flinched, looked around, sniffed the air. What in the hells was happening to her?

On top of a dray, secured with chains, were black barrels sealed with wax. The resinous pitch leaked out the wax, giving off a halo of putridness. There it was. She ignored the pain, pushed it through her like so many other weaknesses. Breathing. She focused on her breathing, as she pulled up onto the dray. The stench tore into her nose. It was like standing at the edge of an ocean drained of all its water, leaving behind only a field of muck and dead fish.

She held her breath, and the pain behind her eyes became worse. She tilted backward and the dray popped off the block it was leaning on. The tray tilted, the barrels rocking as she struggled to keep balance. This dance went on for a few moments as she swore quietly, the ground wavering underneath her.

A clicking noise rang out. She snapped her eyes to the source of the sound, only to catch the wind of a bolt. Her left eye burned in its socket, heat spreading through it. She snarled and jumped for the source, two shadows a hundred feet away, two men with a stink on them, the chemical stink of poison. As she lunged forward, she clipped something hard with her left leg and went sprawling across the ground.

She'd clipped the side rail of the dray. No time to linger on that blunder or she'd be dead. She got up and ran at them, the smells changing, the shadows splitting apart, the left one wafting into darkness. Bolts whistled as they cut the air. They rattled off two, five, eight, slammed into dirt behind her with the rapid clicks and the sound of gas releasing. *Thwock-thwock-thwock.* Drum crossbows. Damn Swords.

She flattened against the ground and somersaulted backward. The last time she'd faced Order assassins, she'd been killed. And these ones had surprised her. More than two likely waited in the shadows spreading across her left side. She pushed backward, flipped up on top of the dray, landed awkwardly, pain ricocheting up her left leg. Bolts one after the other thumped into the wood. Barrels tipped over and tumbled down, rolling towards her. She cradled one in her arms and leaped off the dray, bounding forward on hard dirt.

"You got her eye," one shouted. She whirred her head around, trying to follow the sound, but it was though her left eye was looking through pitch. She breathed in the scent. A shape in her mind's eye, racing along the roof of the farmhouse. She picked up a rock in her claws and threw it the shape's direction. The stone cut the air with a high-pitched hum and squelched as it punched right through the shadow, sending it hurling over the side of the roof's eaves.

The man dropped in a heap a few strides ahead. She saw as she passed that her throw had nearly cut his back in two, tearing up ribs and pink lung out the other side.

She ducked down as another volley of quarrels came whizzing towards her, cutting into a pair of tents in front of her. Springing down the lane, she soared back into the wheat and hoped to lose her pursuers there.

Bells rang out and torches roared to life ahead. Shouting and horns tearing up the lethargy of the night like a bull goring its handler. She paused for a moment, felt her eye gingerly with her hand. Stiff feathers brushed against her fingers, wood stuck half to the end into her eye socket. *Fuck.* She only hoped it wasn't poisoned.

She wanted to roar, tear through this whole camp, gut every soldier who got in her path. She put aside her primal urges. They came from a place of fear, and fear was weakness.

Frix and his cousins were there, waiting, by the pen. The foul smell of brackish water and pig sweat filled the air. She skidded in the mud and put the barrel down, the noise surprising them.

"How the—" Sefinn stared at her with wild eyes.

"The whole camp," Olaf said. Torches burst to life in a ring of fire around them. Horns blasted, disembodied orders shot through the air, men and metal became a thunderhead of noise. "Whatever you're doing, you'd better do it now."

Kyrah tore open the sealed top of the barrel and plunged her hand into the sticky, treacle-like mess. It could hardly be called a liquid, more like a paste as she slapped it on the terrified pigs, coating their backs.

"Help, idiots!" she shouted.

Three soldiers with their pants half-on clattered up, torches in hand, eyes bleary with sleep. They barely screamed when Olaf leapt on them, tore one apart with his hands, bit the second one's head clean off. The werewolf tossed the mangled part behind him like a lord at his dinner table tossing away unwanted fat to his dogs. The third soldier dropped his torch and slapped around his belt with a frightened squeak, fumbling the hilt of his sword. Before he could draw it a finger's width, Sefinn slashed his claws deep across the man's back, tore through his gambeson like warm butter.

Frix was there to her left, dousing up the pigs on that side with pitch. Though she didn't see him. Only heard, smelled him. It was true, then. They'd put a bolt in her eye. And if the sight was gone, just like the pain now, surely that meant it was permanent.

"Demons! Terrors!"

"They mean to eat all our livestock!"

The shouting was on them now, swords ringing, spears clattering, crossbows winding. Surrounded. A sea of faces, washed in torchlight. Orange and spattered with hatred. The nearest to them pushed Sefinn and Olaf back at the end of spears, bristled against them like hunters backing a boar into a corner.

Kyrah snatched up a torch from a nearby post. The flames wavered and she was careful not to get any on her arm.

"Loose!"

A flurry of bolts came at them, slamming into swine flesh. Pigs screamed. Kyrah raised her arm. Metal bit into her arm, skidded off and bounced harmlessly off the ground a few feet away. Another struck her inner thigh. She yowled in pain.

Olaf crashed through the pen in front of her, covered himself in pitch as he rolled along the ground. Three bolts stuck from his chest, one in his shoulder. Swine screeched as they huddled up against each other, their faces painted with terror and black pitch. She had no choice. It was now, or they would all get killed.

She held the torch against the pig in front of her. The pitch went up almost instantly, a flare of almost invisible flame as the animal's skin roasted underneath. It let out horrible noises as it reeled backwards, colliding with another pig, that one catching. At first it was just those two, then the second pig ran from its demise—futilely—straight into Olaf. In refusal of all sense. Being on fire would do that.

Olaf groaned as his arm caught. Fire roiled across him so hot it nearly burnt out Kyrah's remaining eye. She slammed it shut, heard—smelled—the chaos. Soldiers screamed, some yelled, "Fire!" while others just babbled and ran in terror. The heat against her eyelids sent waves of fear crashing through her stomach and her throat. But she couldn't just stand here and wait to die. Her father would say she was being sentimental.

She opened her eyes, and none too soon, since a flaming pig rushed headlong towards her. She jumped, clearing it and landing with a hard thump in the field. She sniffed the air. Beyond the stench of roasting meat, the screams. All blending together now: man, beast, demon. The roar of the fire.

She heard boots behind and whirled, slashed a soldier clean in half, sent the two halves tumbling. Another came in with a spear and she wrapped her hand around the shaft, snapped it into pieces With her other hand she took hold of the gorget around his throat and the soft bits underneath and pulled, yanked his throat out to a soft *pop*, and he stopped coming in, his legs giving way. He landed face down next to her foot, dark, stinking blood gushing out of the hole in his neck. Three more came in at the same time—wisely—and pushed her back at the end of several feet of spear.

"Back, demon!"

Heat spread across her back, the spoor of burning hair and fat cresting like the wave of an ocean of shit. The source of the stench tearing through the field towards them. She turned. The figure's face melted, flesh dripped. It was Olaf. Had to be. He barely had eyes to see, ears to hear, so she couldn't even shout out to stop. Her attackers dropped their spears and ran screaming. Kyrah leapt out of the way as he made it another several feet, then his legs lost their power. He crumpled face-first into the wheat, igniting the dry late harvest.

"Frix! Sefinn!" she roared. Then she turned and lunged through the field, tearing up dry earth ready to burn.

S HE HOWLED AS SHE yanked the bolt from her eye. Hot pain like a brand taken to her orbit burned. Dark blood wetted the steel and two knuckles down the shaft. If she'd been human, she'd be dead. As she sat on the trunk of a fallen tree, she questioned why she wasn't.

She gave a great groan, frustration building inside her. She'd been an inch away from death. Who knew if the god that saved her the first time would think to save her again. Who knew, indeed. Maybe if she died again, the god would see her as unworthy of saving. Just another idiot who got herself killed.

Heroism and bravery are fine, but not if they lead to your death, her father said. Was it bravery that compelled her to risk her life so stupidly like that?

She threw the bolt into the brush, breaking the top of a sapling, and screamed. Not that anyone could hear her. They had bigger problems.

The fire caught the dry wheat, cutting orange ribbons across the camp, equally dry canvas turning clusters of tents into colossal towers of flame. Incorporeal screams filled the night air, music to her ears.

At least these Sigurite bastards were worse off than her.

She transformed to human, the change tearing new wounds in her eye as the ragged skin and muscle tried to reform. She fell in a heap as she screamed, then breathed through it. As soon as she was recognizable as a woman, she changed back again. There was no sense to holding on to an eye that would never come back. And she knew it was impossible now. The flesh in her eye reknitted, skin coming together to leave a cavity.

The pungent stink of a river.

The others bounded into the stand, loping, matted with blood and sweat. Only the two of them. The hope that Olaf had somehow survived, healed from his wounds, hadn't turned into a blazing candle that led to the current situation in the camp; that hope was destroyed just like her eye.

They all changed back, their nakedness the last thing on their minds. Blood and wheat seeds covered their bodies, giving them a kind of modesty. Not that she cared much. When you tore apart your clothes just as often as changing them, you learned to get used to nakedness. And they'd grown used to each other's bits over the last two weeks. Grown close.

Not Olaf. He was a smoldering corpse in a burning field on the horizon.

Sefinn marched up to her, lips curled back in fury, hands extended for a shove. She caught his hands and twisted, flipped him over her hip and he landed with a grunt. His head was the first to transform. She matched the speed of his change and held him down by the throat, his claws tearing into her back. She squeezed, his clawing becoming more frantic, his eyes losing focus.

"Stop!" she roared.

Something hard shoved into her side and she sprawled out, caught herself on the fallen log, turned upright. "He's done," the Frix-wolf yowled.

Kyrah breathed, her back bleeding. Sefinn the man got to his feet and coughed, rubbing at his throat. She changed, then twice again, to heal her back. The others tensed up. Were they afraid of her?

"She killed Olaf!" He turned to Frix. "She saw him in the middle of the pen and threw the torch on him, anyway."

She foamed at the mouth as she yelled. "I did what I had to do to save the rest of us. Olaf was dead, anyway! It was just a matter of time."

Frix just stared at her, his mouth slightly open. Sefinn turned and scanned her face.

"Sigur's enormous cock, your eye," he shouted.

"Two inquisitors took me by surprise," she said, giving them the answer. "I turned and bad luck earned me this. So, you understand, I'm not going to be questioned. I saved our lives."

"Fuck." He shook his head. "But did you—was he really already dead?"

"Yes," she lied. They might've been able to save him. "I did what I did because we were surrounded and had no other choice. Olaf was dead. His body just hadn't caught up to that fact, yet."

Sefinn grabbed the sides of his head and yanked his hair, knelt on dead leaves. "Brother," he yelled, his voice mournful and his eyes filling with tears. The dirge of those left alive. She'd heard that song many times throughout her life.

Frix walked up to her, his eyes avoiding hers. Well, her one eye and the empty hole. "Are you alright?" he asked.

She sat down on the fallen log. "As fine as someone without one eye can be." The words came out harsher than she'd meant. Or maybe she meant them to be harsher. She was in two minds about it.

"Don't worry about Olaf," he said. He reached out and touched her forearm. She let his fingers linger, then pulled away. "He'll be buried as a hero back home."

"That place is your home?" She was surprised.

"As much as anywhere else is." He turned his head, gazing fondly into the flames, his light eyes blazing with the reflection. "Do you think this is enough? They'll turn around now?"

"Yes. Or they'll be angrier than ever, and we'll have even less time to prepare."

He faced bodily to her. His eyes passed judgment over her—whatever he believed about her, it was wrong, she knew. They were nothing to each other. Just a way to satisfy each other's urges. "It's 'we'?"

"I was hired for the defense. When I say, 'we', I mean the defenders."

"That's all?"

She frowned, wondered what the gaping hole in her face looked like as she did. Maybe it was a bit pink, a bit gray, a bit white. Pocked scar tissue. "We are nothing, Frix. When we go back, we'll be nothing. This was a bit of fun and nothing more."

Frix looked at his cousin. Watched him cry as the field blazed behind him, staining the sky, warming their bodies. "Then we should leave." Loss in his voice. Not despair, but it was close. Then it became anger, as he spoke his next words. "If this defense is all you're here for, we shouldn't keep you waiting."

She nodded, couldn't agree more. *I've lost enough of myself for this fucking cause. I don't need to lose more. The slightest sign they're losing, and I'm done. They can fend for themselves.*

VOLUME SIX

18 Fervum, Ae.D. 1045

Your Imperial Majesty,

Andreas Gottscheid, Pontiff of the Sigurian Church, has conveyed your utmost desire to bring the campaign to a rapid conclusion. However, I would advise caution in this endeavor. Because of the lycan attack, many of my men have deserted. I know I am not alone in this, as I have spoken to Lords Kloy, Vantash, and Kronstadt, and they have said that their morale is at an all-time low, and a long march ahead of us leaves more desertion to follow. What troubles me is that the attack bespeaks an intelligence in these beasts we had not known.

I advise the utmost caution, and I would wish to speak to you privately in this matter, though you have been unreachable.

Yours in truth and faith,

Duke Sefinn of the Towers

A,

We found the letter on a courier. Duke Towers has been taken into custody and will be executed for his heretical words, with the letter and his scribe put up as evidence. Lords Kloy, Vantash, and Kronstadt have been questioned about their opinions on the intelligence of demons. They said that Towers did not speak on these matters, and they have been exhaustively informed of the price of repeating such heresy.

We must make an example of him before the entire army, to quell any further doubts and raise morale. The empress must appear before the army, though, to reassure all the men that she is still alive and dedicated to the cause. It would be helpful, also, if she could hold the torch to the pyre and appear the aggrieved party, in lieu of her late husband.

U.

CHAPTER 30

WHEN IT COMES TO IT...

LEVITUM, 1045

Often the worst of the siege comes before any fighting actually commences. Fear and panic set into the defenders and do the work of the attackers for them, far more effectively than if they'd done it themselves.

— DUKE ESTRAD, COUNT PALATINE

THE DULL SHINE OF armor came over the rise, just a slight bump on the horizon at first. Then like a flood crashing over the hillside, more soldiers arrived, and more, and more. Flags of a thousand holdings; of blues, reds, yellows, greens, purples. Northern lords, Annaltian barons, Salzheimish dukes, Sanarikki doyars, Rigan counts. The famously disunited Istryan Empire, all united in cause to destroy her and the Althann. She gave a sarcastic snort. It might've been amusing, if the army arrayed against them didn't stream over the horizon like an ocean of steel.

They came from Avercarn. The land was rocky, windswept, as it moved towards the Bight, where she and the others stood. The Avallano Mountains formed a natural funnel, leaving a spit of land cut through by the river Vesun. Over the Vesun, there was a bridge, and a ford, where the river moved to shallows before it dumped into the Southern Ocean. She thought the army might seize that bridge, giving them full access to the south. Only the forest formed by the heavy rains breaking on the mountains barred their passage, to Palerme within. The heart of the forest, the heart of all their hopes and dreams.

Selene watched them for a moment before deciding they should wait no longer. She looked at Leon when he spoke.

"They'll camp before they cross the bridge," he said. "Put the river between us and them. It makes the most sense."

"Yes," said Rolco. "Any commander worth their salt wouldn't put a river between them and retreat, even one with overwhelming arms."

"Overwhelming, is it?" Selene turned her nose up. There had to be some sense of hope.

"Are we looking at the same army? I've half a mind to turn my men around and go back to Lasterce. By the by, I still might. But we've work to do, and we should let them come to us. An assault now would be suicide."

Frix said to Selene, "Kyrah's plan is still sound. We can weaken any assault—"

Rolco cut him off. "You tried that. Do they look weaker?"

That silenced Frix.

"I'm to inform my men that we are to move into the keep and take up defense, my lady."

"Yes," Selene said, sighing. She knew what that meant. They hadn't been the greatest of companions in the beginning, the mercenaries and the Althann. The months since the dinner where three captains went and only one returned—one loyal to demons, no less—had hardly warmed relations.

"I'll tell my people. Frix, ride back and inform them. Tell them nothing of the Sigurites. Best they hear that from me."

She knew just how well the arrival of an army would send things into a panic. She could ill afford that, not now.

Frix nodded and turned his horse around with scarcely a word. Since they'd returned from the attack, none of them had been the same. Maybe it was the pain of losing his cousin, but Frix's warmth to her had cooled, turned practically icy. Kyrah earned all the accolades of a returning hero, triumphant for losing an eye. Selene didn't see what all the attention was for, since she'd given up many things to be here, but fame was capricious. They needed a hero, and she was jealous it wasn't her.

Meanwhile, Sefinn had lost a brother, and had barely been in the keep, making traps and setting them in the forest around Palerme.

The stallion under Frix's legs pulled him into the shadow of the forest and he was gone. Her hip twinged as she turned in the saddle, the remnant of her injury. Muselio had done his work, and she walked, but she'd been left with a slight limp and a bad hip.

"Then we are done here," Rolco said. He turned his horse to the southwest, to the Thousand Sons camp by the ocean. From here, they looked tiny by comparison to the enormous army to the north. Selene couldn't believe they numbered twenty thousand.

"It looks as though the entire empire is falling on us," she said. A chill climbed up her spine. How could she ever believe they stood a chance?

Leon looked at her, his own horse pawing at the dirt, scraping up a juicy weed. "I've seen greater odds. Rennes stood for nearly two years against the archduke's army."

The mention of Rennes gave her pause. He never talked about the campaign in Badonnia. But now was not the time to reminisce, even though she was curious. "This isn't an archduke, this is the empire. And we're not a city with great walls, and thousands of defenders."

"No, but we have Althann. Look at Kyrah. She alone is worth a hundred soldiers. And she's given them all hope, don't underestimate that."

She couldn't deny the woman's success in building morale. That Althann could take the fight to the Sigurites and *live*. That was not nothing. That was everything. Everything Selene couldn't have done. "Enough about her," she snapped.

Leon nodded and gazed out at the river, the surging army already swelling around it like a kanker, a sore to be removed. They sat in silence, a sad silence. She meant to apologize for snapping when he turned and smiled.

"Well, we'd best return. You've a defense to arrange."

She smiled back, her eyebrows knitted in apology. "Yes, we should. Thank you, Leon."

"For what?"

"For being here. Fighting for us when no one else would."

He gave a half-laugh, half-snort. "What else would I do? I'm hardly good for anything else."

She suspected the truth was something deeper, but she left it at that, and they returned in a better silence.

YOU COULD EASILY LOSE your way in the maze of trenches and traps that they'd dug out the front of the keep. Find yourself fallen into a pit trap, break your leg. Spit yourself on a spike trap, get a nasty wound that wouldn't heal. If you survived the blood loss. A warren of trenches carved up the forest floor, the canopy casting deep, black shadows into them, fixing them in your mind to be bottomless pits. If you somehow made it through, arrows and bolts and cannonstones waited you.

The forest was barely passable at this point, and Selene and Leon had to retrace their path through the trench, following the map that Rill had drawn on a sheet in his masonry shed. He'd designed the plans, of course, and had done so with such verve that Selene wasn't sure if he'd pop an artery with his giddiness. The true path doubled-back on itself, several times. She'd unhorsed and walked alongside the young mare, this one a black Vallonian they'd bought from Rolco when he divided the captain-general's estate.

Giustiniani wasn't married, and so his prizes over the many years of fighting—Rolco said banditry—were numerous and were split among his men. This one, she'd called Eda. What else? The mare was a gentle southern sort, nothing like the wild Vyahtkenese or the high-strung northern breeds.

A hammering sound rang out as she approached the bend, matched by a sawing. The trench swallowed them now, only the glimpse of top branches and the green canopy visible. A bird pecked at the side of the trench, its wings flapping hard to keep it hovering, and sucked out a fat worm. The worm wriggled and writhed, as though it didn't know it was already dead. The freshly dug earth held many wormy, mealy treasures. They weren't the only scavengers about to have a feast. Already, she thought, she could see the vultures and the hawks circling, waiting to receive the fallen.

As Rill hammered the last nail into a support beam, he turned to see her approach. One of the boys from the nearby villages lifted his saw out of politeness, though he spoke not a whit of Osbergian. He bowed.

"Aye, milady," Rill said, and nodded. "Good knight."

"Rill, good morrow," Selene said. "We should like to return to the keep. The path is still the same, yes? You've not changed it?" She offered a knowing smile. He'd changed the plans constantly, though there was a method in that.

"No, milady. It's the same. Though I'm sealing it up, now, so you'd best be through. We're about to be under siege."

"Frix." Leon folded his meaty arms. The man had told them as he passed through.

"Aye."

"I told him not to," Selene said.

"I don't think you were that specific," Leon corrected.

"Shit."

This was a fast way to a panic. *That idiot.* A gentle breeze blew through the trees, pushed wisps of black hair across Selene's face. If it weren't for the army just to the north, this might be any day in the south—warming to the aestas months, now.

Leon snorted. "Guess the demon's out of its cage, now."

"Easy for you to say. You've not fifty angry and scared werewolves to contend with. I'd hoped to tell them one by one."

Leon shrugged. "Nothing was ever done by wailing about it. There's naught you can do now. Make the best of the situation, one step at a time."

Selene nodded. "Then prepare as best you can, Rill, and have it done. I won't have anyone outside the walls come nightfall."

"Aye, milady."

"You're very steady for a mason," Leon said. "Were you a soldier, once?"

"No, good knight. You live long enough in one place, and someone's bound to covet what you have. Seems to be the curse of this whole damned place. Even the Sigurites covet what we got, and they've come to claim it."

"How do you suppose that?" Selene asked. "They would see it destroyed."

The silence of the forest was broken by a sudden shriek from the keep. It rang as loud as cannon, causing a flock of nightingales to take flight. She clenched her jaw. Already the panic was setting in. *Fucking Frix.*

"We've wasted enough time. Rill, seal the trenches as soon as the Thousand Sons come through, then return to the keep, post haste."

"Yes, milady."

Perhaps she should've seen this coming. She'd been through a siege before. The worst part is the anticipation; the anxiety and despair that comes with facing down an army and all that came with that prospect. Killing, rape, wanton violence.

Leon followed close behind her, his sword drawn. He knew what the screaming meant. It came unabated now from behind gray walls, like a woman being murdered.

"Damn these trenches," he said. "It's hard to know which way is the right way."

"Well, we want to be careful," Selene said, tracing the path she'd memorized in her mind. She didn't want to fall in a pit, break a leg again. Once in her life was enough—she only barely recovered from that, and still had a twinge in her hip from keeping her leg straight for so long. Then there were the crossbow traps, rigged up to silken threads, so invisible only the most attentive would notice them. An army rushing through would be easy prey. Then there were the dead ends, of course, and the sheer mud walls that only a few men could climb at a time. But then any who stuck their head up would catch a crossbow bolt or a cannonstone for their trouble.

The screaming rang out three times in a row, then fell silent. It was a hard silence, only their hot breaths, their boots, and their horses' hooves for company. Selene wasn't sure what was worse—the screaming or the silence.

Water splashed up their shins, the recent rains filling the floor with a knuckle's width of water that hadn't shifted. None of the sounds of the forest penetrated here, none of the life, as though the place knew that only blood and death would feed its ground. This was a horrible place.

She felt better knowing that this was what the crusaders had in store for them—raining arrows and thundering stones added into the bargain.

At the end of the maze, the ground leveled out again, the tall castle walls rising to meet them. No one stood sentry, and so they walked up to the gates unhindered. She squeezed her nails into the meat of her palm. Her heart hammered in her chest like an axeman going at a knight's plate.

"There's no sentry," Leon said. "This can't be good."

Selene didn't answer, kept her eyes fixed on the open gate as they followed the wall. Harsh voices cut the air, "...can't do this." A man's voice. "My mother is human, yes, but she ain't an Order lover."

Everyone clustered around the Saburrian named Kyrah. That was no surprise: she'd earned many accolades since her return. Everyone wanted to know her, to talk to her, to praise her efforts. Selene couldn't deny the success of such efforts, if she'd done what Frix and Sefinn said she really did. Burned down half the crusader supplies, destroyed their livestock and supplies, and caused the desertion of near on a thousand of their men. But they still faced annihilation, and whether the imperial army had twenty thousand or nineteen thousand, it didn't matter. They were still on them, and they still covered the land to the Bight like the conifer forests covered the Avallano Mountains.

"What's going on," Selene said.

"Take her," Helge said, letting his finger fly at her as quick as an arrow. "She's killed dozens of us. If anyone's a traitor, it's her."

They looked at her. Many of them carried worry in their knitted brows, faces crumpled in despair. "Milady did nothing," Ottille shouted, slapping Helge's hand down. His eyes widened and he shoved her. Gregor punched him square across the cheek, his meaty fist making a slapping noise that echoed off the gray walls.

Selene drew her blade. "Tell me, now! What is going on!" Kyrah gave her a tired look.

Helena, the mother of Tristain's wet nurse, Galena, and Helge as well, pointed her finger. "Look, she's coming at us with a drawn blade. She means to kill us, even now!"

Selene was stopped. "What?" A shiver stroked her spine like a spent lover. She thought of Helena as a friend. "What is the meaning of this?"

"Stop fighting," Kyrah yelled. "It's settled already. Everyone who isn't a demon gets to draw straws. The short straw's killed."

"This isn't right, Kyrah," Frix said, putting a hand on her shoulder. Selene ground her teeth. He'd certainly gotten close to her these last few months.

Frustration slapped at Selene's cheeks, tingled her lips. "I am the lady of this keep, and you will tell me what you intend with my people, now, Saburrian."

"I intend to kill one of them and hide their body in a crate or a barrel as close to the middle of their camp as I can. It's an old royal guard trick. Foul humors pollute the air and spread disease. The crusaders won't be beaten, not unless we play dirty, and use every trick in the book."

Selene lowered her knife. She couldn't deny the effectiveness of that plan—Sorenius told her that disease spread in camps as quickly as wildfires in a tinder-dry forest. "I wish you had discussed this with me first."

"There's no time." Kyrah pulled the pockmarked, lean Dober by his shoulder. "This one should do."

"But you said, 'humans'?"

"He's human, is he not? Who are the Althann to him? Monsters. Everyone knows the fucking stories—when it comes to it, and we're dying by the dozen, would you trust them not to throw themselves on the mercy of the crusaders? Say they were compelled by us *demons*." She spat the last words with the fervor of a viper.

Selene hesitated. That was also true—she'd had that worry many times. Ginevra's blood, why did this woman have to be right?

"Tell me you're not entertaining this plan, Sel?" Leon said, his eyes widening. "*Sal'brath*, it's murder!"

"You of all people, knight, should know the cost of war," Kyrah answered. "You were in Rennes, too."

"She's right, Leon," Selene said. "Whether I agree with her motivations or not, the plan is a sound one. Disease spreads through a siege camp like wildfire through a forest in summer." She realized she'd echoed Soren's words without meaning to.

"Still murder."

"Have you not the blood of dozens on your blade?" Kyrah said.

"But—"

"Enough." Selene chopped the air with her hand. They needed direction, now. Reassurance. All of them looked at her expectantly. "Regardless, whether the plan is sound, the last thing we need is to fight amongst ourselves. The crusaders will be on us, soon, and we need not be divided. If we're divided, they'll sweep over us without trouble." She looked at Kyrah. "Besides, do we even know if they intend to encircle us? Maybe they'll just assault once they've crossed the river."

"An army of that size creaks under its own burden. Any commander worth their stripes would wait until the supply train's caught up, and the men have had a chance to rest. I'd say we have a couple of days, at least."

"I can keep watch," Frix said, "tell you when they're moving." Selene regarded him coolly.

"Leon?" she asked.

He chewed his bottom lip. "Yeah." He sighed, voice flat. "I'd say that's what they'd do."

"Then I say again: the plan is a good one."

In the silence that followed, an unacknowledged shift in the conversation took place. They were going to do it. It was just a matter of who. Helge seemed to feel the shift, too. He started yelling, furiously pointing at Selene. "Hey! Why not kill her, if anyone deserves it, it's her." Then he shoved Dober forward, yelled, "Or him! He's no one. None of the other miners like him." He didn't look around for support, as though surliness deserved the death penalty, and that fact was so obvious as to be a foregone conclusion.

Selene ground the tips of her fingers into the knife's handle. Ground her thumb into the ring-guard before the blade, that stopped you from lopping off your fingers when you rammed it into someone's guts. If there was a choice to be made, it should be him. *Coward*.

"I'll do it," Dober yelled. "Can't say I've got much to live for."

Selene sighed, felt a guilty pang of relief. The man's forthrightness had spared her the mess of killing a man who didn't want to be killed. Who wouldn't give up a little morality to feel relief, given the situation?

"I'll do it."

"Why, goodman?" Leon said. "This is madness."

"Given the choice between a pyre or a spike and a quick blade in here, I'll take the quick blade, any time."

"We may yet live."

"I know I won't. It's only a matter of time before things go to shit. They've always done, whenever I've been around. That's what my father told me, and he was always right." He gave a soft snort of laughter. "And this is possibly the biggest shit anyone's ever had happen to 'em. Sorry for that."

Selene nearly hesitated, but she knew the soundness of the plan. They all knew the tally, how the pieces would fall. Every single chance needed to be taken, every single trick needed to be played.

She turned her blade over in her hand, offered the handle. Dober caressed it gently. "Are you sure," she asked.

"You'd best leave me to do it before I change my mind." He swallowed. Pressed the knife up to his throat and strained. He let it fall by his side. "Gah, can't do it. Someone do it for me."

No one did. No one wanted to be the one to make the hard choice, but then, she'd long been used to making hard choices. Admitting defeat wasn't something she was used to, though. It had to be done.

"Wait," she said. "If anyone should die, it should be the Order captive." She wouldn't name him. In all the preparation, she'd nearly forgotten about him. Nearly. The man she'd once felt something for, and now had betrayed her just as she'd betrayed the Order.

Kyrah and Leon pulled out Ebberich from the dungeon. He'd become overgrown with hair, matted with sweat, and stunk like a wet dog. Putrid sores over him filled with maggots, and skin pulled taut over his ribs, his sunken chest. He was half-dead, already. The sight of him shocked them; caused shocked sighs.

"The executioner should hold the blade," Kyrah said. She swung her longsword over her shoulder. Ebberich barely reacted, just stared at the crowd.

"Very well. Ebberich, son of a corn farmer and a clothier, I sentence you to death for crimes against the Althann."

"And what of you," he said, staring right at her. "What of your crimes against them? Should you not answer for those? You killed far more than I ever have."

"Enough. Carry out the sentence, Kyrah."

She nodded and put a boot to the back of his knee, caused him to shout and topple to his hands and knees. She came around, brought her sword high, and had his head off in one smooth stroke. Blood gushed across the ground like a cataract, a swelling, spurting mess.

She surprised herself. She felt nothing for him. Thought nothing of their time in the Citadel together. A friend, once. Just another corpse, sealed up in the timbers of her memory.

Selene glanced at Kyrah before heading to the lord's tower to go over the preparations again with Leon before the Thousand Sons arrived. "Get it done."

CHAPTER 31
BROKEN
LEVITUM, 1045

*Another of life's falsities: that a man with nothing left to lose
has nothing left to fear.*

— ANONYMOUS

N O ONE KNEW HIM. He was just another on the march, another lost among faceless thousands, doing the work no one wanted to do, the work that broke other men. Digging latrine pits, burying latrine pits, washing soiled underlinens, hanging them in the wind, fetching them when a breeze freed them from their lines. Most avoided or ignored him. Some stared, some laughed. They saw his horrible, stinking face, his missing ear. The blackened stump where his tongue had once been.

"Just another unlucky soul," some said. "Pauper, beggar," others. "Scum. Oathbreaker."

He got those a lot, from the knights, mostly, when they chucked their filthy clothes at his head. Removal of the tongue was the punishment for an oathbreaker, a little joke. The insult came from the same knights he had rode for, promised their prince he would save their city. The only selfless thing he'd done in his life. But that wasn't the truth, not really. He realized now that wasn't for them. It was for him. It was selfish. He wanted the

Order, thought he could do a better job. That enough wasn't being done, that the crusade wasn't moving fast enough, hard enough.

How wrong he was.

"Get out of my way," someone yelled and shoved him down.

The washbasket he'd been carrying cast its clean, folded contents across the muddy ground. He smacked his head on the side of a water trough and white flashed across his eyes, blood ran down his cheek. He heard men in armor clanking past, gone as quickly as they'd come.

He laid there for a moment, in the mud. Considered not getting up at all, pretended to be dead. Wished he was dead. A hawk glided above them in the warm blue sky, and he envied the creature's freedom. He wished he had a bow and arrow, so it could see how everything comes back to the muck eventually.

But *he* wouldn't. The god that sustained him, kept him alive, wouldn't let him just go to the muck, to death. Wouldn't let him be free. There was a freedom in death that he'd been denied.

As he worked himself up to a sitting position, he realized something.

He'd lost his will, had it burned out of him, by a god. By Vetterand. Whoever he was. Sigur, maybe. Though all the paintings and the icons depicted Him as a glowing, golden-skinned man with a sword of light, that could be artistic license. This midnight-and-white gold-skinned god could change into a human. Did it have to be Vetterand? A middle-aged, hairless man in a white robe? Could the god look like anything, anyone?

And what about the man's daughter? Was that real, too?

Too many questions. Too many thoughts. Richter made it his mission not to have too many thoughts now, since he knew this god and he knew this god was watching him. He smelled the burning flesh, felt the pain of his ear being removed. His skin being peeled like an apple, leaving a rotten core exposed to the air. Flaps of skin sewn back on raw muscle. Cuts made to tendons, pulled until they made limbs dance. And of course, the scoring of his backside, the lance of pain in his anus, turning him inside out. The madgod, the bugger. Did buggery even count among the gods? Likely as not.

He couldn't believe he once thought he'd learned the lesson of pain. That he had somehow mastered it. The Screamer, what folly. Richter was just a novice compared to Vetterand. No, he wasn't even that. He was an ant, and Vetterand was an uncaring, unnoticing boot coming down to crush him.

Whichever god he was, pain was one of his aspects.

The men in armor were in a hurry. They were bringing up the cannon now that a vantage had been cleared through the forest. Only a lonely stone turret of the keep was visible over the trees, but it was everything he'd worked for, everything he'd wanted. Wasn't it? Palerme. The city of demons, about to be breached and broken by an army that surrounded them on all sides. Not a single lycan would escape.

That had been what he wanted, wasn't it? So why didn't he feel happy about it?

A lean woman with dark hair and light eyes extended a hand. "Let me help you up."

He recognized her. *Fehling.* The noise choked in his throat. What could he say to her after all this time? He didn't know if she'd betrayed him or not. But how could he ask? For all she knew, he was dead, or long gone. Buried under a mountain, perhaps, like they'd said. It wasn't as if he could tell her, anyway. Vetterand had won, and Richter never stood a chance.

"Do I know you?" she said. Her skin glowed, had some color on it from the heat of the south. She even wore her hair tied back, similar to how she had it in Annalt, though less fancy. It framed her sharp cheeks and blue eyes perfectly.

Red, full lips closed around his cock.

Pain bolted up his spine as the remnant of his manhood burned, remembering something that had once brought him so much pleasure. A memory could cut two ways.

He shook his head, trying not to keel over in agony. She handed him a rag and four other Swords jogged past. Jogaila, Paun, Bjorn, and Karl. His old companions.

"Leave that oathbreaker, Fehling." The insult stung, coming from Karl. Richter had wanted him by his side at the top of the Order, wanted them all by his side.

"They're bringing up the cannons. They're saying the walls will fall today."

Fehling hesitated, chewed her lip. "Coming." She dropped the rag, ran off to join the others.

Richter groaned wordlessly as she left her scent in her wake, the stump of his remnant tearing him from the inside, as though it was being cut off all over again. Vetterand had left it like that, hadn't been clean about it. If he'd removed the entire thing, left him with a vacant patch, let it heal properly, it might not have hurt so bad every time he caught a whiff of something pretty.

The god of pain. It wouldn't do to have left him numb. At least it wasn't as bad as taking a piss. That felt like a million knives scraping up inside him. He scarcely drank, ate, for fear of more pain, and his body showed the signs of it. His roughspun clothes hung off his gaunt frame, and his breath stunk like grim death.

It was something Vetterand had said. *You're just a shadow of me. A low thing that I fancy only as my pet.* How many others had he taught over the ages, broken, used. How many other pets did he have? Sallust, probably. The torturer was always by Vetterand's side, as far back as Richter could remember. If he was a god, he seemed to have strong attachment to mortals, in his own, twisted way. *A soldier in the coming war.* He needed soldiers for some secret war. A war between the gods? Was that coming?

Too many questions. He realized he'd been standing in the muck, bleeding from the head for a good long moment, now. He fetched up the washing, already browned and stained, and stood up, heading back to the stream to wash them.

Vetterand faced him, human. Stood in the middle of the path, the mucky trail that thousands of boots had churned up, crisscrossing over the land. Stood like he floated above it all. Maybe he did. But then, Richter noticed, mud flecked the bottom of his robe. Maybe he wasn't so holy, after all, so untouchable.

Watching me. Had Vetterand seen him linger? Seen his thoughts? He hid them. Showed his fear, though that wasn't too difficult.

Two inquisitors stood by his side, pneumatic crossbows in hand. The jutting shapes of armor under their jackets. Heavy arms for a heavy task. "Wait here, Jonas, Franz."

Jonas. One of the inquisitors who'd taken him to the pyre, his flaxen hair tied back like a horse's tail. That seemed like an age ago, happened to a different Richter. Was Franz the other one?

"How are you, my son?"

Broken. In agony. Want to kill myself. Want to throw myself into the ocean and never come up. He nodded.

"You look well, considering the circumstances."

No, I don't. I look like a beggar, a man who's had his tongue burned out and his bits cut open and sewn back together for fun. Silence.

"I want you to do something for me, a task that I know only my finest soldier is capable of."

Finest soldier. More silence.

"I want you to attack the rear of the castle while the cannons assault the front. We'll hold their attention while you sneak around. When you get inside, burn it down. Start a fire. That'll pull their attention away from the wall."

As Vetterand detailed the plan, Richter wondered if he could detect some frustration in the god's voice. The Alanian mercenaries had been an interesting development, one they hadn't expected. Siege warfare was an art in Alania, and these mercenaries were some of its premium artists. Their crossbows and handcannons discouraged any frontal assaults with ladders, forced them to clear a path through the forest right up to the walls so they could bring cannon to bear. The only thing that would outrange them.

No one thought to bring trebuchets, which would outrange them all. Some enterprising counts had started building their own, harvesting the forest for the parts, but the engines would take months to build. Months they didn't have.

Everyone, Richter included, expected that they would take the castle as soon as they arrived. They hadn't expected the traps in the forest, the walls to be rebuilt higher and solid. They certainly hadn't expected a mercenary company to offer their services.

Maybe that stung, most of all. That the demons' gold worked just as well as the empire's. But it wasn't just the demons. It was this Lady of Beasts, Diana. Selene Sigurin, an ironic name if there ever was one. She'd been responsible for their frustrations.

Richter made sure to nod, signaled he understood the plan.

"If you see the Lady of Beasts, capture her if you can," he said. "We need her alive."

Richter nodded again.

"Very good. Take Jonas and Franz with you to the forest behind the keep, and I'll send a runner when the cannons are assaulting the wall."

A nod.

Vetterand placed his hand on Richter's shoulder. It took every ounce of will he had not to scream, utter some horrible bellow, tongueless and wordless. A primal scream of terror, heat boiling up from his stomach, making him sick. He tasted bile on the back of his tongue, tried desperately to hold it in.

"Very good." A smile.

That same wolfish grin as he peeled Richter's skin with a huge, impossibly sharp claw, peeled it off in huge sloughs.

Vetterand's hand left his shoulder and he walked off, the two inquisitors going with him. They'd meet him in the forest, at a lightning-struck dead tree two hundred paces from the walls.

Pain wracked Richter's stump as he voided his bladder, piss running down his leg. Tears streamed down his face, and he closed his eyes, sobbed, bent double, laid in the muck, wanted to die, knew he couldn't.

CHAPTER 32
THE SONG OF CANNON
LEVITUM, 1045

*Only the Vallonians would have the idea to put exploding pow-
der inside a metal tube and put a rock in front of it. Crazy
fuckers.*

— Thousand Son mercenary

COOL EARLY MORNING WICKED at her cheeks, turned them pink
in the pale and gray air, the trees whispering a song of coming
violence. By their reckoning, the crusaders would attack at dawn, and so
she watched, bundled in a cloak, leaning on the inside of a merlon. All
told, it was hardly comfortable, and it could not be said she'd slept under
worse circumstances. She'd scarcely slept, unsurprisingly, and watched as
the mercenaries roused from their sleep, and envied them. The soldiers'
boon. The ability to sleep anywhere and anyhow, like a babe in its mother's
arms.

Leon did much the same, snoozing across from her as a group of men
fought for position at the battlements. They clattered forward in tall,
ridged helmets; the open-faced morions of the south. Crossbows unwound
to not wear out the strings, but they were readied with windlasses to be
armed. The Thousand Sons hardly lived up to their reputation, which

surprised her, given their perfidy, and especially given that dinner only a couple months ago. Rolco had brought them in line, turned them into a professional army; something, dare she say, to be proud of.

Their conversation moved to bawdier things, of course. The soldiers' social mores being what they were—humor passed the time. Well, she guessed as much. She didn't understand Alanian, but vulgarity was vulgarity no matter the language.

She pulled her cloak tighter around her. The aestas months had warmed the days, but the early hours of the morning, just before the dawn, were still cold. Hand nestled on her stomach, she idly fingered the layers of steel, padded jacket, linens. Her stomach beneath, flat, and hard. She'd made it so after her leg healed, unwilling to let it stay flabby. Vulnerable, gravid, painful. She still couldn't believe that Trist had come from her; had been inside her. She looked over the yard to the lord's tower, where he'd be rising just now, his cries answered by another woman. A woman who would always be closer to the boy than his mother. Galena. Even now, the woman's name filled her chest with anger.

But she couldn't think of the babe in this battle. Oh, she fought for him, but she knew that any distractions, any fetters, any hesitation, meant death as quick as an arrow. It was hard not to think of him. The Order had proven again and again that they'd do anything to kill him. This battle was as much for the Althann's survival as it was for his.

Selene was confident their defenses would hold, as long as none of them buckled. Fights would break out among the imperial troops, and many of them were diseased, so Frix had it. If she'd learned anything these last few months, not every man believed in the word of Sigur.

A horn blasted from beyond the treeline. Selene's heart jumped into her mouth. She gathered her wits, one of the first to do so, and jumped to her feet. She readied her crossbow, checked her dagger. "They attack," she yelled. "Make ready." A low hum joined the clipped conversation, hurried orders among the mercenaries and the Althann. Leon jumped to his feet, rushed to her side while further down, Rani, Helena, Ottille, and the others moved into position with bows. Kyrah barked something at a group of Alanians, and they made a path for her.

"They're moving up," she roared. "Tell me to strike and I'll tear into their flank!"

Selene watched her. The woman's neck pulsed with a blue vein, darkened by her skin, threatening to burst with anger. "Go, then. Take three with you. Frix, if you will." *He's already done enough.*

Screams rang out from behind the knotted forest. "The traps," Leon said, stating the obvious perhaps, but it gave them a sense of hope.

"Go," Selene said. Kyrah nodded firmly and turned on her heel, running down the stone walk. Frix and Trestinsen followed her. Frix spared her one last glance. Selene forced a smile and wondered if she'd ever see him again.

The first of the crusaders moved out from behind the screen of a yew trunk—a huge man wielding a two-handed axe. Three more joined him, then a dozen, then forty more. Steel crashed into the trench like a wave erupting against a cliff, men climbing down into the gaps.

"*Libera!*" the mercenary sergeants shouted. Strings snapped, bolts whooshed and slammed against shields and armor. A couple of the crusaders dropped but many didn't, and kept on through the trench, surging like water let into a sluice. A pit opened as the huge axeman trod on the right bit of loose soil, and he fell with a scream onto the end of a spike. The wood glistened red through his thigh, having punched right through the armor. His screams were drowned out as some followed after, joining him in the hole, while others just continued over them as though nothing had happened, burying them from view. Disembodied shouts echoed over the clearing, bouncing off the stone. The sea of steel that surrounded the keep looked endless as more and more soldiers filed in.

"Loose," Selene shouted. She took aim and fired, hitting her mark, but it all seemed pointless. There was no end to the numbers against them. A queue formed at the end of the trench. Mercenaries shot crossbow bolts, triggers snapping closed, windlasses cranking methodically in the second line. Casimir and Sesar, the father and son, worked an oiled machine as they shot bolt after bolt, each hitting their target, but the men who dropped just fell under those stepping over them. Crushed them underneath heavy boots, whether they were dead or not.

Something fast glanced off the slanting stone of the merlon in front of her, and she breathed in sharply. Hiding her face behind, the back of her head on the cool stone, she could feel her heart pounding in her chest. She caught a glimpse of something moving fast just in her periphery, and suddenly the world cracked open.

The lower tower's loophole was blasted apart, stone ripped into the air as though an angry god had pushed his finger against it. Chunks of wood and stone dashed out, tearing apart an unlucky mercenary who'd been standing nearby. Happily, for the rest of them, the lower tower was only where they'd had cots, and wasn't where the children were hiding. That was the lord's tower, at the far rear of the keep.

Though there wasn't anything that could be called *happy* about how one cannonstone had torn through a wall as though it was warm butter.

The terrible power of cannon. They seemed to float into view in her mind, like black nightmares. Their walls didn't stand a chance. *How did I ever think we'd stand a chance against that?*

Deep animal roars boomed across the forest, drowning out her thoughts. She turned, daring to glance through the gap in the battlements again. Five black shapes dashed out, blurring between the trees. One slashed apart a ladder team, their bodies and the ladder reduced to ribbons in mere moments. Two of the beasts punched into the side of a team of oxen rolling up a cannon, the ruminants blaring in pain as they were torn apart. The black bronze tube fell off its frame and rolled onto the shin of one of the cannoneers, snapped it in two and dragged him under. A foolish soldier waved his pike at one of the beasts. The other jumped on him—Trestinsen, perhaps. Took his back, split the pikeman open in a cloud of viscera. Ribs and lungs sprayed into the air, pink bits. The other two sped up the ridge behind the first row of trees, the other three joining them. They disappeared from view, the cries of horses and men their victory clarion.

Another bolt slapped off the wall, too fast for her to dodge. It cut across her cheek, leaving a hot mark. She yelped in surprise, dropped to the side again.

Then she remembered she'd seen the black mouth of cannon on the ridge behind the front line.

"Shoot the cannoneers! Now!" she roared. Then the walls trembled underneath her. She lost her footing, fell against the side of the parapet, thrashing her neck. Pain cracked like a whip up her shoulder.

A thunderous crack slapped her ears. Volleys of dark bolts flew down on the cannons, but fell short, planting like blades of grass in the soil.

She pushed herself upright, her shoulder still tender. "Fire the cannons," she shouted to Leon. He nodded and waved his torch. Two, three times. She held her breath. Another cannonball slammed into the wall, pulling loose a chunk of stone. The floor rattled beneath her feet, like the structure threatened to fall at any moment.

She rubbed her shoulder, pushing the pain out of her thoughts. There was no room for aches and pains in this fight. "Arrows!"

Something clattered off the stone, then a cry. One of the mercenaries dropped, catching an arrow in the eye. Another one. Rani, the cook's wife, let out a clipped scream as an arrow cut through her chest.

Selene raced over and knelt down. Rani's eyes stilled. She was dead before she hit the ground. Selene thought of Dunstad, and his face when he told her his wife was dead.

Tears choked the words in her throat. "Keep your heads down—"

She felt a hand on her back. "Tell me what you need, Sel," Leon said.

"Find Rolco. I want to know what his cannon are doing, and why they aren't firing!"

"Got it." He stood and looked down, made a grimace with his face. One of the archers had got a lucky shot on him, the black shaft fitting through the gap in the battlements, punching into his upper arm. The meat tore open like a butcher at a pig flank.

"Ginevra," Leon swore. He brought his arm up and bit down about the middle of the shaft, snapping the other end off with his free hand. "That'll do. Right, Rolco." He turned, then a crashing noise and screams came from behind them.

She wheeled around. Men and stone cast great arcs across the yard below, where a cannonstone had cut through the top of a parapet and taken out several mercenaries standing behind it. Blood still misted in the air, while fragments floated to the ground, descending like morning fog. Below, the men lay in broken chunks. A head here, an arm there. One lucky—or unlucky, really—man had the side of his head torn apart by the impact but remained standing on the wall, walking around in a daze.

Now Selene was sick. Her breakfast came burning up, bits of sausage splattering across the stone. She'd seen death, done her fair share of killing, but this was something else. This was war. Deepest of all, she realized that had she been a few strides to the right, she would've been mist and bits cast across the ground as well.

Steel clattered against the top of a battlement only a few strides distant. Ladderhooks, biting into stone like a fisherman hooking a catch. Another soared into view, spitting pieces of rock as it caught its quarry, then another further down. The ladder in front of her wobbled with the weight of ascending soldiers, murder on their minds. She drew her knife. Now, this, she could do. She could murder. It was practically the only thing she was good at. If nothing else, it would make her feel better.

T HE WANTON SLAUGHTER WAS almost too much. Soldiers in plate and mail fell like grain before the thresher. Before claw and tooth. A shocked group of pikemen wheeled their long poles around, all too late. Kyrah got on their inside, their shafts slapping dully against her thick skin. Her jaw fixed around one helmet, steel and skull bending to the pressure as she bit down. The pikeman's scream was cut short as she tossed him aside, the sudden lurch making a snapping noise, and he crashed into his fellows like a thrown girl's doll. She planted one long claw in the next one's armpit, in the gap between plates, and he made a wheezing noise, like a bellows deflating. His face twisted in pain, legs gave out, and he was just one more dead beneath her feet. She dispatched the rest of the unit with just as much alacrity.

It was never ending. More filled her sight, spanned the gaps between the trees, an advancing tide swelling around the obstacles in their path. It was almost too much. Almost, was the word. When she looked inside, her vengeance and fury were bottomless. It would last the battle, and beyond. Had to.

A sergeant's whistle sliced the air and a volley of dark bolts cut toward her. She jumped into the branches above her, the quarrels cutting into the pile of dead bodies under her, the sound like hitting wet meat. She hung there for a moment, reckoning her best path of attack, when Trestinsen and Gregor punctured the line of crossbowmen, their screams ringing out as powerful muscles and razor-sharp claws made easy work of them.

Kyrah smiled. She could get used to fighting with this bunch. They needed training, but at least they had the talent for murder that she had, on scale. These soldiers were nothing, though they were endless. The Order's fighters were their real test. But they were nowhere to be seen. Men in all colors—browns, reds, greens, yellows, blacks—wearing emblems of horns, acorns, stags, lions, horses. Sigur's beard, it was like a godsdamned menagerie of heraldry. And there was no end in sight to them. But the real worry was the Order. Where were they?

Thunder cracked across the cloudless sky. Something whipped toward her, cut through branches and leaves like a terrible scythe. The branch she balanced on was cleaved from her grasp. A cannonstone. As she tumbled through the air, she saw the ball of iron, pitted with hammer beats, punch into the side of one of the keep's towers, the lower tower on the south-facing side.

She landed on her knees with a grunt. Another great thunderclap and a stone cut the air above her head, blowing through the top of the battlements on the western side, vanishing a few poor souls taking shelter behind. Those Vallonian inventions employed to horrific effect.

She turned her gaze on the ridge. A flash of powder, white smoke, and she leaped to the right on instinct. Where she stood was instantly chunked, dirt blown into great clods that came raining down on the soldiers forming up behind her.

She grinned. They thought to use cannon against them and she was stupid enough to stare gormlessly as they gained aim on her. She had come close to being turned into chunks, and now she'd pass on that favor to the cannoneers.

She ran and leapt over the first line of pikemen, their spears curving upwards as she soared over them. Her hand brushed out and snapped the tops off of them, like a scythe cutting through grass. She landed on the other side, in the gap between the first and second line. Dirt flicked up, muddied the soldiers behind her as they frantically tried to organize themselves. Sergeants only confused their orders, unable to keep up with her movements.

More powder flashed but the aim was off, didn't catch her flitting across the field. She moved like a falcon chasing its prey, single-minded, just a blur too fast to see until it was too late. As the cannonstone slammed into earth and kicked up a great spray before her, she dove onto the ridge, the cannoneers screaming in fear. She could taste it. Smelled like sweat and piss.

She broke the first over his cannon as he threw up his hands in pitiful defense. The six other teams routed, ran screaming. They expected their position to be safe, and now they ran like scared children. She took no pity on fleeing men. It was a slaughter, after all.

L EON SLAMMED THE BUTT of his heel into the hook and the ladder wobbled, teetered tantalizingly closer to the edge. The men on the ladder squealed like frightened girls seeing the long drop below. He saw no reason to give them hope. The muscles in his back squeezed taut as he shoved the ladder to the side. In an absurd dance, the ladder balanced its weight in the air for just a moment, the men on the end of it wheeling their hands around like a mummery. Some jest or a laugh. Then the one at the top, a man with a moustache over his chin, plunged back, screaming as he fell. The sudden plunge in weight sent the ladder plummeting forward again, dashing against the side of the wall. It veered off, speeded the rest of them to a long fall. They fell into broken heaps at the bottom, crushing some of their friends underneath. Leon grinned, made sure to bare his teeth as he looked down on their still, pale faces and the panicked eyes of those who were lucky enough not to be crushed.

Lucky enough not to be crushed, but dead all the same. They'd all find their way to the ground eventually. That was life. You struggled and struggled until you didn't, anymore. Whether it was a stray arrow or a blade or just old age in the bed, death's long arm came for everyone. There was no sense in delaying the cunt.

"Where's Rolco," Leon roared as he approached a mercenary. A flat-nosed man, who looked like he'd had it broken a few times for good measure, he looked terrified. Must've seen the same death's arm as Leon. He raised a shaking arm to the furthest end of the curtain wall, on the other side of the collapsed tower.

There he was. Dressed in nondescript browns, wrangling a set of pulleys attached to a cannon. Leon shoved through a line of Alanians cranking their crossbows. One dropped right as he approached, caught an arrow in the throat, under the chin of his barbute. He made a gargling noise and slapped his hands to his throat involuntarily, then his eyes rolled back in his head, and he stumbled, right into Leon's path. Leon was pushed as he fell back, then the man kept going and tumbled straight over the side of the wall, legs flipping overhead and over again like a ridiculous spinning top.

Leon ducked as another volley slapped against the stone. He peered over the wall, no shrinking flower. It was the point in the assault, the critical point, where the balance of the battle hung like a murderer from the noose.

The defenders would make their stand and survive, or the attackers would overrun them. From the animal roars coming beyond the treeline, it was hard to believe the attackers were running anywhere but home. But then, there were so many.

"Rolco! Alanian!"

The mercenary gave a mechanical look, his lips thin. "I'm busy, knight. What do you want?"

"Why aren't these cannons firing?"

"Are you deaf, hillman? We've fired several volleys." He pointed to the smoking spouts of a few cannons on the other side of the keep's wall, across the wide yard.

The full weight of cannon on the opposing side deafened anything coming from their side. It was then he realized that they had no chance. The walls were putty against that sort of force. Already, the gate's timbers had been blown inward by the force of a stone and would soon fall.

One of the pulleys snapped, sending the moving cannon's bottom scraping against the stone. Someone cried out, and the bronze tube rolled against the ground, its rear moving in a fast arc. It knocked its full weight against Rolco's lieutenant, bending him double. His legs twisted viciously underneath the narrow gap, made snapping noises. It kept coming, knocked the wind from Leon's chest and clear from the ground. He laughed breathlessly as he tumbled from the wall.

Ended by a fucking accident. Of all the ways death's long arm could reach him, in the middle of a pitched battle, he was ended by a fucking accident.

CHAPTER 33
LESSONS
LEVITUM, 1045

Four gods for four seasons—what of the fifth?

— DAMA, THE GRAY RIDER

THE TWO INQUISITORS WAITED by the blackened tree, crossbows propped nearby.

From here, Richter could barely hear the din of the siege camp, the sharpening of swords, the hammering of anvils, the rustling of horses. Only the few disembodied voices of captains shouting orders filtered through the dense firs and shady pines. The pressure in his mind lifted the further he got from the camp, though the weight on his shoulders and the pain remained.

The weight was the knowledge that he was a god's slave, a god's thrall, willing to do whatever it took to please him. The god of pain, the god of terror. He'd been taken apart and remade into a form that was more pleasing. If Vetterand wanted to end his life, he could, as easily as he'd ended that unfortunate inquisitor that stepped into the dank cellar below Annalt's palace. But he wanted him as a soldier in the coming war.

Richter stepped over a branch, keeping low. It was easier to walk hunched now, bunched together like too much sinew. His skin was almost entirely scar tissue at this point, chopped and mangled and sewed a million different times.

A soldier for a secret war. Was that why Vetterand couldn't show his true form? Why he had to make soldiers to do his bidding?

It has suited me to have human identities.

But why? Surely, it was more than just getting to the top of Order hierarchy. To a god capable of such frightening violence, surely it was more than just soldiers he wanted. Why *did* he want soldiers in the first place?

Was he afraid? What—or who—could he possibly be afraid of? He could butcher the entire army in moments if he wanted to, seize the keep, destroy Palerme, reduce it to rubble. That would be nothing for a god like him.

He couldn't possibly be afraid. There was a reason he was hiding his identity, why it suited him to have the leadership of the Order. A reason that Richter couldn't grasp.

Jonas and Franz both talked loudly. Useless. An Alanian mercenary would've found them in moments, pinned them both with arrows. Richter would be shocked if the demons inside the walls hadn't heard them chatting. Chatting about women they'd had on the road, pillage they'd gained. He could kill them both in moments, and they would die before they ever saw what killed them.

Richter came up behind them, cleared his parched throat.

Franz jumped, swung his crossbow around. "Oh, fuck, it's only the creature."

The creature. What some of them had taken to calling him, just a poor beast the Grand Inquisitor had picked up on the road. Like a scraping of shit on the bottom of his shoe. None of them recognized him for Inquisitor Beltrand, the Hero of Ostelar. He never enjoyed that moniker, but it was a sight better than *creature.*

"You scared the shit out of us," Jonas said. Loose brown hair danced across his face as a breeze rustled the trees, kicking up the scent of mushrooms and rot.

"Leave him. We can climb the walls, over there." Franz pointed to a sloping face of the wall, where it had been buttressed and repaired over the years, bloating outwards like a glutton.

You don't think they'd have trapped that? he wanted to say. Couldn't. Didn't know if he wanted to say it that much, either.

Jonas um-ed and ah-ed. "Or we could use our hooks to climb a tree and swing over to the crenellations."

And get shot as soon as they saw you dicking around in a tree?

"But if they notice us, we'll be stuck in a tree. Like pigs at swill. Easy pickings for an Alanian crossbowman."

"Then I say we'll go with your plan. If we're quiet, we could climb into that tower." The fat, jutting wall met the base of a wide tower, bigger than the others, all neat stonework. Probably the lord's tower.

"Probably the lord's tower," Franz added.

"Eh? Might find the Lady of Beasts there." Jonas jabbed Richter in the ribs with his elbow. "Promise you'll get thirds, after we're done with her."

"Vetterand said to keep her alive," Franz tutted.

"Who said anything about killing her? Just want a little hump, that's all. I've always wanted to fuck a one-armed woman, and I hear she's wild from her time with the demons."

"She's likely to die of shock when the creature has his way with her."

"Fair. Alright, fine. Just do what we tell you, and don't hump the lady. Leave that to us. You know what Vetterand will do to you if you don't listen."

Oh, Richter knew.

"Before or after we kill them all?"

Jonas rolled his eyes. "Before, of course. I'm not about to open the gates and let a soldier have his way with her first."

"Fucking knights. They charge in, get all the glory, all the merits, all the land. What do we Swords get? Nothing. Eh?"

Jonas shook his head. "Nothing."

Richter noticed their hands dripped with big jewels, and they'd just got done boasting about the coffers they'd pillaged, the piles of imperial gold they'd seized.

A soldier in a dented bascinet came running up, his boots crunching branches and truly destroying all semblance of subterfuge they might have thought to have. His great thick red moustache fell over his lips, his ruddy face covered in sweat. "Are you the wolf-fuckers?"

"Wolf-fuckers?" Jonas leveled his crossbow at the newcomer.

"Someone's played a mummer's jest on you," Franz said. It was a common enough jest among the army—the Order didn't hunt demons but humped them. "Maybe whoever sent him hoped the poor bastard would be killed. What's your name?" Jonas still had his crossbow pointed.

"Johannes Palladino."

"Well, Johannes Palladino, what do you have to say?"

"They're bringing up the cannons now."

Jonas looked at Franz. "Finally. Let's fucking go." He slung his crossbow over his shoulder. "Run on, bastard, back to your mother's tit, before you get killed." The soldier turned and sped off, tripped over a branch and didn't look back but kept running, likely imagining that Jonas might change his mind at any moment and shoot him in the back.

"Now," Jonas said, "griping about our lot isn't going to get us any love."

"Send the creature first. If it's trapped, at least we'll know, and it'll get rid of him."

Richter was already ahead. He was sick of listening to the bastards, anyway. Wondered if they'd bragged so loudly about being the ones that had taken the feared Richter Beltrand to the pyre. Seemed likely.

The ground was pitted with rabbit holes and fallen branches. He stepped carefully, not wanting to lose his footing, or make noise, especially not in the shadow of the wall. It would be easy to fall into a trap, with all the leaf litter. Too easy. They were only fifty strides distant now. No sentries waited for them, as far as he could see. All the guards would be at the front, arranged for defense of the front wall, against a breach. It didn't hurt to be careful though. He didn't want to make a fool of himself, get pincushioned with arrows.

A fool of himself? Who was he kidding? Spoken like a man with some pride left, some dignity. He'd lost all that months ago.

Still, he stepped over a fallen log, careful not to make noise. Not that it made much difference. The two inquisitors behind tramped over the litter, snapped twigs, broke leaves, like lumbering oxen looking for grass to eat. Franz slipped on a wet leaf and nearly did the splits, Jonas catching his hand at the last moment.

He groaned in pain, clutching at himself. "I think I pulled something."

Jonas rolled his eyes. "Yet you'll still want to be the first to bury your cock in something pretty."

A guffaw, like a braying donkey. "Yeah."

Richter approached the sloping wall. It was built up over the years, a mound of mismatched brick and different colored mortar, all different shades of gray. He was right. It was a patchwork job, remedies on remedies, to buttress this side of the lord's tower against the weather. Easy enough to climb, any child could manage it. These two idiots would have no problem, and Richter still knew how to put one hand in front of the other. Vetterand hadn't taken that from him, happily.

Then why had they left such a gaping hole in their defenses? Surely, they knew it was here. They'd trapped the forest not three hundred paces from here, where a week prior, a poor scout had fallen into a pit of spikes slathered with feces. He'd died of fever not three days later.

He put his hand out to stop Jonas. *There.* It had looked like a part of the stonework, just an arrowloop for vision and for firing out. Unused this side of the keep, where no one expected an assault to come from. In the sun, he hadn't noticed it, but having climbed the slope a little, he saw it now, in the shadow of the tower, in the shadow of the arrowloop. A bolthead, glinting and metal. A light from inside gave it the faintest glimmer.

He wouldn't have noticed it had he not trained his one eye better in the last few months. It was incredible what you took for granted. The use of both eyes made each individual eye weaker, he realized. One eye was all he really needed, though his depth perception left a lot to be desired. Though you could get used to anything, given enough time.

The pain, though, the pain of his stump, the pain of his loss. He couldn't get used to that. How did he still enough pride to be bruised about what happened? He had lost, Vetterand had won. He'd taken on a god and lost. Little wonder.

Richter looked down. Almost invisible, a line of silk wire drew taut across the misshapen stonework, not two knuckle-widths from Jonas's boot. He nodded, drawing their attention, and pointed.

"Sigur be praised," Jonas said, sighing in relief. "I might've died. Fucking demons. Tricky bastards."

"Who knew, eh?"

How many demons have these idiots fought before? Every demon he'd ever faced had tricks. They lived in a world where they were hunted. Of course, they had ways of surviving. Learned ways of surviving, earned by tooth and claw. He admired their will, their anger, their instinct. These two wouldn't stand a chance if Richter wasn't here.

Was that why Vetterand had sent them here? Was this another test?

Jonas slapped Richter on the shoulder. "Guess I owe you my life, Creature. Tell you what, I'll let you have the first wet cunt we find. After me, of course."

"And me," Franz said. "I'm not touching a woman that's been touched by him, first."

"Fine, you can have the first woman we find after both of us are done with her. Sound fair?"

Richter didn't answer, just stepped over the wire. He wanted it to be a false wire, hoped the real wire was up ahead and the bolt would plant itself straight into his chest. Not that he'd die, but at least they'd think he was dead and might stop talking to him.

There was no true wire, other than one they'd stepped over.

At the top of the stonework, they had a full view of the keep's bailey. Empty. Not a soul kept back—they were all at the front, all fighting. Even the women, it seemed.

Horses knickered in the stables, a roughhewn building of new logs. Everything was new, even some of the bricks. They'd built a home here, with their sweat and effort, and made it something enviable. It was nothing like Istrya or Annalt, of course, nor their respective palaces, but it was at least as grand as the march lord's, back in the Cisnistrian Marches. If not grander. Nothing had a sense of murk or age about it, except the keep itself. No tired moss clung to the walls, and the ivy that grew over the stones was well-kept, groomed and blossomed with white flowers. Hard-packed earth sat at the bailey's floor, well-formed, a solid foundation. Cobbled, so the mud didn't get churned up easily, and make ruts in the ground when it rained.

Demons built this place? It almost seemed a tragedy to burn it down, reduce it to rubble. But that was all he was good for. Destruction. He'd never made anything in his life, never created. And he never would. He was a god's thrall. Everything that belonged to him belonged to Vetterand.

The door at the base of the tower was locked, of course. Jonas came forward with the end of his crossbow, smashed open the latch with a blow of the stock.

"This is too easy," he said as the door juddered open. "I'm about to seize this keep by myself."

"Can't wait to see the look on their faces when they see their homes burning down behind them."

Richter went ahead, the two inquisitors behind him training their cross-bows. They swept from room to room, found them all empty. Found a huge larder, stocked full of provisions. If it went to an extended siege, the demons of Palerme would likely be able to last months, if not years, if they rationed carefully. *Good thing we have cannon, then.*

But Jonas, as much as it pained Richter to admit, was right. This was too easy. Where was everyone? Where were the children? The men and women who couldn't fight?

The keep's dining hall was a decent size for such an isolated location. They could entertain a hundred at least, and some tables were set with silver, polished to a mirror sheen. Nothing like the palatial hall in Annalt, the floor was some oiled hardwood, and the walls were polished brickwork. No gilding here, but it was nice enough. Finely woven Alanian carpets hung from the sides, deadening the sound. Had they hosted the mercenaries here? A few goblets had remnants of dark wine in them, dried and stuck to the bottom. Crumbs here and there, like they'd not had a chance to clean up entirely, yet.

Jonas and Franz shouldered him as they passed, slapping down their crossbows on the tables. Started scooping the silverware into pockets sewn into their cloaks.

"If nothing else, this'll fetch a nice price in Alania."

Alania? Why would they be going there?

"You look confused, Creature," Franz said. "Alanian mercenaries means Alanian gold. Means Alania is in league with the demon."

"Means I get some wet Alanian cunt," Jonas said, laughing.

Vetterand planned to claim Alania in the name of Sigur after this? Did he intend for *exterminatus*? The thought gave Richter churning guts. Thousands, millions of people lived in Alania. Did he plan to kill them all?

"You bastards think you can just come in here and take what you want, don't you?"

The three of them looked up. A boy in a dark cloak waved a knife in their direction, his face a dirge of fury. His hands trembled, though, barely holding the knife. He grasped the handle with both hands, so he didn't drop it.

"Well, well, well." Franz drew his sword as Jonas laughed harder. "We got a little demon pup here, have we? Are there any more of you?" The boy backed up, his feet slapping on the flat boards, knife extended but still trembling.

"No, don't go in there," he said. "Take me. No one's in there."

Franz stuck his head around a wooden column. "Ah," he said. "Well, there's a whole godsdamned litter, here."

"Eh?"

A young woman came charging out screaming, wild eyed, dark hair clinging to her face, slapping wildly at Franz with a kitchen roller. He stepped back and flicked his sword with a practiced motion, too fast for the girl to do anything about, and sliced her palm, making her yelp and drop the roller. He pulled her by the arm, twisting, threw her against the table. She crashed into one of the chairs with a hard grunt, slumping to the floor, tears and blood streaming down her cheeks. She took her punishment in stoic silence, nursing her palm.

Franz stepped past the column and dragged screaming children out, two girls—one little, maybe eight, and one in her mid-teen years, curves under her dress showing her budding womanhood. The youngest one kicked at shins to very little effect.

The boy charged Franz, planted the knife in his thigh. Franz shouted in surprise, recoiled. Like it had been a surprise he'd even got that far, the boy stepped back slowly, brows shot up to the ceiling.

Franz turned around and split him open with an overhead chop. The boy thumped onto the boards, stiff.

"Fucking little shit," he roared, holding his leg. "Ah... hold these girls, Creature, make sure they don't do anything stupid."

Doing as he was told, Richter snatched both girls wrists in one fluid motion and held them fast. They were too stunned to respond, didn't even scream. The older girl held her mouth, sobbed.

Limping over to the boy, Franz tore the knife from his thigh. He sunk the end of his sword a few times into the boy's unmoving chest, made sure the job was done.

"Fucking demons. Even their pups are vicious cunts."

"Speaking of cunts," Jonas said. "We got two ripe ones over here."

The older girl's eyes swelled with wetness, and she held herself, realizing her fate. The young woman turned defiant eyes on them, holding her bleeding palm.

"And hey, there's one just for Creature here. He looks the type to like them young."

The two men laughed.

Air cracked with the sound of cannon and men roared, demons roared louder, incorporeal shouts and clashing of steel. They must've been assaulting the walls, scaling it with ladder, trying to take arrow fire away from the cannons. It wouldn't be long, now.

"Let's see if demon cunt is any good before the soldiers get here and ruin them."

Jonas wrenched the older girl by her wrist out of Richter's grasp and flipped her over the table. She shrieked, burbled with tears. He lifted her skirt with one hand, played with his trousers with the other. The youngest girl screamed and pulled Richter's grip. No chance. She would have more luck tearing her hand free from a lion's mouth.

His limp dick like a wet sock, Jonas played with it, cursing. The girl didn't fight it, just laid there. Perhaps she knew it was inevitable. Like a fugue settling over her mind, taking her out of herself, so she could endure it. Richter knew that feeling well.

The young woman eyed the rolling pin, the boy's fallen knife. Went to move when Franz held his sword under her chin, and she froze. "Don't try it." He said it like a scolding governess.

She maintained her stoic silence, though her face was showing all kinds of vengeful thoughts. Or maybe she was an oathbreaker like Richter, too, and had her tongue cut out. Though when she opened her mouth, breathing hard, he could see it was intact. It galled him. This filth had what he did not. But he reassured himself with the knowledge that both older girls were old enough to be targets in a sack, and they knew it.

The youngest had no idea what was going on, it seemed, and shrieked for Jonas to stop, dragging at Richter's hand with her entire body to no avail.

The girl in her mid-teens looked at Richter and murmured something, squeaked, her entire body turning rigid as Jonas shoved himself inside, weight knocking her halfway across the table.

"Help."

He couldn't. Vetterand, the mad god, would have his innards strewn over the walls by sundown, keeping him alive to make him watch. Maybe he'd have his flesh off again, this time leaving him as a horrific creature of only muscle and bone, instead of sewing it back on. He had no doubt that Vetterand was capable of such a thing.

"Help. Please." Bang, bang, bang, against the table. Scrape, scrape of the table legs. The youngest girl pulled at her face with her free hand, screaming, yanking at Richter's grip.

Bang, bang, bang.

Peeling flesh, stinking blood, aching fire. All of it for him. Vetterand had him, and these two knew it.

A soldier for the coming war.

He looked away from the girl, eyes fixing on that boy, red leaking onto the boards. A boy just his age had stolen from a magistrate in Istrya, had his brains caved in by the magistrate's leashed dog sheriff. Been killed for something not nearly as heroic as the boy on the boards.

Bang, bang, bang. Scrape, scrape. Shrieking.

It was Richter's turn to keep silent, to watch that boy die, to let a girl, likely two girls, get raped. He'd done it before, hadn't he? He'd been the raper. But he'd been a different man, then to now. The Gutter had ground away at him. His mother. Then Vetterand ground away at him more, taught him the lessons, the training, came to his bed at night. Made him a sharper man, a man who wouldn't balk at killing, certainly not at raping a girl if it was his due. He'd done more on the mission, the decades of hunting, living like a vagrant, moving from town to town, hunting, killing. The mad god had taken the rest, taken everything left.

Grinding and grinding, like a stone, honed until he became a blade that cut the world. Until nothing remained but pure edge. Until he cut everything he touched.

Richter drew Jonas's blade from his belt and flicked it up, pushed it right through the jagged point of his neck before he realized what he was doing. Richter didn't think he'd do it, either. But that grin, sliding it in that poor girl, as though it was easy as... well, as easy as three feet of sharpened steel sliding through his neck, glistening out the other side with hot, dark blood.

Shouting in surprise, Franz fumbled his sword, dropped it to the ground with a clunk of steel on wood. With a flick of his wrist, Richter brought the blade out one side of Jonas's neck and lunged at Franz, slicing a long gash across his other thigh. He shrieked, legs buckled out from under him. Jonas's body landed with a thump.

His companion shrieked in terror. "I was just joking! You can have the older one if you want. The woman. The Lady of Beasts, even. Just don't kill me!"

Franz's pleading ended with steel between his teeth. He made a bubbling noise, his forest-green eyes rolling into the back of his head. Blood gushed from his open mouth, his thigh hanging off the bone, cut with a barber-surgeon's precision, silver spoons from the pockets in his cloak scattering. Richter let the sword fall from his grasp.

It seemed like something to remember. Was he done with violence? No, he couldn't be. He was the edge that cut the world, cut everything it touched.

"Blaune! Senna!"

A club-headed man with forearms each as large as Richter's chest stormed up the hallway, eyes wide at the grisly scene. It was a moment before he realized what had happened, saw the girl bent over the table, skirts hiked up to her waist, sobbing into the wood.

"Lorela... you fucking raper." He weighed a blacksmith's hammer in his hand. The head was giant and blackened with soot. Blood coated both ends. He'd come from the assault to check on the children, heard screaming, came running.

He swung the hammer in a wide, quick arc. Moved quicker than any block of iron that size had any right to. Richter jumped back and the hammer crashed into the head of a dining chair, turned it into splinters.

The little girl ran up to the man. "Stop, stop! He saved us!"

He shoved her aside, came swinging at Richter again. Richter wanted to explain himself, but he couldn't. Even if his tongue wasn't a blackened stump, he'd seen that look too many times. The look of a man that wanted to kill. Fury, bloodlust. The girl's words wouldn't take. Either Richter died or he did.

The hammer came swinging again, this time only a hair's breadth from Richter's mangled face. He dodged back again, hit his head and spine on the column. His eyes flashed with white, and he tripped over Jonas's corpse, skidded on the wood. The young woman lifted the girl from the table, helped her up, scooped the little girl up in her arms and ran clear from the hall, the little girl shrieking for her to put her down.

No one to advocate for him now.

The man with the giant forearms planted his boot on one of Richter's legs, fixing him in teeth-grinding agony.

He reached out, felt something cold. A handle. The boy's knife. He closed his hand around it.

The man raised the hammer. Even if Richter moved his head, it would carry through, destroy his sternum, cave in his ribs, smash his heart and lungs into bits.

With two quick cuts, Richter buckled the man's knees. Sent him careening forward, down like a felled tree, his foot lifting from Richter's leg.

Richter rolled out of the way as the man with the giant forearms crashed into the boards, and he pushed himself up, and ran.

CHAPTER 34
RETREAT
LEVITUM, 1045

If our gods exist, is it possible that other gods do as well?
The Samarite nomads worship an all-powerful mountain god.
Perhaps he exists, but doesn't care for the imperial west? Or
is it entirely possible that no gods exist at all, and what we
see in the world—the megalith, the Leviathan, the Giant's
Footfalls—are simply the remains of an ancient, all-powerful
civilization?

— APOSTATE LORISTIN

ROARS AND SCREAMS CAME from behind, all around. Ladders came in dozens now, slapped up onto the stone like hooks into the side of a huge beast, bringing it down. Metal ground against metal, steel on steel. It was a mob, now, and she could scarcely tell friend from foe. Stab, stab, stab, and she felt her hand slap hard against someone's stomach. It was then she realized her knife had been ripped from her grasp, clattered somewhere beneath the swarming legs. The contorted face of the man she'd been attacking dropped from sight into the teeming mass.

The ground rumbled. It was all she could do to put her arm up before the man in front slammed backwards, shoving her into the parapet behind.

The breath was squeezed from her lungs. An axe came down on her head. The attacker's wrist struck a shield rim, axehead floating aside. She forced a hand up, her lungs still emptied, breathlessly she clawed at it, trying to grab hold of it.

All then only to have the world struck from sight.

Blaring sound flashed as light across her eyes, dust choked her throat, stone grinded on stone. The weight lifted from her chest and she took in a huge breath on impulse. Coughing, spluttering, her eyes caked with dirt, she stumbled forward. Might've been forward. Might've been backward. What did it matter, anymore? It was elsewhere. She wanted to be elsewhere.

Murder was something she was good at, but this was slaughter. More. Eradication. Her mind swam with screaming thoughts, swirling before her like the dust gathered on the wind. Bits of stone bit into her cheek, her throat as she breathed. Ash, bone. A figure dropped before her. May as well have been made from mud.

She pitched forward, the floor falling out from under her. Tumbling head over feet, she landed hard. White-hot pain wracked her hand, a cracking noise slapped her ears. She rolled onto her back. Rubble littered the ground around her, the wall. The wall was rubble.

A shadow came down on her head, and she blinked back tears as she saw the end.

"Get up!"

Leon's voice. His shadow warped against the gray sky. "Watch your wrist, it's broken. You're lucky you didn't break your neck besides."

He helped her up, his neck running red with blood. Her blood? No, it looked to be coming from him. "Are you alright?" Her voice sounded raw in her ears, and muted, like she spoke under the surface of a bath. He took her behind the stable, where the roof had caved in from a corpse falling through from above.

Despite the risk of raining corpses, it was relatively safe here. As safe as it got in the middle of a battle, she supposed.

"Am I alright?" he said. "You fell from the wall, you *sal'brath*."

"Leon, where is everyone? Frix and the others—"

He grabbed her shoulders. "Forget about them! The castle's lost. Rolco's men are changing sides, the bastards!"

The castle's lost! Of course!

Metal smashed into metal as men fought at the gates, on the walls, howling and screaming. Baying like wolves. Mercenaries broke off and surrendered. More ran. For all their posturing, their reputation, they ran like cravens. The outcome of the battle had changed as rapidly as a knife throw, though maybe it was doomed from the start. The slow tide that pulled out of the putrid beach, leaving only stinking seagrass and rancid bones in its wake.

As her mind reeled, all she could think was that their lives were now forfeit. Palerme was lost, and so were they all. Her head pounded, back spasmed, legs wobbled. There was no dwelling on the past. Her only thoughts were of Tristain, now. The boy and the man, perhaps, but also the child. The babe that carried the hope of them all.

Leon let out a great yawning noise, breathed in sharp. Selene frowned but thought nothing of it. *Tired, in the middle of a battle?*

"Round up any survivors you can find, anyone from Palerme, and get them into the mine tunnel."

"The mine? What mine?"

"What... mine? Are you sure you didn't hit your head?" Another thundering crash and the top of a battlement was dashed from the wall above the gate, the lump of stone crushing a few unlucky souls underneath. The fighting went on, the ones not hit just stepping over the rubble and the dead, detritus under their feet.

"Oh, right, that... the tunnel!" He clasped her forearm. "Aye, I'll do it. Stay safe." He lifted his axe, as though to hand it to her, then paused. "Your wrist."

She looked down. Her hand flopped weirdly as she lifted her arm. "Shit. It's alright. I'll meet you there as soon as I can. Go."

He nodded and turned, and then he was gone as he passed beyond the stable wall. She heard a distinctly Leon battle cry and smiled. *He's just knocked his head, he'll be fine.* Knights knocked their heads all the time in battle, you would think. It was a hazard of the profession.

She peered around the corner. She wasn't useless without her knife and a working hand, but it was as close as it got. Though it seemed the entire thing had gone to shit, and even people with two working arms had as much luck as she did. A mercenary fell flat on his face, scraping up gravel as he was hit in the back with an arrow. A quick, black shadow wheeled across the top of the wall, and two crusaders, clad in plate, almost burst apart. Bits ripped off in a shower of blood and bone, their lifeless bodies falling onto the rubble in clattering heaps.

She ran for it. An arrow in the back, a sword in the guts, who knew what it would be, but her son was worth everything.

A man with half his face torn off stumbled across her path. He raised his sword to strike her, the blade shaking with the effort of a dead man whose body hadn't caught up with reality. She moved aside easily, shoving him down. He had the courtesy to not get up again.

Horns blared and the ground shook with the sound of hooves and a gray wedge of knights blasted through the open gate, punching aside crusaders on their feet, and mercenaries that hadn't got the message that the battle was over. Now it was simply survival. Everyone for themselves.

No one seemed to see her. Her chest ached with the effort of running up the slope of the yard, her lungs shallow, shaken with terror. Her wrist and hand ached from being unable to keep it steady, the appendage moving strangely. She wondered how she was ever going to carry Tristain, but those were details for later. She needed to move. Imagined blades came down on her soft head at any moment, swift and sure. A horseman's hammer, and she'd be just like that man with half a face.

There was a great roar from the keep. A lean werewolf with patchy fur came bursting out of the window on the second level, green glass raining down in little razor shards. Close behind, right on its heels, almost, a bigger one came through the window as well. They tumbled in the air, but the lean one got the best of the big one and threw the attacker down. *Two werewolves fighting?* She had no time for it, and only hoped that their disagreement would take them away from the lord's tower, not back into it.

Screaming followed as three girls came rushing out of the door that opened out to the yard. One tall one—Blauna. And Lorela. And Senna!

"Senna! Girls," she shouted, and the mute girl, running full tilt, crashed straight into Selene. The wind was knocked out of her, but she kept upright. Before her breath came back she saw they were terrified. Blauna wore a brave face, but Selene had worn that same one herself often.

She waved her hand in the girl's face, heaving her breath back, hot pain tearing into her chest.

"Quickly... run... this place isn't safe! Go to the mines, Leon will be waiting!"

"Where's Mama?" Senna said.

"She'll meet you there," Selene lied. She'd lost sight of Ottille long before the battle was lost, and there was no chance of finding her now, even if she had the time.

Before they left, she caught a glimpse of horror in Lorela's eyes. Sunken and black. Something had happened to her.

It has to wait! She went through the door the girls had left open. As she did, she saw the two werewolves leap over the walls and out of sight, and she thanked whatever god looked over them for that.

She still shut the door, anyway. Her wrist ached with the movement of closing the door, her fingers unable to shut properly. She had to catch the doorpull by stiffening her thumb and using her body to slam it closed. The adrenalin had numbed the pain a little, but it still ached.

"Advance," someone shouted. A commanding voice, though deadened by the wood, was no less frightening in the balance. "Burn this demon nest to the ground!"

Fear pricked her neck. She had no idea if Tristain was still here, or whether Galena had taken him to the mines, with everyone else. She knew the escape route—

No. Selene had never told her. She breathed and braced herself as she sprinted up the stairs, taking two, three at a time. *Oh, no.*

Infant screams echoed off the stone. Horrible wails, like he was being beaten. Selene knew she was wrong to trust his care to a stranger. Her heart pounded, harder and harder closer to Galena's door. Sweat dripped down her dress, her pits, her back. Cold sweat.

She had a child! Who had just been weaned but Galena still had milk. It was the perfect thing for him. Her son who needed a wet nurse or he would die. Perfect for Selene. She could feel guiltless about leaving him alone in Palerme while she went to Valenti. It was for him, for all of them. Couldn't she see that?

The stump of her severed arm knotted, white-hot. Twisted, as though knives cut into it. As though the priest was taking to it with the scalpel again. Cutting away the corruption. But demons didn't corrupt. That was a fiction—a lie. Was it infected? Then why not just say that?

Because the priest needed to lie. Sorenius as well; they both needed to keep up the fiction. Lying, just like Galena. Selene would not let that be the end of Tristain, not her baby, not her son. Another scream, a putrid wail, as though her ears were scraped out. She could smell corruption, like rot, like vomit. The vomit of a sick child, and fresh blood.

She shoved the door open, nearly fell over going through, and found Galena leaning over Tristain. In the corner, Galena's child, face up, unmoving. Pale-faced and covered in blood. The baby was on the floor, his eyes and cheeks glistening with tears. She had a knife raised. Selene screamed, felt more fury in her life condensed in that one moment into a beating heart of rage.

Galena turned, wet down her cheeks. "I won't let it happen again! The Order won't take the children!"

Selene lunged and wrapped her arm around the woman's hand just as the blade came down. They wrestled for a moment before Selene realized she was far more skilled than the wet nurse. Using her weight, she hooked her legs around the woman's back and neck, the weight sending her crashing to the ground. Selene tightened, pressed her legs together, squeezed them for all they were worth. Tightened, like a python around its prey. Galena made breathless, choked noises, her face turning purple. Frustratingly, the pain in her hip flared to horrible awareness. Galena pushed Selene's leg up, got free. Bit her calf. Selene shrieked.

"Fucking cunt," she roared. Tristain's wails continued, louder now. They fought almost on top of him, and Selene tried desperately to keep her arm wrapped around the woman's knife hand. She couldn't close her fingers, couldn't tear the knife from Galena's grasp. Her wrist lolled weirdly in the position, almost slapping herself in the face.

"Let me go!" Galena yelled.

"You killed your own daughter and now you're trying to kill my son! Never!"

"They're doomed. They're dead already. I'm just sparing them the pain of what the Order will do to them!"

Selene knew the pain that the Order would do to them. Inquisitors would kill them, beat their brains against a wall, throw them around for sport. She'd seen it happen, made it happen, in the South Hills.

She sank her teeth into the woman's thumb, about the only weapon she had left. Galena screamed and let go of the knife. Raising her good leg high, she wrapped it around the woman's neck, pulled her shin tight in the crook of her arm. Galena made a squeaking noise, her eyes blowing wide with terror. Face turned the color of plums. The woman's movements became frantic, her arms and legs flailing. Her foot struck Tristain in the face, and he screamed, took a huge breath, and went silent for many seconds, his own face turning plum. Selene only saw the woman's death now. There was no other option. A painful, languorous one, preferably, but this would do. Tighter, tighter, tighter.

As Tristain's scream reached gut-rending heights, blood popped from the wet nurse's eyes, her mouth. Like a crushed grape popping its water. Galena's arms and legs slowed, then went stiff. Murderers were hanged. Child murderers were no different, and this was personal. It suited Selene to do the work.

And she did the work. Selene held that position, her head aching, her legs aching, her wrist utterly useless, pounding in agony. Her every muscle clenched, warped in that position but she kept a hold, holding, held, until many moments passed.

Tristain's cries quietened to a low burble, his face still red from the effort. She let go of her leg, and Galena didn't rise. She never would. The skin of the woman's neck was black. Selene had crushed her windpipe, burst blood vessels underneath. Her dead eyes stared to the raked ceiling, into the timbers, just like her daughter.

Selene cursed her for a cunt and took the wicker basket from the wardrobe, the one they used to carry dirty linens down to the stream to wash. She knelt by Tristain and slowly, slowly, hooked her arm under his body. His crying had turned him stiff, though Selene didn't know if she should be thankful for that. It certainly made it easier to get him inside the hamper, and the linens cushioned his fall, since she couldn't lower him slowly like that.

"Fucking useless fingers," she said, and cursed it all. "Fucking useless mother. Can't even breastfeed her child and trusts the task to a fucking murderer." Trist looked at her. Just stared. He didn't cry, just looked with huge green eyes.

Selene wept. She knelt in the quiet room and wept. It was the lowest she'd ever felt, there was no doubt of that. She bawled like Tristain had, thoughtless, desperate. Now all the terror and blinding pain came leaking out like water from a crushed grape. The father of this child was dead, and everything that had been good died with him. Thoughts reeled and clashed in her mind, as deadly and deafening as a charge of knights.

She wasn't the leader the Althann deserved. Who was she to them? No one. In fact, she was worse. She'd killed many of them before she stupidly believed that she somehow knew better than any of them how to rule over them. And all of that hope, everything Palerme was now, was snuffed out, as carelessly as a common candle.

All she knew now was that she had to get out and take Tristain with her. Survive, at any cost.

CHAPTER 35

THE MAN AND THE MOUNTAIN

LEVITUM, 1045

The Gray Rider is a folktale, just like the Althann and the Pallstaff. The only great power in this world is that of the four gods of Istrya.

— HIGH NOTARIUS GIAN ADALLA

FACING DOWN SIX WEREWOLVES eager for his blood wasn't the best start at putting an end to violence. But maybe there was some lesson in that. The more you try to put an end to something, the more it comes roaring back, uglier than ever. He was a bit sick of lessons, really. He was trying something new, seeing if it would stick. This threatened to pull him right back into his old ways.

A pair of thundering arms broke the branch he clung to, sent him twisting through the air. He righted himself, thumped hard into the trunk of the oak and tumbled down some more. Pain lanced across his back, his side. He turned, lashing back, smashed the tan-colored lycan bearing down on him in the mouth. With a roar, the smith lycan filled the gap, sunk razor-sharp teeth into his thigh, tore a chunk out of him like he was a prized cutlet at a banquet.

Richter hit the ground, air puffed out of him, rolled quick, jumped for the nearest tree with his good leg. He reached out for the branch, fell just short, claws scraping the underside of the branch, showering him with bark and leaves. He thought it might be the end of him. This pack was more than a match for him, especially in his diminished state. Maybe they knew he didn't have his killer instinct anymore, his conscience roaring to life again, like a fire that smoldered but had never really gone out, waiting for sustenance. He rather wondered whether that part of him had never really gone away, and he felt sick at the things he'd done when it was only embers.

I'm evil. Maybe I deserve to die. Gods know I've done enough for these demons to want revenge. But then, he could never die. Vetterand would never let it happen.

The trees rustled with a quiet breeze, the sounds of violence and pillage at the keep long distant to the west. He wondered how far he'd gone, chased up into the mountains, where the trees were thinner, and offered less coverage. He hoped they'd give up, unable to hide themselves easily, but it had been the other way around. He had less cover, and they hunted like wolves, surrounding him on all sides.

The black one. The black, slinking one. She instructed them, had some command under her belt, a knowledge of tactics. The short and slender gray one, and the brown one with the scar down his eye came at him from both sides. Lunged. A pincer movement. He flattened himself, let them collide with each other in a snarl, all sharp claws and vicious, biting teeth above, and rolled out underneath.

He flicked himself back up, bound forward. Raced for the nearby gully, slid down the muddy bank, heard the air whistle above him as the block-headed smith soared over. He caught the smith's ankle, drove claws into it and threw him down. Smacked his head against a rock. Enough to daze but not kill.

He had some knowledge, too.

On the wind came the scent of something, like lavender. He'd picked up that scent in the castle, smelled it in the lord's tower. She left it everywhere she went. The Lady of Beasts. Could he parley with her? It would be easier to argue the point with someone who wasn't actively trying to kill him. But his fucking tongue. He couldn't say a word. He'd have to find the girls that he saved, try to get them to advocate on his behalf.

Otherwise, they'd hunt him to the end of the world. Hunters that never tired, never lost track of their prey. Happily, he didn't tire either.

If only he could play dead, let them kill him. But they'd sense his heart-beat, the minutest breath. And the change on his death wasn't exactly inconspicuous, left him vulnerable.

The smith lycan lifted his head, eyes spinning in their sockets, giant fore-arms pushing up slowly, groaning with the effort. He had mere moments before another one was on him—he could smell them, getting closer. But where was the black one? He hadn't sensed her in a while. Could she hide herself, somehow?

He changed once, twice, back to his wolf form again, his leg healed, but the muscle would never be the same. At least it wasn't bleeding, didn't pain him when he stood. It would always be tight, though, and not nearly as flexible or strong as it had been.

Questions of ability had to wait. The smith lycan sat up, fixed his eyes on Richter and growled, baring long fangs.

Richter bound out of the gully, felt the air split behind him, and he raced across the forest floor, uphill, in the direction of the smell of lavender. He hoped to every god, even the mad god Vetterand, that it wasn't just a particularly potent-smelling lavender bush. Ran over a stream, leaped over a puddle where the rains had formed a gulch, stinking and full of worms.

He sensed at least four of them right on him. Smelled them, their fur wet with blood and sweat. His blood, mostly. Further back, the faintest waft of a fifth. But still no sign of the sixth, the black one. Had she dropped back? Fallen back to protect the rest of them, the girls and the ones who couldn't fight?

The forest quickly cleared out to scrubland as he followed the lavender scent east, further into the mountains. A cliff-face erupted from the earth as he cleared a hill, jagged and slick, a long line of it reaching back into the forest and surrounding him, walling him in. Old rock, smoothed with time and wind, with very few footholds that he could see. He'd have a hard time climbing it, but he had no choice. It was this or turn back and look for a better chance to the north or south. Opportunities to be seized.

He started climbing. Easier than he thought, he dug out handholds with his claws. The scraping noise in his ears was like a vice on his spine, pressing tight. He was halfway up when the five chasing him arrived at the base—the slender grey, the large grey, the brown with the scar across his eye, the tan one, and the brown smith with the huge forearms and short body. The slender gray demon sprung up, fell short, screamed in fury. She scraped down the side of the cliff with her claws spraying rocks on the others below, bound off, scattered shingles as she landed.

"Go around," he heard one of them yowl in Hillard. The language seemed to fit better than Low Istryan in their bestial mouths. They scarpered, two to the north and three to the south. He watched them dance up the rocks and disappear into the trees.

He fixed his head up, kept climbing. Nothing had ever been done by waiting around for it to happen, Father Domitus told him. He found himself thinking of the priest, now, and how maybe he'd been the only thing standing between a mad god and a child's destruction.

For a god, he sure does spend a lot of time concerned with the opinions of mortals.

At the top of the cliff, the lavender scent came stronger than ever. A cool lake like glass extended out before him, a copse of sparse trees on the other side, heavy with lichen. Past the trees, he sensed the heartbeats and the breaths of a family of deer, rustling through the undergrowth, looking for mushrooms. This place was virgin, untouched by the morass of stinking bodies in the cities, in the marchlands, it was nothing like he'd ever seen. It nearly made him tear up then and there at the primal beauty of it.

He twisted his body as the black lycan slid up from behind him. Smelled her right as she was on him, hadn't smelled her at all prior. Her claws punched through his bicep, tearing a great gash, nearly ripping off his right arm entirely. He roared in pain, recoiled, grabbed onto her then slipped free, his hands only taking away a smear of mud and lichen.

That's how she disguised herself, by covering herself in mud so I couldn't smell her.

He rolled, arm hanging from the bone like a barber-surgeon half-done. She followed the first blow with a swift second, hitting her mark. His chest exploded in fragments of bone, painting the pale earth red. He shuddered for breath, felt the familiar tingling sensation of his life leaving him, and fell over.

An enjoyable, peaceful moment, looking down on himself, dead in the dirt. If only it lasted.

Fire boiled his skin as he changed, his body pulling itself back together, his heart healing, scarring. His arm knitted back together. Like his leg, they would both never be the same. He tried to move it, tried to flex the hand, but it hung weird, didn't close properly. *You're just a shadow of me.*

Vetterand healed perfectly, grew new parts to fill the void in his cheek. The healing process wasn't perfect because Richter was mortal. It didn't *heal* exactly. It only scarred, like cauterizing the wound. Whatever was left stitched together with scar tissue.

How could he even kill something like that? Each time Richter damaged the mad god, he would only grow back new. If he even could damage him in the first place. Meanwhile, Richter was more and more broken every wound he got, more and more hunched, tighter and tighter like cord over a wheel.

Before he could blink, she was on him again, fangs coming down on his neck. He groaned as she fixed him there with her jaw, her double-jointed body slinking around and flattening him to the earth. She definitely had training. At his full might, before Vetterand had done with him, he might've been able to wriggle out of it. Wanted to. But now he laid there as she tore his throat out.

Blood gushed like a fountain from his neck. The world turned black and he was in that half-space between life and death. A presence stood there, weak, but watching. A figure in the darkness, a shape only observed through obscuring the rest of the darkness. Then Richter was pulled back into his body, his spine on nails, his skin on fire. He groaned as he wrenched the black beast off, but she shoved him back down, tangled up his limbs.

"Don't you fucking move," she swore. Still came out like a garble in Osbergian, but it was a sight better than his attempt at Low Istryan.

The five others bound up, three from the south, two from the north, met them.

"Kyrah," the smith said, chest heaving. He changed back and they all did, even Richter. He knew the game was done, but at least their blood had cooled. Maybe they were hoping for a kill in cold blood.

The black one became measurably lighter as she changed back, but still sturdy. Still looked like she could put up a fight with the best of them. Maybe even take on Richter in his prime.

She's Saburrian. And she's got a freckle on her lower back.

He rather enjoyed that moment, laying there, before she hopped off him with a noise of disgust. She covered herself when the slender gray one, now a tall, pale blonde, handed her a cloak, handed them all cloaks. Except Richter. The cold air iced his skin, made his flesh all goosepimples, hard shingles digging into his back.

"He's..."

"Yeah," said the one with the scar across his eye. It was new, raised white skin, like it had just healed. Something acquired from the siege, perhaps.

"Not intact," the tan one, almost the double of the one with the scar. It was good that they had difference, otherwise Richter probably wouldn't have been able to tell them apart. Least not from the ground.

He sat up. His leg flared with pain, and he looked down. It was a grisly sight. He looked up at them, shook the flapping muscle, hoped his meaning was clear.

"I'd rather let you bleed out," the Saburrian named Kyrah said. The one who had hunted him, taught them how to bring him down. He wasn't sure if he was frightened of her or aroused by her. Maybe both. *Best not linger on that, otherwise I'm bound to pain myself.* Though the pain from his leg numbed his mind to much else.

"Do it," she relented. "Quick. And don't bother running. You know we can catch you."

He nodded. He changed, and his leg formed webs of scar tissue over the deep wound.

He changed back and the smith wrenched him up off the ground. "Come on. Rapists answer to the lady."

"They're not far. Just over the next ridge."

Richter glanced sidelong at the Saburrian. So, he'd been heading the right direction after all. Remained to be seen what waited for him when he got there.

CHAPTER 36
SAVED

LEVITUM, 1045

Then, the question follows, are there gods that we have lost the names for? That hide themselves so well in our world that we could not see them even if they were right in front of us?

— DRAMES, A COLLECTION, 585 AE. D.

THE HEAT SHOVED SELENE back as easily as a hand on her chest. She put her hand up to shade her eyes from the choking, wincing smoke, moving the door very slowly ajar. The kitchen's entrance opened out to a side yard. Tongues of a huge fire licked the air above the wall to her left. Doors juddered and wood splintered as the soldiers crashed into the lord's tower, burning, looting, destroying. She could taste the blood in the air, the killing. Slaughter. She half-wondered if any of them even made it out, or whether she'd find them all murdered at the entrance to the mine.

Goats huddled in the simple shelter in the corner of their pen, as far as they could get away. Soon this yard would be consumed as well, just like the rest. She considered taking one or two of the beasts, since they'd need the food, but she had no idea how she was going to get them to the tunnel. She had no idea how she was going to get herself there, let alone with a baby on her back.

Tristain cried. Her eyes widened with panic. His crying was the only noise in the silent yard and would quickly alert anyone within earshot. Even the goats had the good sense to remain quiet, huddled in their shelter.

The heat made him restless. She couldn't do anything about it. It was let him cry or smother him.

She heard shouting. A scream as someone was stabbed, turned to a wet gurgle. Boots and metal rattled towards her, and she kneeled, flattened herself against the side of the thatched toolshed. She eyed one of the spades, the picks that were used to break the ground, to bury the posts for the goat pen. Easily able to crack through a man's ribs, get between the gaps in their armor, in the right hands. Well, her one hand was useless, broken and mangled, while her other hand was likely bone and mush now, thrown in with the priest's waste, if it hadn't been used as feed. So, it could never be said it found the right hands.

"Is she here?"

She recognized the voice. Frix and Trestinsen both emerged from the archway at the end of the yard, opened out behind the buttery to the inner bailey. They were covered in blood, gore running down their shirts, from their mouths. Dried, most of it, and they were naked from the waist up. A rush of fear made her lightheaded. What had they been through to get here? What did they intend for her? The status quo had been washed away in the tide of slaughter, and she knew just how quickly old ties could be severed in that wake.

Trestinsen's bloody sword lifted towards her, his pockmarked face scanning the yard. "I can smell the babe," he said. His voice harbored a dark intent, she thought. It made her flinch. "She's here."

"Selene," Frix said. "Milady. Are you here?"

She stepped out. Frix's brows shot up. Trestinsen remained cool and even, guarded. The man she'd once had feelings for ran over. She backed up, turned the baby on her back away from him.

Frix stopped. "What happened? Are you alright?" He looked down, passed his eyes over her. "Your wrist is broken."

"I'm aware," she said, voice level though she knew both of them could tear her apart in mere moments.

"Some of us made it to the tunnels, though we can't find Helena and Helge. The ostler and his son. Galena and her daughter. If you're here with the babe, where—"

"Galena's dead. I killed her because she killed her daughter, slew her before the Order had the chance. She tried to kill Tristain, too."

"She..." He wiped his mouth, face paling. "Gods, Selene. I'm sorry."

"It's done." She pressed her mouth into a hard line. "Let's go."

T HE ENTRANCE TO THE tunnel was secure, all told, and looked as important to a raiding army as an empty coffer. While the soldiers were busy ransacking the lord's tower and the smithy and the inner buildings, they kept to the narrow rain-ditch between the wall and the outer buildings. Tristain settled once they got far enough from the fires, stopped crying. Selene thanked all the gods for that. It should never be underestimated just how loud a crying baby is. But now escape was before them—all that remained was to make it across the back of the yard, and the postern gate.

Frix peered around the corner. His shoulders crusted with dried blood and ash, the soot falling from the air now, into her hair and on her tongue. It tasted foul, like the dead. On balance, likely a sizable portion of the ash clinging to the air came from burning bodies. The crusaders were piling up the dead in the yard, a mountain of them. Men took to them with axes, taking them apart, piece by piece. White-robed clerics stood over the men as they prayed, exalting the god of war, dousing them with pungent smoke. The god she once worshipped, the god she once bled and killed for.

She didn't want to look, though she couldn't look away. They kept low as they approached the postern gate. Opposite the main yard, a hundred paces between them and the waste of a lost battle. Groans of the dying rang out, cut short by bloody, thumping sounds. Steel sliding through flesh. They were killing the wounded. She gasped as she saw the ostler and his son, Casca—their dead eyes staring pale among a pile of bodies ahead of her.

Frix pulled open the gate slightly, just enough for them to step through. Selene held her breath as she went over the stone, and down the rocks on the other side, shivers running down her back.

She worked her way down the slope carefully since moss had crept up the sides in the miners' absence. Since their preparations for the battle, everyone had been induced to work on the traps and the trenches. And for all their effort, they were left with nothing. The total of a year and more of hard living, neatly accounted for by its complete loss, like a notary taking cruel, unfeeling stock. Life was a shattering after all, and like broken glass, grief tore its way through her chest. She could name that grief now, though that made it no easier to deal with. She wanted to lay down and die, but she had a child now. Those that depended on her. Leon—her constant companion through this horror. Senna, Ottille.

The leafy ground crunched under her boots. Trees thick with yellowing leaves, the first hint of auctumnitas, broke wide trunks to reveal the mine tunnel, a solid frame of wood around stairs cut into a mound of earth.

No one spoke. The only noise in the forest was chanting, and the constant *thump-thump* of axes.

S ELENE'S ACHING FEET SLIPPED across the shingled ground, the tunnel and the forest having long given way to mountain. Her shoulders and waist chafed with the strain of the linen sheets she carried the basket with. She gave one last look behind. Palerme's walls were swallowed by the canopy, while the yard was engulfed with putrid smoke. The crusaders had built their pyre. Only the keep's tower extended like a slender finger. The castle was smaller than she realized, and it overwhelmed her to think that it would soon be ruined. It was where Tristain was born, where so many had made their lives, and already she imagined it being torn down, stone by stone. Taken apart by brutal hands; with iron staves and axes.

A year to be built, a day to be destroyed.

Gray clouds held the threat of rain, like a knife to the throat. Before, they could just take refuge in the keep, in safety, but now they had nothing. They'd have to find shelter, before long, but where was that? Any villages around would hand them over to the crusaders. They could trust no one.

The mountain before her gutted the steel-colored sky with its white, jagged peak. The Fall, it was named. Where the Great Devil wounded Sigur after the latter was tricked by his son, Veles. Or so the myth went.

"They're just over the next ridge," Trestinsen said, his mouth moving around the words awkwardly as he changed back. He went from loping along the slope towards them in his werewolf form to walking in one smooth motion. Frix looked at Selene, opened his mouth. It looked as though he had something to say ever since they'd gone through the tunnel, but he couldn't force himself to say it.

She couldn't care less. Whatever he meant to say to her, it mattered as much as a wet shit, now.

"Good," she said. "There's—"

A woman's scream rang out across the barren slope. They ran, the two Althann transforming and racing off. Frix, his rust-colored fur swishing as he turned back, gave her a pained glance. It was a lot to read into a man who'd lost all his features and now looked like an overly muscled, huge wolf on two legs, but she can't have imagined it was anything else.

Then he was gone over the ridge, and Selene sighed. Her feet slipped on the rocky ground, and she slowed. What did it matter, really, if she was there? What if she were to leave, now, and descend the mountain, leave the Althann far behind? Once, she imagined them as victims, as the downtrodden, worthy of saving. But now, amongst all the horror, they had themselves. They had each other, at least. They weren't alone, anymore.

But she was. Leon was the only piece to her past that she knew. Everyone else was gone.

She continued up the rise. There were thirty, maybe forty of them, a couple of goats. They gathered around a single man, a scraggy, bite-ridden, long-haired man, who looked as though a knife had been taken to every part of his jagged, emaciated form. She didn't recognize him.

"He's a raper," Gregor bellowed, his voice echoing across the stony ground. "We should kill him!"

"He was with the Swords." Ottille added. She had a furious, guarded look, and held Senna tight around her thighs.

The girl looked up. "But, mama, he saved us. The—"

"If he's a raper, we should gut him and leave him for the birds," Kyrah said.

Selene wandered in behind Trestinsen and Frix, who had since transformed back to human. The others didn't see her, nor paid her any mind. Maybe it was better this way. Let the Althann settle an Althann dispute.

Voreld, one of the miners, cut the air with a chop. "Cut his cock off. That's what a raper deserves."

She looked over the wretch's body. He had no shame baring his naked form, though it was clear that someone took to him with a blade at some point. One of his ears was a stump, cut off at the root. His hair was patchy and white, his pale lips broken and bleeding, hanging open slightly. It was then she saw the blackened stump of his tongue. *An oathbreaker?* She looked down.

"It looks like someone's beat you to it," she said.

"Lady Selene," Ottille said, bowing. "I didn't see you there."

The others made shocked sighs when they saw her. She probably looked half a corpse, though it surprised her to see they cared. Leon smiled at her, then flinched, pinched his face as he rubbed his nose with his fingers. Was he hurt? *Who isn't?*

"You have the right of it," Kyrah said. "I would know the truth of this matter, but he can't speak, either."

Ottille yelped, and Sanna ran forward. The girl had struck her mother in the shin, the latter hopping around in a circle. "I'm telling you," she cried. "He didn't rape Lorela! He didn't rape anyone. In fact, he stopped Lorela from being raped. Gregor just came in at the wrong time!"

Lorela—Selene looked around for the girl, saw her hugging Helena tight. She wondered if Helena knew what had happened to her daughter, though those concerns washed away as she saw Lorela's stark eyes, the long, blank stare. It sent chills through Selene, made her neck hairs stand. She'd heard of victorious armies taking liberties with the women of the cities they'd assaulted—certainly she'd heard enough out of Ostelar. It made her hate the prince even more than she did already. But to see the result first-hand—her heart poured out for the girl.

"Is this true? Who else was there?"

"Blauna, she knows." The girl pointed to the mute. The older girl nodded.

"Then," Gregor said, "why was he with the Swords?"

"I don't recognize him," Selene said. "But then, I didn't know every Sword there is or was. He could be from the north. He looks northern."

"It's settled then," Leon said, lifting his fingers. "He's no raper. In fact, he's a hero. We need to keep moving if we want to stay ahead of the army."

Kyrah nodded. "The knight's right. If we make it across the mountains and south, we'll get to Alania. The duca'll give us refuge."

Selene pursed her lips. She meant to speak, to say the duca would more than likely surrender them in exchange for his city's safety, when Frix spoke.

"What makes you so confident?" he said. "The southerners are all snakes. Can't be trusted."

"I'm a southerner. Am I a snake?"

"That's not what I meant."

"What did you mean, then? Look, we don't have any other choice. We need to keep moving, go across the mountains and south. It's a hard trek, but the season hasn't brought the snows too far down the mountains, just yet. If you want to stay here and die, get impaled or burned at the stake, be my guest. If you want to live, come with me."

Selene shook her head. There had to be another option, but they were all out of allies. The duca wanted to make Palerme a bastion against the imperial armies, and the castle had been taken in a day under the might of an empowered pontiff and all the lords under his banner. So much for that idea. If the crusaders were unsatisfied with the meagre holdings of a wolfman castle, as he'd intimated, then they'd easily move on Alania. The riches of the Jewel of the Bright Sea were well known.

They grumbled their assent. Leon moved alongside Selene as they moved into a column, Kyrah at the front.

"She's ineffable," Selene said. More to herself than anyone else. "The leader the Althann need."

"She's... invertible."

"*Inv*—What?" Selene looked at him. His neck was still covered in blood, and his eyes rocked back and forth in their sockets. "You're hurt, Leon."

"Nonsense. I need to rest. We've all been through stinking shit. I'm no worse than the rest of us."

"Where's that barber, Muselio?" She glanced around. They were far fewer than she thought. Forty, at the most. Gregor stumbled along, she noticed, a twinge to his ankle. Many more just had haunted looks to their eyes. The barber-surgeon was nowhere to be seen.

Tristain woke with a sharp, shrill cry. It was time for his feed.

CHAPTER 37
FELL

LEVITUM, 1045

A rumor persists that some of the demons are unkillable: that they cling to life despite drowning, or dismemberment, or poisoning, or through any varied method of death. These rumors are patently untrue.

— High Notarius Gian Adalla

THEY WOULD BE HIS army. The mad god might fight off ten, a dozen, two dozen, but not forty of them. Six of them had hunted Richter like he was a rabbit, what could forty of them do? Surprise was on their side. They'd heard no sight nor sound of the crusaders since they escaped from the keep, and it was likely Vetterand didn't even know where they were. Richter had surprised him when he took a chunk out of his cheek, so the mad god couldn't see the future. There was that blessing, at least.

With the element of surprise, and with this Kyrah and her training behind them, what weren't they capable of?

He couldn't believe that less than a year ago, ending the demons was his life's work. Now he wanted to help them and hunt the mad god that fathered him, at least in all the ways that mattered. It was his baser instinct, after all. Vengeance. What was baser than cold, hard violence in the service of revenge? The primality of it, seated deep in the make of every man and beast.

You take something of mine, I'll take something of yours.

Stupidly, Richter allowed himself some hope. For now, he would have to play the role he was given, like a good soldier.

The goats bound ahead over the shingled ridge. The creatures had no problem navigating the pitted landscape marked with mountain rains, and it was his job to keep them in sight. On the horizon, the spine of the Avallano Mountains like a dead giant's back, knobbed and white-bleached in the sun.

Cold air washed between the cloak and his skin, made him shiver, but the boots they'd given him kept his feet warm and dry at least. They'd taken all they could carry from the castle, which wasn't much. Fleeing a sack didn't exactly leave you a lot of time to grab things, and certainly not the right things, either. It was likely the fully stocked larder he passed in the keep remained, if it hadn't been picked apart already by Vetterand's soldiers.

It was hard going, and go they went. Over the mountains, it seemed. No word on where they'd make camp, and Solni had nearly completed his journey, the wisps of afternoon all that was left. The little girl took it in her stride, though, racing ahead, proving a headache for her mother.

Ottille was her name, the slender gray lycan. "Senna! Don't go too far ahead! The goats are better at climbing than you."

She scowled at him when she caught him looking.

"We'll have to stop soon," Selene said. "It's getting dark, and we'll have to make fire and set up camp."

"This is open country," Kyrah replied, adjusting the longsword she balanced over her shoulder. "If scouts spot us, they'll ride us down within moments." She shook her head with a frustrated grunt. "Too bad we had to leave the horses behind."

Richter often found that she contradicted Selene, or always had a word to say edgeways. He wondered why it mattered if scouts ran them down, then remembered that the children hadn't come into their changes yet. Maybe they weren't lycans, just that their parents were. Sometimes it missed a generation.

"Wouldn't matter." Selene set her jaw to the horizon, the lean muscles in her neck working a swallow. The basket on her back looked to be burdening her. A babe, from its shrill cries. Now, it slept, but it didn't look a happy sleep. The Lady of Beasts looked like she might topple over at any moment, and she didn't seem to be willing to set it down.

"There were never enough horses for all of us, and the children can't ride. Goats can't ride, either."

"If we had horses, we could forget the goats and the mountain. Go south, to Alania."

"And stay one step ahead of the crusaders? How long before they hear we've taken refuge in Alania and decide to attack? The duca's just as likely to sell us out, just like his mercenaries."

"Mercenaries blow with the wind, failing that, blow with the coin. It should've been no surprise." Kyrah grunted, wiped her thick black brows with a thumb and index finger. "Where do you suggest we go, then? Starve in the mountains? Freeze to death when bruma comes?"

That cast a pallor across them, a low murmur, looks of concern. Senna, just ahead, stopped her play on the rocks and the two boy twins that had been tossing stones playfully in her direction turned, worry knitting their faces.

Kyrah was right, of course. But people often had trouble accepting painful truths.

"Enough," the smith said firmly. "We'll find a safe spot to camp and figure it out in the morning."

"There's a good idea," Ottille said. "You." She pointed to Richter. "Round up the goats."

Richter nodded. Better he played the role he was given, for now, even if it was to be goatherd. The more he ingratiated himself, the better. But how was he to tell them of the mad god? Draw a picture?

When he'd rounded up all six goats, clapping his hands and beating his thighs and shouting tongueless—quite the strange noise—they took shelter under a leafy oak, heavy with orange and brown foliage. He tied the goats to a nearby sapling, sturdy, but bare in the cold. A brook of icy water trickled just over a fallen log, and a fern stood alone in the shade of a twinning birch. Come a few months, this place would be completely bare and frozen. For now, it offered shelter, though not much if it rained. Happily, it looked as though the sky had cleared, and the only gray on the horizon was the smoke of the burning keep.

Well, unhappily for them. It was a bittersweet notion.

Gregor the smith and Frix and his cousin rounded up wood for the fire. Everyone avoided Richter, which suited him fine. The little girl seemed to be the way in. She was beloved by everyone. Blauna, the mute, didn't bear to look at him. Lorela hadn't said a word to him either, though he'd saved her life.

Ottille and Selene cooed for the little girl as she swung her leg around the tree. She dropped upside down a stride from Richter's face.

"Hello," she said.

"Come down from there," Ottille said. The girl's mother, the girl had none of her lean features, with chubby, rosy cheeks that bloomed as blood pooled in her head. Took after her father, perhaps.

"Hello. Why don't you talk? Are you like Blauna?"

Richter shook his head and opened his mouth.

"Ew! It's all black!" The innocence of children. The only thing that bothered her about his tongue was that it looked bad. Which it did, no doubt, but she didn't understand the implication. At least it wasn't pity. He didn't know if he could take pity from the girl.

"What's a rapist? Was it what happened to Lorela?"

"Senna," Ottille scolded. "Away, now!"

"Sorry, Mama," she said, and flipped down with the acrobatics of a monkey. She slumped her shoulders and tramped over to the budding fire, where the smith and the cousins two were arguing over the best way to build it up.

A hard hand came down on his shoulder, made him jump. The Saburrian. Her hands were not like a farmer's, with the calluses around the fingertips. She had the calluses of a warrior, hard, pale skin around the webbing of her fingers and thumb, across her palm. Her steps were silent, an achievement considering the floor was littered with browning leaves.

"You might not be a rapist," she whispered in his ear. "But I don't trust you."

You be stupid to.

He gestured to her sword, now resting on a nearby log. It was Alanian make, as long as she was tall, and she was taller than Richter. Wide, sturdy quillons before the twisted guard, made from one single piece of metal, running up to the blade. A hilt of wrapped lambskin, run through with a cord of twisted red samite and goldthread, topped with a fluted pommel, fat, and steel for counterbalance. Beautiful. Master swordsmiths make and would've cost as much as a duchy.

"I worked for the duca. Still do, I suppose. Lady Selene bought my services for the kingly sum of one ducat."

She's an Alanian Marine. That explains the training. I wonder if Alberracin knows she's a werewolf?

Selene gave the briefest of smiles to Kyrah, turned back to her vigil. She was fiddling inside the basket, now set down on a flat rock. It was hard to see inside the tightly woven wicker. She lifted a babe out, a tiny little boy, pale and blue in the cold, despite the thick woolen suit and hood he wore. It was likely the babe wouldn't survive if the temperature dropped much further.

"Get him by the fire," Kyrah said.

"I know what to do," Selene snapped. That broke the low murmur of conversation. They all glanced at her, then went back to their own jobs in silence.

Kyrah sighed and grimaced. She scowled when she saw Richter looking. "Don't you have goats to watch?" she said, and thundered off into the brush, snatching up her sword as she passed.

At least they don't call me Creature, *here. Could be worse.*

J UST AFTER DARK, THE fire cracked and waved beyond the trees, vigor and violence. Strange that such an innocuous thing, that warmed and comforted in small amounts, destroyed and hungered in tall amounts. A lesson in moderation, he supposed, though that was cold consolation to him and the lycans here, where fire had brought them all so low in their lives of late.

If nothing else, he'd certainly become more cautious, more introspective of late. The inability to speak turned you inward, he guessed. He certainly wasn't the same man that killed lycan babies in the womb, in the crib. Wasn't the same one that burned at the pyre, nor even loved Fehling on that wondrous night in Annalt, before it all went horribly wrong. He didn't pity himself. He knew they were all part of him since what were you if not your memories and your experiences. But he also knew he was a different man. Not a better one. Just that he felt guilt, for once in his life. Enormous, soul-crushing guilt. Maybe that did make him better, but he was no priest. Domitus would know.

Domitus. Fehling. Karl. His old life quivered up before him in the dancing flames. A life that had been killed by a mad god, but it was own selfishness that had beaten it halfway dead anyway.

Piss spattered the trunk as his muscles unclenched, a dull ache now instead of a million knives. It sprayed out, went over his boots and his cloak as much as the tree. He let out a low groan. While he stood there, the fire's warmth had faded, and it was only a matter of time before frost set into his fingers. He needed to find clothes, but there were no spares. Spare clothes hadn't been a priority fleeing a sacked castle.

He could steal some, but if they went missing and he magically had some, that would be tough to explain. And he needed their good will.

Their good will.

He took off the cloak, the boots, and went hunting.

T HE BEAR CUBS WOULDN'T see out winter without their mother, but that was the way of the world. The wolf wasn't bad for killing the sheep, it was just doing what it needed to do to survive.

He hauled the dead bears into the camp, bleeding a little from the back. The father had caught him off guard as he was tearing out the mother's heart with his claws. So much for quick, merciful deaths. Happily, his fur was armor, meaning the bear's swipe was only a few scrapes rather than gaping, life-threatening wounds.

The smith was the first to see him, fifty strides distant in the inky blackness, fire low behind him. Of course, he didn't need a torch. Their senses were heightened, even in their human form, and Gregor was first watch.

He nearly changed before Richter shouted. That strange, tongueless noise in his throat.

"Oh, you," he grunted, sat back down on the fallen log. "Is that..."

Richter dumped the corpses at the smith's feet and changed back. Cold iced his skin, raised it to gooseflesh. The heat of the hunt had long subsided, so he found his cloak and boots, put them back on.

He warmed himself by the fire as the others realized their bounty, a slight smile on his face. Grinning seemed a bit too much, and it might freak out the children.

"Are you sure? It was him?" Ottille said.

Gregor nodded. Frix and his cousins laughed, came over and slapped him on the shoulders.

"Well, fuck me," Frix said. "Who knew the not-rapist here was useful at something?"

"Any one of us could do it," Kyrah said, leaning on the oak, picking dirt from her fingernails with a knife.

Frix shot a look at her. "Then why haven't you?"

She didn't answer, just looked at him. Didn't rise to the criticism, calm as a veteran under crossbow fire. She had her reasons, felt no need to share them. Richter found himself more and more frightened, and more and more aroused.

"Can we refrain from using the word 'rapist', please?" Ottille whispered. She nodded in the direction of Lorela, who was sleeping with her back turned to them, another woman curled up behind her. "She cried herself to sleep. Helena had to hold her, otherwise she wouldn't go."

"Fine," Frix said. His cousins clapped their hands together like diners at a tasty banquet, climbing over them and surveying the offerings.

"The meat'll feed us for a week. More if we can dry it," one of the cousins said. "The skins'll make cloaks more than warm enough."

"You did well, flaxen-hair."

Richter looked up. Selene's eyes danced in the light of the fire, her pale neck covered with fox fur, but the slightest silver of her collarbone was visible. The smile of a refined lady. Restrained and proper. A year ago, a few more times than was healthy really, he imagined opening that pale neck and seeing what goodies came out. Now he was trying to win her approval, win her trust.

This had won him a way along that long, long road.

LOOKING AT THE TRAPPER'S cabin, it wasn't much. The roof sagged, thatch poking in places like porcupine quills. Water had soaked the boards beneath where it opened to the elements, swelled them until they were cracking and rotting. A weathervane in the shape of a dolphin, its head snapped off, gone. Like a beast had come along and decapitated it, taken its head for keeps.

But it was shelter enough. A light drizzle had moved in, dripping water from the eaves. Most of them moved inside, though the cousins three went for firewood.

Kyrah turned at the front, put herself in the path of the door.

"You've got first watch," she said.

He nodded. He went back down the steps to the hard-packed earth, looked out on the vista. They'd already climbed high in the mountains, and the keep was gone, the smoke just a shadow of a pinprick on the horizon.

Fir and conifer hugged the land like an old lover, thick and impenetrable. He couldn't even see where they'd stopped the day before, by the icy brook.

It would take months for the army to cross the forest, if they ever did. If they were ever found. He noticed that the Saburrian often went back to cover their tracks, bury their footprints when it rained, smear out the dirt and break foliage every direction, so only a master tracker would know which path was the real one. If that.

"We could fix the roof before the rains set in," he overheard Ottille say to Selene as they emerged from the cabin. "It'll be a cozy winter, but at least we'll be safe."

"We need to stop somewhere. Tristain is losing heat every time we move." The lady had taken to wearing the babe across her chest, but it still wasn't enough, and he looked as pale as Luni. The cold of the mountains could be unforgivable to the unprepared.

"Then here is as good as it's getting," Kyrah said. "It's been long abandoned, there's no one coming back. Once we fix the roof, we can even hang the bear meat and dry it out. Have supplies for months." Richter felt her eyes on him. "And we can always hunt more, before the animals go in their burrows for bruma."

"Very well." Selene sighed. "Is this alright?"

She sought approval from them all before she decided, often. Fairer, Richter supposed, but leaders often had to make decisions that went against the grain for the good of the group. As it was, the cabin was a fine place to stop.

"It's well, Selene," Ottille said. "There's enough time left in auctumnitas to find the supplies we need and make the rest. The bear skins go a long way to making blankets that'll keep us warm."

"I can make potash and seal the gaps in the floor, make new boards to fix the rotting ones," Gregor said. "So the wind doesn't get underneath. Retar the roof if we find enough sticks to fill the gap."

"There we are." Ottille gestured, more for Selene's benefit than anything else.

He'd seen her face in Swords after their *Velitore* enough times. The first time they'd killed a beast and come close enough to dying themselves. She looked ready to scream and curl up into a crying ball, as those novitiates often did.

But she's lost her home and now she's on the run with her infant son, having to keep it together for everyone else.

Kyrah tramped over to him, jerked her head sharp to the left. "Come with me," she said, not waiting for an answer.

He followed. They rounded a small stand of pines, shingle crunching under their feet. The trees were stunted by the winds and the biting frosts that were all too common up here. As it was, he had to pull his cloak tighter around his shoulders just to stop feeling the cold. Everything cleared out up here, the top of the world. High places nearer to heavens untold. The Fall, where Sigur had struck the final blow on the Great Devil, sent him tumbling to the ground, defeated.

But the battle had cost Sigur, and now the gods were gone. But that wasn't true, not anymore. Vetterand had at least returned, and if you believed him, never left. Who was he? Sigur did seem likely, but then why would he have to hide his identity? The Great Devil? It was possible, and that would explain why he had to hide. But that would mean that Sigur hadn't defeated him after all, and the entire thing was a lie.

I'm not sure what's worse.

Kyrah marched ahead with the speed of an alcoholic marching to a tavern at the first sign of opening. Richter almost had to run to keep up with those long, strong legs, her hips swaying something between a bedwife in the Gully District and a dockworker carrying a heavy load. Not unerotic, just confusing.

He put those thoughts to bed before they developed further. He was still aching from that morning's piss.

Kyrah looked back as she climbed over a boulder just ahead, an outcropping above where a giant, flattened, gray rock balanced on the edge. Gray, that was the world. A world of gray, where the color drained from the land, leaving only dry tedium. Living here wouldn't be much, and how long before the cabin proved small and cramped? Fifty people in a trapper's cabin in the depths of winter? Even with the few improvements they could make, a recipe for murder. Kyrah and Selene looked ready to murder each other of late, and things would only get worse.

Where the hells has she gone?

He looked around. The Saburrian had cleared off, gone too quick for him to keep up with. What was she playing at? He'd have to find her now, and he'd get blamed for not keeping the first watch. Whoever took over from him would give him the cold shoulder, and he'd have to start all over again.

It's not my fault, he'd try to explain, then remember he'd had his tongue burned off by a mad god.

Bitch. Saburrian dog.

Cracking noises rang out. A shadow moved across his periphery. No, moved on him. He looked up. All he saw was gray, a world of gray as the boulder crushed him, his head punched into the dirt, skull shattered and his mind shattering with it. He died, instantly.

It didn't take.

He breathed shallow, all he could manage as he was pulled back into his body, fire and needles across his skin. Anger flared in his trapped chest, his lungs and stomach burning with rage. His legs felt crooked, bent at weird angles. Not that he could look down and see. It was darkness for him, cold stone against his furry cheek, but he heard something. Deadened by the rock around him and the dirt under him, it was the sound of claws scraping up the shingle as she walked.

"I would say I'm sorry," Kyrah said, voice muffled. Sounded like she might be speaking right to the rockface. "But I'm not."

Why?

"I can't trust you. You're Order, and that makes you my enemy, even if you're a lycan, even if you hunt bears for us. That makes me trust you less because now all I think is that you're trying to make us trust you so you can betray us later."

It wasn't far from the truth, but the accusation still burned red hot in his throat. He wanted to rip her to bits, but he couldn't move a muscle. He could scarcely breathe, a constant pressure against his ribs.

"The lady might welcome any stray dog from the cold, but I know better." He thought she might've left him, done with talking, when she spoke again. "If you're anything like me, I know you can't be killed. Whichever god keeps you alive, pray to them now. It's all you have left. If you somehow make it out of this, at least you won't be able to find us, follow us. If you do—just leave us alone. Let go of any petty revenge you might hold for me. Just know I'm doing what I'm doing for our survival." She meant the rest of them.

Then her boots ground up the shingle as she walked away, the sound fading out and leaving him cold, stuck to the ground, trapped, unable to breathe properly, unable to move, unable to scream. He wished he would die and knew he couldn't.

CHAPTER 38
LOW MORNING
LEVITUM, 1045

How can something so eager to kill itself be so key to humanity's procreation?

— ANONYMOUS

TRISTAIN'S CRIES FELL TO a low burble as they woke in the morning, and she didn't know what was worse. It was an awful night, preceded by an awful day of trekking through cold forest. What rest they had was broken by the shifting and groaning of forty stinking bodies in the small hut as horrid, icy winds howled outside. And the crying. The babe would keep even the deepest sleeper awake. More than once, she'd pressed him to her breast just to quiet him, and he sucked for comfort, though there was no milk. She hadn't made any and couldn't. It wasn't possible.

Something was wrong with her, she'd long thought it. She couldn't even do this one thing for him. Any comfort the sucking might have had on the child lasted mere moments before he was flailing his arms again, wailing for milk she couldn't give. The only person who could she had killed. It was excruciatingly painful for her since she'd started bleeding from his vigor. But it brought him comfort, and quiet, if only for a few precious moments.

In the morning, a pale day outside poured with rain. Her eyelids fused together, crusty, and it took effort to open them. Or maybe she didn't want to open them, afraid of what she might see. It was, in some ways, easier to lay there in that half-space, propped up between a leg and an arm. The boards were hard under her though the flesh was soft and warm. Leon slept next to her, as still as the dead. *At least some got their rest*, she thought.

She lifted her head. The babe in the crook of her arm slept, his soft nostrils whistling with breath, and she sighed quietly in relief. She unraveled herself, as a hangman unravels a murderer's knot. Careful not to disturb the sleeping, as though she would disturb the dead. Trist's face was pale in the morning light as it streamed in through the cracks in the door. Her eyes caught the briefest glimpse of Luni on the western horizon as she made her final descent. As to a grave.

She heard thumping outside. The noise of an axe chopping wood. Someone was up, cutting wood in the rain. A futile attempt at starting a fire since everything was saturated. The hut was hardly weatherproof, and drips fell from the ceiling, waking Ottille and Trestinsen, and some others, and they started, rose together. She caught their eyes. None of them looked better for the rest—what little there was to be had. They'd be looking to break their fast, to eat the last of the bears that had been hunted. But soon there'd be nothing left, or what was left would go bad. They couldn't cure the meat until they weatherproofed the hut, and that's if it lasted that long. No meat, and certainly no bread. The larder in Palerme was fully stocked and yet it was entirely out of reach. If it hadn't already been raided.

She offered a leaden smile. The last goat, the last of their livestock, was the only thing feeding Tristain. Guilt needled at her cheeks, tugged at her lungs, stole the breath from her throat. She'd done this to them—she'd been unable to save them, and had doomed them all to a frigid, wet, hungry death in the mountains. It would've almost been better if they'd all been slain by the crusaders. Might've been quicker than this walking death.

But then Kyrah had headed them down this course and shared an equal portion of blame. They'd better cross the mountains, soon, otherwise they were all going to die.

As though by clockwork, Trist's eyes squeezed tight. She took a sharp breath, anticipating the horrible wail.

He gurgled instead. A horrible, thready sound, as though he had spit caught in his throat. Or he was simply too weak to cry. It slapped her ears, pitted her stomach. It wasn't a sound a babe should ever make. His head was cold to the touch. She picked him up. His face turned veiny, splotchy, and she frantically put more bedding around him. Ottille came up to her shoulder.

"What's happened?"

"He—" She pressed the back of her hand to her mouth, bit her hand, forced down a scream. Her eyes wetted with tears unshed. "He's dying."

"Come," she said, and picked up the child, helped Selene up by the shoulder. Her wrist still ached from its break, and it was likely she wouldn't be able to use it normally ever again, unless she was able to get treatment. She bound it with cloth and a block of wood in a splint, and her fingers still worked, but the bones likely wouldn't heal properly. The tendons around the joint were weakened, flared in pain each time she flexed her hand. Made worse by the fact that it was simply her only option.

"Thank you," she told Ottille. Gave a glance to Leon, who slept soundly. He wasn't bleeding from the ears, anymore, so there was at least that.

The woman gave her a comforting smile. "We'll try and feed him. The goat is still making milk." *For a kid that has been left behind.* One child was sacrificed so that another might live, and maybe not even then. Trist's appetite far exceeded that of a goat youngling, and it never seemed enough.

Outside, gray, drab rain met them, the dirty sooty smell of the fires at Palerme washed away by the deluge. It wet her hair, soaked her jacket. Ottille shielded Trist in the crook of her arm, pulled over the fabric of her loose dress. They went out to the goat, the animal penned in the small outhouse. A privy, of sorts. It seemed extravagant for what amounted to a huntsman's lodge.

She wondered where the goatherder had gone. The mutilated man had been missing since yesterday evening.

The goat looked at them when they opened the door, shut it behind them. Selene wondered if the mother knew her babe was dead, and Trist was like a parasite, sucking what was meant for the kid.

Ottille knelt down, Trist's burbles turning to soft groans. "Here we go," she said. "Go on, child." The babe's mouth formed a ring around one of the teats and started sucking. Relief washed over Selene like a warm ocean wave.

"He's not too weak to feed, thank Ginevra," she said. She knelt down beside them, and watched her child feed for a long while, until he gave up, and turned away. He cried as he did, the pressure from the goat's nipple spraying him in the face with milk.

They laughed. The goat just stared.

She looked at Ottille, the woman wiping the babe's face with care. The woman's light brows dripped with wet, droplets running down her cheeks. She tried to understand what the woman was thinking, how desperate things had become in their minds.

"It's good I should see these things, before it's my turn again," Ottille said, preempting any words Selene had on her tongue. "It's been a while since I had Sanna."

Realization struck her like an arrow to the soft bits. "Truly—?"

Ottille smiled broadly. "Yeah."

She hugged her friend. It was awkward with the broken wrist, and Ottille holding Trist with both hands, but no less warming to their faces when their wet cheeks touched. "How wonderful."

"Thank you." They embraced there for a while, a patch of warmth in the frozen day.

When they broke apart, Ottille was grinning. "Did I tell you about the time Sanna nearly lopped her finger off?"

Selene chuckled. "No, you didn't."

"I left a knife out on the counter, and there were just... a million things going on—and she was at that age where you can't stop them from getting into everything." She breathed. "I turned around for a second, and she was already sawing her finger off."

Selene grimaced. "Damn."

"Yeah. Tristain's a bit hungry, but at least he's not hurt." Ottille squeezed Selene's shoulder. "I think you're doing just fine."

Selene sniffed, tears running down her cheeks. She sighed, and the pain and anguish of the last few months left her a little bit, left a warm feeling behind, like a hug from a mother.

She thought it was time, time for the truth. "Do you think you should leave us humans behind?"

Ottille looked up, lines scored across her forehead. "What?"

"There's no reason to wait for us. You can transform and get over the mountains easily, go wherever you want. You could go to Vallonia."

"Vallonia, why?"

Selene swallowed. "The duca gave me a strongbox full of papers when I left Valenti. They're old documents and notes by some historian. The notes say that the royal line of Vallonia is Althann. They're all lycanthropes, Ottille. Every single one of them, unbroken from the first king."

Ottille stared, her eyes inscrutable until they turned down, her mouth dropping. "You're saying... you left Valenti months ago. You didn't think to tell us in the meantime?"

Trist whined at the sudden change in her voice. It was a cold kind of anger, not blustering or aggressive, but enough that a child could tell the difference between the gentle Ottille and this one.

Selene's cheeks burned red. "I... didn't know what to make of it at the time. We don't even know if King Cartenas would welcome us knowing or whether he would just kill us all and cover it up."

"Shouldn't that be all of our decision? I know you're the lady, mistress, but..."

Now it was Selene's turn to get angry. She needed to defend herself, that pit in her stomach yawning open again. "I did the best I could, given the circumstances. We all make mistakes. I've given up so much for all of you."

Ottille grunted her sarcastic support. "Indeed."

"If I could go back and change what I did, I would."

"Where is this strongbox, now? Where's the proof?"

"In Palerme. I couldn't have carried it by myself."

Ottille's eyes unfocused, fixed on something distant, beyond the walls of the stinking outhouse. "I see," she said after a while.

"I'm sorry," Selene offered. "For what it's worth."

Her friend smiled. "Yes." The sun peeked through the window as the eaves dripped, water gathering up in giant beads to fall to the ground. The rain had stopped. "We should go."

CHAPTER 39
OF GODS AND MEN
LEVITUM, 1045

There are no names in any language for what he is.

— APHE, THE MIND

THEY NOTICED THE CREATURE following them not long after they left the hut. It appeared at the periphery, catching tufts of white fur on branches, dropping balls of it on the path. Kyrah kept her head on a swivel, catching sight of the wolf following their path. It kept its distance, waiting for the opportunity to strike.

Strangely, the forest also changed its mien, becoming darker, more dead, yellowing leaves stopped abruptly, leaving the forest looking like a grave-yard of unearthed skeletons stretching to the sky. Along their path, they found trees cut in half like this. As though half the tree had suddenly died.

"We should turn back," someone said. Frix, maybe.

"No, we keep moving." Kyrah dragged them on, knowing that if they gave up now, they would all die. She didn't much like the Lady of Palerme, but she wouldn't forgive herself if she left her and the babe behind. *I'm a cold-hearted bastard, but I'm not that cold-hearted.*

Though they would all get much better sleep if the babe stopped crying, however that happened. Already, it was starting again, an insatiable appetite for milk that its mother couldn't give.

The ground had turned to peaty mud from all the rain, and it was hard going. The sun barely touched the cold ground up here, this high, and it was easy to get lost. She sniffed the air. Ahead, a fallen carcass of some animal fouled the air, made her wrinkle her nose. Her mouth watered. They might be able to scavenge what they could off its bones.

She looked at Gregor. The only one who knew what she did—burying another one of them alive under that boulder. He hadn't cared why, only she knew that he didn't like him. He didn't take much convincing.

"There's a stream up ahead," he said. "And a fresh kill."

"Meat," she replied. "We should make camp up ahead," she told the rest of them.

T HE NIGHT GAPED ITS black maw for all of them to see. Silently, the wolf moved into the camp, its white fur a beacon, Kyrah's remaining eye burning with the sight. It wasn't the same thread-pulling that she'd felt in the crusaders' camp. It was more like looking directly at the sun.

The creature limped into their midst, its white eyes passing over them coolly. Kyrah saw that the pupils were a pure milk color, and what should've been the whites were as dark as pitch. "It's you," she said. Though in her dreams, or whatever that space was between life and death, the god looked much more like a... well, like a god.

This one just looked pathetic by comparison. The black sky opened, a dazzling array of colors shooting across the field. She looked up. She'd heard of the borealis in the north, in the Geisteschreien, but she'd never seen it herself.

The rest of them made awed sighs, but she just watched, and waited, kept her hand on her blade.

"You know this creature?" Selene said. Kyrah hadn't realized she'd come alongside. "I've seen him in my dreams."

"I've seen him in my death," Kyrah replied. "He told me he has grand plans for me. Well? I'm waiting. What fucking plans have you got for us, then? To starve?"

"YOU KNOW YOU CANNOT DIE," the creature said. It spoke directly into their minds, like metal scraping against bone. Emptied its fury into their skulls like a hammer. Kyrah howled in pain, clutched her head. Selene did the same, the rest of them. "THIS BODES ILL. THAT WAS BUT A VESTIGE OF THE PAIN THAT YOU WILL FACE."

They went silent, the forest air swelling with the pause, as though the whole world held its breath. Above, the sky continued to crash in dazzling blues, purples, reds, like a war erupted up high.

"YOU KNOW WHAT YOU MUST DO. THE MAID WITH THE LITTLE GIRL KNOWS." A pause. They looked at Ottille. "AND THE LADY. THE ONE WHO HAS BEEN HIDING EVERYTHING FROM YOU."

Kyrah's nostrils flared. "Hiding what?"

"THE SECRET OF YOUR LINEAGE. THAT A ROYAL LINE IS AMENABLE TO THE CAUSE."

"The—cause?"

"I TIRE OF THESE INANE QUESTIONS. I OFFER YOU THE LAST OF MY BEQUESTS BEFORE I MUST ANSWER FOR MY CRIMES. MY FATHER HAS RETURNED, AND YOU HAVE ONLY ONE CHANCE. SEIZE IT."

Kyrah shook her head. "No, I tire of these fucking riddles—" Her mind burst into agony, as though put in a drum and pounded on. Blood fizzed from her nose, her ears. The world turned upside down and she thought she might've hit the ground, it was hard to tell.

The god spoke into her mind, overrunning the pain, tearing her to pieces. "HE IS MORE POWERFUL THAN EVER AND HIS ARMIES WILL RAZE THE CONTINENT TO THE GROUND. SO, I OFFER YOU ALL ONE BEQUEST. THE LAST OF MY STRENGTH."

"What is it?" Selene said. The voice fuzzed in Kyrah's ears, as though the woman was speaking underwater.

"No, don't," Kyrah yelled, but her breath was choked in her throat. *She's lying, she'll take from you all. We can't trust this god, whatever he might be.*

"METAMORPHOSIS."

"Metamorphosis?"

"EVERY WARRIOR ON THE CONTINENT WILL ASSUME THEIR TRUE FORM."

"Every Althann?"

The god flinched at the mention of the word. "YES."

"She's not one of us," Ottille said. "How can she decide for us?"

"Because you can't decide for your fucking selves," Selene yelled. Colors danced across her pinched features, the babe in the crook of her arm shrieking at the shouting. Started crying. Kyrah had never seen her so angry, especially around the child. "So much disagreement, so much infighting... you would all be dead back in the Citadel if it weren't for me. You need a leader, someone who's not afraid to put you back in line."

"That's not fair, Selene," Leon said.

"Aye, that's not us at all," Frix added.

"Aye," came the rest of them, shouting now.

"How dare you decide," Kyrah said. She stood now, her senses returning. Selene stepped back, guarding her child. *I've seen that look. She's afraid, though she might not show it. The dog that barks loudest is the frightened one.*

"ENOUGH." A low buzz tingled Kyrah's senses, a small touch of pain compared to what the god had done to her just before. "HUMANITY HAS FAILED, THAT IS CLEAR. THE CONTINENT MUST BE PU-RIFIED. MAN AND WARRIOR CANNOT LIVE SIDE BY SIDE."

He keeps repeating the word, warrior. *Is that us?*

"METAMORPHOSIS, CHOOSE. NOW."

"Why do you need our choice? Why can't you just do it?"

"BECAUSE THE LAWS OF THE LAND ARE CLEAR. IT IS NOT WITHIN MY POWER TO DECIDE, I CAN ONLY OFFER IT. THE WARRIORS MUST DECIDE."

"What would it mean?" she asked the others. "Every wolfman and woman would turn, even those who hadn't known they were."

"Imagine the carnage," Frix said. They nodded in agreement.

"Then who is this god with all the armies?"

"YOU KNOW HIM AS SIGUR."

The blood rushed from Kyrah's face. "We... fight against Sigur?"

"THE AGE OF DISCORD HAS COME TO AN END, AND THE AGE OF LIGHT WILL RETURN."

"Then I say do it."

"What?" Gregor shouted. "No," Frix said. The others shouted and bick-ered.

"Enough. You want a leader that puts you all back in line," she said to Selene. "Well, do it. Start the metamorphosis."

The creature closed its eyes for one moment, opened them. Above, color faded from the sky, turned the black of night again. "IT IS DONE."

Then the creature was gone, the heaviness returning to the forest. Kyrah fell to her knees, suddenly light-headed, the blood rushing from her head. Someone screamed.

Gregor's twins were the first to turn. Their clothes tearing open and limbs pushing outwards. Over by the fire, the little girl Senna transformed too, her fearful cries turning to wolf-like yawps in her twisting mouth. Like a ripple of primal fury, the feeling spread outwards, and even Kyrah had to struggle to maintain her composure.

Helena and the mute girl were easy pickings. They scarcely had a chance to defend themselves as Gregor and Trestinsen gutted them and started eating them.

Selene was gone, she noticed, and she smelled the woman's fear as she ran into the dark. Another woman and a man ran with her, their footsteps and heartbeats as clear to her as a falcon spotting mice in a field. She could chase them down, easily, and thought she might, just for sport, until something hard raked across her back, and white-hot pain slid down.

She turned. Frix roared as he reached up triumphantly, holding up a flap of her skin. *What? No! Every one of us has become an unthinking, primal warrior, feeding from god-given rage!*

Dodging another blow, she twisted her body and punched her claws under his chin, grabbed hold of his throat and pulled. Bones popped and tore free of flesh, his windpipe flapping uselessly, spurting gouts of blood. Frix clutched at his opened throat, stumbled back. His legs collapsed out from under him.

Gregor's twins raced off into the forest, chasing down the three humans. But the rest fought amongst themselves, their eyes only hungry for death, killing to feed their rage.

If she couldn't save them, she realized, she'd end them all.

CHAPTER 40
GONE

LEVITUM, 1045

It is as though whoever made the lycanthropes—be it a god or a curse or nature—left a particularly convenient weak point on the back of their necks. Almost as though it is a built-in failsafe.

— DRAMES, A COLLECTION, 585 AE. D.

SELENE HURTLED ACROSS THE black, only the slimmest margin between running head-first into a tree or a fallen branch or slipping on the muddy ground and ending the babe in her arm. The moon was a pale finger in the sky, casting the scantest light on the forest floor. Lorela ran alongside her, Leon a few paces away, though it was hard to tell, and she dared not look back. Her death was coming, what difference did it make if she knew what form it took?

Stupid dog. Promises from a god. Powers and bequests. Metamorphosis. Selene knew what it was when a wolfman transformed without training and knew it would be a bloodbath. She saved the girl, about the only one that could be saved, since she was to hand when they ran. Leon protested, but when he heard the roars, he knew Selene was right.

Her legs burned, breath steamed against the night air. She dumped the basket on her back, unable to keep it propped on her shoulder anyway.

Lorela screamed in the sharpness of the panic, a thousand knives to Selene's ears. Trist wailed, his cries a beacon to the hunters behind her. And they moved faster than their prey ever could. She turned, caught her breath, back pressed against the tree she put between her and the werewolves. Leon and Lorela shot past her, and she hissed, "Stop!"

They skidded to a halt, and Lorela let out a sharp yelp, colliding with a bramble, a face full of cuts. "I'm—sorry!" Selene wasn't sure if she apologized to the bush or to her, though it hardly mattered.

"There's no escape, we have no choice. We have to kill them."

"Kill—*kill them?*" she barked.

Leon drew his axe and sword. "They might've been our friends and family, girl, but they ain't no more."

She heard rustling in the distant trees. The roars were quiet now, and that was worse. There was no way to know how many of them were chasing them. But she did know how to kill them—that was one thing she was certain of. *How quickly I've turned on them...*

But the god was right, in a way. Humanity had failed them, and now the Althann sought to destroy them. The warriors of the gods had metamorphosed. Into killers, primal hunters.

She took a hard breath. Pushed her baby into the girl's chest. It broke her heart to do so, but there was no other choice. They needed time. "Take the child. Run. Surrender to the crusaders, tell them you were hunted by the demons and now you're running scared, and didn't know what to do other than to give yourself and your child to the imperial army." It was only a knife's edge from the truth.

"What are you going to do?"

"Buy you time." She looked at Leon. "Go with her."

"No fucking way. I'm—" Two roars shook the trees, the leaves. Closer now.

"Go, girl! Run!"

Lorela shrieked, then turned and ran, bounding off into the dark, pressed the babe to her chest tight. Selene's ribs tightened, breath choked in her throat. She was going to make sure that it wasn't the last time she ever saw her son.

"Push me up into the tree," Selene said. "Do you remember what happened in Rennes?"

He nodded. "We got our fucking arses kicked."

"Yes. Do you remember why?"

"The Annaltians—" Realization dawned on him, as bright as the beautiful morning sun. A morning sun that she longed to see again, preferably with Trist close to her chest. "Yes. I get you."

"Do it, then." She bent down and smeared herself with mud, covered her plates, her jacket, her pants, her skin, her face. "You know what to do. I don't want any doubt, just because they were once our family."

"I know. It's fucking awful. But I won't hesitate. You know me, Sel."

"I know you." She kissed him on the cheek, a gesture of all her thanks. He lowered himself to a knee and she jumped into his waiting hands, and he flung her up, up, far above the branch she meant to climb up on, until all she had to do was catch herself on the branch above, perfectly placed at hand height. *Gods above, he's still as strong as the stories have him.*

"C'mon!" He smashed his axehead and the sword blade, bangs of steel. Sparks shot out. "Come get it!"

She swiveled around, drew her dagger. Below, a dark shape thundered through the brush. Two. The second one, identical. They both had fur that caught Luni's light, silvered on their coats. Branches flattened as the first one crashed through with all the grace of a rampaging bull, and Leon dived to the side. The werewolf swiped air and skidded along the ground as it missed. The second one lunged at Leon, caught him on the ground.

He put the sword up and the beast clumsily shoved itself on the blade. The other one came around and she waited, waited to see if any more were coming.

Leon roared as the furious beast shoved itself further on the blade, blood showering the knight underneath. The other one came around, came down on his axe arm with its teeth, down on his big bicep, hooked into flesh. "Selene!"

She pounced, landed on the second's back and plunged her dagger right between the upper vertebrae. Just below the skull, right where her instructions had told her. Her hand twisted weirdly from the movement. Agonizing pain jumped up her wrist, jarred her shoulder. It jerked, its mouth suddenly forced open in shock as it let out a soft gurgle. Then it collapsed, and she rolled off, her hand all cramped up. She thought she felt something snap in her wrist. Her fingers didn't close anymore. She had no choice but to leave the dagger in the beast's neck.

The first one looked up, distracted by its companion's death. Leon roared as he brought the axe up, slammed it into the side of the beast's neck. It was all he needed. Gouts of red covered his face and his neck.

It collapsed on top of him and he turned it aside. Selene breathed, her side hurting, her legs aching, her hand twisted and broken. Standing slowly, Leon pulled himself up using his sword, his other arm gushing with blood. The bite had gone to the bone.

"Fuck," he swore. "*Sal'brath*. I'm gonna fucking die. Of all the fucking things." He fell to a knee, groaned.

Selene rushed over, caught him with her arm, her wrist flaring with pain, her flinching. "No, you are fucking not. We're going to the crusaders and surrendering. They'll have much bigger problems than an ex-knight and an ex-Sword, now."

He looked at her darkly. "We ended the world, Sel. I don't know how many of us are Althann, but even if it's one in ten, they're going to kill everyone. No one's ready for what's coming."

"Then we need to make the gods answer for this. I don't know how, but I know that the leader of the crusader army is Sigur Himself. You heard that wolf-god."

"Sigur—" He coughed. Foamy blood mixed with spittle flew from his mouth. "Shit. Don't worry, I'm just gonna... lie here."

"No, Leon. I need you."

"I got knocked in the head, you know. I could tell. I wasn't going to make it, anyway. Even if I die now or in a few days, it's over for me."

"No. That's not true, we can... we can get help." The words died in her throat. She didn't believe them any more than he did.

"The world's got bigger problems, Sel. We're days from civilization, anyhow. If civilization even exists, anymore. I'm done, Sel."

Tears broke the dam that she'd erected until now. They leaked out of her just as easily as the red gushing from Leon's wound. Flooded her eyes, her lungs, until she felt like she might never breathe again. Blood continued to inundate the ground, feeding the loamy, dark earth like a glutton. His face paled in the moon's light. Pale as a ghost. A heavy breath left his chest, his eyes turned glassy, his movements stopped. She sobbed, and as she did, she crossed his sword and axe over his chest, since he still held them, some last dignity that she could offer. A burial for a knight.

The monsters turned back. The twins. Gregor's twins. Selene felt a twinge in her guts, of guilt, but then, lingering on guilt was what got her into this mess in the first place. It was time to move on; think of her own survival, think of Tristain's survival.

She stood and wiped her eyes. "Goodbye, Leon." Then she ran after Lorela.

EPILOGUE

PRIMA, 1046

FIVE MONTHS LATER

Of ALL THE LESSONS Richter had learned, how to die wasn't one of them.

It came as the frosts descended on the mountain, the snowdrifts piling in like the hate of a betrayed man. The boulder lifted, only just, hair's breadths over days, and days, weeks, and weeks. Richter suspended in that crushing, squeezing feeling, and his eyes would fill with blood, gush from his mouth as his ribs broke inward, piercing his lungs, over and over.

Then the snow piled high enough, filling the spaces between him, his fingers and toes freezing off, felt like they burned off. He moved a knuckle's width, and another, and another. When he turned, skin that lifted upwards and inwards to make room for the fur peeled from the ground, leaving shreds of him on the stone. It was like being flayed, all over again.

But it was easier to move. The boulder was an unmoving beast, the weight like a bull sitting on top of his chest. Breathing came a little easier, though he hadn't had a full breath in what seemed like months, though what was in all likelihood only a couple of weeks.

More snow piled in. It encased him now, his eyelashes, his mouth filled with it. The faintest of light came in, dappled across his eyelids, the smell of fresh pine and water. He sucked the snow around his mouth to salve his thirst, the trickle down his throat sweet like honey. Sweet like Fehling's mouth.

No. Those days are long gone. If I ever make it out of here, I'm done with that life. Or maybe that life was done with me, the moment the mad god caught me.

The mad god. Vetterand. A holy army at his disposal, a fanatic Order at his fingertips. How could Richter ever face down something like that? And even if he could, who knew if gods could be killed?

No, it was better to die, or at least some semblance of that, and lay under this rock for all eternity, and when the rock weathers away, find the deepest pit he could find and jump into it.

It would only be what he deserved.

Let go of any petty revenge you might hold for me. Just know I'm doing what I'm doing for our survival. The Saburrian woman's words rang clear. He didn't hold any vestige of revenge, not anymore. That desire faded quickly. The time under here had given him nothing but time, to think, to reckon with his life, and his death, and what had brought him here.

One night, he thought he might've heard howling, baying across the mountain, the strange noise like a pack of wolves tearing each other to bits. The sound faded as quickly as it had come, and he was left with a silent mountain for company again.

There were moments when he thought he could hear the mountain, and it came like a thrum, a deep, deep humming noise like it was breathing underneath him. Breathing with him. It was strange; gave him that feeling of peace he'd felt in the Schwarze, but this time it didn't make him feel uncomfortable. No, he'd been through far too much to feel like he'd put on a too-small glove.

Maybe it was all he could hope for, if he dared allow himself a touch of hope. That whatever god the mountain was had opened its heart for him, and would welcome him soon enough.

It wasn't to be.

He woke with a start as cold slammed into his face, wet and blinking, he opened his eyes to find his breath steaming in the air. Blinked his eyes again. Light danced across white snow, pale and thick. He took a breath, filled a space in his chest that he hadn't felt for an eon.

What?

He reached a hand up, snagged it on the rock, tore a great gash along his forearm, and dragged himself. Dragged himself towards the light. Wasn't quite sure why. He thought he would just fade, stay in that living grave, buried until the end of time. But the light called to him, the breath, and the fury—

The fury. As his lungs expanded, as he scraped himself, tore chunks from his skin, his fur, whatever remained of his fur after Vetterand had done with him, they filled with something more than just air.

They filled with rage.

Rage for everything, for everyone. Anyone that had ever done him wrong; Fehling, Karl, Jogaila, Bjorn, Paun. The names of friends, the names of those that had abandoned him to his fate. The name of the god... *Sigur.* It had to be. Golden skinned, that hole in his gut, where the Great Devil had done with him.

Blessings come in all forms and sizes and at the most unexpected times, for He is good.

Nothing could be truer. It struck him like a quarrel to the ear, the steel eating into his skull and the pink bits within.

He pulled himself forward, and forward, got the other arm free, his mouth, chin pulling, scraping, leaving more of his skin on the stone it was so cold, *so so* cold, his breath misting, ears pounding with his heartbeat, his fury unending now, building until his skin tingled.

His head poked through a snowdrift, and he looked up. The sungod hung low in the world above, peaky face cowering as though from Richter's sight.

Richter was the one who could not die. What was he afraid of? Not even the weight of a mountain could stop him.

He was the one they should be afraid of. He was pain, and he knew pain, he lived in it. Heated in it, forged in it, his face held to the grindstone, ground, honed until he became a blade that cut the world. Until nothing remained but pure pain, pure death. Until he cut everything he touched.

If there was one thing he was good at, it was killing. Let the killing begin, then.

LIST OF CHARACTERS

In Palerme

Selene Sigurin — disgraced Inquisitor of the Order, Countess of Palerme, known as the Lady of Beasts

Leon Vorland — former knight of the realm, known as Leon the Strong

Ottille — Selene's lady's maid

Frix — factotum

Sanna — Ottille's daughter

Lucia — Ottille's mother and Sanna's grandmother, trusted elder

Gregor — blacksmith

Ulie and Lugen — Gregor's twins

Dunstad — cook

Rani — cook and butcher

Blauna — mute, kitchen helper

Rill — mason

Galena — Tristain's wet nurse

Helena — Galena's mother

Helge — Helena's son and miner

Dober — miner

Trestinsen and Tomas — guardsmen

Roland Denerim — Annaltian ex-merchant

Lorela — wool carder and spinner, Roland's daughter

Roland — stablehand, Roland's son

In Istrya

Richter Beltrand — inquisitor, the Hero of Ostelar, renowned for his brutal methods in despatching demons

Ulrich Vetterand — Grand Inquisitor of the Order of the Golden Sword

Andreas Gottscheid — Most Holy Pontiff of the Sigurite Church, head of the Order of the Golden Lantern

Franz II — emperor of the Istryan Empire

Melusine — empress of the Istryan Empire, Franz's sixth wife and ex-dancer

Nials — inquisitor, known as Nials the Bitten

Karl — ex-squire, novitiate of the Order

Fehling — novitiate, known for the unique scar across the top of her scalp

Bjorn — Salzheimish and novitiate

Paun — hillman and novitiate

Jogaila — novitiate

In Annalt

Reynard of Annaltia — prince of the Lion Throne, ruler of Annaltia

August of Annaltia — prince of the Lion Throne, count of Annalt, Reynard's son

Roberg — Duke of Annaltia

In Valenti

Kyrah Al'Lami — Sergeant of the Alanian Marines

Constantin Alberracin — Duca of Valenti, known as the Eyes of the South

Gothenburg — Sigurite priest

NEAR THE BORDER OF ALANIA AND OSBERGIA

Casimir — crossbowman

Sesar — Casimir's son

Muselio — physician trained in Saburria

ACKNOWLEDGMENTS

Firstly, I'd like to thank my incredibly supportive wife, Shannon. She is my foremost alpha reader, and came up with character of Richter ("what's the most fucked up thing you can think of?" — in a character). Of course, my editor, Sarah Chorn, who made a diamond out of a hot mess of a draft, and whose inline comments give me life. Lee Seater, for their speedy, accurate proofreads; your patience with my lightning-quick schedule is deeply appreciated! Thanks is due to my writing partner, Michael Sala, who gave me the courage to put gods in the book.

Thank you to Kian Najmechi and Tom Baldwin for their enduring enthusiasm for my career. Thiago Abdalla, Krystle Matar, John Palladino, Zamil Akhtar, Gregory Kontaxis, Michael R. Fletcher, and many, many others for their advice and support.

I want to thank my amazing ARC readers: Boe Kelley, Javier Vaquera, Eddie Castro, AndDown, Esmay Borst, and so, so many others that it would be impossible to list them all.

And finally, to you, my reader. If you enjoyed this book, please consider leaving a review on Amazon or Goodreads, or whereever you like! It really helps me out, and allows me to keep doing what I love, and what you (hopefully!) want, which is to keep writing.

About Author

NC Koussis was born in Perth, Western Australia in 1993 to Greek and Gamilaroi ancestry. He has moved all around Australia, settling in Newcastle for the moment, where he lives with his wife, son, and staffy dog, Nala. He's been writing fantasy books since he was a little boy, after falling in love with Lord of the Rings, Realm of the Elderlings, and Deltora Quest. He decided to publish a book in 2019, and it only took him three years. He considers himself an enthusiastic amateur of medieval history, historical battles and tactics, and food. When he's not writing, he's making sourdough bread and working on a PhD in neuroscience.

For more, check out art of characters from this book, and a high-resolution version of the map at https://nikitaskoussis.com.